THE HIDDEN GRAVE

LEGENDS OF NOLA

BOOK FIVE

Books by the Author

LEGENDS OF NOLA SERIES
The Lake, Book One
Lovers in Stone, Book Two
The Pirate Laffite, Book Three
Enemies and Allies, Book Four
The Hidden Grave, Book Five

Published under the name Susan Elliston

The Wardrobe

There's No Explanation

THE HIDDEN GRAVE

LEGENDS OF NOLA

BOOK FIVE

A Historical Time-travel Adventure

BY

D.S. ELLISTON

Elliston Entertainment • Florida

The Hidden Grave

Cover Image: Dylan Daniels
Cover and Book Layout/Design by The Book Team
ISBN 978-0-9854801-8-9 (Original Paperback)
First Paperback Edition: October 2022

Contact the author
On Facebook:
https://www.facebook.com/Author-DS-Elliston-287604241632452/

Book Series on Facebook:
https://www.facebook.com/Legends-of-NOLA-149136808530163/

Twitter: @Ldylstn

NOTE—ADULT CONTENT: Book contains profanities, harsh
language, violence, and sexual abuse and is intended for adults.

This book is dedicated to my brother Roland,
who as a child, sat for hours listening to my stories.

For all the scary stories I frightened him with,
I beg his forgiveness.
but for all the adventures we went on,
I will forever be grateful.
My first fan,
my best childhood friend
and confidant.

You are forever in my heart.

My Lady,

Time is as fluid as the sea I sailed upon. Its currents like the days washing you along on life's journey. The kindest, most beautiful gift time ever deposited upon my shore was you. The cruelest its waves ever became was the day it swept you from my life. And now it seems, in its grandest moment, I am to be put adrift in the mystery of its depths. Or rather, set free to sail upon heaven's ocean above.

Upon which star I wonder, will I wash ashore? Wherever time and tide take me, I go full of love and in peace. Let me no longer be an anchor to you. Instead, let the memory of us calm your soul, and set you free to sail the most glorious ocean of them all . . . the one called life.

Jean Laffite

⚜ One ⚜

When Jean and Tori arrived at General Andrew Jackson's headquarters, the hour was late. The building had been hand-picked by none other than his old friend Edward Livingston and New Orleans Mayor Girod. Its location on Royal Street was easily accessible, unseen by prying eyes under the cloak of darkness.

As they approached the house, both observed that no lights illuminated any window. For all practical purposes, the place looked like the occupants had retired for the night. If Cisco had not explained, in great detail, the circumstances of the meeting, Laffite may have turned and left, but he, like his wife, knew they were expected, regardless of the absence of activity. Just because the place seemed to be asleep meant nothing; it was but a ruse to fool those who may happen by at such a late hour. No soul in the city would dare disturb the American General, especially upon seeing the man's establishment had retired for the day.

Tori inhaled slightly, then she looked into Jean's face and witnessed his lower lip twitching. His features showed no expression, his breathing was steady, and the only indication she had of his hesitation was his continued silence. At that moment, she speculated, Jean was going over every detail of what could occur. The possible outcome of what they were about to face, whether good or bad, was out of his control. He was not a gambler when it came to such consequential decisions, and once he made his mind up to act, it was a fait accompli. Slowly his head turned away from the building he had been studying and looked into Tori's eyes, holding her gaze steady as if he were about to say something, instead he just winked. Jean's mind was set; the meeting would go ahead regardless of the danger. So, with a steady hand, he reached out for hers, and without uttering a word, the pirate stepped forward.

Once they reached the side of the building, they approached the gate to the courtyard, knowing it would be open. Jean had been instructed to go to the back door, which would be left ajar if everything was secure and the meeting was to proceed. Every detail had been arranged well ahead of their arrival, and so far, everything Cisco had told them was correct. Once inside, they were to make their way to the only room with a light shining from within. Their friend had insisted that they could not mistake which room this would be once they stood inside the long hallway. Jackson would be waiting for them in that room with a few of his most trusted men.

Tori's stomach was in turmoil, and her nerves were visibly on edge as they made their way down the narrow hallway toward the only sign of light they could detect. The yellow beam shone out into the hallway from under a closed door less than halfway to the front entrance. It was far too dim to be seen by anyone walking by the establishment, but like a lighthouse beacon, it illuminated the small area in the dark hall indicating which room they were to enter.

As always, Jean seemed utterly in control of himself and did not even attempt to hide their arrival. His long heavy strides echoed loudly on the wooden floor as they made their way directly toward their destination. Tori had thought she heard voices when they first entered the house. Whoever had been talking, though, had stopped at the sound of their arrival. Maybe she was wrong; she told herself, but then, why would a room full of people sit in silence waiting for their guests? She only hoped the greeting they were about to receive would be friendly and not turn out to be a trap. After all, it was common knowledge that Jackson was no fan of Jean's, and the Governor could have set up this arrangement to get his hands on her husband. Would history be on her side, or would it again prove to be somewhat different from what she had learned?

Jean didn't even look at Tori when they reached the only door with the thin beam of light shining out from under it. He knocked once and immediately pushed it open, allowing his wife to enter ahead of himself. At first, she was amazed by this bold act, but Jean never did anything without reason. She knew that he would never put her life ahead of his and must have known that this simple declaration of trust was necessary and an excellent way to begin their relationship with the man they had waited so long to meet.

The room was dimly lit by a few candles and the firelight that emerged from the logs, which crackled as the flames licked hungrily upward toward the chimney. The burning wicks of each candle swayed and flickered in the breeze from the open doorway, causing the shadows to move in the room's interior. So far, every indication was pointing to a friendly meeting. Even the small but intense fire that burned in the hearth gave the atmosphere a cozy glow. Tori could tell that there was no trap here; no soldiers were jumping out to arrest the most wanted man in New Orleans.

Jean's instincts told him that, for now, they were safe. Besides, he had entered the room knowing that the odds were even. There were two of them, against Jackson and a few men. If Jackson had thoughts of arresting him, he would find a none-too-willing participant and a lady who could fight better than some of Jean's men. Still, he kept his guard up and squeezed his wife's hand to let her know he was aware of his surroundings and in control of their situation. However, at this precise moment, everything changed, and control was no longer his to dictate.

The tall figure standing before the fire turned to face them, and showing no emotion, he spoke in a reassuring tone. "Ah, Mr. and Mrs. Laffite. Please, do come on in." He took one step forward, looking at Jean intently. "I have been expecting you both." Jackson smiled briefly at Tori but quickly returned his scrutiny toward the pirate he held no respect for.

The General's voice sounded friendly enough, but the instantaneous activity in the room warned both the Laffites that they were on shaky ground. From out of the shadows stepped two giant figures, who reminded Tori of mountain men, and before she could say or do anything, they both stepped toward Laffite, placing themselves within striking distance.

One held a pistol which he aimed at Jean, and the other had a long ugly knife tapping at the side of his thigh. Behind them, in the hallway, came the sound of more footsteps hurriedly approaching the room. "All secure here, General Sir," said a man, suddenly popping his head through the door. "They came alone."

"Very good," Jackson replied. "Man, your post, and keep a sharp eye out." The General then faced his men in the room and uttered his next order impatiently. With a nod of his head in the direction of the still-open doorway, he continued. "You two can put away your concerns and join him; I wish to talk with our guest alone."

"Yes, Sir," the man in the doorway answered, but not before sending Laffite a warning through the threatening look in his eyes. He then nodded affirmatively to his companions in the room who joined him. The door closed behind them; however, this time, no sound of footsteps echoed from the hallway beyond. It was evident that the men were remaining just outside, close enough to help Jackson if he called out.

Tori could not help but wonder why? Were they there to protect their General, or were they standing there for a far darker reason? She, Davis, and Cisco had been so sure that this meeting actually took place, and that Jean won the General's support. Could they have been wrong, Tori wondered? Did they make an error in judgment because right at this moment, it was beginning to feel more like an ambush? Had they just been taken into custody? Tori looked from Jean to Andrew Jackson, and her expression clearly showed she was worried.

"You must forgive my men," said the General, his voice surprisingly sincere. "On the other hand, I would not be much of a soldier if I did not take precautions, now would I? Your reputation precedes you, Mr. Laffite, and even if I have been informed that you are on the same side as this uniform of mine, until I am certain of your loyalties, your ties with the enemy cannot go unsuspected."

Laffite nodded his head. "You have not done anything that I did not already suspect you would. I do suggest that the poor boy, sitting up in that large magnolia outside, be let down, though, especially on such a cold and damp night like this. No one will be following us, and if they had done so, your men along the street would have been the first to know."

Tori looked at her husband in astonishment. She hadn't seen anyone watching them as they walked through the dark streets and then inside. Yet that was beside the point; more important was the man who stood facing them, the President, or would be President Andrew Jackson. What struck her more at that moment, though, was the man's appearance. He was a mere shell of what she had expected to meet. He was pale, terribly thin, and his eyes burned with what she assumed was a fever. This was no robust soldier ready to battle the British; this was a man with one foot in his grave.

Jackson smiled slightly, nodded his head, and softly uttered his following command. "Go to it. We don't need the boy getting sick. We need every soul we can muster." Jackson turned his head to the side, then coughed slow and deep before continuing. Looking again directly at the man he hoped could help him, he spoke louder. "We are going to need every able-bodied man, young and old, in the days ahead."

Tori once again was shocked as she had thought them finally alone with Jackson, but upon looking around the dimly lit room, she spotted the tall buckskin-clad man standing in the darkened far corner behind them. Stepping forward without any hesitation, he quickly departed the room without so much as 'yes, Sir.' She heard him give orders to someone, but he did not return like she thought he would. After looking around the interior once more and observing her surroundings to confirm they were now alone with Jackson, she relaxed. The imagined hostilities were just that, imagined and for the time being, the thought of her husband ending up in jail again left her mind.

Laffite's wife turned all her attention toward the frail-looking man standing before her. She didn't look at Jean; her interest was with the American General. Here before her was the man who would make history, become President, and he stood only feet away from her. A flash of memory filled her mind; it had not been that long since she stood before his statue in what was known as Jackson Square. Blinking to clear her mind of the image, Tori observed the man closely. She was near enough to see every detail surrounding this historical character and try as she might not to be rude, Laffite's wife continued to stare.

Tori was horrified by the sight she beheld but quickly hid her emotions as she watched Jackson struggle to remain standing without swaying. She was about to suggest that they all take a seat when she witnessed the American casually reach his hand out and rest it on the back of a chair. She was sure that he had done this to help give himself a bit more balance. Again, he coughed, only this time it was so violent that he bent forward, visibly trying to gain control over the wave of nausea and weakness that threatened to engulf him.

Neither Jean nor his wife needed a doctor to explain that the American was gravely ill; it was way too obvious. However, it did not surprise Tori to see this man, a legend in her own time, still remain strong in character and very much in control of his surroundings regardless of his weakened condition. The way his men obeyed his every command proved he was the leader she had read about, but anger filled her; no one had said that he was ill. Livingston had not mentioned it, and to her knowledge, history had not indicated such. Looking toward Jean, Tori wondered if he understood that the General was in very feeble health; however, Jean did not show he was concerned; his face remained blank.

Jackson, having gained his composure, spoke his mind. "I had started to think that you were not going to arrive." His fevered eyes were riveted on Jean, then shifted to Tori. "Forgive an old fool his manners, will you not, my dear?" He indicated a chair with his hand. "Please do come and join me. I have always found that under the circumstances such as these, it is best to try and act civil." He was smiling broadly, but his expression was weary from lack of sleep, and his attempt to conceal his condition was not working. Still, he continued to try and lighten the atmosphere in the room, and he seemed genuine in his actions. "Mr. Laffite, let us get directly to the point, Sir. I am not one to beat around the bush, nor will I. It has come to my attention that you may have certain information that you think is vital to my campaign here in New Orleans." He held up his hand to stop any reply that the pirate might give. "Before you speak on the matter, I would like to warn you, Sir, that it is against my better judgment to associate with the likes of you. It is only because of the insistence of close acquaintances and the dire situation that I now find myself in that I agreed to meet with you." He looked at Tori. "Again, I apologize to you, my dear. I have no such feelings of animosity toward you. I most heartedly assure you that you have nothing to fear in that direction." He raised his hand to his mouth and coughed again.

Jean nodded his head and escorted Tori toward a chair placed in front of the fire. Looking directly into the General's eyes, he said, "Monsieur Jackson, General, Sir. We have much to talk about, you and I, but time is not about to allow us that liberty. I am confident that you will have a far different view of both your seemingly grave situation and your opinion about myself by dawn's light. Monsieur Livingston has spoken to you about our short trip, *oui*?"

"He has, Sir," Jackson said, his hand visibly shaking as he raised a half-full glass of liquor to his parched lips. "Though, at this time, I have to inform you that unless you can present valid information which I might add, can be confirmed, altering my present views about you, I will have to decline such a trip."

Jean could see for himself the state the General was in and silently cursed Cisco and the others for not informing him of the man's poor health. It was clear to the pirate that the American was not in any condition to ride off in the dead of night, let alone survive a harrowing ride into the backwaters and bayous beyond. "I see your point." Jean stood looking directly at the General. He was playing with his mustache, and not a hint of how he truly felt right at that moment showed in his expression. "Just how much have you been told, may I ask? You yourself would never have agreed to a meeting with my wife and I unless you had more information than you are letting on. Or…unless I am now captured and no longer a free man?"

Jackson looked angry for a split second before quickly composing himself. "I had given my word that we would meet and discuss whatever it is that you think pertinent: that, and only that… no tricks. I have been informed that you are as much a man of your word as I am. It would seem, Mr. Laffite, that you trust me about as much as I trust you at this point in our relationship. At least we have that much in common for now." Once again, he began coughing. He was putting up an excellent front for their benefit, but Tori could not let the man continue.

"General Jackson, may I be so bold as to suggest that you accompany me here by the fire. Please, Sir, take a seat, and Jean, you could sit there," she said, pointing to the empty chair close by. "I don't think either of you will be taking any trip this evening. I see no point in it anyway. You can just as easily tell the General what you have come to offer, and he can verify it by sending one of his officers instead." She witnessed Jackson's shoulders slump slightly. He either found relief in what she had just suggested or had suffered another terrible wave of weakness. She hoped it was the former.

Jean walked to the empty chair and indicated his wife by leaning his head in her direction. "I have learned never to argue with my wife when her mind is made up. Surely you understand such matters?" Jean took a seat and continued to hold the American's attention.

Jackson chuckled, "Indeed I do, Mr. Laffite; indeed, I do." He hesitated no longer and took a seat opposite Tori. "Some refreshments are in order. Mr. Sims," he called out, "bring us some of that fine bourbon that we had earlier, and then I think you and the others may leave us. Standing there listening is not warranted or needed, may I add. Wait, Mrs. Laffite, may I enquire about your beverage of choice? Some wine maybe, to still the night's chill?"

"That would be very considerate of you. Yes, either a glass of wine or bourbon would be acceptable."

Jackson chuckled. "You heard the lady, Sims." Although he had not spoken the words as an order, they were followed as such. In minutes, Tori watched as the man Jackson called Mr. Sims reluctantly entered the room and did as asked, then exited, leaving their leader in the hands of what they all assumed to be little more than a pirate and a possible traitor at that.

Jackson had seen Tori watching his man and wanting to assure her she had nothing to fear, he leaned forward and touched her hand lightly. "Do not let him concern you, my dear. My men are at times out of place, such as now, with their concern toward my safety, but then, they are also the finest fighting men one could ask for."

Tori smiled. "I'm sure you are right, and please forgive me if I looked concerned. I do understand their position. But, Sir, I can tell you truthfully, they have no need to fear our reasons for being here this evening."

"And just why are you here? What exactly is it that I should know?" He looked from one guest to the other.

"Jean, I think you had best tell the man before he begins to think us a waste of time. He looks as if some good news would, at this point, be most welcome, don't you agree?" Tori was beaming, her smile adding a certain cheerfulness to the gloomy atmosphere.

"I think you are all but bursting with the information yourself, my dear," Jackson chuckled. "Yes, indeed, these old bones could use some good news. Please, do go ahead, by all means, Sir."

"Oh yes, go ahead and make his day," Tori said lightheartedly, not being able to help herself.

Jean flashed his eyes at her. He had no need for words; his expression, a dark scowling one at that, was a warning. This was serious business, not some silly fancy, and most definitely acting like Cisco was something his wife knew better than do. Tori understood like he did that the next few hours held not only their fate in its hands but the future of America as well. Making light of the situation was not going to be tolerated.

Her husband's glare conveyed his unspoken feelings, and Tori quickly fell silent. She understood that her nerves had gotten the better of her and was determined to overcome her anxious thoughts and actions. It was at this instant that Tori pulled herself together. Instead of allowing herself to feel awkward after Jean's apparent reprimand, she decided to study the man they had come to talk with. Maybe if she understood this historical individual and his intentions better, she would become more comfortable around him.

The General was nothing like she had thought he would appear. True, he was tall and his hair, mostly grey, was longer than she had seen in paintings. His eyes bore into her as he spoke, but they had a subtle glaze about them, and there were tiny beads of sweat on his brow. This last observation indicated to Tori that there was a good chance he had a fever, which was something to take note of. His face was slightly scarred on one side; a thin red line ran along his cheekbone. This in no way detracted from his handsome features or demeanor, but it did make her wonder. Had she ever seen a painting depicting this flaw on his otherwise perfectly chiseled face?

Jackson stood up, intent on domineering the moment. The man had seen how his female guest was studying him. What he needed right then was to take command of his situation and get to the bottom of what it was this pirate had to offer. He pulled himself up and squared his shoulders as he turned to face Laffite.

Jackson was attired in his military uniform, minus his sword, which Tori had spotted laying on a tabletop across the room. She watched him as he poured himself a drink before asking Jean if he cared to join him and then added his apology to her. "You must forgive me, Madame; I had not thought to consider your needs before ours. An oversight, I assure you, that will be rectified. Bourbon is not for such a genteel female such as yourself. I admire your wanting to oblige me, but my manners won't allow such. Sim's send the boy to Livingston's and have him acquire a bottle or two of his best wine for our guest and make haste."

The sound of running footsteps echoed once more in the night, followed by the slamming of a door. The General grinned briefly. "That should not take long. Mr. Laffite, would you care to join me?" He held out the bottle and reached for a glass when Jean spoke up.

"I think not at this time General. I will need to keep my wits about me."

Tori closely observed the American and guessed that Jackson had chosen to meet Jean in full military dress to intimidate him. Little did the future president know that it would take much more than presenting himself in such a manner to rattle her husband.

The American was in command of his intentions and spoke honestly and upfront, but again she could not ignore that his appearance betrayed his weakened physical condition. The General was too thin, and the flesh that should have filled out the space between his cheekbones and chin was lacking. Though cleanly shaven, his face had a somewhat gaunt look about it, and even though after each coughing fit, a deep red flush colored his face, this quickly disappeared, leaving an almost ghostly pale complexion behind. Her eyes left his face, and for a brief second, Tori noticed how his hands trembled before he placed both arms behind his back. He stood at what she thought would be called 'at ease.' His legs were slightly apart, and his shoulders were straight, not slumping in any way. Her admiration for him grew as she realized the man's actions indicated that he did not wish anyone to know or guess how weak and tired he was.

Andrew Jackson stood and listened as Jean made his proposal.

Never did the man's expression change or give any hint as to what he was feeling. His only movement was to shift one foot forward at the mention of the powder and flints. It was the only physical indication that Jean had hit a raw nerve. When the room finally fell silent, Tori looked at each man in turn and watched as each summed up the conversation and its implications.

Jackson spoke first. "If what you have just told me holds to be true, then I give you my word, as an officer and a gentleman, that as soon as it is verified, you will have my gratitude and my full support. Also, I give you my word that I will endeavor to see your side of the bargain met." Jackson reached out his hand. "I offer you my hand on it, Sir."

Jean stood up and walked to Jackson's side. He took the General's hand, and they shook.

"Mr. Sims," Jackson's voice rang out, and no sooner had he spoken than the door flew open, and two men immediately appeared, guns raised. "For God's sake, men put those weapons down. Mr. Laffite here is not the enemy, far from it. It turns out he is our savior. You will accompany him and return and report to me as fast as possible. I mean to hear what I already know to be true from your lips." He smiled at Tori as he continued. "You will explain to the men on the way, Captain Laffite. To have me do so at this stage will only serve to delay your mission. Your wife will keep me company until you return. I assume this detail was explained to you. Livingston's idea and a most welcome one. So, Captain Laffite, are you ready?"

Sims's eyes shot open at the reference to Jean as 'Captain.' He looked at the pirate and then back to his General. "We will depart right now, Sir." Moving toward the door, he looked at Jean and said sharply, "You heard the General. Are you ready or not?"

"I have been ready and waiting for weeks, Mr. Sims. Let's not keep the General waiting any longer than he has to. Tori, you keep Monsieur Jackson company. I will be gone for some hours." Then before anyone could utter another word, Jean spun around and marched out of the room, causing Sims to run after him to catch up.

Tori noticed the look of amusement on Jackson's face. It faded as the room slipped once again into silence. He was bone-weary, and though glad not to have to make the trip himself, he would not rest until he had verification of what Laffite offered.

"General Sir?" Tori asked. "May I send for a friend of mine? She is a healer of sorts, and I am sure she can help you. Please, Sir, you need help, and I can't just sit here and not do something. In fact, I won't."

He smiled at her and her concern. "I appreciate your offer, but I assure you, it's nothing a good night's sleep won't cure."

"Begging your pardon, but I'm not stupid, nor am I about to give in. You are ill, and you do need my friend's help. Please, just let me get word to her. I won't rest until you see her, and I think you know it."

"If that is how you feel, and you do feel very strongly on this, don't you? You are very much like my Rachel, and I know better than to argue with her. I will have your message taken to your friend. For you, my dear, only for you, I will agree to see her." These Laffites were both strong-willed and stubborn, he thought, and very much like himself. He liked that very much as he had little time for those who did not possess the same attitude, drive, and determination. "Jefferson," he called out, and before he could continue, the man's head popped around the open doorway.

"See to it that Mrs. Laffite's message is delivered, as well as anything else she wants. I will rest here if that is all right, Madame?" Forcing a smile on his lips as he took his seat next to the fire. "You and I may talk a while; it makes the time go faster I have found. If one keeps busy and not only in one's head, that is to say. I have so much to ponder that I find it exhausting. Maybe our chat will take my mind off such complicated worries that encompass my thoughts."

Tori frowned. Jackson needed medical help. It was plain to see that the man was physically ill and mentally worn out. Again, she found herself facing something that the history class in school had not told her. He was gravely ill, and if not helped, he might not fulfill his historical role. They had not waited this long for him to let them all down, no matter his condition. "Marie is most qualified to aide you, and I know she can be trusted." She turned and faced the Kentucky man she had seen several times that night as Jackson spoke to him.

"Mr. Jefferson, if one of your men could find Mr. Livingston and inform him that Mrs. Laffite wishes a friend to attend me, he will understand. I assume Madame that Mr. Livingston will know how to reach this person in question?"

"He will know." Tori looked toward Jefferson. "If you will tell Edward…Mr. Livingston, that it is urgent and that Marie and her herbs are needed right away, she will come. Oh, and when she gets here, could you please see to it that she comes right in." Jefferson nodded his head, and without a spoken word, he departed and closed the door behind him.

Tori watched as the General stood briefly to place two more logs on the fire, and once satisfied that they would burn, he returned to his seat. "Come, my dear, let's get to know each other, shall we?"

This time Tori smiled brightly. "I would be honored, Sir."

"Please, not so formal. I would be most happy if you were to oblige me and call me by my given name, Andrew." He had another coughing fit and struggled to stop it. Tori remained quiet and waited for him to compose himself. At last, after several minutes, he took in a deep breath and mopped his brow. "You know, from the second I saw you I felt a wave of familiarity sweep over me. You remind me of my Rachel in your actions and demeanor. But, also in your face, there is a resemblance to my dearly departed mother." He coughed once and turned to face the fire that now burned brightly.

Tori looked into the older man's face and saw a pain there that could not be denied. "I am sorry for your loss, Andrew. Please accept my deep condolence, and please do call me Tori. I agree, an unusual name, but it is the name my friends prefer to call me. Victoria has always seemed so formal." What else could she say, she wondered? The moment was awkward. This was something she had not expected. Talking with Andrew Jackson about personal matters was mind-blowing, let alone being on a first-name basis; that was far more than just mind-blowing; it was incredible. It was then that Tori reminded herself she had to take care of what she spoke about or acknowledged. Cisco had warned her that this man was brilliant, and he would pick up on anything out of the ordinary.

Jackson looked at her with a kind expression on his face. "That is most kind of you. She died when I was but a boy. I was orphaned when she did not return from a trip…" he fell silent for a bit. "I lost my older brother also. He was everything a younger sibling could ask for. The British killed him. Gave me this to remember them by." His hand touched his face, and then he held the same hand palm up to show Tori another long scar. "They took so much from me, but they will not take this land by God. I will find a way to stop them; it's as simple as that. Then he mumbled under his breath, "Or I will die trying; you can count on that." Jackson looked into Jean's wife's eyes and saw something that comforted him. She was not shocked, nor was she afraid. There was no pity there in her expression either. He smiled slightly. "Begging your pardon, I should not burden you with my sorrow or shortcomings. It is not right to do so. I have no idea what came over me. I never talk about that which has driven me all these years. Of my disdain for the British, disdain, which I freely admit borders on hate."

"You have no need to apologize, and I will not speak of that which you have chosen to share with me. However, I think I can ease your fear of the battle, which surely is coming our way. Jean will return with what you need; in fact, I know he will return with not only ammo and flints but with men who will fight alongside you."

"I am grateful to you for divulging such positive details, facts that allow me the confidence to stand by my own assessment of Mr. Laffite. I am confident that your husband is telling the truth. His word was given, and I took it to heart. The mention of men, well, that does in of itself, help ease some of the worries. Finding good men to fight alongside me has been a burden. I have seen the river, visited the forts, met the men, who are even as we speak making preparations. However, I have known I needed more to join those I already have. Men who have no doubt fought and have an understanding of what we face—men who have experience in battle and what it brings. Forgive me, but those I have met here in this city are gentlemen. Many are willing but not prepared, I think. What we will face demands much, and I fear greatly…I have more marching our way, but I fear they may not reach us in time. Please, I do not wish to burden you with such grave matters. Please, Tori, make yourself comfortable. If you would allow me to help you with your cloak?"

"That is not necessary, Andrew; you remain by the fire. I am quite capable of seeing to my needs." She smiled gently at the man while removing her winter cloak.

His head dropped down until his chin hit his chest. "Forgive me, my dear; I need a short nap. You will wake me upon the return of your husband or that of who you have sent for. No doubt, it will be your friend to raise me from my slumber." He had spoken this last statement to himself and no sooner finished than a soft snore escaped the exhausted man's lips.

For a while, the house would sit in silence as they awaited the return of Jean, Mr. Sims, and also Marie. Tori hugged herself as she watched the General asleep in the chair.

Sat before her was a man who would be president if history allowed. So much was riding on a fine thread of what three people could remember from their history lessons and memories. Tori was beginning to understand that what they knew and what they did not was daunting.

She realized that not one of the three had known that Jackson would arrive on December 2, 1814, and that shortly after his arrival, he'd depart downriver to see for himself the forts and protection they'd offer the city. He would be gone for close to two weeks and made his intentions clear on his return. In those long agonizing two weeks, she and Jean had speculated, plotted, and planned, but most of all, they had done their best to keep up with what was going on.

Upon Jackson's return to the city, meetings were held at his headquarters and in the Masonic lodge, whose members, like Jackson, included Edward Livingston and Claiborne, among others. Many facts would be made known to Laffite through Livingston. He had been informed their friend Jacques Villere now held the title of Major General and had departed the city. He'd left escorted by the Louisiana militia that he commanded into the bayous to cut down trees and block the waterways. Jean had sent out word that his men were to help in the same manner and not accost those who remained to guard the numerous channels. Now sat waiting for her husband's return, Tori found herself praying that the so-called blocked bayous would not hinder the stash he had gone to retrieve.

The long night hours crept by, and though she wanted to sleep, there was no way her anxious mind would allow her the peace to do so. The worried female looked at the room's closed door and hoped Marie would hurry up.

⤜ Two ⤛

The gray light of dawn crept between the curtains, where someone had hurried the process of covering the window but missed the small opening. Two thick panels hung with a sizeable gap between them, and Laffite's love was glad of this because she could gage the early morning hour. It had been a long night and one that was filled with anticipation of its outcome.

Tori sat up all night opposite the General, watching him sleep restlessly. His fever was up, and his respiration was labored. It was as if he was fighting with each breath to fill his empty lungs with air. She thought that by exerting such energy, the man would look flushed. Instead of having a red hue about his cheeks, his face maintained a bluish-gray tint. Suddenly she recalled that the last time she had seen someone with that appearance had been when Leone died. This thought terrified her. Surely it was not possible for Jackson to be that close to death. Tori would never allow herself to believe such a thing possible; because history said he fought in New Orleans. History, however, was a fickle thing, though, and no one knew that better than herself. Anxiously, she kept listening for the sound of Marie's quickstep, announcing her arrival and her help.

However, hour after long hour, the house remained still. Once or twice one man or another would step just inside the room to see that their commander was alright. Quietly they would add wood to the fire and, without speaking, leave her and the General alone. A few hours ago, two bottles of wine were brought in, and Tori made a note to thank Livingston for his generosity when next they met. After the wine arrived, visits to the room ceased, and the only sounds came from the sleeping hero-to-be, whose wheezy chest and light snoring filled the room. Not one sound beyond the closed parlor door invaded the tomb-like stillness that enveloped her.

Tori remained ever vigilant, her eyes shifting from Jackson to the door and back. If help did not come soon, she would have to do something. There was no doubt that it would be up to her to take this desperate situation into her own hands and act no matter the questions or resistance that would most certainly come her way. The next time one of Jackson's men looked in on them, she would inform him of her decision and tell him what she needed but what she needed most of all was for Marie to arrive. Then, as if God himself had read her mind, she heard the door slowly creaking open, followed by whispering voices.

"I have no time to argue with you about my identity. The fact of the matter is this. I was sent for, and I'm here. Plain enough for you? Now, I highly suggest you move your carcass and let me by."

Tori recognized the voice immediately and noticed the determined look on the man called Jefferson's face; she admitted that Marie had a lot of guts to stand up to him like that.

"Jefferson, let the poor woman pass before she brains you one," growled Jackson, who then mischievously winked at Tori.

Marie moved past the man in the doorway and, taking the initiative, pushed him out of the parlor and closed the door. "Now you stay put, afore you make me really mad like," she hissed at the door before turning with a slight smile on her lips while walking toward Tori. The two hugged and then together turned their attention toward Jackson.

"I can see with my own eyes, why you sent for me. Thought I would have been sent for days ago, though. By just looking at you, General, I can see your head must feel ready to explode, and as for them bones, that ache something fierce, well I say you be one stubborn man to put up with it, that's all."

Andrew Jackson had seen some sights in his time, but looking at this slip of a girl, who stood before him, telling him how stubborn he was, raised color to his deathly white pallor.

Marie was glad to see this because it indicated that the man had

the strength to fight because what she needed now was his co-oper-
ation, not his anger or stubborn ways. "Now, don't you go a getting'
yourself all worked up. Miss Tori here sent for me and by the looks of
you, none too soon." She shook her head and spoke to Laffite's wife.

"I'll be needing some things. That Jefferson better be a-doing as I
ask, or things is going to get loud around here, and that ain't a-going
to please the General none," she laughed, walking back toward the
closed door. "Now, let me get ready." She removed her cape and then
walked to her basket, pulling off the cloth covering.

Tori grinned at Marie, who was talking somewhat odd, but then
she always had a reason for what she did, and her friend knew what
she was about. Ignoring her for the moment, Laffite's wife went to
Jackson and knelt by the side of his chair. "General Sir, please excuse
Marie; she means well enough. I sent for her late last night, as you
may recall. You said I could remember?" She watched as recognition registered in the man's eyes before hastily continuing. "Marie
is very good with herbs and tonics. I would trust her with my life-
have done just that, in fact. The doctors try, but Marie, well, she has
her ways that, for the most part, heal faster and with less stupidity. I
disagree with bleeding a person to get them better, and I bet you see
the insanity of that too. If we called a doctor, it's my bet that would be
the first thing he would do. Trust me, Sir, Marie will have you feeling
much better in no time if you will listen and do as she says. Please,
General Sir, you must get well and fast. Marie is the only chance
you have right now to do that." She grabbed hold of his hand and
squeezed it tight to re-enforce what she'd said.

He looked down at his hand in hers and then back up. His
instincts told him that she meant well enough and that just maybe
if he listened to this Marie, all would be as it should. "Mrs. Laffite,
forgive me, Tori...first, I would like to thank you for your concern,
and second of all, I believe that we know each other well enough to
drop the formalities as we agreed last night. Please do me the honor,
and I will also abide by our arrangement. We are, after all, friends,
aren't we?"

"That we are, Andrew, and it would be far more of an honor than you could guess for me to call you by your first name." God, how she wished she could talk to this man and tell him what she knew and who she was, but that could never happen, and the modern woman knew it.

"You two finished with your visit 'cause I got to get this here medicine down his throat. Ain't got no time to fuss about. Time is not what we got if we are to get you healing." She shot Tori a knowing look.

"Excuse me, Andrew," added Tori. "I had better let Marie here do her job. Just trust her, and you'll see; everything will turn out as it should."

Andrew sighed deeply; his lungs crackled as he exhaled, causing him to cough. When he managed to control his breathing, he spoke. "Tori, how could I not accept her help? Your word is good enough for me. Now, Miss…"

"Marie is my name."

He nodded. "Marie, shall we begin."

Tori watched as Marie gave Jackson three different drinks, and by the look on his face, each tasted worse than the other. Still, he put up no fight, and after the last glass was empty, Marie put his head back on the chair and told him to sleep for a while.

"We will be right here, Andrew," said Tori from across the room. "Please try and rest. I give you my word; as soon as Jean returns, I will wake you."

Marie took the tray with the empty glasses on it and walked to the table by the window, signaling Tori to join her. "We won't be needing any light for a while, so leave these here curtains drawn over. Don't need no light to talk by, and that's what you are wantin' to do now, isn't it?"

"I suppose it is, but what I really want to know…will he be all right? What's wrong with him, Marie? He looks just dreadful, and I'm sure he feels worse than he looks."

"That be the truth of it for sure. I know'd some of the reason he is the way he is, sick and all, but, even with Cisco's help, we can't be certain of all the reasons." Marie saw Tori's puzzled look and smiled gently at her. The young healer patted her friend's hand. "He's going to be just fine if you ask me. Just takes some time, and that's what's worrying me and all." Marie looked back at the sleeping figure in the chair by the fire and frowned. "I asked that man of mine. I say, Cisco, how much time d'we have to get this here, General Jackson ready for the battle? And you know what he says? He goes and tells me he don't know. His best guess not long. Not long, he says, and how I supposed to cure a man, with not long to do it in, I asks you?" She rolled her eyes and then closed the lids and squeezed them shut with her fingers while she continued to whisper. "I just know he won't be fully well in time, but he be well on his way. That be the best I can do. For him to rid his self of all that ails him, well, that will take months. I kin get him to feeling much better, even stronger, but no cure."

"I believe you, my friend, but you still did not answer my question. What's wrong with him? Surely you and Cisco have some idea, and why are you talking so strangely?"

Marie opened her eyes and grinned. "Oh, that, just playing my role," she giggled. "As to what's wrong, Cisco and I talked. He has a case of the fever you call malaria; we call it Swamp fever. Cisco says you have a medicine called quin, quinin?"

"You mean quinine. Yes, we have that. I took it myself when I went to Africa on a trip. You don't have it here at this time, though, or do you?"

"Reckons we do. Ain't sure it be this here quinine, but the tea comes from tree bark. The tree ain't found here, no way. It come from South America way. Good thing the bark keeps for a long time. It be so hard to get some years. Your man, he is the one who finds it and sees to it that I get it. Not that he finds it easy to supply me with what I need. He has someone in one of the ports that sells it to him, and you know, your man never asks me to pay him."

Marie had a faraway look in her eyes and seemed lost in a

daydream for a few seconds as if remembering just such a time. Then she shook her head and continued. Cisco says the base of the medicine he would have used as a doctor comes from a plant, and so it could be the same. Strange, it is, the things my man explained to me. He said that your menfolk got themselves a way to make what nature makes. Said, plenty of your pills and potions are made by man, but they all used nature's secret to start. Don't know why anyone would want to try and match nature. Anyway, we used it." She pointed to the bottle that contained the first potion she had given Jackson. "If the General has the swamp fever, this will cure that. His head and his pains be taken care of by the second drink. You know'd about that one yourself."

Tori grimaced, thinking of the horrible taste that Marie's form of aspirin had. Still, she knew it would work and felt a slight sense of relief.

"The third be my own making, and I know that the man be needing it bad. He ain't been eating or sleeping good for weeks, and if he is going to have to fight, he will need his strength. You call it what you want. I ain't a-going to tell you what's in it, but know this, he's about to have himself a real good lift of energy." She slapped her leg and laughed, putting her head close to Tori. "I give it to Cisco once. Once be all I could take. That man was on me day and night like he was a dog in heat. Lord, he almost killed me. It was fun at first, but then he came to wanting way too much, so I had to send him away till it wore off." She was giggling like a schoolgirl and had to turn away from Tori.

"Oh, stop it, Marie," Tori laughed. "You are just impossible, you know. We need to be quiet… we can't wake Andrew. Look at him. I think he is resting more comfortably, don't you?"

Marie looked over at the man and nodded her head. "Yes, he be resting real well. Now, what are we going to do for you? You look as if you need some of my powders."

"Oh no, you don't. Don't you dare try and give me any of that energy-boosting shit. I know Jean would love you if it had the same effect on me as it did Cisco." She was chuckling again. "Shit Marie, stop this before I bust something." Tori was choking and trying desperately to stifle her laughter which turned into coughing.

Marie pushed a cup of tea toward her, and Tori downed the warm liquid, extinguishing the coughing fit.

Gratefully she smiled at her friend while wiping the tears from her eyes. "God, Marie, I didn't think you could choke to death on your own spit." She sipped again from her cup and sat back in the overstuffed chair, satisfied that the coughing had ceased.

"All I need is some sleep, and I just might be able to take a nap if you are quiet." Tori was trying to sound firm, but her smile betrayed her.

Marie grinned. "You listen to me. Reason you all but choked on your spit, as you say, is plain as can be. Your body is telling you it's just plum tired out. You need sleep as much as that there, man. Now, you make yourself comfortable in that big old chair, and I'll stay and watch over you both. Go on now; listen to me. I know what I be talking about."

The thought of sleep, if only for a short while, sounded wonderful, and Tori knew she needed the rest. "Thank you, Marie. I think I will take a short nap. You'll wake me, won't you? I mean, if anything happens?"

"Yes, um, I'll wake you. But it won't be necessary. You will wake yourself when you are needed; you'll see." Tori rested her head back against the chair, and before she could think about all that was happening around her, she fell into a deep, dreamless sleep.

"Marie picked up Tori's cup and put it on the tray next to the teapot. As she did so, she smiled slightly and whispered to herself. "And the fourth potion put him to rest for sure, just like you." She chuckled softly. Cisco was right; you did need to sleep some. All you needed was a little help, that's all. Just a little help for a few hours of sanctuary, that's it. Sleep is the only place you are worry free," she said to both of them. "I ain't a-goin' to be able to help you none in that department again," she added sadly before heading to the door with the tray of glasses.

"Jefferson, you be there?" she softly called. "I have more for you to attend to, and these glasses need cleaning. In hot water, not cold, you understand. That's very important. Also, a fresh pot of coffee will be nice in a few hours, and I know the General is particular to his being strong. Not that he has need of it; he will have all his strength without no black mud, as I think of it, but some habits are hard to stop, and I reckon he has a habit of having more than one cup at a time."

Marie sat quietly and watched over the two sleeping individuals in the hours that followed. Jackson's breathing was a bit easier, and Tori had not moved once, proving she was indeed in need of rest.

Jackson woke first, and upon seeing Tori asleep, he spoke softly so as not to disturb her. "How long have I slept?"

"I would say for as long as you needed. The sun is up, and Laffite should return soon. I have some coffee here if you would like some."

"Indeed, Madam, that would be most welcome."

Marie handed him a cup and a small glass with an amber-looking liquid filling it to the rim. "If you would drink this down first, it will take that headache away and ward off the chills you are feeling. It's not that bad; gulp it down and then enjoy your coffee."

Without so much as a word, he took the glass and did as instructed. Handing the empty glass back, he added his thoughts on the substance. "May I add, you may not think the concoction is vile, but I can assure you it is most unpleasant. Still, I am under your care, and as Madame Laffite told me, you are a most talented healer, and healing is what I require. I trust, however, that you will keep our arrangement and my condition between us?"

"I will." She took the empty glass from his trembling hand and smiled. "You should feel better in a short time but not healed; I am sorry to say. I will do all I can, and Tori will expect me to continue."

"I will see to it that my men know you are free to visit my office and me whenever you require to do so. Ah! Tori, you awake. I do hope we did not disturb you."

Tori sat up and looked toward her friend Marie and frowned. "You slipped me a Micky; I mean, you snuck some of that sleeping whatever in my drink, didn't you?"

"Guilty as charged. Jean made me promise if I could get you to rest, that I would, and Tori, you needed it as much as the General here."

"Maybe, I suppose so. Any word from Jean yet?"

"No, but the sun is up, and it can't be long now. How about joining us and have a cup of coffee. This blend should wake you up if nothing else."

"I will take a cup, thank you. I need to get rid of this groggy, ah, sleeping feeling. Coffee always helps."

Marie was filling another mug when the sound of footsteps approaching echoed in the hall outside the room. There was a brief knock on the door, and then before any one of them could say enter, Tori watched as Jean entered, followed closely by Jackson's men.

Tori stood up and faced her husband, who was grinning ear to ear. "I take it that all went as you planned. Dominique did good; the powder and flints are where he said?"

"They were, and as we talk, the General's men are moving everything from the bayou to town."

"Excellent!" It was Jackson's turn to stand and face the pirate. He extended his hand, and Jean stepped forward and took it in his. Laffite's grip was tight as he shook the American's hand. What he needed now was for the man to honor their bargain. "Mr. Laffite, I am in your debt. You, Sir, have proved your worth and kept your word. If I can entice you to join my men and me…"

"I will most certainly be honored to do so."

"Good. With that settled, I feel coffee and something to eat is in order. Then we shall begin to make arrangements. Plans need to be set in motion and agreements met." Jackson looked toward one of his men. "See to it that all of Laffite's men are released from custody and while you are at it, tell Claiborne that as of now, the city is under martial law. Tell him I expect him and his council to meet here in two hours. We have much to do, and I fear little time to accomplish what is necessary."

The man turned and left the room as another entered with a tray of food. "Thought you would be wanting something, General, you and your guests." He placed the tray on the table. "More coffee is brewing, and if you allow me, I shall return with more food and plates."

"Excellent. Madame Laffite, would you care to join us, or are you anxious to spend time with your husband?"

"General Jackson…"

"Andrew, please."

"Forgive me. We did agree on that last night, didn't we? Andrew, it is. I would be honored to join you, and then I shall depart with Marie and let you gentlemen have your meeting. Jean will talk with me later."

"That is what I had hoped you would say. A lady's company is always welcome, and yours more so right now. You can say you are standing in for my beloved wife. Now, let us eat before the food goes cold. Captain Laffite, you can tell me of last night's adventure as we eat. I am sure the story will be most entertaining." He chuckled at the expression on his men's faces. They may not like that he had a pirate as a friend, but they sure as hell understood that the man had delivered what he promised and, in so doing, just might have given them all a fighting chance.

EDWARD stormed into Jackson's headquarters; his expression was one of sneering as if he had a bad smell up his nose, and his eyes held a look of pure anger in their depths. For the dandy, the day had been going just fine. Every plan had been expertly implemented and executed to perfection. Why was it then that just when all seemed to be in hand, everything had fallen apart once again? There was no doubt as to the authenticity of the news. Dominique You, along with the rest of Laffite's men, had been released.

Not only released, but some given high ranks in Jackson's army. He had seen all the activity on Royal Street with his own eyes, especially in front of the so-called, headquarters for the Americans. Had the whole city gone crazy, he wondered? Just what was going on and why? Two questions he demanded answered, and Edward was determined he would not leave the building until he had a valid explanation.

THE entrance to the house was blocked by a small group of men, most of whom Edward recognized and some he did not even want to acknowledge. Those were the so-called Kentuckians. These men seemed to be more savage than the few Indians with them; not only did they look evil, but they also smelled rank. They were unshaven and unkempt. Hell, even the way they spoke was filled with such uncouth language that he wondered how the American Jackson, who seemed so refined at social gatherings, could stand to listen to them, let alone make any sense of their babbling.

Edward had met a few of them standing outside the house. At first, they had barred his way, but upon an explanation of who he was and who he needed to talk with, they had stepped aside. 'Stupid men, letting anyone in, he thought; why he bet any one of the pirates could do the same, and then where would they be? With a dead General, that's where he told himself.

He'd had difficulty understanding the two guards, let alone accepting them as so-called men of undying loyalty. Clad in animal skins and wearing animal fur on their heads, instead of gentlemen's hats, proved to him they were heathens and nothing more. Though he did suppose wearing a fine hat dressed as they were, would look even more ridiculous. He had proceeded to the parlor where he was told the Governor was, but assuming he would be alone with Jackson, was a mistake.

Jackson's men looked as if they only cared about themselves, and the way they turned their backs on the dandy when he entered the room was just unacceptable, in his opinion. How Jackson could entertain having these men as a part of his entourage baffled him. After all, when introduced to Claiborne and his friends, the American had proven himself a gentleman of high standing. His manners were impeccable, so it made no earthly sense that such an educated individual would lower himself to converse with such inferior idiots.

Claiborne saw Edward enter and smiled brightly at his Creole friend. "So, you have heard? Who would have ever thought? Laffite has saved the day. That is, at least he has given us the means to provide it with a hell of a good effort."

The Governor saw that Edward had no idea what he was talking about and left the group of men around the table to explain to his trusted friend just what had happened.

"Laffite has saved the day?" Edward spit the words out as if they were dirt in his mouth. "Just what does Laffite have to do with anything, let alone the release of his slime from the Cabildo? They are supposed to hang, remember?"

"Please stop before you venture any further," Claiborne said none too quietly. Holding up his hand to silence Edward, he strode forward. "It is only your unfamiliarity with the facts that have your judgment clouded. Walk with me. I could use some air." The two men left the room without a further word and strolled out to the courtyard. "I tell you, I would never have believed it myself, but these are the facts. General Andrew Jackson himself has verified it, and it was on his orders that we released Laffite's men." He looked at the stunned expression on Edwards' face and felt sorry for him, and knew he needed to dispel his confusion. Claiborne placed his hand on the younger man's shoulder, guiding him toward the stone bench. "Here, sit with me, and I will explain it further. You are well aware that our forces, small as they are, had an even graver problem than size. The need for flints, powder, and weapons was desperate, as you know. It was an unsolvable problem, I say. However, the problem has been…"

Edward had a sinking feeling about where this conversation was leading, yet he still clung to the thread of hope that he had not guessed right. Quickly he interrupted the man and spoke in a harsh tone, hoping to deflect the impossible. "Did I hear you correctly? I fear your excitement, which I see on your face. That you are having difficulty containing your feelings indicates more, much more. Just what are you trying to tell me?"

"Calm down, my friend, and I will explain. I did indeed say there was a problem. That's because, thanks to Jean Laffite, we no longer have a shortage of flints, powder, or men willing to fight. We also have a stock of weapons, and I hear maybe a cannon or two. At least Laffite has been on top of the situation, which is more than I can say for us. No matter what we did or didn't do, Laffite kept his head and waited, biding his time until Jackson arrived."

"More likely, he was waiting for the British, and Jackson lucked out and got here first. He took the waiting opportunity to his advantage."

Claiborne interrupted him immediately. "I... Jackson and his men, we all believe Laffite. He has integrity... he told us the truth in those letters. I only wish we would have trusted him then. Edward, we need to thank God he is on our side."

"The man is a pirate, a murdering bastard who has on many occasions made you look like a fool. Have you not forgotten that? He roams the Gulf and has met with the British; what more proof do you need that he is in league with them?"

"He could have helped the British by now if he chose to. Jean and his men's knowledge of the backwaters is extensive. Laffite has bought Jackson time by having his men stall the British. They refuse to show them the way through the bayous. The very mouth of the Mississippi and surrounding areas, including Grand Terre... what's left of it... well, it's now guarded by his men and ours. We have been fools, I tell you, not to have listened to him or respond to his correspondence. Such fools. He and his letters were all genuine, and I regret what we have done as far as Grand Terre. Still, it is done, and we move forward. Laffite has done so for the betterment of our country, and so shall we all."

Edward was sick to his stomach and had to try to reason with the stupid American Governor. "I can't believe what you are saying. You are sitting there, telling me that this pirate, this traitor, has bought you off with the offer of his supplying flint, powder, and men? William, are you blind? Has it not crossed yours or anyone else's mind that the man could be working with... is in league with the British? I would bet my life he is."

"I am not blind nor stupid. I am grateful for your concern Edward, but Jackson has verified the supply of flints and powder, as I have already told you. He has Laffite's pledge of loyalty, along with those of his men. The very fact that his men have not shown the British through the waterways only goes to prove that Laffite is not in league with them, does it not?"

Edward was highly agitated, and thinking that the dandy's actions were out of concern, Claiborne tried to calm him further. "Jackson is no fool, Edward. I'm sure that if, for one second, the General suspected Laffite to be anything but what he seems, he would never have acted as he has. Jackson's reputation, both as a fine leader and fair judge of men, proceeds him and gives credence to his actions. Others of fine standing, John Grymes and his partner Livingston, who it turns out, is a long-time friend of Jackson, known each other for years. Many others, too many to name, have all stepped forward, stating the very same facts. Jean is not our enemy, never has been."

"You can't believe them, not a one. The pirate has paid them off... fooled you all."

"No, Edward, you are wrong on this account. I met with Laffite face-to-face only a few hours ago and have to admit that even though I still find the man and his piracy deplorable, he is forthcoming in his desire to fight and protect this city from the enemy. I wish I could divulge more." He looked as if he was about to say something else but quickly changed his mind. "You will just have to trust me on this." He stood up and looked toward the parlor while speaking. "There is much to do yet, and I'm sure you will excuse me. I can only hope that with men such as Laffite and yourself, we will have a chance at pushing the British from our shores, should it come to that." The Governor never looked back at Edward as he left. He simply called out as he walked toward the house. "We will talk later. Stop by this evening with Simone. Cayetana would love to see you both." With that, he was gone.

Edward sat still on the bench and felt a sharp pain in his chest which he chose to ignore. That fool actually had the audacity to compare him with the likes of Laffite. Laffite, the despicable pirate, had once again pulled himself free of his demise. He had the whole city believing his story of loyalty, and now he would be heralded as a hero for his supply of weapons and fighting men. Damn the man. Edward put his hand to his now-throbbing head and squeezed his eyes shut. Simone would help him figure a way out of this mess. If anyone could help him, it would be his wife. She had never failed him, and he doubted she would now. The dandy knew only too well that Simone was at her best when things seemed at their worst. Edward opened his eyes as a sinister snarl curled his lips. "I'm not done with you yet, Laffite," he mumbled.

JEAN and Tori were often seen coming and going from Jackson's headquarters, and the city streets were now filled with Jean's men from Barataria. They may be pirates and rough bastards who sailed the high seas, but in the hour of need, these men had been accepted by the people without question. Tori had met with Dominique and Beluche, only briefly before they departed, on what they called essential duty. Both had been given the rank of Captain, and as skilled artillerymen, they were being treated with great respect. Dominique hugged Tori as he would a daughter and then, laughing out loud, proclaimed that he, Dominique You, would be a force to reckon with when he returned. However, he would not give any hint into what it was that he alone seemed to know. Dominique just winked and chuckled, "it is good to have planned ahead. The Redcoats will soon understand that to go against me is foolhardy."

JACKSON and his officers, along with Laffite, spent hours planning and plotting each move. Even with the added number of volunteers, they were aware that they would be vastly outnumbered. Worse still, Jackson knew, they would be up against the world's strongest fighting force. All of the British militaries were filled with seasoned veterans, and all Jackson had that he could count on were a few men who had seen action with him and Laffite's pirates, all of whom he was pretty confident were ready to kill and relish doing so. The men who knew how to fight were backed by willing and eager greenhorns, most of whom had not even shot a gun, let alone killed someone. True, he had some plantation owners, who had hunted for game and thought that qualified them, but shooting deer or birds was far different from shooting another man. The very thought that he could be sending these men to certain death in weeks, or even days, weighed heavily on his conscience.

Marie had continued to pay the General a daily visit, and she always brought her powders with her. To many there, who saw Jackson, he showed slight improvement. To Marie, he was growing stronger and healthier each hour. Whether he himself felt any difference was not known, not even to those closest to him. He would smile and gratefully take what was given him and then once more proceed with whatever he had been doing. Tori watched and prayed that the British would wait a few more weeks before arriving because Andrew Jackson needed time. Time to build up his strength and time for the tonics or whatever Marie was giving him, to work.

WITH Christmas approaching, Tori, like the rest of the town, felt that they had to do something. Could they plan any celebration knowing what was coming? Tori and John Davis had met and decided to have a small gathering of friends for Christmas dinner and not worry about what the rest of the city was planning.

"It's December 23rd already. I don't suppose even the enemy would want to fight on Christmas day, do you?" Tori had half-jokingly asked John, who stood looking out the balcony window.

"I suppose not. We have bought time for Jackson. Have to hand it to the General; his idea of sending a few men to be caught by the British and convince them to approach New Orleans by way of the swamps and not just sail up the river was brilliant." He looked back into the room and continued, his voice sounding full of admiration. "Those brave souls allowed themselves to be caught and then tortured by the enemy to convince them that what they were eventually told under duress was the gospel truth. I did not think it would work; still, that's a moot point now. The British bought it. They believe a large force protects the river and that surprise is the best option they have. By moving their men, equipment, and such overland toward the battlefield is happening even as I stand here. A miracle, if ever there was one, and a huge error on the enemy's part. I often wondered why they didn't just sail up the river and take the city? Now, I know, but one thing I have learned in my life is never to underestimate your opponent." After pausing a moment, he looked back at the street. "Cisco is coming, and by the way, he is running up the street; I think he has something of great importance to tell us."

Tori looked at John and let the pen in her hand drop to the desk. All thoughts of writing out the dinner invitations fled her mind. Cisco only ever ran when he was excited or had something of great importance to impart. If John had seen him running down the street, it meant something was up and that something had to be grave news. Before Cisco even entered the room, Tori knew deep down that time had just run out for all of them.

The door burst open, and Cisco flew in. He stood looking from one to the other, and then he spoke. "The British have been spotted and get this; they are only nine miles south of here. Seems we can't stall them any longer." Tori grabbed the side of the table, gasping. "Nine miles? That's too damn close. Oh my God!" She spun around to face John. Did you know they got this close? You did, didn't you? I mean, that's why you are not that upset, right? You have been waiting for this moment."

"As I said, never underestimate your opponent." He looked directly at Cisco, and with concern filling his voice, he spoke. "I, unlike either of you, paid a visit to the battleground in our time. Shame I didn't research it more. After I saw the site, I sort of forgot about it. One fact is correct; it is about six or seven miles away, so history is still on track. Now, Cisco, my friend, do explain how you came to learn of this latest development?"

"Jackson just got the word, and I came here right away. It seems they are not on the move, the British that is, but have camped on the Villere plantation. They had arrived early this morning and get this; they put the family of the plantation under house arrest. That did not sit too well with the owner Gabriel Villere. He escaped out a window on the second floor. Jumped down, landing on two Redcoats. Bet that hurt," he laughed. "Then, he ran to the wooded area he knew well and ran as fast as possible with the British on his heels. He knew he had to hide, and this is the sad part. His dog followed him, and he had to put the poor animal..." Cisco looked away from Tori, whose expression told him his following words would be more than upsetting. "Well, he had to kill it. Hit it with a branch from the tree he climbed up into." He looked away from John and spoke to Tori. "The dog, you see, would have given him away. He said it broke his heart, but it was quick, and one blow to the head is all it took. He climbed way up in the tree and hid there. The soldiers could not find him and gave up. When they left, he climbed down and ran to Jackson's headquarters and burst in to tell them all that the enemy was on his land and had taken his house over. All hell is breaking out down there at Jackson's. I thought you should know. I've got to get back. Plans are changing fast, and Jackson is giving orders. He plans to hit them first; at least that's what I think he meant. You coming, John?"

"Need you ask?" he said, grabbing his coat and taking a pistol out of his desk drawer. Tori, who stood frozen on the spot, did not want to believe what was happening. However, she quickly made up her mind to act. "I'm coming too."

Seeing the instant horror register on both men's faces, she added, "Only to see if I can wish Jean luck. He will be fighting too. We all know where I have to go and what I have to do. You were right, John, to make plans early. Don't worry; I'm not stupid. I'll do my part. Let's go, shall we?" She grabbed her cape and took Cisco by the arm. "This is it. Let's make history." hit them first; at least that's what I think he meant. You coming, John?"

ROYAL Street was as active as a beehive in summer. Swarms of men were coming and going, all rushing in different directions, determined to carry out whatever orders they were given. Tori had seen a few women here and there waving goodbye to loved ones while still others stood crying openly on the verandahs overlooking the street. Chaos seemed to reign around them the closer they got to Andrew Jackson's headquarters. Cisco or John had to pull Tori out of harm's way several times. Wagons were rushing by, intent on their mission. Men and soldiers marched down streets, calling out for anything that could be used to dig. If signaled, they would pause, and once the shovels, hoes, or other implements were loaded up, they moved on.

By the time Tori, Cisco and John actually reached the front of the headquarters; Tori had been pushed and pulled so much that she was not even paying close attention to those around her anymore. Her one thought was to reach Jean before he had to leave to defend the city, so one more man, bumping into her, didn't surprise her in the least. However, Cisco's added grip on her arm caused her to look up into the face of the individual who had nearly knocked her over.

"Edward!" Her voice was more shocked than fearful. "What are you doing here?"

"Tori. Gentlemen." He bowed slightly. "I was leaving on a mission for the Governor. Now, I ask you the same, but then I think I know why you are here." Edward leaned forward slightly and spoke directly to Tori. "He's already gone, you know. You're too late. Headed out with his men on orders from Jackson."

Something inside her churned as she struggled to keep control of her emotions. Her eyes filled with tears at the thought of having missed Jean. She had so wanted to hug him and tell him to stay safe and come home to her when the battle was over. Now it seemed that chance had gone.

The dandy spotted her upset and delighted in it. "I wouldn't worry if I were you. Seems your pirate always gets himself out of difficult situations. Still, there is the chance that this venture may be the one to undo him. Tell me, my dear. Have you considered what you will do when the British win? I have no doubt they will prevail, and your Jean will be a prisoner or worse yet, dead. Oh, forgive me; I see you have not. Well, let me assure you, I will be…"

Cisco's punch came out of nowhere, landing squarely on Edward's jaw, knocking him backward with such force that the dandy lost his balance and fell flat on his back.

"That, you slimy little bastard, is not only for the lady here but for Jean as well. I have to tell you that I have been waiting for some time to have the opportunity to get my hands on you." John Davis's firm grip held Cisco back, and Tori, who did not want any further confrontation, spoke up.

"Don't bother yourself with this scum, Cisco. You have put him where he will no doubt end up after all this is over. It suites him, don't you agree? In the gutter is a good choice. Well done." She turned her back on the spectacle Edward was making of himself and spoke to John. "Look, we are needed right now. Let him grovel his way around amongst the muck. Shit begets shit, does it not?" She pulled Cisco and walked past Edward, deliberately kicking at the dirt as she went.

"You think you have won?" Edward screamed. "Just you wait and see who grovels next." Seeing some people staring at him, he pulled himself up, and while brushing some dirt from his sleeve, he declared in a loud voice, "This whole town has gone quite mad, quite mad indeed." With that said, he headed home.

ONCE they were inside the house, Livingston met the three of them and ushered them to the back room, where the General was preparing to leave. Livingston sounded out of breath as he spoke. "He had hoped you would come by and asked to speak with you if you did. Hurry this way. You just missed Marie. She was here with her potions and insisted he take them. Gave him extra too."

Tori entered the room, and two things hit her at once. First off, Edward had lied. Jean was still there. He was talking with Jackson while putting a piece of paper into the inside coat pocket of his jacket. It was not a fancy gentlemen's jacket, more of a coat a pirate would wear. Something was going on, but she'd not question him now; he'd most likely not divulge any information anyway. Besides, she had other things to ponder right then as she realized Jackson looked weaker than she remembered. Tori stood transfixed by his sickly appearance and watched him drink the last of whatever Marie had given him. His face contorted while swallowing the contents of the glass, and not wanting to give away his true dislike of the liquid, he coughed and hid his frown behind the palm of his hand, which was covering his mouth.

Turning toward Tori, he straightened himself and brushed off any sign of his weak condition. His eyes were brighter than they had been. He did have some color back in his cheeks, but Tori knew that this man was living on pure willpower and inner strength, which came from his dedication to his job and knowing how many people depended on him.

"Tori, my dear. I must confess, I am so delighted you have come. Please come over and join us." He held out his hand, and she took it. "I just wanted to thank you for all your care and concern. My wife, God bless her, could not have done more. I have to confess that you were right about your friend Marie. Her potions, or whatever they are, have helped me tremendously, but do remind me never to try her cooking." He laughed, his eyes sparkling and winked at her.

Tori found herself laughing with him. If only he knew that his estimation of her friend's cooking was so out of the ballpark. She laughed even more then because the man would not have the slightest idea what a ballpark was. Every person seemed in high spirits and not in the least bit fearful, which to her was pretty strange considering the circumstances.

Jackson hesitated before speaking. It was as if he loathed telling Tori and her two friends what he felt and understood to be true. "I take it you are aware of the unfortunate situation we are in? At least I can stop guessing which way they will come, and they have obliged me by showing themselves during daylight hours and not moving under cover of darkness. My men have confirmed they came via land; marched through the swamps from Lake Borgne. They assure me that those who now camp not far from here do so because they require rest. Bone weary are the words used to describe their condition. Like I told those who have just left, they will not sleep easy as long as they are on our soil." He looked toward Jean and nodded his head to confirm something that Tori and her companions were not yet aware of. "I know I ask a lot of you, Captain Laffite."

Jean placed one hand on Jackson's shoulder, and the other arm went around his wife's waist. "Nothing more than you will of others."

"True, I ask much of all who will face the enemy. Tell me, the ships; they will be in position by the time we have a need? You know the river, Sir. Is it possible to man them and have both underway within the hour?"

Jean took a step back, and with a genuine look in his eyes, he answered. "General Jackson, Sir, you can count on it. They will be where they are required and will follow orders. My men are among those who crew each vessel, and I would bet my life, if nothing else, they will see to it." Jean smiled as Jackson seemed satisfied by his answer.

The General let a slight smile tug at his lips. "So, it begins, and we, Sir, will give them a welcome they never expected. It seems that our plan to maneuver them into the most desired position has worked. Indeed, Laffite, it is my fondest wish when this is over that I can shake the hand of the men who dared to carry out my orders. I pray they survived their ordeal."

"I am with you there," Livingston spoke up and gave Jackson a heartfelt slap on his shoulder. "It was a stroke of genius if I may say so, a plan fraught with risk but successful nonetheless."

Laffite left Jackson's side to pick up one of the maps on the table and study it. While examining it closely, he added his thoughts allowed. "I would never have thought the ruse, the outright lies told to the British, would work." He put the map down and faced Jackson. "Honor, it seems, is still held high with the British when it pertains to rank. After all, as you said, an officer and gentleman would never lie. On that merit, those involved gambled much, and it is obvious they succeeded."

It was Claiborne now who spoke up. "Forgive me, Laffite, but I am at a loss as to that which you speak of. Maybe someone could explain?"

It was Jackson who faced the confused Governor. "William, forgive us, but such was the nature of the plan that only a few were privy to the details. In short, after my visit to the forts down-river and upon my return, it greatly worried me that the British armada would sail right up the Mississippi and take the city with ease. After all, with Laffite's home destroyed, they faced little to no resistance." He faced the former Captain of the ship, the Carolina, with a frown filling his face. "No fault of yours, Captain; you were, after all, following orders."

The captain nodded his head and then turned to face Laffite. "I do hope you know how I regret those actions, and I give my word that after this is over, I will do my best to rectify your losses and have your ships returned to you."

Governor Claiborne inhaled deeply and then cleared his throat. He was most uncomfortable but still had no idea as to what had transpired among Jackson, his men, and Laffite. Without looking Jean's way, he spoke to Jackson. "I also regret that action. For now, General, we need to apply all our attention towards what will transpire in the days to come, not of those actions that have passed. You were explaining…"

"So, I was. I shall keep it short, and we will talk of it in greater detail when time allows. It was a plan devised by myself, Henley, and Livingston. Henley volunteered for the mission. He had no higher rank than Captain, but that was solved by Laffite, who suggested that Captain Henley could make use of another's uniform, and thus he obtained the higher rank needed to convince the British that he was someone to be respected and thus believed. The plan was for this brave soul to sail the Carolina into the Gulf, harass the British and allow his vessel to be taken. Once a prisoner, his job was to convince those who would question him that what he divulged was God's truth. He was to outright lie. Something that goes against the grain of those who would question him."

"Forgive me but convince them of what? I still do not grasp what was to be gained by letting the British take one of our few ships, let alone have a volunteer masquerade as a high-ranking naval officer."

Jackson placed his hands behind his back and paced the room as he continued. "I know, as most in this room do, how interrogation can be violent under such conditions as Henley and his crew would have placed themselves, and I also know that our man would not have given his story up too fast. I would expect that he suffered at the hands of those who questioned him. As an officer and gentleman, his final explanation and details given under duress, would have been accepted as true. After all, no office and certainly no gentleman would lie. He would have told them that the river was well protected, that our defenses were strong. After all, the city had guessed that they would be attacked sooner or later. Regrettably, he would have also begrudgingly told them that our defenses had one weakness. The only way to surprise us was to go overland and attack us from the very spot that they now hold."

Claiborne's mouth opened in stunned silence as the understanding of what Jackson had told him sunk in. "You planned this and carried it out?"

"We did, and it would seem that our intentions and deceit have succeeded. We now have the British right where I want them. They are in a bottleneck, with the river on one side, swamps on the other, and our forces, becoming increasingly well dug in, are stretched across the land to which they will have to march to reach the city. Now, I am in a hurry and need to get to my men and see the rampart they are still constructing."

Jackson didn't have time to explain further as one of his men strode into the room, ignoring everyone but his commander, and calmly announced what he had to say.

"General, it's time, Sir. Your mount is ready, and the men are waiting."

Jackson looked at his officer. "I'll be right with you."

"Yes, Sir. I shall wait with your horse out front."

Jackson nodded his head and then turned his attention to the only female in the room. As he pulled on his gloves, he spoke in a kindly tone. "Now, Tori, my dear, you take care of yourself and keep the home front safe. Jean has informed me that you will be staying in town with some of the fine genteel ladies. I think maybe, your job will be far harder than mine." He took hold of her chin with his trembling hand. "Permit me?" He leaned forward and kissed her lightly on her cheek. "You do your job, and I will do mine. With

God's help, we will be together again soon."

Then to Tori's amazement, he seemed to suck into his body all the strength and vitality he needed. He strode from the room with an authoritative aura about him, and she witnessed he was full of the charisma he was well known for. He was General Andrew Jackson to most, but to his men, he was 'Old Hickory,' and it fit. His last words sounded from the hallway beyond the room.

"Don't take long, Captain Laffite. I'm counting on you."

Jean turned and looked at his love. If all went as it should, they would be together soon, and not only would he be forgiven of past crimes, he would be awarded what he desired most; he would become an American citizen as well. If that happened, Laffite swore that he would be a different man. He would settle down and raise a family with the love of his life. He could do that without his ships because there was the Duval Plantation that he and Tori could claim and claim it they would. As for the lake and her returning to her own time, he decided he'd face that when it came.

"Something on your mind?" she asked.

"Only you, as always. I have to leave now... you stay safe and try not to worry." He took her into his arms and pulled her close to him. "I will have you with me, here in my mind and my soul. I will make history, just the way you want it, and then together we will decide what to do." He kissed her long and hard, tasting her while holding her closer. The sweet aroma of red wine lingered on her breath, and it pleased him. He would have kissed her longer, but they were interrupted by an urgent call.

Cisco spoke as he re-entered the room, "Jean, come on, man. We have to go. You two are always acting like you need to get a room."

Jean let her go and put his finger on her lips, silencing her. "Don't say anything. I'll return as soon as I can. You can count on that." He backed out of the room slowly, remembering each detail of the image before him. Once satisfied, he could recall the moment and see it like a painting in his mind; he turned and walked to the doorway.

Once there, he looked back at her for a few short seconds,

and Tori could see the mischievous smile she had grown to love so much. Before she could utter a word of encouragement, he was gone. Never had Jean's wife felt so helpless as she did at that moment, knowing what was about to happen and realizing all she could do was wait. But she also knew waiting was not her strong point. This thought reminded her of her next move. She was due to arrive at Madame Poree's house, just down the street. Tori and quite a few ladies had all arranged to be there together. It had been Marie Destrehan's suggestion, and having agreed to join them, Tori found no way to back out. Besides, Marie had been such a good friend to her; it was the least she could do. She would comfort her friend and pray J.D. would be among the few not to be hurt.

JEAN and Cisco made their way to the edge of town, where they met up with a small group of men. Thiac was waiting there, as were a few other free men of color. Some Jean knew, some he did not. All were on foot, and more than one looked at Cisco and Jean's horses with envy. Laffite saw the side-glances but chose to ignore them. Instead, he brought his mare around once he had passed by the small group and faced them. He spoke, looking at each face that watched him. The only one he did not have to look at was Cisco.

"I have my orders and yours from General Jackson himself," he announced as he moved his horse a few steps forward. "You are to go with Cisco here and report to the main group south of here. I will not be joining you right away, as the General has other plans for me. Let's show him what we are capable of, shall we?" he cheered.

The men shouted their support and then rallied around Cisco. All except Thiac, who stood by himself looking worried; then, as if he knew what was needed, he stepped forward. "I ain't goin' to let you go off by yourself." Thiac had called out to Jean over the rukus. His voice had thundered so deep and loud that all around them fell silent, and they turned to look at the massive man.

Jean kept calm as he answered back. "You have no choice. You and I have to follow orders. Follow Cisco. There's nothing else you can do." Jean rode his horse right up to Thiac's side.

The black giant reached out and grabbed hold of the bridle. "That is where you are wrong, Boss. If I can't go with you, then young David here will." He reached behind him and took hold of a young man's shirt with his free hand. He then pulled the tall, lanky coffee-colored lad to his side.

"If you won't let me join you, then you have David. If you don't take David, you won't go. I mean it, Boss, and you know I do."

Jean had seen this side of Thiac before and knew that the man could be just as stubborn as himself. Once he got a notion into his head, there was no changing his mind, and he was sure this was one of those times. Jean looked at David and, seeing no fear in the lad's eyes, asked him straight out. "Why should I take you, boy?"

David stepped forward, looking him squarely in the face. He pushed his long curly hair aside, and with an earnest and confident voice, he spoke. "Because you need me. Someone has to watch your back."

Jean grinned. "I think maybe I have been able to watch my own back over the years, don't you?"

"It be true enough, but I also growed up in them backwaters. Been goin' up and down them on barges all my life. I know'd these here parts better'n you, an you need a guide. Thiac said you needs me." Bolstered by Thiac, he put his hands on his hips in a defiant act as he continued. "Should be reason enough for you to has me come."

Jean wanted to say no, but the truth of the matter was that he did need a guide, someone who knew his way around the backwaters, as the boy had said.

"Thiac, do I know this boy?"

"No, Boss, can't say you do. You do own him, though, and he be the best working boy on the river you has. More'n that, he can be trusted if you get's, what I mean."

46

Jean knew he'd been ambushed into taking the boy with him. He didn't like it, but he had to agree; it made sense. "Fine, fine. But, David, if you slow me up or get in my way, I'll leave you for gator food, got me?"

David's face lit up. "Yes, um, Boss. I won't be slowing you down, none an I will do as you say's."

Thiac added to David's enthusiastic outburst. "Anything he orders, you do it, but don't leave the Boss's side. You done know'd what I told you, and boy, I meant each and every word. You can do as the Boss says for you to do, but you ain't to leave his side," Thiac's growl hit home as the boy looked toward him. Still, he stood up to the large man.

"I know'd what you done told me. All the way here, you told me an explained an made it clear like."

Jean had had enough. He turned in his saddle and called to Cisco. "Let's move on out of here. We can keep each other company some of the way. Thiac, when we get to the parting of the way, you will have my horse. Where David and I have to go, well, we have to go on foot."

Cisco moved his horse up alongside Jean's, and the two led the group, whose size was expanding all the time. More and more able-bodied men joined them, some carrying guns, others spades and picks. It was a group made up of such a mixture that Cisco had to smile to himself. He had never thought that he'd live to see the day when all seemed friends and with one goal.

Most were silently walking along as if they had nothing to say and much to ponder. Each man or boy was keeping a lookout, as if they expected the British to appear at any second, and kill them in their tracks. The tension was such that it made Cisco so nervous he couldn't stand it any more. He began to softly hum a tune to both boost his nerves and lighten the moment. He murmured on and on, and then, looking at Jean, he broke into part of the song. "The hounds couldn't catch them," he laughed at the expression on the pirate's face, "down the Mississippi to the Gulf of Mexico."

Jean put his finger to his lips, chuckling as he did so. Cisco fell silent, knowing that he had better stop singing a song from his time; after all, they were there to make history, not change it and singing a song with a catchy tune that would not be written for years and years to come, could have a bad outcome if it caught on. Someone could hear it and begin to sing it, and that would never do. He frowned Jean's way; the man must have realized what was happening and silenced him before he could make a bigger blunder. The pirate was not upset, though, because he was grinning and looked amused. There was one thing Cisco knew; Jean never smiled when he was pissed off and when amused, he'd be full of questions.

Laffite leaned closer to Cisco so as not to be overheard. "Suppose that's part of a song from your time?"

"Yep, sure is."

"Don't suppose I'm in there anywhere, am I?"

"Nope, not that I can remember."

"Thought so. Nice tune, though," he said, laughing. "Damn good words too." He lowered his voice still more as he continued to talk. "Shame you can't sing them all." He pulled his horse to a stop. "Maybe, John will when we meet him again. Well, Cisco, my friend, time to part company." He dismounted and was immediately joined by David. "You take care of yourself and old Thiac," he added.

Cisco saluted Laffite with a grave expression. He spoke up and sounded very sincere even though he felt far from it. "You can count on it. If I were a betting man, I would say we will all be back together real soon. You can count on me to keep an eye on Thiac. We are, after all, well acquainted."

Jean grinned at him, "Just the same, take care. You ready, David?" The pirate did not look back or wait for an answer. He moved off, following a small trail into the dense scrub, and was quickly out of sight.

Cisco turned toward Thiac. "Guess you had better mount up. We should get a move on. Still got some miles to go until we reach this Rodriguez Canal. I hear Jackson's told old General Humbert that he wants to make the first strike tonight. Said he wanted to begin adding to the fortification as fast as he could, right along that canal. Wants it done like yesterday."

Thiac's eyes widened at this, but no emotion was heard in his voice as he spoke. "No, Sur. Ain't got many miles if you follow me. I say we have more like just under three miles. Not easy going, but still faster, and we ain't a likely to run up 'gainst no enemy neither. We be there long before you think, that's for sure. In plenty of time to start building whatever the man wants. I even took it upon myself to send some lads to fetch us all the shovels they could git. They be coming along real sharp like and them boys be ready to do whatever we say for them to do. So, Cisco," he grinned as he whispered the man's name. He'd not said Mr. Cisco, no Master Sir, just plain Cisco. They were friends, after all, and he'd been told he could use his name. The thing was, up until now, he'd only used his name when no one was around. Now he'd done and gone used it in front of everyone. It felt right and good. "Just follow me, and you men, you pick it up. We ain't out for no stroll; we be goin' to a battle.

❧ Three ❧

Tori looked around Madame Poree's parlor at the small group of ladies. Nightfall had come, and oil lamps and candles lit the home. The ever-familiar glow from burning logs that crackled and sparked added to the soft-lit rooms. As far as Tori knew, just about every room she had entered had a fire, and each fire was attended by its own keeper. Young black slaves would be seen now and then as they deposited more logs to take the place of those allowed to burn low before adding another. Their job was also to shovel out the ash below the iron grate and remain close by to ensure no sparks flew out onto the carpet. This part of their job seemed easy enough but not one that lasted longer than needed. More wood would be required throughout the night and days, all cut into suitable sizes. Then to make sure they never ran low on supplies, the older slaves chosen could be seen pushing a cart in the direction of the edge of town. They had one ax between the four of them due to the need for implements at Jackson's ditch, a project, a burn of sorts, built to keep the Americans safe from British fire. Also, it would be these garden slaves, as they were referred to, to allow an inside slave to accompany them. The trusted house boy would have the cash to buy logs from those who gathered cords of oak to sell. If the supply was depleted, they would send the house boy back to inform the mistress that they would locate a sizeable tree to chop down and use.

It was easy enough to see who worked at what job. The way they were dressed and sometimes the injuries they suffered, such as burns on their forearms, was a hint that could reveal this. The younger boys who tended the fireplaces inside all had such scars, and a few had their hands wrapped up. These boys would still be told to shovel the hot ash regardless, and Tori found that anger filled her more than once as she witnessed these young slaves struggle with their tasks.

Upon her arrival at Madame Poree's home, everyone warmly greeted Tori. Laffite's wife had met most gathered there and was welcomed by all in the same manner, with no one trying to outdo the other for once. Many thanked her as if it had been her flints and powder that had saved the day. Often, she was told what a hero Jean was without a single hint at how they really felt. These same women were among those who had turned their backs on Madame Laffite, when her husband had been placed in jail. The same ladies who bought merchandise from the sales Jean held. They were all about appearance and decorum, two acts that they lived by. Often without so much as a second thought, friendships could be denied, and those chosen to be ostracized would find themselves outcast. One such lady, known for her dislike of many, had greeted Laffite's wife as if they were best friends when in fact, Tori knew her to be fickle and condescending. If it had not been for a timely inter-ruption from a friend, there was no doubt that Tori would have snubbed this particular woman's greeting, and that would have caused an ugly scene knowing how she would have felt slighted. Instead, Marie Destrehan called from the top of the stairs and waved, motioning for her to stay where she was until she came down. This intervention gave Tori the perfect excuse to walk away from the other guest without causing too much of an upset.

Once Marie stepped off the last stair, she began talking to Tori. Walking toward her, she ignored the few ladies who looked her way, listening to what she had to impart to Laffite's wife. "I have put the small ones down for the night. J.D. wanted me to leave them at the plantation, but Lord, how could I? Men, I ask you. They don't understand us, do they?" Not waiting for a response, Marie entered the small room and greeted the ladies with an affirmative nod. She turned and faced Tori, who was following close behind. "Of course, I left the older children, but then I don't think we have that much to worry over, do we?" To Tori's ears, it sounded as though Marie was trying to convince her lady friends, as well as herself, that they had nothing to fear.

"I think you are right. I am sure it will all be over soon, and we will be victorious." She was about to continue with her reassurance when a voice from behind filled the room.

"I beg to differ with you on that matter. I, for one, feel we all have a lot to worry over," sounded Simone's cold voice.

Tori turned to face the one woman she had not counted on being there. She had not seen her when she entered the house, but sure enough, the bitch was there. Before her, standing only a few feet away, was a beautiful, elegant woman, almost regal in her appearance. Yet, Tori knew behind those large tear-filled eyes lay nothing short of a vicious, conniving imposter.

Simone looked around the room as she spoke softly. Her voice trembling with emotion, and as her tears fell, she delicately wiped her cheeks with the linen handkerchief. "I have spoken with the Governor himself… and my darling Edward, who is very close to William. He told me much, much more than you could know. May God please protect my darling husband; he has confided in me. Are you aware of the enemy and its size?" Again, she looked around the room and saw a few women shake their heads no. "They are reported to be greater than twelve thousand and more to come."

One of the women gasped and promptly fainted, while still another, falling to her knees with a rosary in hand, openly began to pray.

Simone went on, seemingly untouched by the panic she was causing. "Edward was informed that our forces amount to just over two thousand, which he thinks is an exaggeration. He has prepared me for the worse." She dabbed at her eyes with the hanky. "I know I should keep these things to myself, but I simply cannot. My darling Edward, and all our dear husbands, brothers, sons, and friends, have gone to fight a battle they surely can't win. Like lambs to the slaughter, they are."

A woman behind Tori responded, sounding hopeful. "But we have that fine General Andrew Jackson, and he knows what to do, assuredly?"

Simone retorted, "Why, may I add, you would think so, wouldn't you? However, he has to deal with many of our men and boys, who have never seen war, let alone carried arms against another man. He will have to give orders to those who are far from familiar with military actions. On the other hand, the British are nothing short of... how do you say?" She inhaled loudly and, on the exhale, spat out, "Well-trained, blood-thirsty murderers."

Another woman moaned and fainted, and still more started to cry openly. Simone was indeed in her glory, and no doubt enjoyed putting the fear of God into those gathered there. Tori was about to confront her when, as if on cue, the sound of distant cannon fire reverberated in the heavens.

Like many of the women who had fear and horror etched on their faces, Marie looked away from Simone and toward the open French doors in surprise. It was, however, Madame Poree who was the first to act. She walked over to the doors and pulled them shut. "Enough of that. We don't want to upset the little ones, and besides, it's just too chilly this time of year. I don't know why they were open anyway. We shall pray. Yes, that's what we will do. For those of you who want to join me in my vigilance, come this way." She led a few of the ladies from the room. "Maybe Marie, we can have someone tend to those who are faint of heart and lay upon my floor. When they regain their senses, please send them to the library. Come, ladies, let us pray."

Simone had not been amongst the group who departed, choosing instead to stay and sit facing Tori. She fully intended to make the wait a living hell for her. Then, when the British marched into town, she, Madame Duval, would turn the bitch over as Laffite's spying wench. Oh, she would enjoy that very much. It was going to be a good Christmas, with a lot to celebrate, she told herself. Until that time, though, Simone intended to make Tori suffer. She would tell the bitch, that her darling Jean would most likely be killed or caught and tried as a traitor. Not that she believed for one second that he would be hurt or caught; he was too damn lucky for that.

As for her Edward, she could smile, safe in the knowledge that he was far from harm's way. He was at their plantation, making arrangements to entertain the victorious British. He would not be a subject of their wrath but rather their praise for not bearing arms against them. It was a perfect plan. Edward had even come up with a backup version, should the British somehow not be victorious. He could slip back into town, claiming he fought hard and bravely. Who could prove him wrong in all the chaos? Who would even think to ask?

"You seem to have something on your mind, Simone. Correct me if I assume it has nothing to do with your little display just now."

Tori's words slipped softly across the room, unnoticed by the few women left there, who were aiding those who had fainted.

Simone stared at her and put on a sad and pitiful look. "Why Tori, my dear, you are so perceptive. I declare it's as if you could read my mind. I do have so much to think about, just as you do. You must be so worried about your precious Jean. If he is not injured, he still could fall into enemy hands, could he not? The very thought of that sends chills up my spine. Do you suppose they hang or shoot spies? Oh, but don't let me upset you." She dropped her head down, feigning regret. Then looking at Tori through the slits of her snake-like eyes, she all but hissed as she spat out her next barb. "Jean can take care of himself, I'm sure. He knows the waterways so very well. Escape seems to be that man's second name. You, however, are so brave to remain here in town. Why I declare, if I were you, I would have never had the courage to remain here. I wonder what the British will do with the likes of you? I mean, you are the wife of the pirate who supplied Jackson with what he needed. I wonder if in their eyes you will be as guilty as your husband?"

Tori had had it. She stood and walked right up to Simone and calmly put both hands on her shoulders. Very softly, she spoke to her without a hint of how upset she was. "Why, Simone, how nice of you to be so concerned about my well-being. You are such a dear." She then pulled the woman close, as if hugging her, and whispered into her ear.

"You won't understand this but listen closely; you are coming with me right now." Tori pulled Simone to her feet and led her from the room out of hearing range of anyone else. Laffite's wife thought Simone seemed far too smug, and she intended to wipe that feeling away immediately. "I'm not the least bit worried about Jean, nor am I worried about the outcome of the battle. We will be victorious; you can trust me on that. We will all live to see our men march home. From which direction will Edward come; I wonder?"

Tori saw Simone stiffen slightly. Strike one, she told herself. It had been a guess that Edward would not fight, and now she was sure of it. "You can try to upset me all you want. I can live with that, but if you so much as try to upset these poor women again, I swear to you that I will personally shut your lying mouth and don't think I can't do it. I have learned well while living with pirates," she said this while slamming one closed fist into her other open hand. "Just don't push me, bitch, got it?" Tori pushed her backward, smiling at the shocked look on Simone's face. "If you will excuse me, I think I had best go and help Marie calm the little ones. You look like you could use a little calming yourself. May I suggest you sit a spell."

On her way upstairs, she breathed deeply and prayed that she had frightened Simone into behaving herself. It was not going to be comfortable living in the house with her. But it would be even more challenging if she had to put up with twenty or more frenzied ladies.

How could she explain to them that the battle they now heard in the distance was not the battle that would bring them victory? This was the first of many to come; she knew that much. The date was only December 23rd, 1814, and the decisive battle would not be fought straight off. She wanted to hear pre-dawn booms that didn't stop until mid-morning. That would be the signal that the final Battle of New Orleans had begun. John had been very clear about that one fact, just not so clear as to when it would happen.

It had taken Marie and Tori well over an hour to settle some of the children, but in the end, the late hour won out, and the exhausted little ones were left to sleep. Marie had volunteered to remain with them, and several other ladies offered to do so also. Among them was a volunteer that neither of the Laffites had met before, so it was Marie's delight to introduce Tori. "Tori, my dear, please let me introduce you to Dr. Rankin's wife, Cameo. She accompanied her husband here from Baton Rouge. The doctor thought he should come as there are no doubt going to be many in need."

Tori placed her arm around Marie's shoulder for a second to comfort her, and when she turned to face Marie's friend, Cameo held her hand out. "I am very pleased to meet you, and may I add, we have heard a lot about you and your husband's efforts to aid the General. For that, we are most grateful. I also understand that you have some experience with tending the wounded yourself?"

Tori liked her right away; this new acquaintance was someone she felt she could trust and not a woman to ignore. She was forthright and better still; Cameo was not a Creole who let her emotions run her. She had greeted her as an American would have, and this act had bonded Tori to her right away. "I am honored to meet you, and yes, I have a little experience with wounded men. I shall tell you about one in particular if you care to know the details. But first, do tell me, Cameo, that is an unusual name. I like it very much."

"As I yours. Tori is also unusual, is it not?"

Marie laughed, "It is so, but only because it is short for Victoria. Silly me, I should have made the proper introduction, using your rightful name."

Laffite's wife laughed out loud. "Oh, Marie, please, we are friends, and all my friends use Tori." She smiled brightly at Marie and then turned her attention back to Cameo. "I do hope you consider yourself my friend and will call me Tori."

"I most certainly will if I can ask you to help me in my task that lay ahead. Marie will take care of the children, and it is up to us to prepare to take care of the wounded, be they British or our own. I require many sheets to make bandages, and Madame Poree has kindly donated all her bedding for the task."

Tori had not thought much about the results of the battle, just that they would win. Now, she stood with the doctor's wife, ready to get to work and prepare for what was to come. "Of course, you will have my help, but maybe we should work downstairs so as not to disturb the little ones."

Cameo nodded her head in agreement. "Madame Poree and I planned on such an action; the sheets await us in her dining room, and more will be delivered when those sent out to gather donations return. I have also asked for more scissors and baskets to put the bandages in. I am certain many will be needed at the frontline after it is over."

"Well then, let us go and begin. I think we shall have plenty of time to get to know each other, and I do so look forward to learning more about you and your husband." Tori meant each word, and she was thankful to have something to do other than sit and wait. It was Marie who would be sitting up here waiting, with nothing to do but watch the children and keep them in line. Tori looked at her and knew right away that Madame Destrehan was exactly where she wished to be. "We shall go down now, Marie; you don't mind if we leave you? I think we shall have a lot of work by the sounds of it, and it's best we get started."

Marie was already thinking about the children and not in the least bit worried about whatever it was Cameo and Tori were about to tackle. "You go on; I will be down later. Maybe a glass of sherry to settle the nerves will help. Be sure to put some aside, my dear." She hugged Cameo. "We are so lucky to have you, Cameo. You and your husband are most generous in joining the fight, and you do so with so much at risk. I will pray for you both. Tori, you are in good company, and Cameo, I trust you will be entertained while you work. Tori has many stories she can share, and some I tell you are quite remarkable. Now, if you will excuse me, I shall attend to the older children who still refuse to sleep." Without another word, Marie left the hallway and entered a bedroom that had been put aside for those too young to be left unsupervised and yet not old enough to fight.

Cameo smiled and turned to leave, her long skirt in one hand, and using the other; she pushed back a long strand of chestnut hair that had fallen free of its updo. She was striking to look at, and as she walked ahead, Tori had more time to observe her. The doctor's wife was taller than most and dressed for comfort, not for show as many of the ladies in the house had. Simone came to mind briefly when Tori made this observation. Edward's wife had chosen a gown to show off her figure, and as far as Tori considered, it was a garment that was inappropriate for the cooler season. Simone was the total opposite of Tori's new friend; she was always seeking the center of attention.

On the other hand, Cameo was more practicable and carried herself with purpose. She had an air about her that spoke for itself. The doctor's wife was in control and self-assured, and not in a bossy sort of way, far from it. She acted in a no-nonsense kind of manner, knowing just what needed to be done and willing to do whatever it took to complete the task. She was confident in her appearance, which gave Simone a run for her money as far as Tori was concerned. Cameo had no need to dress to draw attention; she turned heads whenever and wherever she went. Her smile was radiant, and her porcelain complexion glowed. Her lips had no need of color to exaggerate them; they were full and accentuated her exotic appeal. It was going to be interesting getting to know her better, and Jean's wife looked forward to passing the long hours with someone she could rely on.

THE sun hung low on the horizon, its weak light making work on the rampart difficult. It could be easier if torches were utilized, but orders were to delay that action until word came from those in charge. Everyone guessed that no orders would be released until news from the scouting party Jackson had sent out was relayed. Those who had taken part had not been gone long when word of their return spread throughout the defensive line.

Cisco looked over at one of the men who had bravely mounted his horse, along with several others, and he, like many, wondered what they had seen. The Kentucky-born man seemed unfazed by what they had encountered, and seeing many looking his way, he took it upon himself to talk of what had occurred.

"We split into two groups and rode as close as we could without running the risk of being shot. My group rode close to the river bank before going to our left. The others rode close to the scrub and almost rode right up to the break in the tree line. They were a smaller contingent and had the opportunity to survey the British camp near the area where the force had emerged from the swamps onto the very spot that General Jackson had hoped they would. It is safe to say we were able to give Old Hickory the news he wanted. Having said too much already, let's wait and see what will come of our excursion."

"Wise of you, Sir." All turned to face Andrew Jackson, who had joined his forces. "I am pleased by what I have been told, and as you know, as a military strategist, most of my men will boast that planning a strategy is my best trait."

"Bet the Misses would say it was something else," laughed the man known to Cisco as Jefferson.

"My Rachel might have other opinions, I agree. Mr. Sims knows how my wife's disposition rules our home but never my military responsibilities." He chuckled and then turned to face those gathered around Cisco. "I can tell you now that I am gravely aware of what we will be up against tonight, as I also am aware that the British will never know what hit them. We will attack them under the cloak of darkness. A tactic that their commanders will find offensive. I have chosen the man who will stand atop the rampart and signal the Carolina. She will then begin her onslaught. That should distract them from our approach, and God willing, we will raise hell on earth for each of them before we return."

Cisco had no idea the Carolina was going to fire her cannons into the enemy, and once he grasped that notion, he could not help but question the wisdom of attacking a camp under fire, for surely if they did, many would fall to friendly fire. "May I ask what advantage we will have riding into the line of fire from the ship?"

Jackson showed no emotion and kept a calm tone as he answered the man known to him as one of Laffite's friends. "We will not ride into the hell; all that onboard ship will create. When we are upon the enemy, close enough for them to see us approaching, Mr. Sims will send a signal. The Carolina will stop her attack, and we shall begin ours. May I suggest that those who plan to join my men and I let Mr. Jefferson know and add your name to the roster. The finalization of plans will be accomplished in an hour. Mr. Jefferson will tell those who he deems not necessary for this night's raid to remain and the rest to prepare for tomorrow. Until I give orders to join me, I suggest you rest, eat and make ready. Mr. Jefferson, you have my permission to describe what you and the others witnessed on your scouting mission. No one will ride or walk alongside me without knowing what they face." Then without another word, Jackson and Mr. Sims left those at the rampart to ready themselves for the night's raid.

Cisco looked at Jefferson with admiration. It had taken guts to do what they had, and he respected the fact that the General trusted his man to give an accurate and fair description of what they had learned. "Someone, hand the man a hot cup of coffee and something to eat. Mr. Jefferson, please begin. I really want to know what I will face, what we all will face tonight."

"Right, you are then. It's this simple. The British campsite is of considerable size. The area reaches from the river bank one mile across the open fields to the dense underbrush beyond. That area is nothing more than Cypress swampland. Before we left to see just what the Redcoats were up to, I was told that they disembarked their ships in the bay referred to as Lake Borgne. It seems that Lake Pontchartrain is too shallow for their vessels, so they chose to do as the General had planned.

A few are aware that our man Henley allowed himself and his crew to fall into the enemy's hands. It was he who convinced the British to travel the route they took, to land up where they are now camped. Old Hickory had worked out the details of what he was to inform the British, and I would say it worked. They are camped in what they were told was our weakest defensive area; they had some resistance, some gunboats were taken, but again, all part of an intricate plan. That is as much as anyone needs to know about that."

Cisco grinned. "I get it; they were fooled, but how the hell did they find the way through from Lake Borgne to there?" He had turned and pointed his finger at the British camp shaking his head as if in disbelief.

Jefferson chuckled. "Locals in that area were very instrumental. It was not an easy journey for them to make their way through the swamps. Took them five days of brutal traveling, and in miserable weather, with no comforts and little food. That alone has them worn out."

Cisco looked back at the men standing by Jefferson. "So that's why they did not make an attempt today to march on and claim victory. They are resting and, dare I say, waiting for more troops. Sitting in an area they think is our weak spot. Brilliant, it's just brilliant. After all, if they had just sailed up the Mississippi full force, I dare say they would be celebrating today. But again, how did they know where to march, crawl or float up too?"

"As I said, they had some local fishermen help guide them through the backwaters and swamps. Those fishermen risked much to see them trudge through such an unfriendly landscape. Those men chosen have no love of the Redcoats, and having been aware of Jackson's plans, it was simple enough to arrange without the British being the wiser. So, they sit by their campfires, waiting for supplies and more battalions to arrive, confident in victory but in no hurry. After all, this most welcome respite in their objective was, I am most sure, welcomed by all of them. I saw myself, as others did, more than we expected; many were sleeping, totally worn out."

"Then that should make our job easier. Worn out, military men don't fight so well." The Tennessee boy who had interrupted Jefferson was laughing but fell silent when the older man looked his way.

Again, as Cisco liked to think of him, the Kentucky mountain man continued. "Soldiers were seen making themselves as comfortable as possible and seemingly with no fear of the American foe that sits waiting for them across the river or behind this, our ever-growing rampart, whose construction until tonight had continued none stop. It is paused now for a good reason, but on our return tonight, we will begin again in earnest."

It was Livingston who spoke up then. "Best to let them think we are retired for the night. I assume tomorrow they will send out troops to learn the lay of the land and how many of us there are. Tonight, if we do the kind of damage that the General wants, it could make a difference in their course of actions. The British never enter a fray that they have not prepared for. So, you have the gist of things as they stand, Cisco. Several thousand troops are camping on our doorstep, and God willing, we will show them that they are not welcome, nor, as the General said early today, will they find rest on our land."

"Did they not see any of you spying on them," a young voice called out.

Jefferson turned to face another young lad. "The British had posted a few sentries who alerted their comrades of the approaching cavalrymen, and then they set about firing on those considered to be part of our reconnaissance party. Upon becoming aware of the insurgency, and possible attack, an alarm was sounded. A bugle called men to arms, and shouts of commands filled the air, but no panic was observed in their camp. Knowing the routine, many soldiers scrambled to prepare to fight, and rapidly three columns of soldiers formed lines awaiting further orders. Having gained the knowledge we set about to learn, I ordered our party to turn their horses and make a hasty retreat before any engagement could take place. It's safe to say that the Redcoats think of us as cowards or overwhelmed by the sheer size of their force."

"What happened next," asked Cisco?

"The British soldiers cheered. When the all-clear sounded, and their commanders were undoubtedly satisfied that there was no further danger; so, the camp relaxed and returned to preparing food confiscated from the plantations downriver. Little did they know that the information we gained confirmed Jackson's decision to attack but not until under cover of night."

One of the younger among them looked upward to the moon. "I think I shall ask God to dim that light, a few clouds, no rain mind you. Clouds to cover our approach would be most welcome."

"I second that," said Cisco, "and no doubt the weather and God is on our side. You wait and see."

THE scouting mission was the second time the soldiers had been interrupted. Earlier that same day, many in the British camp took time out from their assigned duties to watch the movement spotted on the river.

A large ship sailed down the river's slow-moving muddy waters until it was directly opposite their position. At this point, men on deck were seen stowing the sails and dropping anchor. This action kept one side of the vessel horizontal to the British side of the riverbank and safely out of gunshot range. Once all was completed aboard the ship, the decks cleared, and no further action was taken.

The vessel was going nowhere, and no amount of calling or signaling got a response. This was concerning for the two highest-ranked officers as they observed the craft, which they knew was out of their musket and small cannon range. Until their reinforcements arrived with the larger cannons, they could do nothing but keep a watch on the ship.

Both General Keane and Admiral Cochrane decided that the vessel had to be either an American military or a civilian ship with a crew that was supporting the feeble attempt to prevent the invasion. Any hope of it being British and from the large armada in the Gulf was dashed when no communication occurred. For Admiral Cochrane, it was clear that the enemy had placed it there to spy on the encampment. He negatively shook his head. "They will learn what they already suspect, and that is how large a force we have that is preparing to march on the city."

General Keane nodded in agreement. "I agree; we have no need to conceal our numbers or position, as I am certain it is currently known by the city's population and surrounding areas by now."

Keane was in complete agreement. "The interrogation of the American Officer that was caught when his ship was taken was most helpful. He revealed that our large British force had been tracked ever since it left the islands. No doubt the pirate Laffite had informed his fleet to follow and report to him." Keane frowned and looked back toward the Carolina. "Laffite would have been a helpful ally, but now the fool will be caught and hung for the pirate and traitor he is."

The Admiral took a step toward the river and looked at Keane. "It took some time; they said to get the man to talk, the officer that is. Under duress, he broke and told us all he was aware of. The promise of immunity and the safekeeping of his family also helped. He gave his word as an officer and gentleman that the facts he divulged were as accurate as he knew them to be. It is this interrogation that bothers my mind. After today's arrival, I have seen no sign, either on the river or on land, that a substantial force awaits us as he described. It could be, as he said, the large force guards the river and is not overly protective of this stretch of land. At least they weren't until we arrived. "

Kean agreed and added his insight to the Admiral's statement. "The track through the backwaters has proved to be profitable then. We are in a prize position to march on the enemy's rampart and continue on into the city itself."

Cochrane grinned before turning serious. "That is our plan, but plans can and may be affected by what happens tomorrow. I suggest we talk to the men and then sit and go over our mission as we have been instructed."

"A splendid idea, if I do say so myself. I shall have the troops close to us ready for your address. They can share what you say after to those along the line. Spying eyes and listening ears might pay attention if we rallied all."

"I agree, Sir. Not that it worries me any. Let us both address the men then."

KEANE began his speech that was intended to raise any low morale. "As you see," he pointed across the cane field, "the mighty army we face is busy digging what one can only presume is a pitiful trench, and behind that is what I assume is a rampart. Both of these are poorly constructed obstacles and will be nothing more than a slight hindrance when we march on the city. We have caught them off guard; indeed, their need to know more enforces that. Once our victory is accomplished, I assure each of you that better sleeping quarters will be obtained, and I hear that the food is enjoyable, as are the local females."

A few soldiers let out a cheer, and more than one raised their arms and shook their fists at the American side while laughing among themselves. Sleeping on the cold ground in a foreign land was not desirable but being victorious and enjoying whatever this New Orleans had to offer was.

Admiral Cochrane waited to address the men until order had been regained. He confidently spoke to those gathered around. "Tomorrow, we intend to send out a reconnaissance team to spy and report back as soon as they have any pertinent information. If any one of you would care to volunteer, come to the headquarters after the evening meal. Lower-ranking sailors are excluded from this mission as I shall require those who are trained in such matters." He looked into the faces of those listening and saw several younger men not looking at all happy. "I think General Keane will be most agreeable, that double rum rations for all, to ward off the chill tonight is in order. You have earned it." He looked out over the small crowd gathered and acknowledged several officers with a slight nod of his head in their direction. "I have noticed several enterprising soldiers have acquired poultry and other foods from local establishments, all commandeered in the name of the crown; enjoy your spoils, for tomorrow, our work for the King and country begins in earnest."

Having said his piece, the Admiral looked at his counterpart and spoke under his breath. "I do hope our dinner will be as pleasing as theirs. One always draws up plans far better on a full stomach."

To which Keane added light-heartedly, "I agree, and might I add, one fights better when rested, and his backbone is not knocking his empty belly." They both chuckled and looked across to the Americans and sneered. "So much for their massive army. However, until we know what we are really up against, it's better to be more prudent than not." Without another observation or comment, Keane and Cochrane departed for the plantation they had confiscated for their use.

GENERAL Jackson walked behind his ever-developing line of defense, knowing he was only a few hours away from leading his makeshift military force into battle. He'd told his men that the British would fight using the old tried and true ways they had mastered over the years. First off, they would fight only during the day, and second, they were set in their ways to do battle. The fact that they had not advanced toward them or the town since they arrived was proof.

He stopped not far from Cisco and spoke to a few men waiting to follow him. "The English military will not break from tradition, and that will be their downfall. They are highly trained to fight a battle in a highly regimented way. You will see how they march in columns, and they will fiercely advance on our position and far smaller force. They will fight until we surrender or until not one of us is left standing. But take heart, not a man among them has ever seen what my men, what all of us are capable of. We will not fight by their rules of engagement, and we will give them much to ponder."

His speech was not very reassuring, but at least the volunteers knew that good old Andrew Jackson would lead them, and he was known to be quite the strategist in warfare. If anyone could guide them to victory against all odds, it was Old Hickory himself.

WHEN the British first arrived, and during the daylight hours, they had set about to dig their defensive line but were in no hurry to do so. All had welcomed the rest and relaxed atmosphere. The men relished the idea of eating fresh meat taken from the plantations along the river and other goods that they considered were delicacies, such as cheese, bread, and other numerous items. Not all the food was known to them, yet they took what they wanted regardless.

Camping and even sleeping on the cold ground was highly desired as exhaustion wore on them. Fighting was the furthest thing from their mind; that would happen in the days ahead, or so they thought. There would be plenty of time yet; they told each other while standing in line to receive their rations of rum. More campfires had been lit to ward off the cold wind's bite and make-shift spits set up to roast the many chickens. Most ate quickly and then made what beds they could to sleep. They had not transported tents and the like through the swamps; those would be coming with the next group. The British camp was peaceful by late nightfall, and then without warning, the quiet night exploded into mayhem.

CHAOS inside the British camp followed as the unexpected bombardment rained down on the soldiers. There was no place to take cover, and just when they thought it could not get any worse, it did. The British soldiers began shooting blindly into the night in desperation, mistaking every shadow for an advancing foe. Cries and screams were heard as men called out, "I am friendly, not foe!" These soldiers had hoped to save themselves from the friendly fire only to give away their location and be taken down by those that had come to conquer them in the darkness.

IT had been evident that Jackson's nighttime raid was working. Many soldiers were killed where they slept by the cannon blasts. Still, many more of their comrades ran in confusion from Carolina's thunderous blows and quickly realized that they were going no place. Everywhere they looked, dead bodies lay, and worse still, bits and pieces of fellow soldiers littered the blood-splattered ground.

Everything had seemed surreal as Cisco made his way across the open cane field to engage the English. Watching the blasts ahead of him tear into the camp and hearing the calamity of frightened and confused men terrified him. The closer they got to the British, the actual reality of his situation became clear. He saw men blown to bits, and by the light of several fires, Cisco, like his friends, witnessed others drop to the ground in agony from flying shrapnel or run while their uniforms burned them alive as the barrage continued.

AT first, having been distracted by the firepower of the Carolina, no one witnessed Jackson and his men silently making their way toward them. They were not spotted until they were less than five hundred yards away. The few that had their guns at the ready turned their attention to the rapidly advancing foe. They stood their ground and did their best to ignore the incoming bombardment.

Gunfire and cannons echoed in the night along with blood-curdling screams of those injured, and still, Jackson pushed forward, knowing the Carolina would stop its attack at any moment. Cisco found he kept glancing at the river and back ahead of him where the hellfire rained. He could only pray that the General had told the truth, that the ship would see the signal and cease its bombardment because running into the area that the cannons were blasting to kingdom come would be suicidal.

UPON spotting torches wave from the back of Jackson's advancing group, the lad up in the rigging called down to the crew, "The signal, I see the signal. Stop now, or you will blow up our own." Upon hearing the young sailors call, Carolina's crew ceased their bombardment. Andrew Jackson was about to storm the British camp, and all on the ship knew that for the raid to succeed, they had to give their men a fighting chance, which meant silencing the highly successful attack from Carolina's guns. It was going to be up to the General and his men to inflict as much damage as they could from there on. Maybe even push the British back into the swamps from where they came. All they could do was watch the confusion and deadly attack, which was nearly impossible to do as the darkness hindered their view.

THE enemy's army had been stunned when they got hit by cannon fire in the middle of the night and then shocked when the guns fell silent for no reason that they could determine. In seconds though, seeing what was about to happen, bugles sounded, calling the Redcoats to arms. What was left of the camp scrambled into action. The well-disciplined military raced to do what they were trained to carry out without hesitation; regardless of the hour or the mass of confusion surrounding them, they began to form their lines of protection.

THE young lad in the crow's nest could have come down, but he had such a clear view that he remained and called down with descriptions of what he could make out. "It's hard to tell who is who, and the fires, those that we did not hit, are being extinguished. I see flashes of muskets firing, campfires blowing up, and spreading flames everywhere. Some of the men are on fire!" His running commentary spurred the crew to cheer for their side. "The General," he shouted down, "is on his horse and leading the front line. He is with them, and he is running the Redcoats down if they get in his way." This last statement caused the crew to cheer even louder.

BY the time General Jackson reached the enemy's campsite, hand-to-hand combat had ensued, and all along the mile-long stretch of the encampment, one could see the bloodshed that followed.

Leading the way were the Kentuckians, followed closely by the citizens of the city, a few armed with guns but most had knives and garden tools. Cisco had seen how the Native Americans, and those from Tennessee, had moved around the already fallen and, using their knives, they inflicted many mortal wounds without hesitation. They spared no one and even attacked those who were trying to drag their fallen brethren to safety. Upon entering the camp, they struck down the soldiers trying desperately to extinguish the campfires. The fires were seen as beacons guiding the Americans to their targets in the darkness. At the rate they were putting out the flames, it was not going to take long before all were fighting in the total darkness. Even the almost full moon had slipped behind clouds that threatened to rain at any moment. Fighting in the darkness seemed insane to Cisco, but onward he went.

The pre-emptive strike launched so late at night was genius as far as he was concerned. The ambush had given Jackson and his men the dominance they needed for the first foray. The guerrilla tactics caused grave concern among the enemy as they battled mercenaries who fought with no dignity or honor by their way of thinking. These Americans were breaking all known combat rules of engagement. Many had resorted to fighting with their fists, and one was seen kicking with his feet like they were his hands, punching those he encountered!

Not a one expected the younger man, dressed in fine garments, to use his strange way of battling the enemy. He could take a man down in seconds and move forward to confront the next. He spun around, using his arms to lash out at the next victim, and then just as swiftly, he would raise his leg and connect with the next soldier in his way. The younger man, following this wild American, unbeknown to them, was a pirate, and he knew what was needed of him without being told. He would ram his knife into the men Cisco took down, and they pushed forward, working as a team together.

Cisco looked toward the river and the Carolina who had begun the onslaught. She was still anchored safely out of reach of any reprisal. The plan had worked so far. Under the cloak of darkness, they had loaded their cannons with grapeshot to maximize the damage and aimed them at the Redcoat's campfires onshore. The area he was now fighting in was a blood bath, and many things he witnessed, Cisco prayed he could, in time forget.

How long had he been fighting, Cisco wondered? How many had he killed? All he knew was that every Englishman he came across or that came his way was killed or seriously wounded. However, the tide was changing as the war-hardened British rallied far quicker than anticipated. These fighting men had gathered themselves and followed the orders of their commanders without hesitation. Two battalions were rapidly and masterly formed out of nowhere, and once in position, they marched toward the American insurgents just as Jackson had described they would.

The General was a true leader, fighting alongside his forces until he judged it was time to retreat. Jackson's command of "save the guns… at every sacrifice" was called loudly at this turning point. Then the General rode at full gallop toward his retreating men ignoring the oncoming Redcoats. He was placing his life in danger, but this action served its purpose and rallied his troops. Many could be seen picking up fallen soldiers' weapons, and one or two long rifles were rescued before the enemy could gather them. Sadly, this was not so for their owners, who lay dead next to their weapons.

During the rapid retreat, Cisco continued to witness all-out hand-to-hand battles being waged. They fought bayonet to bayonet, and knives were being thrown with deadly accuracy. Others like Cisco used their gun stocks as clubs to defend themselves; he had bashed many heads before stopping to pick up several fallen guns himself. These he handed to the young pirate who had followed him throughout the attack. "Take these back; I will follow you. If you see more, show me. Together we will return with extra guns. Let's get moving as I am not ready to die by one of those bastard's hands, and Jackson has given the order. He wants to get us away from those marching our way. You better pray that they do not follow."

THE fighting had ended hours ago, and still, Cisco's hands trembled. He'd been lucky and got away without a single scratch. Even Andrew Jackson had returned unharmed, but many others had not. Sadly, there would be no more fighting from them, and he knew it would be days, maybe even weeks, before anyone would learn the identities of the dead.

Like the majority around the American camp, sleep was impossible. They had withdrawn behind the Rodriguez Canal and were back hard at work building and digging what Cisco knew would soon become the last line of defense.

He could only hope that his close friend John Davis was all right and that all his friends would remain safe in the days ahead. Odds were in their favor, he knew that, but still, he found a deep fear climbing inside of him. He shuddered because now he knew, first hand, the meaning of cold dread.

Cisco looked out into the darkness beyond and envisioned the British disembarking from ships like a swarm of ants. By the thousands, they would come, marching toward the small but determined few, and for the first time in his life, Cisco bowed his head and prayed. He prayed for history to turn out as it was told in the modern era, and then he prayed for all those on both sides that he knew would die.

Slowly he sat down on the earthen bank and took a deep breath. He was so fatigued but still wound up. "Come now, pull yourself together and look at this from a historical point of view. There is no need to get all tore up, and I better stop talking to myself too." He looked behind him and seeing no one was paying any attention; he looked back toward the enemy's darkened camp. Most of the fires that had burned so brightly had been extinguished, so further movement by the foreign force was impossible to make out.

The few small cannons the Redcoats had dragged through the swamps did not have the firepower to reach the ship that had bombarded them repeatedly or the rampart he sat behind. Cisco recalled Livingston's words. "The cannons I saw were not even set up to do battle, let alone accomplish hitting their targets. The Carolina had even destroyed several of those. After tonight's efforts, though, there is no doubt that the enemy will make haste to set those weapons ready to use. Hell, they could be doing that right then, and there is nothing to stop them."

By the light of day, many hoped that they would be able to determine how much damage had been inflicted. With any luck, many more silent cannons would have met an untimely fate and rendered useless, very much like the numerous British soldiers who had met their death or were gravely injured.

In his mind's eye, he could picture the bloody mess they had created, and a part of him, the doctor part, wanted to help those they had injured, but again he pushed this sad thought immediately away. Any such ideas could wait, but right then, he tried to recall everything he had learned from Davis and Tori about the bloody Battle of New Orleans. As horrible as this first attack had been, if history was correct, then what they had just fought was not the battle to win all; no, that was yet to happen. What troubled him was not knowing the date or time of the big one. Davis had mentioned that there would be a few skirmishes before the victorious conflict, but even he did not know how many or when they would be fought.

It was inconceivable such an onslaught would occur without warning, but it had, and now the British huddled behind their line of defense and regathered their units. They took their wounded to be treated and ventured onto the cane field to pick up their dead. All fires were forbidden for the remainder of the night, and many were heard grumbling among themselves. The English officers held a meeting in the Villere Plantation house and argued about the right course of action to be taken next. One thing they agreed on was that reports had to be dispatched regardless of the hour.

The encounter with the Americans had left many of the enemy's leaders temporarily paralyzed. They had never expected to contend with such a lethal force. Jackson's men, they determined, were comprised of a rag-tag collection of individuals, and not trained in any form or fashion. They should have easily been defeated, but they fought with a strategy that could not be deciphered or defended against.

They were nothing more than heathens who were sure to fold before the might of the British military; at least, that's what they had been told. However, what they engaged were men who were bloodthirsty and determined to succeed in their endeavor. Their marksmanship was brutally accurate, sparing no one they set their sights on. Proof of this were the dead in the camp and the open field they had briefly marched in. Hundreds had fallen, and still many more were injured to the point of being rendered useless.

The British commanders also learned the truth behind the long guns. The weapons shot further than the British muskets, and Jackson's men would have the advantage of firing those shots from behind the rampart they had been building.

THE General was proud of his men and what they had succeeded in doing. He guessed that they had dealt a deadly blow and shown the enemy that they were willing to fight against all odds. It was but one battle, though, and all knew the next one would prove harder to fight. Never again could they use the cover of night because the British would keep a sharp eye out for just such an action. Once prepared, they would be a force to reckon with, and they still had the numbers to succeed, even without reinforcements that were sure to be on their way.

The battle-weary General stood facing his cheering men, who were celebrating their win. However, Jackson would not give them an inch to relax or let down their guard. The General explained, "With its ruts and low vegetation, the cane field is in need of illumination. The military might of those we face will cross that expanse when daylight comes and not attempt to do so before then. The first round has given the British something to think about and maybe shaken them up, but it will not stop them. We all, every one of us, need to prepare as best we can. Continue to reinforce the rampart and take turns resting while you have this opportunity. If you are injured, come to the Macarty house. If you find a comrade who can't walk, carry him. All will be treated. Mr. Livingston, you will join me as I require counsel on how to defend our location best. "With that order given, he turned and led his horse behind him as he ambled back to the Macarty mansion where he had set up his headquarters. The loss of men always weighed heavy on him, and tonight was no different. What he also understood was that the worst was yet to come, and he was determined to protect the city at all costs, even if it meant dying to do so.

CISCO again looked out across the cane field, where among the trampled cane stalks he knew lay the mangled bodies of their side, and he let the horror of the moment set in. The greenhorn, as a few Kentucky fighters had called him, trembled as he recalled what the General had said right before they carried out the surprise attack. "There was no honor in war, just winning and win they would."

Jackson had gone to the Macarty Plantation home after the last of his men returned from their surprise assault. Others from his unit, who had come with him, were put on guard duty as they were combat-ready and understood what was needed. The plantation slaves were helping those who worked continuously reinforcing the rampart or digging the ditch deeper. They did so under torch-light, as all agreed the Redcoats would not attack at night; it was not how they handled warfare.

There were four plantation homes between them and the British. They were Charlmette, Bienvenue, De La Rouge and Lacoste. The next day all would have a notice hung on their fences or porches. The papers read, 'LOUISEANIANS! REMAIN QUIET IN YOUR HOMES. YOUR SLAVES SHALL BE PRESERVED TO YOU,

AND YOUR PROPERTY RESPECTED. WE MAKE WAR ONLY
AGAINST AMERICANS.

A mere two miles stood between the enemy and the American
line. The land was open, and only the odd canal or ditch broke
the landscape. Cisco looked down at the Rodrigues canal and
wondered why it was called such. There was hardly a drop of water
in the darn thing, so in his mind, it was nothing more than a vast
mucky ditch. It was four feet deep and twenty-foot wide, and right
on the other side of this ditch between them and the British was
the Chalmette plantation house; it would not survive the ravages of
time. As for the other plantations along the river, they, too, would
not be so lucky.

The house that visitors would see when visiting the battleground
in the future was not built until 1830, many years from right then.
All that he saw, all he was looking at, would be gone, just like those
men who would fight in the days to come, just dead and gone.
Cisco sat down and tried to put all this out of his head. Were they
right, Tori, John, and himself? Allowing the battle when they
knew a treaty had been signed, could they have told the truth of
the circumstances and made both sides accept it? He shook his
head no; in an age where time was against you, where word of
what happened took weeks, not a matter of minutes or a phone
call away, it was impossible. Jackson would never have understood,
and the British, well, maybe they already knew but chose to fight
anyway. They fought knowing that along with victory—which
was most certainly theirs for the taking—would come what they
most needed. It would give them control of the Mississippi and the
advantage to win back what they had lost after burning down the
capital and the White House.

Word came to those working on reinforcing the rampart and
spread rapidly. They had lost a handful of men; good men and over
a hundred were injured. Some were taken back to the city, but most
remained, insisting they would stay and fight despite their wounds.
Those reported as missing were assumed to be killed and lying in

the fields beyond or taken prisoner. One could only wonder about their fate. It was just too awful to think about, and Cisco knew that there were going to be more days like he had just witnessed. He realized that he knew the total price that would have to be paid for victory, which terrified him. Slowly he stood up and looked at the rising sun, and for the first time, he hated being a time traveler.

AT two in the afternoon on Christmas day, the American side heard an uproar coming from the British camp. Pistol shots rang out, and an artillery salvo was fired, and everyone snapped to attention. Were the British about to attack?
Davis looked over from his vantage point, and using his spyglass, he saw that the commotion was nothing more than a celebration. The Honorable Sir Edward Pakenham, Major General, had arrived at long last. "I'd give anything to hear what he has to say and what they will no doubt be planning. With any luck, Laffite may be able to find out."

LAFFITE and David had been crawling around the swamps and backwaters for days, many times coming precariously close to the enemy but always able to outmaneuver them and get word sent back to the front line. A few of Jean's men had formed a network of spies who could relay Jean's information on the British movements. With the river now under constant surveillance and the British closely monitored, it was time to head back to Jackson.

JEAN reached a fork in the path, and there he met up with one of his men, an old acquaintance of his, General Humbert. The two spoke together briefly, trading information while those around them took the time to drink and eat. David had water offered to him while the men talked and was happy to take it. However, he never once allowed Laffite out of his sight and refused their offer to go with them.

Humbert told Jean they had won many of the more minor battles and managed to hold off each attempt to breach the rampart. One skirmish had happened on the night of December 23rd, just beyond the Rodriguez Canal. "We lost some men, but many more of the British were taken down. I was told around five hundred or more fell to our boys," gloated Laffite. "Never saw anything like it, and these old eyes have seen a lot in their time. You have no idea how much I wanted to fight, but my orders kept me from enjoying myself. You know, I like Jackson, have no love of the British." He looked at Humbert and frowned. "You know, the only reason we have a chance at saving New Orleans is because we hit them first. Took the wind right out of their sails. Since then, however, they have been like a stirred hornet's nest, and the whole area has become a perilous place to go wandering around in. May I enquire where you are heading?"

"I am taking my men and crossing the river as fast as we are able. We will be moving carefully until then and vigilant on the other side. Thanks to you, Jackson is aware that the Redcoats have men over there. I was told they sent them over, but the current of the river, she was not kind to them. They ended up further down than they had planned. That gives me and mine the time to cross and be ready."

Jean looked at David, who was listening to the conversation. The lad looked concerned. Jean lit one of his long thin cigars and offered one to Humbert. "How many of them do you think are there?"

Humbert refused his offer to smoke. "No, thanks. I'd rather a drink but won't take that either. Got to keep my wits about me. As far as to how many are over there, well, not as many as on this side. We can handle what we find. You go careful, my friend."

Jean understood only too well about being careful, for he had been doing precisely that. Suddenly, Cisco's strange saying jumped into his mind, and he chuckled as he hit Humbert on the back and repeated it. "I would say that they are well and truly pissed off! Jackson is not fighting by their rules." Humbert may not have understood Jean's statement, but he did get the jest of it and found himself laughing, along with the rest of those who were standing close.

He looked at Jean. Still chuckling, and added, "I would say you have about summed it up. I suspect you heard about the racket Dominique You gave them. Damn good shot, you know. He was loving it, talking to his cannon like it was his lady." He threw back his head and laughed heartily. "Bet not a woman in any port got as hot as that cannon did." Again, he laughed and was joined by many of his men.

Jean grinned at the mention of Dominique and his antics. "It would take a hell of a lot more than a few British cannons to get Dominique You dislodged from behind Jackson's ditch; I'll tell you that. Once that old fool gets his mind made up on something… well, you know him as well as I do."

"That is true enough. I talked to the stubborn fool myself not long after the Redcoats tried to breach Jackson's earthworks. He was hopping mad that the cowards broke and ran once he started firing his cannon."

"I heard about that myself," smiled Jean. "Seems they were smart though, not cowards. Would you have done any less, my friend, seeing your men being so easily picked off?

David and I had a damnable time after that, trying to learn their next move, I'll tell you that." David nodded his head in agreement but let Jean do all the talking.

"We were able to get word to Jackson that the British were planning to hit them with heavy artillery fire. Got that straight out of the horse's mouth. Caught ourselves a real talker." Jean carried on with his explanation. "So, sure of himself, he was, and of the outcome, too. Guess they never heard of our Dominique and his talent, huh? I thought that day was going to be a serious attempt. The big battle, but since then, we have seen for ourselves that it was not. I have spent so many days spying on them and harassing the bastards. Always trying to stay a jump ahead, but I tell you this, a big battle is coming soon."

Jean's smile disappeared from his face as he fell silent, lost in his own thoughts. The blue smoke slipped out the corner of his mouth and floated upward in the cool air. He took one last inhale and then dropped the remainder of his cigar on the dirt and put his boot on it. While he stood there, he covered the butt with dirt and spoke as he did so. "Can't have the enemy finding this and figuring out that folks are spying on them so close, can we?"

Humbert did not answer that question but started to give orders to prepare to move out. "Gather up; we are moving on to the location where the barge will pick us up." He watched briefly as those in his group began to pick up their supplies and weapons. "I do know one thing Jean, and that's the British are not going to take it much longer.

They have lost face too many times, and the longer they wait, the less confident they become. Jackson figures they will make their move real soon.

"Then I had better get to Jackson, and you had better follow your orders and prepare, my friend." Jean shook Humbert's hand as the two nodded in agreement. Nothing else was said as each man turned and headed out in different directions, determined to carry out their missions.

AFTER leaving Humbert and many hours later, true to his word, once again, David was able to find his way in the darkness and take Jean and himself into Jackson's camp undetected. As the headquarters had been destroyed, Jackson had set up a makeshift sort of tent and gathered his officers there. It was set back a short distance from the rampart and guarded by both his men and free men of color. One black child, and he was that, in Jean's opinion, was proudly, tending the General's white horse. He had not paid any attention to the two strangers as they approached the area, so intent was he on his duty.

Jean's meeting with General Jackson had been both intense and informative. Jackson's praise and admiration of Jean's men was one of the first matters he discussed. "You had not told me, Sir, that your Captain Dominique was such an artilleryman. His handling of the cannon has put the British to shame. Never will I forget how he entered the camp here, riding on his cannon as if it were a horse." Jackson's weary grin briefly erased the deep-etched worry lines and put a light of mischief in his eyes. "He came in sounding like the boom of his weapon, shouting his orders, and if I might add, causing quite a welcome relief to the tension amongst my men." Jackson's face went stern as he turned and walked toward a small wooden table and chair.

"Here, Mr. Laffite, please come and join me. There is a very grave matter which we must discuss."

His walk seemed a little slow but other than sitting down heavily and sighing as he did so, there was no other visible sign of just how tired the man was.

Jean's admiration for this American continued to grow as he listened to him. He knew only too well how sick he was and how little sleep he'd had in the past week, if any, and yet the man continued to do his job and be the leader his men expected.

"The tension is high, Mr. Laffite. You only have to breathe the air to realize that we are on the very brink of the fight of our lives. I agree with you wholeheartedly that the enemy is ready to strike. With this very dawn's light, I believe that the British will advance upon our position. I would expect nothing else from Pakenham. His reputation as a fine soldier proceeds him. His men will do as he commands, regardless of the risk. A risk that will become clear as my men will not stand down. Neither, Sir, will I do so. I intend to die trying my best to protect the city he wants so much. To allow him to take it would give the British an advantage, which would be impossible to take back. America's future lies in our hands."

He rubbed at his eyes with his long bony fingers as if trying to wipe away a vision he was seeing. "We have received reinforcements, and our standing is far larger than I had dared hope for, but still, we are spread thin. My men have to make our stand and pray to God that we can endure. Look here," he said, pointing to a map sitting on the makeshift desk. "My line is here, just about five miles from the city itself. We have Mr. Laffite, a crude defense at best, which has been thrown up and reinforced several times. This parapet," he said, running his finger along the line, "is all that lay between us and the enemy's fire. In some places, I estimate it to be a good twenty feet thick and five feet high, but that's only in a few places, I'm afraid." He shook his head sadly. "The parapet extends from the bank of the Mississippi to the swamp to here."

His hand hit the spot on the map and stayed. He then seemed to repeat himself. "It is nearly a mile long, and all along that distance are my forces. So, you see for yourself; we are spread thin. I worry that the British will take full advantage of this fact and use it against us." Jackson then pulled a letter from his jacket pocket and placed it on the table in full view, pushing it slightly toward Jean. "I have already deployed General Humbert and his men to where I believe a breach could occur across the river. I do not, however, have any knowledge if he and his company have reached their destination or made the information available to Brigadier General Morgan."

"Begging your pardon, Sir, I may be of some help there. I saw Humbert on my way here. We talked briefly, and he headed out right after. I am sure that he has indeed reached his destination by now."

"That is good news, but it is of the utmost importance that this message," he said, tapping the letter hard with his index finger, "reach our forces. They are situated on the far side of the river." He softened his look briefly, his lip almost curling up in a slight grin. "You, Captain, are the person I have chosen to deliver this message. You and your lad there will depart immediately. See that this falls into the hands of the commander there. It is not to fall into enemy hands. On this, I can't be any clearer." He stood up and extended his hand.

Jean rose and, with one hand, took the document off the table and with his other, shook the Generals.

The grip was a firm one and genuine in its friendship. Jackson's words matched the gesture. "Good luck to you, and Godspeed."

Jean said nothing. He just turned and called David over his shoulder as he made his way out of the camp. While still on safe ground, the pirate explained their mission briefly to the boy.

David understood the importance of following the General's orders, but one thing bothered him, and he just had to ask before they started traveling in silence.

"Boss, how'd you plan on crossing the river once we git there?" David's whisper sounded a little ragged, his voice coming and going in sharp, shallow breaths.

"That, my lad, is the least of my worries right now. If the General's information is correct, a small flatboat is hidden on this side with some of his men. I have a pass here from the man himself; should we be questioned. It's getting across right under their noses that worries me." Jean put his hand in his pocket once again, checking to ensure that Jackson's message for Brigadier General Morgan was still safe.

"By there, you mean the enemy, right? If the boat ain't there, then what? I mean, we aren't going to steal no boat, are we?"

Laffite looked at the boy and frowned. "You are with me to show me the way, not to steal anything unless it's something of the British making." He placed his hand on David's shoulder and squeezed it lightly.

Jean knew Jackson was right. The British would try to advance at daybreak. They had the numbers and the experience, but they did not have Old Hickory. How ironic it was that he, Laffite, would not be there after all this planning and waiting. He shook his head in disappointment. The pirate had wanted to stay with Jackson and his men and face the British. However, the General's trust in him had made Jean both proud and humble before the American.

He had found, like so many of Jackson's men, that it was easy to follow the man's orders, even if it was something you didn't want to do.

JEAN walked, thinking things over in his mind, trying to put it all into perspective. Over the seventeen days since December 23rd, they had fought minor but intense skirmishes and played the game of cat and mouse and hit and run, but now it all had become apparent. The enemy had somehow managed to pull their big cannons to their camp, and with those, they had blown both the Carolina and Jackson's headquarters to smithereens. The other ship was anchored in the river, safely out of range. That was until the more significant firepower had arrived. When the big guns came and turned on the ship, it was clear safe distance was no longer theirs.

The Louisiana had been a sitting duck. Even with all her sails unfurled, there was not enough wind to move her upriver and out of range. The ship would have been lost if not for the brave men aboard her. They had taken to small boats, and some men on shore had used their strength and willpower too. All in the smaller boats had rowed and pulled at the larger vessel; other men walked the river banks and pulled, till in the end, slowly and painfully, they had moved the ship half a mile upriver and out of range. Jean had never witnessed such heroic actions, and he guessed neither had the British.

The Americans had ignored the cannon fire and put their lives in jeopardy to accomplish what seemed impossible. The crew who survived the sinking of the Carolina had been those onshore, and they were determined to see not one cannonball or hot shot hit Louisiana's deck. For them, it was a matter of pride and showing the British that they could not sink the last ship between there and New Orleans.

After that defeat and unable to breach the rampart, the British were ready to commit all their men to the final battle. There was no doubt in Jean's mind they were going to advance against Andrew Jackson and his line of defense very soon, possibly at dawn like Jackson had said.

❧ Four ❧

While Jean and his young companion made their way out of camp, less than a quarter of a mile away, along the ditch, Dominique was trying his best to keep those around him calm and ready for the bloody battle ahead. The tension and the fear were palatable, and more than one inexperienced young man sat looking at the sky above or at their hands, which held the guns they had been given. One of the young men, a Creole and obviously from a wealthy family, looked at Dominique and asked him almost in a whisper, "They will all come at once; I heard they would. There are thousands of them, and only a fraction of that number stands against them. I am worried; we all are. So why do you look so calm, may I inquire?

Dominique grinned. "You know this here time reminds me of something that I find I wish to share. I think it will answer your question."

Cisco looked at the older man, whose skill with the cannon had been seen by all, and questioned him. "What might that be?"

"Well, hand me a sip from that flask you have hidden, and I will tell you."

Cisco grinned. He thought he had kept his whiskey hidden, and yet the pirate had taken the time to see what he had. Just how in the hell the old man had done so proved to him that there was more to Tori's friend than he knew. He handed him the flask and waited.

Dominique swallowed the remainder of the contents and handed back the now empty flask, and as he did so, he began to tell his story. "It was not long ago that I fought with Napoleon. That is where I learned to fire with such accuracy. I had not known that the Emperor had heard of my skill, but when I was invited to a luncheon, a true honor, I assure you, I understood he had been informed. The gathering was in July of 1807, and I will never forget it. The highest-ranking officers and elite attended the affair." He looked around at the small group of men and saw that still others were joining them. All wanted to hear his story, and Dominique could see that his idea was working. They were, for the moment, distracted from the horror of war.

"The Chief of Staff, Alexandre Berthier himself, had arranged the event. It included a hunt for rabbits. Well, now to the point of the story. We all began the hunt, walking toward this open field. Napoleon and his beaters, with his gun-bearers, walked not far from me. A proud moment in time...Oui." He was lost in thought for a moment, with a faraway look in his eyes. No one spoke a word as they waited for him to continue. One of the free slaves who wanted to know the rest of the story coughed, and it was enough to bring old Dominique back to the present and out of his daydream.

"Well, back to the story." He looked at the small crowd gathered around him and smiled. "As I said, it was to be a rabbit hunt, but those who planned it found that one needs rabbits to have success. They scoured the countryside, every farm was asked to give them their rabbits, and gladly they did so. Poor domesticated bunnies would get revenge, I tell you, and wait until you hear how.

But I digress. Where was I? Ah, yes, we headed out alongside Napoleon, and it was at this time that the cages on the far side of the field were opened. Three thousand rabbits ran free. At first, it was a grand time, and the slaughter of rabbits was great, but the animals did not run away in fear for their lives. No, they ran toward us. Thousands of the furry buggers there were, and in minutes, they were on us and all around us. Being short in stature, Napoleon found them climbing up his pants legs. He swiped at them with his riding crop while some of the beaters began to use their bullwhips to try and scatter the swarm. That was what it was, a swarm of rabbits. Anyway, Napoleon had had enough and ran for his coach. He climbed in but not fast enough to escape some of the determined rabbits, who climbed in with him. I tell you, I have never laughed so hard." Dominique slapped his leg as he chuckled, and a few of those around him laughed too. The image of what the old pirate had told them was vivid in their minds.

"I say it was a sight to see, as the coach pulled away and raced from the area. We all witnessed rabbits flinging from the windows of the coach as it hastily left us behind." The old pirate slapped his knee and laughed for a few seconds more before continuing.

He took a deep breath and continued. "You see, it was all Berthiers fault. He had got the rabbits from local farmers. They were tame rabbits, who upon release had seen Napoleon as someone who was going to feed them." He laughed even harder. "I tell you, the man should have caught wild hares, but no, he got domesticated bunnies, and his mistake cost him, I am sure. The bombardment of rabbits was a sight to see, and our Emperor running for his life, frightened to death of the animals, was... well, it was humiliating for him, I am sure. It was, for me, entertaining, I can tell you that. The animals had the coach surrounded in seconds and had it not sped away as it did, I think the buggers would have jumped inside the windows to get to their food. You see, they had been caged for days, and they were starving. These rabbits were hand-fed, so... that's what happened."

Now those around Dominique were laughing at his story. Many knew about the hero Emperor, and the idea of Napoleon running away from thousands of rabbits was an image they found amusing. If it was true or not, the story had done its trick. Hot coffee was handed out, and men sat talking and retelling Dominique's story. Up and down the defensive line, chuckles and laughter filled the pre-morning light for a short time.

"I think maybe we had better watch out for the rabbits now." Dominique had stood up, looking across the foggy field. "I am going to think of those Redcoats as rabbits running toward us. Pick them off easily. They are coming soon, I tell you. Thousands of them will march across that field like the rabbits headed toward Napoleon. Only we won't run. Stand your ground, men. Wait for it and be ready."

A hush fell all along the American line in both directions. Up and down the ditch, men stood up and followed the example of those before them. Words did not have to be spoken; it was clear the time was near.

Cisco stood and faced the field. Once again, he softly hummed the tune of a song not yet written. 'The Battle of New Orleans' was a great song; what words he could recall mentioned rabbits and had the Americans winning. It sure fit the moment. He couldn't remember all the words. Just bits and pieces of it, and he told himself if he lived through this, and John also managed to survive, he would ask him if he knew the song and get him to sing it. For now, he clenched his gun and watched as Dominique lowered the aim of his cannon so he could fire directly at the soon-to-be oncoming enemy.

Time slowly slipped by, and Cisco wished the battle would begin; the waiting was the worst it seemed and looking up, and down the ditch, he saw the faces of many who no doubt felt the same way. It seemed impossible that the British would march their men through the early morning fog blindly toward death. Maybe they would wait until the fog burned off? It seemed reasonable to think so. Dominique had told him they fought by traditional rules of engagement and that he wondered if they would continue to do so this time. The old pirate was standing ready and nodded his head; his hand patted the cannon he had by his side. The men behind the barrel took their places as if given orders, but none had been spoken. Then as he looked intently into the grey-filled morning, the sound of rocket fire filled the heavens. Above him, he saw the burning flares and then heard the booming cannon fire echo from the British side. It had begun, and ready or not, he had no choice but to do as Jackson was calling out.

The American General rode up and down the line of defense

on his white horse, seemingly unafraid of what was coming. He called out to all, "Hold your fire till you see them, then by God, let your aim be straight. We fight to save our land. I will not let them pass. I will die rather than allow our soil to be taken by the bloody British. Fire when you are ready, Captain Dominique; the others will follow once you fire. You have command, Sir. We will follow your lead. May God be with us all."

JEAN and David continued to push on towards the river. The going became slower as they approached the riverbank. Finding their way by moonlight was becoming almost impossible. They had to travel as silently and as quickly as possible, which took a tremendous amount of concentration. It was something that Jean was, at that moment, not doing. He would later realize that it was David's actions and alertness that saved not only the mission but their lives as well.

"Boss, stop!" The words hissed close to Jean's ear as David grabbed his arm and pointed off to the distance. There, silhouetted in the fog, a small garrison of British soldiers moved their way in the early morning fog.

Laffite reacted without hesitation, pulling young David with him. In seconds they lay flat on their stomachs, crawling and inching deeper into the dense underbrush. Dirt filled Jean's mouth as his chin dragged along the ground, his head barely clearing the scrub above him. The Palmetto's scratched and tore at his skin, but still, he pushed deeper into the tangle of trees and undergrowth, praying that David was close behind him. Then as fast as he had moved, he stopped.

David did not have to be told to stay perfectly still and silent; he instinctively knew it, and he dared not say a word for fear of the Redcoats hearing him.

"This is going to be close," whispered Jean. "Remain still and pray they pass."

Close or not, David found himself ready to follow Thiac's words: "You take care of the Boss and see he gets back." Slowly his hand reached down to his waist, where under his shirt was a knife he would use if he had to. The boy would fight to the death if he needed to. Laffite was going to live one way or the other. He shuddered at the thought of fighting, having never done anything like it. Still, he was determined to do his duty. Listening to the sound of the British patrol as they got closer and closer, David carefully watched Jean, who suddenly took the letter from his coat and hid it under some dirt and palm roots. This was not a good sign for David. The Boss, he realized, feared that they would be caught. His hand gripped the hilt of the knife tightly, and the young slave swore under his breath that the enemy would not take them easily if found.

Noticing how frightened the boy appeared, Jean winked at him to ease some of his tension. Keeping eye contact with David, Jean rested his head down sideways, his cheek on the sandy loam. There was no place to go and nothing left for them to do but wait.

Both of them held their breath and stared at each other.

A few of the British men had indeed heard something moving in the underbrush but weren't sure exactly where the sound came from. For a brief time, the soldiers had ventured a short distance into the brush, on each side of the small trail ahead of them, but soon determined that a search would prove most difficult, if not impossible.

In whispered tones, one spoke to the soldier next to him. "Bloody hell, I tell you it was a deer," said one of the soldiers to his companion. "Had to be; there ain't no way a human could go in there. Having us push after the deer is not good. Could be if we had a chance to kill the animal, but we can't, can we? No weapons used until further orders. Bloody oath, what the hell are they thinking? We have to use our bare hands to grab them?"

"Stand and halt! Attention. Silence!" The commander's voice had called out loud and clear, and his orders were obeyed. These men were well trained and veterans of war. They knew how to obey orders, no matter how difficult to follow.

FOR what seemed like a disturbing amount of time to Laffite and David, the soldiers stood silently listening. A pair of these soldiers stood uneasily a few feet away from those they sought. The morning was chilly, and fog-filled dampness filled the air. They could see their breath, and the idea of clambering through the surrounding underbrush was not something they relished doing.

Suddenly the call from the man in command echoed in the foggy morning. "Form a line. March and keep your eyes open. The enemy could be any place, and we give no quarter to any."

Laffite had listened as the order to head out had been given. However, the soldiers had given up too quickly to his way of thinking. Jean knew from experience that this was something the British did not do. He looked at David, and signaled with a stern gaze for him to remain lying where he was, without making a sound.

The time seemed to be dragging by to David, but Jean still did not stir. The British had moved out at least thirty minutes ago, and not a sound of another man could he hear. The call of a large bird answering its mate indicated the morning sun had climbed above the horizon and that dawn was in full bloom. Nature was waking, and soon it would be light enough for anyone to see them in the brush, where they lay hidden or out on the trail.

The continued silence was most unnerving to David, and he wished that the pirate would make a move. Then to his surprise and horror, he heard the first man-made sound echo in the stillness. Cannon fire rumbled across the heavens like thunder, and he looked to the pirate for a response. Surely, they would leave now and make their way to the river's edge, but Laffite signaled him to remain where he was. Again, David obeyed. All he could do was remain still and listen to the noises that filled the heavens above.

Laffite was not surprised to hear the cannons. A few hours ago, Jackson told him he thought the British would attack at dawn, and now it looked like he had been right. He looked at the area where he had buried the orders Jackson had given to him and thought about how long they had remained still. Time was running out, the document had to be delivered, but he remained feeling a certain unease. They both continued listening to the rumble of cannon and the whistling of rocket fire and judging from the roar of weapons filling the air, both sides were firing at each other. While the initial bombardment had been slow, the engagement was picking up. How either of them hoped to hear any sign of the British now was, to David, impossible. Even though no other close noise of the enemy assaulted their ears, Laffite remained vigilant.

Occasionally, there were crashing sounds of frightened native animals fleeing the terrible noise from the battlefield. Even the screeching birds taking flight, their flapping wings, were heard directly above them, but it seemed nothing, and no one else stirred close by.

David felt it was unquestionably safe enough to come out of hiding. Twice he had started to ask Jean, and twice, the flash from the man's eyes had silenced him. So, he continued to remain and wait.

Jean was not about to leave their cover. At least, not until he was confident that they had not been detected. In his mind, a little longer than one hour would prove him right or wrong. Patience was on his side, not the enemies. If the British suspected someone was there, they would wait, hoping to catch them as they emerged, but they would not stay long now the sound of the battle rolled across the heavens. Jean decided that if nothing or no one else moved in the next ten minutes, they would hasten on to the location they were headed toward.

Time crept slowly onward, but in the end, having no indication that there was anyone around, Jean was ready to leave. He had made his mind up on this and was just about to make his move when the sound of men's voices reached his ears. The rustling close by was undeniably the sound of men moving about and reforming their marching column. The shuffle of feet and grumbling of voices filled the air. Then the words, 'move out,' came floating on the morning breeze.

He had been right! Not all of the bastards had left the area right away. Some had remained in hopes of catching them after all. The man had to give them credit for following orders so precisely. They had stood the whole time silently, not even moving a step until told to do so, and regardless of the battle that ensued, they had held their position.

Running rivulets of salt-stinging sweat began to drip into Jean's eyes. He knew now how truly close the two of them had come to being apprehended. If the British had waited for a few more seconds, they would have had both he and the young boy dead in their tracks. The thought of what would have happened if David had not seen them coming and warned him... Jean squeezed his eyes closed and then slowly reached up with his hand to wipe away the beads of sweat on his forehead. Thinking about what could have happened was nothing to worry over; thinking about the now and what to do next was.

Laffite had laid in the dirt, wide-awake, safely hidden, listening to the noises of men fighting for at least ten minutes after the soldiers had left, and still, he had not moved.

He knew the sounds that filled the heavens came from the battle he was supposed to have fought. The Battle for New Orleans had begun at last, just like Tori, Cisco, and Davis had told him it would. It could be no other. They had waited days for this, fought minor battles, and now, he was safe from harm while his friends, his brothers, and citizens of New Orleans fought against thousands of British soldiers. Making a fist, he squeezed his fingers tightly in both anger and frustration.

The constant sounds of cannon and screams filled the air around him. Drums beat, and bugles sounded; even Scottish bagpipes drifted on the breeze. Was it turning out as Tori and her friends had predicted? He could only hope so.

"David…" Jean's voice was so low that the boy was not sure he had spoken. "We will stay here a little longer, just to be sure."

"If you say so," whispered David. He was feeling the dampness of the sandy soil, and his legs were cramping, but he did not move.

Jean closed his eyes and seemed to be resting, something that the younger lad could not do. David only hoped that the pirate would not sleep long because they still had to finish their mission and return to Jackson's rampart. More than anything, he wished he was fighting alongside his friends, but his word had been given to Thiac, and he intended to honor it regardless of what he wanted.

It had been a long thirty-six hours, and he closed his eyes, thinking about all they had experienced together. They had worked well together, and maybe what they had accomplished had helped prepare the Americans. Thirty minutes later, much to David's surprise, it was he who Jean was waking up and not the other way around. He watched as the pirate unearthed the document and put it back in his jacket. It was time to back out from under the brush and pray they were not seen.

By midday, they had safely delivered Jackson's message; then, not wanting to waste any time, they had headed back to what Jean knew was going to be the victorious front line. He had tried to get David to remain securely behind, but the boy insisted on accompanying him, and no number of threats or orders could sway him. The date was now January 8th, and by the time Laffite and David arrived back at Jackson's last line of defense, the famous battle was history, and everything had turned out as his love had wished. Not all, though, survived the carnage she had not wanted, and looking at the sheer number of dead and injured that lay before the rampart, he was glad Tori would never have to witness it.

Thinking his part was over, Laffite was surprised to see Andrew Jackson walking toward him with yet another document in his hands. It could only mean he had another letter to deliver before reuniting with his wife or checking on his friends and brothers.

FOR days and nights, Tori listened to most women cry and pray. On the first day, there had been twenty ladies to deal with.

Now, she estimated that around one hundred of New Orleans's female society had gathered behind the closed and bolted doors. The only light in the place was from a few candles that they kept burning around the clock. The curtains had been drawn closed as if they could block out the terrible and horrific noises from not so far away. The days were long, but the nights were longer, as they had nothing to stop their minds from thinking about what was happening. Laffite's wife had worked steadily, assuring the ladies that Andrew Jackson and the city's citizens would prevail. Her suggestion was that they continue to pray and trust in God and his will.

THE fire had burned low, leaving only orange glowing embers, where dancing flames had ruled most of the night. The room had a chill about it that Tori's way of thinking had nothing to do with the lack of a roaring fire and more to do with the atmosphere, which had enveloped the residence since receiving the news from Jackson's camp the day before.

Looking around the parlor, she could tell that most of the women were asleep. Those who were still awake, and as far as she could tell, only three of them remained so, sat in continued silence with their demons and fears.

Tori had walked into all the downstairs rooms, while Marie

had remained upstairs with the children. After seeing that all was secure, she had returned to the main room. No one acknowledged her arrival, and Tori was thankful. She needed a break right then because remaining strong had taken its toll. The past few hours had been no different, as hysterical women needed comfort that, for some reason, only she, Marie Destrehan, and Cameo had to give. They trusted them and looked to each of these strong women for everything. Most would look at Tori and gauge how things were. Tori was, after all, Jean Laffite's wife, and look what he had done for the city. Besides, she was someone who received information now and then from the front. So far, she had only shared the messages with Cameo and Marie Destrehan, who then would console those who needed it, assuring them that the news had been most hopeful. It did not occur to any of the women that not all the facts were shared with them, nor would they be. They trusted, and they followed the lead of the stronger women, thus passing hours with hope and anticipation.

Briefly, Jean's image filled his wife's mind, and she wondered where he was at that moment and if maybe he was thinking of her? How did he sleep outside in the cold and the damp? How much rest had he had? At least she was warm, fed, and could take a break now and then. However, rest for her had consisted of catnaps here and there, and even those were filled with nightmares. Rest was a luxury, and Tori guessed for her and Jean that rest would remain so until the battle was over.

Tori walked to the French doors and looked out at the grey foggy morning. There was not a soul on the street, not that she had expected any. Looking up and down the narrow road, then across at the building before her, she frowned. Unlike the one she was in, most homes had pulled their wooden shutters closed. It was as if the whole city was now holding its breath, knowing that all hell was about to break free, and then it happened. The heavens echoed with the sound of numerous large cannons firing, which made the glass on the doors and windows vibrate. At first, it had been one or two blasts, as one side fired and the other responded. This steady back and forth action, was quickly followed by a non-stop barrage from both camps.

Shuddering, she wrapped her arms around her body. "Please be safe. God look after them," she whispered. Then as if on instinct, she listened carefully to the disturbance outside. By the sheer amount of noise that swept over the city and beyond, there was no doubt in Tori's mind what was happening at long last. It didn't take a genius either to know that both sides were firing everything they had. Not a single second passed without the thunderous fury filling the morning air. It was just one continuous roar that filled her ears. Hell on Earth was occurring less than five or six miles away, and there was nothing to do now but wait.

The cannon fire destroyed any semblance of tranquility left in the house. The moment the cannons sounded, footsteps running from one room to another could be heard throughout the house, followed by screaming women calling out to each other or their children.

Like the rest of the home, everyone in the parlor was wide awake. The only difference was everyone in the room looked her way as if she had the answers to their questions. One of the women didn't wait for Tori to speak; she stood and faced Laffite's wife and spoke for them all in the room.

"Lord Miss Tori, this is it. I mean, I declare after what news we received just yesterday, those British are surely making their way toward us. To this very home, they march." Her eyes were full of unshed tears, and with a voice that sounded on the verge of sheer panic, the individual turned to look at a small group standing in the parlor doorway. "Pray, ladies, we need to pray. I tell you, our dear Lord and Savior, is the only one who can help us now. Pray that God, in His wisdom, keeps our dearly loved ones from harm. Come join me, won't you? I can't just stand here waiting. Miss Tori, please excuse us; we have the Lord's work to do."

Without missing a beat and calmer than she felt, Tori spoke up.

"Please, you do as you feel you must. Prayer is always a good and positive action. It helps calm those of us who are in need to find the courage to continue to help others. I welcome your help. I will remain here, should you require me."

Cameo spoke up and, in a firm voice, added, "I will remain here with you. Now, ladies, I suggest you follow the others calmly." She ushered the remaining females out of the parlor and toward the study, which they had converted into a prayer room, complete with a priest and two nuns.

Once the door to the hallway was closed, Tori turned to look at the empty street without really seeing it. On her mind was the news from yesterday. A boy, of not more than twelve, had arrived to inform her what was happening. More so, he told what was going to happen. The information had come from John Davis himself, so she put stock in everything the lad had to say. Closing her eyes, Tori envisioned the meeting in detail.

"You see, Ma'am, I was to tell you first and no one else. We got word from your husband, Mr. Laffite, and now I come here from the front lines to tell you we have been pre-warned."

"You saw my husband?"

"Not me, no ma'am. Just told Laffite was with the General sometimes, don't rightly know when, but his spying got the news that Old Hickory was waiting for. Everyone thinks that tomorrow or sooner, we will have a major battle. 'A decisive battle will soon be fought,' were his words." Looking at the women who stood by listening to each detail, he frowned. What he had to tell next were for Madame Laffite's ears only.

He had taken her out of the house and given her the last of his message in a hurry. "Miss Laffite, Mr. Davis told me to make sure you got this next part alone." The young man looked behind him to make certain they were well and truly alone before continuing. "He said you were to tell no one until needed... if at all." The boy looked both ways as if once again making sure he was not overheard. "You see, General Jackson, he has men around the city, and

if the battle goes wrong and the British are victorious, the men...
well, they are instructed to burn the city to the ground. His orders
are everything, the docks, the shops, these homes... all of it must
be destroyed. General Jackson says no quarter given to the British,
and you and yours are too..."

Tori's mouth dropped open as the implication of what the boy
said sunk in. "Are you certain of this?"

"Yes, very. Mr. Davis said you would know if things were lost.
Said, you are to get the ladies and as many as you can to leave
and head up the river road. I reckon if the city is ablaze, you won't
have much persuading to do. Baton Rouge will be the next line of
defense if needed. He did not think it would be but wanted you to
know ahead like."

"Thank you. Would you please tell him I understand? Now, I
must go back inside and keep the ladies calm without letting on
that there is more news other than what they heard before. I shall
tell them I was asking about Jean, and you had nothing much to
report on that matter."

The image and thoughts of yesterday vanished when Cameo
joined her and spoke softly. "This is it then, the big battle that will
decide our fate. I pray my husband and yours... that all the men
remain safe, but that is wishing for something that is impossible
against so many, isn't it?"

"Not impossible but worrying about it won't help. Cameo, you
and I have become dear friends these past few days, and I know I
can trust you. I have a bit of information you need to know in case
Jackson and our men do not win the battle." Tori turned to face
the road as she carefully formed the next sentence in her mind. "If
they don't win, Jackson has men all around the city, and they have
orders to burn everything to the ground. It will be up to us to get
as many as we can to leave and head up the river road to Baton
Rouge." She turned to look at Cameo and see if she had understood
what she'd just divulged.

"I see. That's what the boy told you yesterday; why he took you outside?"

"It is. Will you help me?"

"I will. It won't be easy to leave, but I will if I have need."

Tori hugged her. "Thank you. I knew I could count on you." She turned back to face the empty road and listened to the cannon fire. The pirate's wife could see the horrible battle in her mind and prayed that the outcome would be as history wrote.

The doctor's wife did not want to guess what was happening; she just prayed that it would be over one way or another and soon. She looked at Tori Laffite, and still, the woman said nothing. Tori kept on looking down the street as if willing something, but Cameo had no idea what she was thinking or what she was looking for.

Suddenly Tori's daydream shattered as she realized that someone was running up the empty street and another was following him close behind. Both were yelling at the houses they passed for everyone to stay inside. Then they were gone from sight, but their warning had remained, and the vicinity of the home she had taken shelter in looked very much like a ghost town. Not a solitary soul was anywhere. Not even standing in front of a window or door like she was doing. Indeed, it was a very grey day, and the ghostly mist continued to sit upon the land with no sign of dissipating. Tori looked upward and wondered how long it would be before the sun burned off the fog? Quite some time, she bet, as the pale orb had barely climbed in the morning sky yet, so it had no heat to clear the air. Looking back at the street and beyond, Tori could tell the fog was thicker than any other morning so far. Usually, everyone could see the crossroad, which was less than a block from where she stood, but today the landscape had disappeared, shrouded by nature's blanket.

As Tori watched and listened, so did Cameo. Wanting to add support for Laffite's wife, the doctor's wife reached out and took Tori's hand in hers. Together they would face whatever happened next, and either way, she understood that they would need each other's help in the days ahead.

Tori pulled the French door open and stood still, listening and hoping it would end quickly. She looked down at their joined hands and squeezed her new friend's hand. She was grateful for her added support but did not utter a word. They both looked back down the street and listened to the rumble of cannons and shuddered.

Tori told herself surely those fighting needed to see what they were up against? Firing blindly ahead of them to her way of thinking was nothing short of stupid. Friendly fire could, under these conditions, prove to be a problem for both sides. Stepping back from the open doorway, she pulled it closed and then pushed her face right up against the glass and squinted, trying to see if the grey soup-like condition was lifting. Could be the fog had already thinned down by Jackson's line. If that were true, then they would be ready to fight face to face. Her hand gripped the cold brass handle and again pulled open the French doors to listen. Not sure of what she was listening for, but certain she'd know it… she'd know when it was finished.

Over the past week, they had all grown accustomed to the noise of battle, but upon hearing such a commotion, and at such an early hour, it could mean only one thing: The Battle of New Orleans had indeed begun. It was just like John had said, the British would march at the break of day. It was happening, she told herself, closing her eyes briefly. Realizing the final battle to be fought on American soil against a foreign enemy was underway, a cold dread dug deep within her. Fear, as she had never known, gripped her.

One way or the other, history was being made that morning, and all the praying and crying in the world wouldn't take her terror away. For Tori, for American history, they had to win. If they didn't, and the British won, her future, the future of the country, would be radically changed.

"Stop it," she hissed to herself. "They will win; it is destiny." Tori closed the door again and lay her forehead on the glass for a second time, and then she turned and faced the few women in the room that had returned. Her job now was to lie to their faces if need be, but most of all, she could not afford to show her own dread. These ladies needed her, and she had given her word to Andrew Jackson himself that she would take care of the home front. Looking at Cameo, Tori nodded her head. "Time to prepare for what will be. Let's at least begin to ready ourselves."

FOR the next couple of hours, the sound of cannon fire reverberated over the land and continued unabated. There was not even one second of silence to indicate one way or the other that there had been a resolution to the conflict. Tori walked from room to room until, in the end, she stood again in front of the glass doors, silently praying the fury would die down. Her mind wandered now and then as she envisioned what hellish conditions all the men, both English and American, were facing. Both sides would fight until one emerged victoriously. It was who was winning that plagued her mind. Then, without warning, Jean's love felt a difference in the air; it was the sound that made the difference. The repercussions of thundering rolls no longer sounded like one enormous roar. The bombardment was slowing; she was sure of it. Tori could now hear distinctly each cannon fire one after the other. Separate from each other, they echoed from the battlefield toward the city.

At first, the change was subtle, then slowly, as the seconds ticked by, the firing of cannons became audibly more sporadic. One could almost count between the booming, as there seemed to be a more extended period of silence with each blast. Then as suddenly as it had all begun, it was over. The silence was deafening and what it meant was, at that point, anyone's guess.

DURING the hours of waiting for news of any kind, Tori had tried to calm the most hysterical and comfort the genuinely distraught, who, upon hearing the sudden silence, took it to mean the worst. They knew the odds had been against their men from the beginning. Now, they assumed that all was lost because the mighty battle was over so quickly. What else could it possibly mean, they had whispered? No sooner would Tori and a few of the older women calm everyone as fear began to rise than another distraught female would carry on as if the end of the world was upon them.

Simone, who had behaved herself after her first encounter with Tori, now came alive. Confident of the outcome that faced them all, she left her place in the study and entered the parlor. "I have no idea why we remain sitting here and waiting. It is surely over. Why else should the cannons have ceased so suddenly?" She clasped her hands together and looked truly worried as she addressed the women. "To be up against such a force, they must have been overwhelmed and surrendered before being slaughtered. Ladies, I think we had best prepare to welcome the British and their rule."

Madame Poree gasped at this, followed closely by Marie Destrehan's declaration: "Never!"

Simone would not give up so quickly, though. She looked around the room at the shocked and tear-filled faces. "Come, come, ladies. It is the only possible way we can help our husbands now. Our gallant but foolish followers of that stupid American General Jackson," gloated Simone, "have lost. However, if we present ourselves as loyal citizens to the victors, the British will surely not harm our beloved sons, brothers, and husbands or us. However, they may do otherwise to those who pose a threat, don't you see?"

Not only was Tori astounded that Simone was at it again, deliberately upsetting the ladies, but she also couldn't comprehend how the woman seemed to believe what she was saying.

"I would be wary of what you choose to tell all of us, Simone, and so boldly. We have no indication one way or the other of what our situation is, let alone the situation of the fine and brave men at the front." She was about to soothe the women's fears by asking them to have patience and think positive thoughts when the sound of cheering people outside on the street filled the room.

In seconds, not wanting to wait, Tori ran to the French doors and flung them open, knowing already what the cheering meant. They had won, it was clear, and to hell with Simone; she couldn't destroy this jubilation. Calling to the ladies, she beckoned them to come and see. "Come join me, look, see for yourselves. It is over, and we have won! Come, come step outside; I am sure this will ease your worries and fears."

What was plain as day was the sound of joy ringing in the air. Women were standing on their balconies. All up and down the street, they were waving to each other thru tears of relief and happiness. The word 'victory' was called from one person to another and passed quickly throughout the town and beyond. Even Baton Rouge would receive word of the victorious outcome before the day's end.

Tori laughed triumphantly and stepped back into the parlor and right into the open arms of Marie Destrehan. "I told you, Marie did I not? It has happened. Jackson has saved the town, saved America, and it is over. We have won!" She could not help but cry tears of joy as she danced around the room with her friend. If anyone thought it un-ladylike for Marie Destrehan to act so with Laffite's wife, no one said so. Instead, a few others, including Cameo, joined in, and still more in the hallway beyond began to dance and cheer.

Dizzy from the spinning and excitement, Tori stopped and sat down in a chair facing the open door and hallway beyond. She saw Marie Destrehan heading upstairs, no doubt to tell the children, at least those who were old enough to understand. She could not blame her for wanting to be with her brood, as she called them, and so Laffite's wife looked around for someone else to celebrate with. All the women in the hall had stepped outside, and some in the living room departed to join them. One, however, among them stood gazing out with a most severe expression. "Cameo, please do come and join me; we may sit a while and gather what must be done next. Our time to celebrate will be in the days ahead, will it not? Your expression tells me that you have other thoughts, more profound than a mere celebration… am I right?"

"You are indeed correct, and there is much to do, but for a few minutes, I shall join you. The idea that it is over has not quite sunk in, nor can I allow my emotions to gain the upper hand. I still worry about those who will be needing us. Be them British or American. We are victorious, but at what cost, I wonder?"

Tori frowned. She had allowed her emotions to soar without any regard for what the victory entailed. A dark cloud engulfed her; however, what Laffite's wife witnessed next made her laugh once more. She observed a very embarrassed and, by her expression, an infuriated Simone quickly depart. The high and mighty left without so much as a word of thanks to her hostess, or any one of the ladies for that matter. "Good riddance is what I say," Tori giggled. "Don't let the door slam you in the ass," she mumbled. Nothing was going to ruin this moment for her. They had worked so hard for so long to reach this glorious outcome.

"Ladies, ladies, please. May I have your attention?" said Madame Poree standing next to Mrs. Destrehan. Both her tone and her expression were solemn. "We all know how happy we are, but Marie here and I can't help wondering about the condition of our dearly beloved and brave men. Last night we talked for hours about this and pondered what should or should not happen if we were victorious. Our brave men and their battle is over. Our participation and contribution, however, has just begun."

Cameo spoke then, relief filling her tone of voice. "I agree, Marie and I propose to aid our wounded and help those of the defeated also. Our battle has only begun, as you have said. It is our duty to help heal those in need, is it not? It is, after all, the only Christian and charitable action to take. As a few of you gathered here know, my husband, Dr. Rankin, has been at the front to help those injured. I know he will remain there as long as he is needed, and one can only imagine the carnage he is amongst. It will not be easy, but a few of us should proceed to the battleground and help in any way we can. Others here, return to your homes, but be ready, I beg you. Open your hearts and your homes. Take in those who most need to be cared for. If you have a mind, too, the nuns, I am certain, will not turn away a helping hand. Tori and I can leave a few baskets of bandages for you to share. Many saw how we made them, should you require more, and I believe you will be in need. Madame Destrehan will distribute items and oversee what else needs to be accomplished. Come, Marie, and you to Tori, please join us. I have a few ideas to share on that which we can expect." Cameo stepped close to the older woman and spoke softly of her plans for the first time.

Tori had not thought about facing the carnage or dealing with those soldiers on both sides who would need medical help. She had known the battle's results would be horrible, but the idea of seeing it with her own eyes had never entered her mind. This realization sobered her mood, and for a brief second, fear gripped her, and then she felt shame. "Cameo, I do most certainly agree with you," she announced, standing up. "I am humiliated, to have to admit, that the thought of doing such a kind and selfless act, such as you now call for, never entered my mind. I take it that you plan to go to aid your husband. You did tell me you have done so in the past. I will join you if I may, and now seems as good a time as any. Shall we begin?"

Cameo smiled, "I had a feeling you would, and might I add, you are most welcome."

❧ Five ❧

By the time the sun was low on the horizon, the light was dimming across the battlefield. Many women of New Orleans had arrived by the wagonloads. Each set about helping re-load the wagons with those who could travel and escort them back to the city where they would find lodging and further assistance. Still, others helped put together a makeshift hospital. The surrounding area was set up, split in two, and quickly filled. On one side were men who were hurt and could wait; the other side was for those hurt seriously and in need of immediate care.

A British surgeon oversaw one section where the injured were taken. Though if not for his accent, one would have been hard-pressed to tell that he was a soldier. His uniform coat, which would have distinguished him, was long ago discarded because it was soaked through in blood. Now, his shirt was in much the same condition, and still, he diligently continued his duty, helping all that were brought to him.

This British doctor had been one of the lucky few on the British side to remain off the battlefield, remaining behind to tend those who would be brought to him after the victory, he had been assured would be theirs. By this placement, he'd survived unscathed. However, the doctor would later explain that while his body escaped harm, his mind had not. Never in his career had he witnessed such a blood bath as he had that day.

He recalled how British officers had argued over the idea of retreating, but Sir Edward Pakenham had decided they would advance regardless of reports that they would face many losses. He had at his command the might of the well-seasoned British force and felt confident of the outcome. The enemy would stand no chance against them once they breached the rampart. After that, he declared New Orleans would be theirs to take. As the commanding officer, his orders were followed. If any had doubts, they were squashed by those whose support was behind Pakenham. After all, the man had always led them to victory, and this battle was to be nothing less than victorious, they assured themselves.

So it was; the English doctor had watched in total disbelief as hundreds were slaughtered while the Americans continued to hold their positions. Standing safely in the British camp, the English doctor watched as the columns of men fought the way they had been trained, in the old style that had served the crown well for many years. However, he also witnessed the Americans fight a different kind of battle in a manner that was as shocking as it was successful.

True, both sides had the loyalty of their men, and both had men ready to die for them and their country, but only Andrew Jackson's men broke the rule of combat to fight with a tactic unknown to him or his comrades in arms. The Americans would not march to their death upon a field of engagement as the British did. Instead, they would remain behind their rampart and fire discriminately upon their enemy with both guns and cannons. The barrage was continuous and deadly; no one escaped a bullet, knife, or arrow. They were cutting down men long before they reached the rampart and continued to do so easily.

Looking through a spyglass, the doctor saw a few men who had somehow reached the top of the rampart. He held his breath and, for a brief moment, thought they would breach the defense of the enemy as they had planned. Then he witnessed the cutting down of each soldier. They were struck by swords, shot at close range, or pushed off the rampart by fist or other implements they had at their disposal. Once down, if they had not been impaled on one of the many spikes set up in the ditch, they had no chance of recovering their fall; their own oncoming comrades trampled them while trying to climb up and over the enemy's line. After viewing the carnage taking place, the doctor lowered his spyglass and prepared for what could only be a tremendous loss when the bugles sounded the retreat. When no sound came, and the men kept trying to advance, the doctor once again viewed the carnage through his spyglass.

He witnessed Pakenham valiantly fighting before he was killed on the field. A bullet had found its mark, and the officer was dead before he hit the bloodstained earth. The doctor continued to observe and watched as a young soldier picked up his unit's flag, marching forward a few steps, only to be shot seconds after. The cannon fire ripped continuously into the columns of men, some of whom were now trying to retreat regardless of no orders to do so. They stepped on the body of Pakenham and other commanders, knowing they had lost and no longer willing to risk their lives. A few made it out of reach of the long guns and away from the cannon fire, but thousands of others would not be so lucky.

ONCE the fighting had stopped and the American victory declared, the British doctor was one of the first to venture onto the disastrous battlefield and begin the horrible task of trying to locate those who lived or could live if tended to. At first, he had been overwhelmed, but by early afternoon, he found himself working alongside those he had thought to invade.

The time for war had passed, and he, like many, stood only to help and heal now. It was then that the British doctor learned those lucky enough to have sustained only minor injuries, or nonlife-threatening ones, were being loaded into wagons and taken into the city to the Ursuline Convent. The Convent had been converted into a hospital, but after so many cartloads of men arrived, this space filled quickly. That was when to his amazement, he'd learn the doors of the very citizens, who only hours before had been the enemy of the British, were opened. They did not turn one soldier in need away, no matter whose side they had fought on. His admiration for these Americans grew with each hour and honorable deeds; it seemed they intended to save as many as they could no matter what.

HAVING witnessed the American side tending to all, the British doctor made himself known to a young Spanish man walking among the fallen and showing those who followed him which man needed to be carried immediately off the field. What surprised him was how he quickly assessed each fallen man he encountered. Furthermore, it surprised him when this man called out to him for help.

Cisco looked up after finding a young soldier in his late teens. His leg was clearly broken and twisted at an awkward angle; his other leg was hanging by the skin only. Someone had already applied a tourniquet, and though it had saved his life, the boy needed attention. No one was close by to carry the lad, no one from the American side that was. Cisco called out to the British soldier kneeling by a fallen boy, whose lifeless hand still held the flag he had marched with. "Hey, I need help here. That one is dead, and this one will die if we don't get him help. Can you carry him with me? Come on; there is nothing you can do that will help your men more than getting the living to our doctors."

The soldier stood and stepped over and around the fallen, which was no easy task, and reached Cisco's side. "Dr. Taylor, at your service. May I enquire to which side we will carry him?"

"Did you not understand me? We go to the winning side and the best doctors New Orleans has to offer. You have no need to fear; in fact, I say we could use your help if you are a doctor, as you claim."

"I assure you I am, and I fear not. Helping is what I am sworn to do and help I will. Our side of this field sorely lacks what is needed for those like this. Let us carry him. You show me the way."

DURING the hours that followed, Dr. Taylor worked in the makeshift tented area, where he gained respect for what he saw. The man introduced to him as Dr. Ranking and whose wife was assisting him spoke volumes of their dedication. Dr. Rankin, unlike himself, was not a military man but had volunteered knowing he would be needed, regardless of who won. His wife, and many other ladies of New Orleans, also helped distribute bandages and buckets of clean boiled water. They washed the saws that were bloodied from amputations before being used again. Then they saw those men who had received help move out while the next victim moved in.

A huge black man called Thiac was tending a fire with the aid of several younger boys. The flames were hot and never allowed to die down. Into this fire were poked long pieces of metal. Some were swords; one was the head of a flat hoe, customarily used to till the garden and now used as a medical instrument. These white-hot irons were used to cauterize the limbs where moments before amputations had been performed. The smell was horrendous, burning flesh had a way of nauseating those not accustomed to it, and it amazed him further to witness that not a single woman floundered. They ignored the screams and the stench and kept on helping in any way they could.

As soon as the doctor had finished his task, they began theirs. The wound would be dressed, and the soldier carried to a waiting wagon. Not one place he looked could he see confusion; all seemed to know what was needed and trained or not, they worked tirelessly on supporting both each other and those they doctored.

TORI'S eyes had filled with tears again and again at the bloody sight that met her gaze in the area just beyond the hospital tent. Walking in some spots was dangerous, for the blood of so many covered the ground. The stench of blood and death hung in the air, so thick as to make it hard for her to breathe.

At first, she had found it more deplorable than she thought she could bear, but the painful and pitiful calls for help had forced her to cope. Alongside Cayetana Claiborne, Mrs. Livingston, Cameo

Rankin, and many others, she bandaged and cleaned wounds on both the conscious and the unconscious. Cameo would disappear at times into the tent that the severely injured were carried. Her assistance was needed; she'd tell those close by, leaving the women to do their best.

With gentle hands and caring voices, they applied all the aid they could. Those who could talk thanked Tori repeatedly for her kindness, something that she felt guilty about, and as the hours passed, her guilt grew.

The sheer number of injured, and their ages, never stopped amazing her. It seemed to her that most of them were nothing more than young boys, but she also realized that their age was not the issue that bothered her the most. It was in knowing that the battle had been fought when peace had already been declared. The peace treaty had been signed at Ghent, and copies were on the way. However, the distance between Europe and New Orleans was huge, and time again, had spread her wings and delayed the knowledge that could have prevented the slaughter.

They had all fought a war that should not have been. John Davis had told her this fact, and now Tori stood wondering if she could have prevented the needless slaughter of so many? She told herself repeatedly that she had no way of getting that news to the right people to stop the massacre. It would have been a fool's errand had she tried, and if she had done so and they listened, history would have been changed. There it was, the most extensive guilt trip ever! Tori Laffite had not wanted to change history, and the guilt was almost too much.

With her emotions and thoughts fighting each other, Tori continued to guide each soldier to the designated area to await a doctor's service. Cisco called it triage, and he decided whose lives hung in the balance. If one died before help, it was up to Tori and others tending the fallen to have the body removed.

It was also her job to see that drinking water or hot coffee was taken to those inside the hell tent, as she called it. Food was impossible and not asked for, but coffee was gulped down and appreciated while the new victim was brought in. Often screams of agony would fill the air, as the sound of a saw cutting a limb off filled the silence when the patient fell unconscious. Laffite's wife did not linger in the area when such was happening; it was too much to deal with. So much blood, so much gore, and not enough modern-day knowledge or drugs to help those fighting for their lives.

During one of her times into the tented area, though, Tori saw Cameo holding a young soldier as the doctor she was assisting stitched his gut wound. Doctor Rankin's wife kept talking, and her manner was such that a total trust was formed, making the procedure endurable and easier for both the soldier and physician. During such a procedure, Tori found the time to bring what she could to all who were working. Thinking of night falling and seeing no slack in the numbers of injured, Tori had arranged for oil lamps to be delivered, something that had been overlooked but would be sorely needed. Tending the wounds in the dark would be impossible, even with candlelight. The lamps were many and helped tremendously.

As darkness began to fall, Tori ventured back into the tent. In her hand, Laffite's wife had a fresh pot of hot coffee and in the other, a basket of bandages. "I have coffee and bandages..."

"Tori," interrupted Cameo, "please, my husband could use some coffee when we finish here. Only a few more stitches to go, and I could use the bandages and your help dressing the wounds."

Without hesitation, Tori answered. "You have it." She placed the basket of torn cloth strips on a stool by a bucket, in which, God forbid, were an arm and leg sticking out. Quickly, Laffite's wife looked away and spoke to the doctor. "Do you have a cup?"

He had finished his last stitch and turned to face Tori. "Indeed, I do. It's over here, out of harm's way, and my wife is correct; I could use a cup or two. Bless you for thinking of it."

Cameo spoke up again. "Tori, this is my husband. David, this is Laffite's wife, Tori."

He smiled slightly but made no offer of his blood-covered hand in a formal greeting. "Not the best circumstances to meet, but I trust we will do so again in a few days under more pleasant conditions. Let me take that pot, and you can help Cameo bind up this lad's wounds."

"Dr. Rankin, I will do my best, and yes, I do look forward to meeting again when we are back in the city." She tried to smile but found her eyes welling up again as Cisco helped another man.

"Doc, this one has a gash that needs to be fixed. He has a broken leg, and the other... well, the tourniquet can't stay tight much longer, or he'll not have a chance of keeping it... We found him like this, don't know how long he has been unconscious, my guess it saved his life... passing out that is..."

David Rankin didn't flinch; he handed back the coffee pot to Tori and helped Cisco move the man onto the table. "Here, let's take a look, shall we? Cisco, if I didn't know better, I would say you have knowledge of the likes of myself. Ever thought of becoming a doctor?"

"Nope, not for me. Like I said, my father was one, and that's how I know a bit, right Tori?"

"I guess." She put the coffee pot down next to several metal cups and one wooden bowl full of honey. "You help the doctor, and I will give a hand to Cameo." She picked up the bowl and approached the doctor's wife. "We will have to send for more soon; the honey is good, right? I used it on Dominique's arm, and it worked. It can't hurt, right?"

Cameo just smiled and continued to hurry, knowing that, more than likely, her husband was about to take yet another limb off.

THE injured kept coming because those who searched among the bodies always found more to help. Way after dark by torchlight, they searched and would not stop until they felt not a single person was left alive. Every fallen soldier had to be checked for breathing and then loaded up onto the makeshift stretchers to be carried over the rampart. All those that could walk or be moved came over the ditch. The spikes upon which many had been impaled while trying to topple the defensive line were pulled up and used to help stabilize the temporary walkways across the muck-filled ditch.

The ground before the ditch was soggy and impossible to maneuver over. Jackson and his men had placed cotton bales, mud, and water, which they covered with hay, grass, and corn stalks to camouflage the treacherous ground. The whole area was rendered most unstable and acted like a bog or quicksand in places. Once a soldier stepped into the man-made swamp, his boots would sink, and the more he struggled, the deeper he went. The muddy bog had helped tremendously in slowing down the enemy; now, it hindered those who needed to cross.

Cisco watched as he drank some coffee. The battle was playing over again in his mind's eye. All who reached this trap were shot where they stood or taken down while struggling to push forward. Now, those bodies had been respectfully moved out of the way for the living to pass. At Livingston's suggestion, wide planks crossed the blood-filled muck, and onto these small causeways, the injured were escorted.

THEY had been tending the hurt for hours, and with darkness close at hand, Tori had to see for herself, the field of death, as one of the men had called it. Now that the rush of victims had slowed to a trickle, Tori felt she could safely leave the area without abandoning her post. No one stopped her as she climbed to the top of the rampart not far from Dominique's cannon. Many before her had taken a break to view what was left of the British army, and all had left looking shocked.

She stood there as the sun began to set, looking on in horror and sadness. As far as the eye could see lay bodies, bits of bodies, and among them walked Americans and British, searching and hoping to find another living man in need.

Tori looked away from this sad sight and down toward the ditch that had stood in the British way and saved America. It had a horrible odor she could not deny, and sadly she realized that until now, she had never known that blood and death had a nauseating stink. She had not known either that the ground could turn from crimson to burnt orange in color as the sticky substance aged. The old blood and the fresh were slippery and far worse than ice to walk on. It was all too ugly to look upon, so her eyes again looked out over the land. Far too many bodies lay beyond the embankment and now beyond help. The field was covered with the remains of different regiments in different uniforms. They were not all dressed in red coats as she had assumed. They were army, navy, and others seemed to be civilians, while some even wore kilts; their bagpipes silent by their side. Flags and banners, torn and broken, lay close to those who had gallantly carried them into battle. Why did they march so blindly to their deaths? She couldn't understand it. To have died so far from home… never to see their loved ones or their homeland again, was almost too much to cope with. They were English, Scottish, Irish and Welsh, and God forgive her, she had known! They died for nothing! The words reverberated in her mind until they became unbearable. At that instant, Tori knew she had to get away from there.

Laffite's lady did not remember walking away from the area behind the rampart. Nor would she recall how long she'd walked before stopping. All she knew was that it was pitch dark and she was alone and crying. She'd fallen on all fours first and then had sat with her head resting on her knees and continued to cry for all she was worth. Thoughts raced in her mind. Could she have told them about the peace treaty? Or was she guilty of allowing it to happen because, more than anything, she just wanted to go home? Go back to her world, where this battle was nothing but history. She did not belong here. God help her, she, Cisco, and others; they had done what she had told them they needed to do but at such a cost. It had all turned out as it should, but Lord, could she live with it? Either here or in her own time, she'd always have to face the fact that history might have been changed and was not. Such was the state of her mind when a hand touched her lightly.

"Ma'am, you all right?"

Tori looked up into a young Kentuckian's face. The manner of his dress told her this much without asking.

He wore a buckskin coat and tall leather boots, a long rifle at his side in one hand, and a lantern in the other. Its soft light was reflecting off the blade of his long bone-handled knife, which rested in place on his hip, held snuggly against his body by his leather belt. The boy looked to be not much older than sixteen or seventeen at most, though it was hard to tell in the dark, with only the light from his lantern to go by. She stared at the bloodstained bandage around his head and shook her head no.

Tori was so upset, and she had every right to be to his way of thinking. The surrounding area was no place for a lady; it just didn't seem right. He was amazed at how so many women had come to help and managed the hell around them so bravely. Instead of breaking down and crying, they had rolled up their sleeves and attended to so many maimed and bloodied bodies. Maybe he had not seen them cry because they did it in private like the lady before him. He put his lantern down by her side and spoke softly, as he would to his own mother.

"Mind if I sit a while with you, Ma'am? I think we both need some company and maybe a shoulder to cry on."

She smiled. The boy was trying to be brave and be the man his body had not yet grown into. However, after today, Tori did not doubt that he had earned the status of adulthood for himself. She nodded her head, and he sat next to her, letting her lean up against him.

From all around them came the sound of men calling to each other. Torchlight flames flickering in the wind would stop moving as another body was found to be alive. Tori had not realized that she had wandered so far into what was referred to as the death zone, and right then, she didn't care; she just cried without shame and without the need to stop.

FINALLY Tori had stopped crying and looked around. At first, the distraught woman thought she was alone, but when she looked to her left, it was to find her young companion sitting patiently, waiting for her to speak. The first thing she realized when she looked at him was that his hand had somehow taken hold of hers. His grip was light, and his thumb was stroking her fingers. Then before she could react, he started to cry himself, and the roles reversed; she became the one to offer comfort and a shoulder.

Through his ragged sobs, his story unraveled. "I didn't think it would be anything like it was. I can still see them Redcoats coming at us, wave after wave. They just kept coming, and we just kept shooting," he shuddered. "I saw them blown to bits by cannon fire, and still those that followed; they marched right over their dead companions. I shall never forget it, not for the rest of my days. It was hell, just pure hell. I even saw the man next to me get shot. His blood is here, see?" He pointed to the side of his leg. "He was my friend, you see; he got shot. Won't be coming home; no, he won't."

He sobbed, taking in big gulps of air, no longer caring or talking. Tori just held him, not saying a word. He had to get it out of his system, to let go or go mad. After a few minutes of heart-wrenching tears, he was wrung out. The tears stopped, and through hiccups, he started to talk again. He looked into Tori's face and admitted to her and to himself for the first time, something he found shameful. "I was so scared, and admit I'm still scared. I got hit, see," he said gingerly, touching his head. "Doc said I was lucky the bullet bounced off me." He cocked his head to one side and continued, "I woke up after it had ended. The battle was over, and some man was carrying me to the doctor. That's all I clearly remember." Fear covered his face as he grabbed Tori's arms, pleading with her. "Tell me I'm alive, Ma'am; please tell me, I'm right?"

She drew him into her arms again and rocked him, whispering over and over as she stroked his back that he would be just fine. "Look at me," she demanded when he had quieted down. "I think you and I had best introduce ourselves. Friends need names, you know? My name is Tori, and yours?" He wiped his nose on the back of his sleeve, "Robert, Ma'am. I mean to say my name is Robert Evans," he held out his hand.

Tori took his hand and shook it. "Well, Robert, I'm here to tell you that you are not only alive but are going to recover fully from your wound. You will be home safe in no time and a hero at that."

He looked at her and half-heartedly laughed. "My mother will be happy about that, and my Jenny too, I suspect."

"I'm sure they will be. Today's battle was one that will go down in history, you know? You and all of Jackson's men fought a courageous fight, and against all the odds, you won. You can be very proud of yourself. I am honored to have made your acquaintance." She smiled fully at him. "You have made me feel a whole lot better, and I hope I have helped you?"

"Yes, Ma'am, you have. I'm not so sure that you should feel so honored, though, me crying like a baby and all."

She laughed lightly. "Now, don't you go and worry about that. I know many fine brave men who have cried." He looked doubtingly at her. "Really, I have. Do you know who Jean Laffite is?" Robert nodded his head, his eyes growing large at the pirate's name. "Well, Robert, if you give me your word, you won't tell; I'll let you in on a little-known fact about that man." Once again, he nodded affirmatively. "Well, I have seen him cry. We were at sea, and his dear friend got hurt badly in a fight, and when the fight was over, Jean cried."

"How do you know that?" he quizzed. "You're just making it up to make me feel better."

"No, I'm not. And I know it to be true because I was there. You see, Jean Laffite is my husband."

Robert was dumbfounded. His mouth hung open, and he held his breath, afraid that if he moved, he would wake up from this fantastic dream.

"Oh, Robert, I wouldn't lie at a time like this and not to you. Trust me in what I'm telling you, will you?"

Somehow, he knew what she was telling him was the truth, and he did trust her. "Thank you, Ma'am. That means a lot to me an all. I best be trying to find my uncle now, him or my friends. I know they must be looking for me, and I would hate for them to worry."

"Soon as you find them, you will be headed home?"

"Yes, Ma'am, I sure hope so. Nothing to keep us down here any longer, as far as I can see anyway." He stood to go.

"Robert, where is home for you?"

"That be up Tennessee way, Ma'am. My family has a farm there. Nothing like this here country, I can tell you that."

Tori had not meant to offend him and sort to set things straight. "Oh, forgive me my mistake. I took from the way you are dressed that you were from Kentucky. My mistake: Tennessee is lucky to have you."

Another thought crossed her mind as she sat by him. "You don't happen to know a Davey Crockett, do you?"

"Yes, Ma'am," his face lit up. "Well, that is, don't rightly know him personally like. Know folk who do, though. He was with the General, that be Andrew Jackson, and we had to try and save a fort from the British. We lost that fight, that's when Old Hickory, that's what we call the General, on account, he is so stubborn and strong like, gave the orders to march. We had a long way to go to reach New Orleans, Ma'am, and it was hard going, but we did it. The General gives his word, and that's that. He fights right alongside us. He and old Davey… they know each other really well. Mr. Crockett fought right alongside of us all, and when it was done, he got his orders to head north. Try and see if he could get us more men and supplies. Good man and brave like. He a friend of yours?" He was looking at her strangely.

"Oh gracious, me, no. I've just heard about him; that's all." She fell silent, wondering if she should do what she wanted or not. Then without further doubts, she just knew. Robert deserved to have a long and happy life, and she could try to ensure he did.

"Robert, I'm about to ask you to do something for me. Something that might sound strange and not make any sense." She was trembling. "Do you trust me?"

"Yes, Ma'am, I reckon I do."

"Well, I want you to promise me something and know that what I am about to ask you to do, is very important."

He looked at her, almost fearing what she was about to say.

"Robert should Mr. Crockett ever ask you to join him on a trip to Texas, I want you to promise me you won't go. I know this sounds strange, but I think God put us here together tonight so I could give you this message. No more battles for you, all right?"

"Ma'am, I would be only too happy to agree to no more battles." He actually smiled, then reached up with his hand and scratched the top of his head. "You really think old Davey is going to go to this here Texas place to fight another battle?"

"I know he will, Robert, and I'm asking you not to go."

She looked so beautiful, sitting there in his lamplight, pleading her case. Her face was almost like that of an angel, and his eyes widened as this realization hit home. That was it! His mother had a picture of an angel in her Bible at home, and looking at this woman now, he was convinced that she was one. She had to be.

Tori wanted to say something but watching his face and the strange emotions he seemed to be experiencing, she decided to keep still and let him be the one to talk. He looked like he was about to get up and run. Who could blame him? She must seem like a strange woman, claiming to be Laffite's wife and telling him not to go to Texas. He probably thinks I'm crazy, she thought. Best I let him figure things through and keep my mouth shut, or really frighten him.

Robert had been raised to be a God-fearing man, and once his word was given, it would be kept. A man's word was his word, after all. To break it would be a sin. He would never know why he agreed and gave his word that night. He just decided that he would remain on the farm. "Yes, Ma'am, you have my word if it means that much to you."

"It does," she said with a tone in her voice that backed up her statement. Then softly, she whispered to herself, "Finally, I get to change something and set it right." Her eyes were glazed with unshed tears. "God, go with you, Robert, and be happy."

She hugged him, then quickly stood up and walked away. She was ready to head back to the make-shift hospital and those that needed help. Tori felt stronger somehow, and that feeling was helping her heal in a strange way.

Robert watched her disappear and felt that he had been helped. He could not explain it, but he knew that God had sent her. She was no wife of the pirate Laffite, he told himself. In his mind, an angel truly had touched him, sat with him, and comforted him. The young soldier turned and headed toward town, where he knew his uncle and friends would be waiting. His fighting days were over. He was ready to go home and settle down. No more adventures for him. He had all he wanted waiting for him at home. Her name was Jenny, and the thought of her was more exciting than any adventure.

❧ Six ❧

T ori and two other ladies headed back into the city with a
wagonload of the injured soldiers. The three women had
traveled in silence, too exhausted to talk and stunned by all they
had seen. Tori had been amazed at how well the ladies of society
had taken control of themselves among the bloody mayhem. She
compared them to others earlier that day; like so many others, they
had been hysterically shrieking and fainting. These ladies had not
fallen apart; they had pulled themselves together for the betterment of the injured. Never would she have guessed they would
have been capable of such bravery and unselfish acts of heroism. If
Tori had not witnessed it herself, she felt sure that she would have
thought it impossible and nothing more than an exaggeration.
Now, she knew the truth; she would tell Jean what she had seen,
and there it was. Jean, where was he?

Mrs. Livingston felt Tori's concerns and raised her head, looking
curiously at her. She was almost too tired to speak but weakly
smiled as she did so. "I am sure he is all right, Madame Laffite. I had
heard some of the men talk of him earlier and how they had seen
him with the General. I did not hear any mention of any injury. It
is your husband who you are thinking of, is it not?"

"That is so kind of you. It is. Actually, I was not wondering
about Jean; she lied. I was sitting here thinking of the miracle I
had witnessed today. You have to admit that to see so many of
the ladies, working there among the blood and pain, after such a
display of helplessness this morning." Tori took in a deep breath
while shaking her head. "It was just so amazing, was it not?"

"I believe, Tori... I can call you Tori, can't I?"

"I would be happier if you did."

Mrs. Livingston nodded her head and continued. "Well, like I was saying, I believe that under the circumstances, such as we have been experiencing for the past hours, we were able to carry out our duties because we were in control, don't you see? It's the unknown that tends to make one edgy."

"I think I do understand," Tori replied, a tired smile crossing her lips. I have learned so much today with all I have seen, and I have to tell you, my respect and admiration for the women of New Orleans has grown immensely."

Mrs. Livingston just nodded her head and smiled. The sway of the wagon was rocking her body back and forth as if on a boat at sea. She seemed lost in her thoughts when she looked across at the third companion, who was deep in sleep. "I have to agree with you. My own opinion has taken such a shift. Who would have ever thought it?" They both laughed softly as they recognized each had been feeling and thinking the same thoughts. "You are not American, are you? My husband told me you come from Europe. Her question came out as more of an expression than a question.

"Well, I can say I'm just an American. An exhausted and happy-to-be-alive, good old-fashioned American-as-apple-pie girl."

If Mrs. Livingston was going to pursue the line of conversation or question Tori's strange remark, she did not have the chance. A voice rang clear in the crisp night air. It was a most welcome sound to Tori's ears, and seeing her reaction, Mrs. Livingston smiled all the more. The wagon driver pulled his team to a halt as the mounted rider approached.

As tired as he was, Jean could not rest until he had his lady by his side. For hours he had searched and questioned her whereabouts, finally learning that she was most likely among the last of the ladies to leave the battlefield. He had been on his way to collect her when he spotted the wagon making its way slowly up the road. Her laughter had carried in the air, like welcome music to his ears, confirming her presence aboard."

Jean?" She stood up, turning to face him. He did not speak, just pulled his horse close to the wagon's side and reached out to her.

Tori took hold of his outstretched hand and let him pull her up onto the animal in front of him, where they both hugged each other.

Jean looked over at the puzzled wagon driver. "I have what I came for. I suggest you continue and get these other ladies to their husbands and these men to the hospital, where you will find those willing to have them in their homes. Ladies, if you will excuse us, we have to leave your company for now. Good evening to you." With that, he turned the horse and spurred it off, holding his lady close to him.

"Was that Jean Laffite? The man himself," asked the shocked woman across from Mrs. Livingston?

"It most certainly was. Dashing, isn't he?"

"Why Mrs. Livingston, I declare you are making me blush. I declare such thoughts and from a married lady like yourself. All in all, one still would have to agree with you, though," she giggled. "I dare say my husband would never agree to pick me up so and riding away with me like that. My, it is romantic. Now, don't you go saying anything. I will deny it if you tell anyone that I agree with you on that pirate." A grin filled the woman's face, and softly she added her last remark on the matter. Well… maybe. I mean, I think I shall tell a few close friends how dashing he is."

FOR the first time in what seemed like forever, Jean and Tori were able to return to the townhouse. There they were welcomed and fussed over by a very emotional and happy Bessy. She insisted on feeding them while hot water was taken upstairs to fill the bath.

"Now, I's won't be takin' no for no answer. You both just listen to me and know'd that I be takin' care of you. You just be too tired to think clear like, and I know'd what you be needin' and all." Her hands were placed on her hips as her head swayed from side to side. She could be a powerfully persuasive person when she put her mind to it, and no amount of argument was going to change her course of action, not when one of her stubborn moods hit.

Jean and Tori let her have her way, knowing that she was probably right. Neither wanted to talk about what they had seen or been through. However, slowly as the hours ticked by, they spoke and learned what had occurred since they were last together. When at last they found themselves in each other's arms in bed, the talking stopped. They were content to lay silently. It was early morning before they finally drifted off into a deep and peaceful sleep.

VOICES from downstairs broke into her barely wakened state, one that she longed to stay in. Pulling the covers up over her head, she struggled to remain in that blissful place, warm and cozy, right next to her man.

The only problem was as she reached across the bed to find the space that should have held a warm body, it lay vacant. Tori sat up and listened intently to the now distant voices below. She was trying to determine who had come calling at such an early hour but was unable to do so.

Downstairs, Jean and Cisco sat drinking coffee and talking about the past few days and what was occurring even as they sat across from each other.

"Jackson will remain at the battle site until the British withdraw completely. It is an uneasy truce that has taken over down there, but it will hold." Cisco was trying to put it all into perspective. "You don't have to worry. As far as Davis and I can recollect, both sides will avoid any further confrontation. Besides, the British have so many dead to deal with.

The count is in, you know, at least on our side. We have thirteen confirmed killed, thirty-nine wounded, and nineteen missing. Jackson estimates the British losses to be nearly three thousand, an estimate that will be damn close when all is said and done." Cisco took a long sip of his coffee, watching Laffite as he continued.

"You know, in my time, we have a saying-it's shell-shocked. Our men, who saw real bad action in war, would sometimes suffer from this condition.

Anyway, this morning as I left Jackson's men, I looked across at the Redcoats and would say that, in my opinion, many are suffering it, shell-shocked, I mean. They are so stunned at having lost, and Jackson's men are just as amazed at having won, but no one down there is acting any way but shell-shocked. Do you understand what I'm trying to say?"

Jean had an excellent idea of what it was Cisco was trying to tell him. Even knowing the outcome of the fight, he himself had been shocked when it had finally ended. However, this shell shock his friend talked about did not play with him or his emotions.

Tori entered the room hurriedly, wanting to know what was happening. Upon seeing Cisco sitting with Jean, she broke into a huge smile and extended her arms. "Come here, you crazy fool. I have been so worried about you. Is there any news about the others? How is John?"

"They are all fine, as far as I know. Davis is at his hotel helping supply some of the food for the hospital, and Livingston and Grymes were still with Jackson when I left early this morning. We have done it, Tori. We have kept history intact but at a price."

She looked at him and could see the sadness in his eyes. He had been there, seen the battle, the killing, and all the ugliness of war. Her happy-go-lucky Cisco would be changed forever.

"Davis and I talked late into the night, and I have to let you know what we decided. Whether or not you join us is up to you, but we intend to keep our promises to ourselves." He sounded somber.

Tori frowned. "I think you had better sit down and tell me; it sounds serious. Jean, could you fix me a cup of coffee, please?"

"You know, I would be delighted to do so if it was broken. Jean grinned briefly. "If you two need to talk alone."

Cisco looked away from Tori and faced Jean. "No, please stay and listen to what I have to say."

"If you want me to. But before you start, I have a question for you both. It's something that has been on my mind for some time. I have not wanted to ask until now. If I may be as bold to come forward and put this question to you?"

Tori took a seat, and having no idea as to what was on Jean's mind, she spoke. "Yes, of course."

Tori took hold of Cisco's hand, and the two of them laughed at each other. To Jean, it was as if they held another secret, and his question was most serious and nothing to laugh about.

"You may not laugh when I ask my question, but I have to ask. Now that this great Battle of New Orleans is over and all has happened as planned, well, now what? What do you know about what happens next to me? Or dare I ask?" Tori looked at Jean's face and could clearly see the complex emotions behind his eyes. He wanted to know and yet was afraid of the answer. She wished she could ease his pain and suffering, but he would not find an answer coming from her.

"Jean, Cisco, John and I have spoken about this… mind you, only briefly before we left the rampart, and well, each of us only knew about the battle. John did know a bit more, didn't he?" She looked at Cisco who nodded in agreement.

"Yes, just a bit. That's part of the problem. It always has been, hasn't it? We only know bits and pieces. All we have are some dates or approximate dates. We know about events in history that will yet happen, but we don't know any accurate details of everything that has occurred. We got lucky here, just fortunate, that's all."

Cisco's face was quite serious. "We can tell you this, Jean. You will become the hero of the day. It's like we told you. You will be known as the Gentleman Pirate in the history books and certainly in New Orleans. You, along with your men, will receive a full pardon from the President, and that's about it. Sorry man, we don't know anything further than that. We did not study about you in history. Our history lessons did not contain the information that you are seeking. What I do know, for now, and forever, is that you are a fine friend and a true American."

Tori watched Jean's eyes. She saw the shadow of disappointment and then the all-over happiness that washed it away. Ever the optimist, he laughed at them both. "Well, maybe it's for the best. From here on out, I can make my own destiny, and the outcome will be as it should, no doubt."

"I'm sure of it." Cisco stood and gripped Jean in a hug, slapping him on the back. "I'm glad that you feel as you do because it has a lot to do with what I wanted to tell you both. John and I have made a pact with each other to keep all our knowledge about the future within our minds from here on out. We have had quite enough with this history-making business, and from now on, we intend to let the cards fall as they may." He looked back at Tori. "I don't know where you stand on this. It's something you have to deal with yourself. But from now on, the future is the past for us, even with you. You will always remain our dear friend. Nothing can change that, but we will not discuss or talk of that, which is beyond the now."

He had changed from the carefree man he used to be. It showed in his manner and sounded in his tone of voice. Tori had no doubt that he spoke the truth. For her two time-traveling friends, the future was finished, and of that, there was no doubt. From now on, any talk about the things to come would have to be between her and…who? Panic flickered inside her as the implications took hold.

Cisco could see the pain in her face. "Look, Tori, it's just that we feel that we have done quite enough, and we just want to settle down. We want to live the remaining years of our lives without complications if you know what I mean?"

"I do," she spoke softly. "I don't blame you or John. It's just going to be hard not talking about… I just don't want to forget." Tears started to fill her eyes. "Look, if that is what you want, then I will have to live with it, that's all. I may not agree with you, but then I can't live your lives, can I? As to what or how I will deal, with what I know, I can't say right now."

Jean admired John and Cisco's decision, knowing that it was not going to be an easy promise for either one of them to keep. As for his lady, he found himself hoping that she would continue to tell him her stories of the future on their quiet days alone together. He did not always understand or like some of the things she'd told him, but how he loved hearing about the great and strange inventions.

"Look, you two, I have got to go," said Cisco. "Davis is waiting for me to get back. Take care of yourselves and stop over soon. John would love to see you both." He hugged Tori and smiled his old Cisco smile. Then he was gone, leaving the room silent.

Jean sat down next to her and slipped his arm around her waist. "You know that you are not alone and never will be, don't you? No matter what you decide, whether you talk to me about the world you came from or not, I will abide by your choice. But, if it helps you any, I, for one, adore hearing about your time."

She kissed him gently and nodded her head. "I think I shall always want to tell someone. There is so much…"

Bessy entered the room, making as much fuss as she could, just so the two of them would know that she was there. Tori grinned at her, knowing that Bessy never interrupted them when they were alone unless she thought it was necessary. "What's up, Bessy?"

"Nothing important, Mizz Tori. Just ain't a knowin' what to do with that there, David. He, be a standin' around, fidgetin' about like a dog with fleas. He done asked me to ask the Master, what he supposed to be doin' now?"

Jean had forgotten the boy, and now that the matter had been brought to his attention, he knew he had work to be taken care of.

"You tell that lad to stay put and rest up for a while. I'll come for him when I'm ready."

"Yes, Sur Massa, I'll be telling him right away." She left happy at having solved one more household problem.

"Now, my lady, as much as I would like to stay here with you, I have a few ends to tie up." He chuckled and then continued. "I am sounding like you now. Have to take care there. Now excuse me, I'll explain when I return. You, on the other hand, have just about enough time to dress for a nice evening dinner. Grymes has invited us to join him, and I'm glad, as I have some papers for him to draw up for me. Don't ask me about it now. I'll explain when it's all taken care of."

Like always, when his mind was set on something, there was no stopping the man. Tori was glad when he quickly departed, leaving her alone with her thoughts. She needed some time to sort out a few matters of her own. One such thought kept niggling at the back of her mind, refusing to go away. It was the question of her own promise to return to the lake.

DAVID walked with Jean for the first time in many days. The streets of New Orleans were preparing for Jackson's triumphant return, and every person they passed was either consumed with that event or the opportunity of shaking Jean's hand. The entire city seemed to want Jean and his lovely lady to join them for dinner. This was a far cry from only a few weeks ago when he was a wanted and hunted bandit.

David realized that it was going to take them quite a bit longer before reaching the blacksmith shop. "I had best be goin'. Thiac, he'll be needin' my help and all."

"That he will, my lad. More and more orders come into the shop each day." Jean turned around to look at the boy, who was walking a few steps behind him. "David, you did a great job when you and I were together. You know that, don't you? You are to be proud of what you did, saving my life and the mission, as you did. I will never forget that."

"Boss, it's I who will never forget. You saved my life it seems to me. Keeping me still and all. It be me who will not forget. You saved me, sure'n you did. I owe you, not d'other way. Yes, Sur, one day, one day David Jackson, he's goin' to find a way, to pay you a back. I swears it, on my own soul you will be paid back."

"So, it is David Jackson now, is it?" Jean put his head back and laughed, temporarily standing still. He continued his walking when he realized that people were staring at him. "I assume that the choice in name had something to do with the General?"

"Yes, Boss. It be his name and all, but he won the battle and kept them, Redcoats, out of this here city. So, I thought that I'd be a takin' his name and do good by it and all. Sort of thanking him and reminding myself of him every day and such."

"I'm sure the General would be honored, but then we can't have a slave with his name now, can we?"

David's bright young face fell. "No, Boss, I guessin' we can't." His young head hung down. Once again, he was reminded of his position. What would he be needin' two names for anyway? He was stupid. He should have known better.

Jean softened toward the boy, who had no way of knowing he was teasing him. He couldn't drag this out any longer. "You had best go on ahead and tell Thiac that I think he had better consider hiring you. I want you to work there for me, Mr. Jackson."

David looked up at Jean, his face full of wonder and questions. Had he heard the Boss, right?

"Well, go on, jobs are not easy to find, and you had best take advantage of my offer before I change my mind." David spun on his heels, ready to take off for Thiac's, when Jean's stopped him. "Wait just a second there, don't be running off till I am finished. What I have not explained to you is simple enough. You will find that Thiac has your freedom papers waiting for you. I saw to it that you would have them, that is if it is what you want?" he asked jokingly.

Amazed, David looked at Jean, the man he owed his life to and now his freedom! A huge grin filled his young face. "Yes, Boss, it be just what I be wantin'. I'm a-goin' right now. I will make you proud. You see that I will."

"I have no doubt of that. You are already quite a man. Now, if you don't mind, a lady awaits me." Jean turned and walked away. He couldn't wait to give Tori this piece of news. She loved it when a slave got his freedom, said it made her feel good, and Jean guessed she was right after all. He felt just fine, more than fine. He felt free.

David ran off down the street, also feeling free. He made up his mind that one day he'd pay back all that he owed, but how do you pay someone back for giving you your life and your freedom, he wondered?

JANUARY 19th, Jean and Tori learned that the British had given up and set sail. Ever the cautious man, Jackson was going to remain at his post with his men a few more days to be sure they had indeed departed.

"You know Jean, that the British tried to take the fort down-river, but after many attempts, they gave up. I am amazed that they would continue to fight after such a loss." Tori continued to look at the many invitations which had been delivered since the victory.

Jean looked up from his desk and spoke with an edge to his tone. "They never just give up, and I, my love, am surprised they have left. My bet is that Jackson is too. That's why he remains. Never trust them… It's why this city is still under martial law and will remain so until the General and his advisors know we are finished with the British completely."

"Well, I think this time, it's safe to say they have given up. With their dead buried either in dirt or at the bottom of the grand Mississippi's murky water, those in charge must have felt they had no choice anymore. But a watery grave is not in the cards for General Pakenham; Davis said his body was put in a cask of rum and taken home for burial."

Jean chuckled. "Trust them to come up with such an idea. Bet rum rations are cut, and the sailors, what's left, will not be so happy…" he was grinning as he spoke. "Let's not waste time on the British anymore. We won, and that's that. I have much more serious matters to attend to, and Grymes is going to ask Livingston to help in my appeal to have all that is rightfully mine returned. Might even get my ships back." His attention was back on the paperwork before him, and so he missed Tori's worried frown.

THE city had continued to stay in full readiness when at last, on January 23th, 1815, General Andrew Jackson and his men triumphantly rode into New Orleans and into the biggest victory celebration, anyone had ever seen. On the steps of the Cathedral, in an area that would later become known as Jackson Square, Mr. and Mrs. Livingston greeted their old friend. Filled with enthusiasm and caught up in the moment, Mrs. Livingston placed a laurel crown upon Jackson's head.

The large crowd roared its approval, and Jackson, although thoroughly embarrassed by such an act, had a good sense of humor and joined the laughter with all those surrounding him. He waved to all, and standing there like he was, proud and humble at the same time, Tori found herself thinking he would make a good President. She wondered if he would approve of the monument that would be erected in the future and the area surrounding the church being called Jackson Square. She could share so much with the man but knew in her soul that such things needed to remain untold.

"Jean, I am glad we came to witness this; it seems the whole city has come out to do the same."

Laffite looked around and nodded his head. "It would seem so. Jackson deserves it, but there is still much to settle." Jean frowned, and then not wanting to spoil the historical moment for Tori, he changed the subject. "I am grateful you agreed to witness this event from back here. I feel as though joining them up on those stairs would not have sat too well with Jackson's wife. Rachel Jackson is a woman who has every right to be by her husband's side, but like us, she does not like to be seen under such circumstances. Livingston was telling me that we will see little of the pair now she is here."

"I don't blame them. Andrew explained his wife's discomfort with crowds and hero worship. She is fearfully protective of him, you know, and like us, they are made for each other."

"I would agree there. Come, let us leave this celebration and visit my brother. I doubt we will be missed, and my affairs concern me greatly. This city owes me, and yet they have not moved a hand to pay me what is due. Let us hope Pierre has information about our ships and merchandise."

"I hope so. You have not acted yourself for days. Maybe the upcoming ball will cheer you up. I am sure Grymes is going to get you everything you lost. I think Andrew will help you too." Tori was uncomfortable talking about the subject, so she changed her topic of conversation. "Mrs. Livingston and Mrs. Jackson have planned a grand ball together. It is to be a celebration for all. For the first time in the city's history, all cultures will come together for one joyous occasion under one roof. Think of it... the people of this city partying together without any hostilities, and better still, all your men, they will be there."

Laffite laughed at that statement. "I shall endeavor to make a showing for my men, but until matters between the city and I are settled, I won't be enjoying myself or staying late. Besides, like Rachel Jackson, I prefer at this time to remain in the background and try to remain optimistic."

Now it was Tori's turn to laugh. "You remain in the background... you who is a showman and hungers for the spotlight! You better be careful, or your nose will grow."

Jean had no idea what she was talking about, and for the first time, he did not question her. Instead, he took her by the arm and made his way through the crowd to the open streets beyond. His wife may not be worried, but he was. They had promised to return what they took, and yet, nothing had been done, and it seemed nothing was going to happen anytime soon.

THE American victory at Chalmette was supposed to have been the reason behind the celebration ball, but once Laffite and his men appeared, it quickly took on another tone. Now, the city had the real heroes of the battle to thank, and thank them they did. With welcome arms, they accepted the pirates. Jean and Pierre were no longer to be avoided or shunned. Indeed, many tried to be among the first to invite or be invited to future dinners and gatherings with the couple. Laffite's men, who would have stood no chance at ever walking the streets of New Orleans again, now called it home and its citizens, friends.

However, lost in the uproar and rabble-rousing were two very disgruntled people. Edward and Simone had hidden their hostilities well, smiling and joining in the celebration. They avoided any contact with the Laffites, choosing to bide their time as to what should be done about the 'deplorable situation,' as they called it.

Simone told Edward, "Let them have their moment of glory. The higher the Laffites climb, the harder they fall. I don't think it has crossed anyone's mind, my dear husband, that Jean and his men are still wanted, pirates. We shall have to remind the Governor of his duty once the General departs. All is not lost yet, my love."

Edward, who had been feeling defeated, found himself snickering and feeling decisively better. Once again, his darling Simone had boosted his morale, and he had no doubt that this time, with careful planning, Laffite would see the end of his so-called hero status.

"Yes, my darling Simone," he cooed into her ear, brushing the hair from her neck. "You are right once again. All is not lost. Let us forget about the fools and have our own celebration. I've been thinking, how would you like to be married to the next Governor?" His question caused her to giggle. "Once we get what we want, I feel that fool William should lose his position for taking such a damnably long time to accomplish such a simple task. The fall of Laffite and his wench should have happened long ago and if he had not been such a fool, it would have, don't you agree, my dear?" His breath was hot on her neck, his lips wet and warm.

"That I do, my love, and what a glorious idea, Governor" she responded in a sexy voice. "Why didn't I think of that? You will make a great Governor, and I will help you any way I can."

Edward touched the side of her cheek and let his finger trace the outline of her lips. "I can make these turn up in a wonderful smile, and I think I shall do that now. I have an invitation to dinner at Williams's home. Hard to come by invitations..." His finger continued to trace the outline of her bottom lip as it turned upward in a huge smile. I have it on good authority that only the most important and close friends are invited, and we, my dear, are still close friends with those who count."

Simone hugged him close and then faced him with pure joy filling her face. "People who will help us gain all we want and more. Right now, all I want is you... let's plan later. We always plan better after we have enjoyed ourselves. Besides, I have to show you how grateful I am for this latest surprise, don't I?"

THE invitation, dated February 10th, requested the presence of Mr. and Mrs. Jean Laffite to attend the farewell dinner for General Andrew Jackson. It was to be held at the Governor's house and would be well attended. At least that was what Cayetana had told Grymes.

Tori had wanted to see Andrew Jackson just one more time before he rode off into history and out of their lives. She had promised herself that under no circumstances would she allow herself to reveal any knowledge about his future, no matter how tempted. He would find his own pathway to his Presidency with or without her help; she was sure of that. No, Tori wanted only to talk with him and his wife. Not a long talk that would be dangerous. Andrew Jackson was a shrewd man, and he was also a good judge of character. He paid attention to the small details, and now that war was no longer on his mind, Tori understood that she'd have to remain on her guard and not let anything slip or give away her identity.

Jean had listened to her talk for hours, over the past few weeks, about history and the future, but as the days slipped by, she talked less and less about history and even changed the subject when he brought it up. This action puzzled him, as she had always been more than eager to describe all the events, inventions, and miraculous medicines she could think of. Tori always laughed and joked as she shared her knowledge with him, knowing how ridiculous some of the things she told him must have sounded. Some stories had been wondrous and exciting. He enjoyed hearing about space travel and ships that sailed under the waves, and men and women, standing on both the North and South Poles and climbing to the top of the tallest mountains. All of these recounts of the future and more had taken his breath away. Then without thinking, she mentioned something about the Civil War and the fall of the Confederate South.

After the mention of this war, which seemed to be something she hadn't meant to tell him about, it was as if a curtain had come down on all that she knew, and nothing he could do or say would allow it to be raised again. Some inner instinct, or fear, had forced her to finally agree with Cisco and John's decision, to remain silent about what was to be, and no amount of probing on Jean's part could change her mind.

Jean had worried at first. The Tori he loved and knew so well had buried a large part of herself by denying the opportunity to discuss her life in an era he could only imagine. In doing so, she had become more somber, seeking time alone to sit and contemplate whatever it was she was struggling with. He often caught her staring ahead, looking at nothing but seeing a daydream world of her own thoughts. No doubt, Tori's visions were miles, if not years, away from him and his love. His lady seemed to be growing even more distant, but when caught off guard, she would conceal whatever it was she'd been thinking about and act as if nothing was wrong. Jean knew she was only fooling herself when she claimed that everything was all right. Behind her eyes, he would catch a glimpse of the hellish turmoil his wife was in and knew a storm was brewing. When or if it would break would be entirely up to her, and like a sailor at sea, all he could do was prepare for whatever it held in store for him.

As far as Laffite was concerned, the Governor's dinner party could not have come at a better time. His lady had seemed to come alive with the news, and whatever had been plaguing her; had for the time being, died down. Marie had helped her prepare for the gala. A new gown had been delivered, something that Tori had never expected. After all, the seamstress would have had to work around the clock to produce the dress so soon, and Tori knew that cash was tight. This expense was something, had she known about, would never have been added to their growing debts, but seeing Jean so proud of his surprise, she decided to say nothing along the lines of money, debts, and what they would do about it all.

Upon seeing Tori descend the stairs, all smiles, and laughter, he dared to allow himself the luxury of relaxing. For now, he had his lady back, the one he had fallen in love with. Maybe the storm had blown by, and now with a bright future ahead of them, they could settle down. Pierre had told him that he had petitioned the courts to return all the government had confiscated. He had seemed most hopeful that very soon, the ships, those that were left, would be theirs once again. Knowing this, Jean and Tori departed for the dinner, happy in each other's company.

Compared to the chill of the February evening, the house was warm and inviting. Cayetana had gone all out for the affair and was repeatedly rewarded by many positive compliments about how splendid everything looked.

Nothing had gone unattended, from the smallest detail of flowers placed in strategic positions to the choice of music. The guest list had been hers to attend to, a matter that her husband usually had more control over. This time, however, he had not cared so much as to who or why certain persons had been included, trusting instead in his wife's knowledge and ability to host the perfect sendoff for the General.

WHEN they arrived at the house, Tori and Jean beamed as they realized that more than one or two of their close friends were in attendance. Tori tugged at Jean's sleeve as they entered the large parlor, and giggling; she whispered, "Seems that Dominique has the General's ear already. Just look at the two of them. One would think they had been comrades in arms for years, not just weeks. Do you suppose Mr. Jackson needs a break?" Jean raised one eyebrow and grinned. Then they both nodded their heads in unison and, laughing lightly, walked up to Dominique and the American.

The relief on Jackson's face told Tori that she had been right in her assessment. The poor man had been cornered, it seemed, by the well-meaning Dominique. The Frenchman had insisted on once again telling his tale of the battle and how his cannon had not let him down. He had just begun to explain how he had kept his weapon hidden until needed when a friendly voice interrupted him.

"Andrew, it is so good to see you again." Tori extended her hand toward him, only to see it snatched up in Dominique's eager grasp.

"Tori, you are, as always, the belle of the ball, and you make this old man's heart flutter like the wings of a butterfly." He kissed the back of her hand and then leaned over and placed a light kiss on her cheek, causing her to blush. "Ah, Mon General, she is like the daughter to me, as Jean is like a brother. To see these two together is like the meeting of the ocean and the sky on a tranquil horizon. They become one, oui?" He was beaming and obviously enjoying the moment. "I should tell you about the time this woman surprised us all and saved my life. I have the scar to prove so and..."

"Dominique," Tori broke in, "I think maybe that can wait until another time."

His face fell, and for a second, he looked so downfallen that Tori was going to agree; he could tell his story. However, the old sea dog pulled himself up and transformed back into the jolly fellow he was. "I agree; this is not the place or the time. I shall excuse myself from you and the fine General, Cisco is motioning me over his way, and by the looks of things, this single gentleman is about to be introduced to some fine-looking wench's, ah, excuse my manners. Fine ladies, I mean proper and... oh just excuse an old fool." Embarrassed by his blunder, Dominique took his leave and crossed the room to join his friend and the small group that surrounded him.

Jackson smiled at the Laffites and knowingly looked into his wife's eyes. He had looked forward to this evening all day and to the announcement that he would make in his farewell speech. Lives were going to change this night, and people were going to be very happy. If there was one indulgence he truly enjoyed, it was bringing happiness to those he cared about.

Laughter and a carefree spirit filled the atmosphere. Men and women mingled and talked freely, enjoying the company and the new acquaintances they made. Creoles actually found themselves in conversations with the dreaded Americans. Jackson's men presented themselves as gentlemen, and many younger New Orleans males engaged themselves in descriptions of the battle and other such subjects. Things were changing, and all wanted to be a part of the future and possibilities that it held.

Edward Livingston and his wife had joined the Governor and the Laffites, leaving Edward's law partner John Grymes to escort the Governor's wife onto the dance floor, where the two seemed to enjoy themselves and the music unnoticed. Grymes was a happy man and would have forgotten the circumstances under which he held the woman of his attention if it had not been for the arrival of

Edward and Simone Duval.

Nothing or no one else could have distracted him as fast as that pair. Just seeing them enter the room made him nervous. While observing them, he stepped on Cayetana's foot, causing her to stumble and nearly fall. Shocked at how clumsy he had been, Grymes set about to make things better. "Please forgive me, my dear? It seems that I am a little out of practice. Maybe we should sit for the remainder of this dance?" He did not wait for her answer but instead guided her to a side chair, where he seated the limping but smiling lady. "I shall fetch you a cool drink right this second and maybe something to prop your foot on. A small stool, maybe?"

"Oh really, Mr. Grymes, that is unnecessary. The stool, I mean. A cool beverage, on the other hand, would be most welcome, though," she laughed.

Grymes was off at once but not toward the direction of the table containing the punch bowl and assorted bottles of liquor and wine. Cayetana frowned; 'what could he be doing,' she wondered? Then before she could reflect on his change in mood, Simone's laughter crossed the room, announcing her arrival. This single event gave her a clue as to why Grymes was acting so strangely. She looked at Edward and his wife, and then she watched as her lover slipped up to Jean. Immediately he took his friend aside to inform him of the latest guest's arrival.

Jean did not even turn to acknowledge the despised couple. Instead, he stepped next to Tori and drew his lady closer to him by placing a protective arm around her waist. This was done so subtly that no one in their small group seemed to notice his change in mood. Satisfied, Grymes took two glasses of champagne from one of the silver trays carried around by the Claiborne's servants and returned to Cayetana.

"I assume, Sir, by your roundabout manner, in obtaining my beverage, that you had an ulterior motive?" she grinned. "Need, I guess? Or better yet, let me say, does the name Simone or possibly Edward have you scurrying across the room, I wonder?"

"You can wonder all you want, Madame, and not be any closer to guessing the truth of the matter than you already have." He scowled in the direction of the small gathering around the Duval's, which was at the far end of the room. "I had no idea that those two had been invited to this affair."

"Believe me, John, it was on no account of mine. I had every intention of omitting them from the guest list, knowing the history between the Laffites and Edward, not to mention of your own animosity toward them both. You have to believe me," she said, touching his arm gently and bringing his attention back to her. "I tried to leave them off the guest list, but William would have none of it, so convinced is he that Edward is a true and dear friend."

Seeing the plea written on her face, so clearly etched alongside her love for him, he had no reason to doubt her. "I would never consider otherwise, my dear. Put your fears to rest." He patted her arm and raised his drink in a toast. "Here's to hopefully a calm and uneventful evening." He smiled briefly and then looked back toward the two most despicable people he knew. He would keep a close eye on them for the rest of the evening because where they went, trouble always followed. "If you would please excuse me for a moment, my dear? I think I had better alert the rest of the troops as to the location of the enemy." He was chuckling, but the undertone in his voice told her he meant every word.

She nodded her head in agreement. "I shall endeavor to do my part. After all, those two still think of me as a dear friend and confidant," she said laughing, and then leaning closer, she added softly, "If you will excuse me, I shall go and greet my guests and see what the enemy is up to. I am sure my glass will need refilling shortly." She gave him a meaningful look and winked playfully.

Grymes watched as she made her way toward Edward and Simone with a delighted smile on her face. Just what those two scheming individuals would think about their hostess if they knew what she was up to made him grin. Fill up her glass indeed. How appropriate for her to contrive a way for him to approach her again without raising suspicion. He would play the gentleman, and she would play the spy, telling him just what was going on. Till then, he would have time to alert Cisco and Davis, but that was going to prove more problematic to do than he thought, as both were surrounded by the fairer sex and continually on the dance floor.

EDWARD and Simone had received their invitation to the dinner and had accepted immediately. Neither had guessed that the Governor had invited the Laffites. They knew that Livingston would be there and his partner Grymes, who they both hated, and agreed that Grymes was nothing more than a minor thorn. They were there to see the American General off and then to start in on the Governor about Jean and his men. They had agreed to begin their new plan of action that very evening by dropping sly hints and small reminders of the crimes committed by the pirate. Crimes Laffite had been charged with and not yet paid for. They intended to set Jean and his men up and show New Orleans how inadept at his job Claiborne was.

As always, if Simone could not be the first to arrive, she would be the last. Staging a grand entrance, she swept into the room simpering and flirting, posing at every turn and demanding, by her very actions, to be the center of attention. She had the act down so well that many, if not most, did not even realize what she was up to. Simone was splendid in her attire and manners. The woman was a beautiful, self-assured young female on the arm of her dashing, wealthy husband. She had everything she could want at that moment. To her delight, the compliments were flowing in her direction like water down a stream, smooth and constant. Each gentleman tried to outdo the other in his description of what a vision she presented and how lucky Edward was to have such a wife. The ladies, though slightly jealous, vied for her attention and company also. They swarmed around her as if she were a queen bee. They moved away begrudgingly; however, when Cayetana's greeting overwhelmed the conversations, the small group was caught up in.

"Simone, my dear friend, welcome. I had begun to think that something serious had detained you, but, no matter, you and dear Edward have arrived." The Governor's wife reached over and placed a light kiss on Edward's cheek, something she had never done before. "I do hope you know that William and I consider you both family... after all, we have been through so much these past few months together, have we not?"

Edward recovered from his surprise at Cayetana's outpouring and was truly happy that she felt as she did. He would manipulate her toward their goal a lot easier with her feeling as she did. He gave his wife a knowing glance.

Simone looked around her and continued to smile. Fools, she thought; they meant nothing to her. Well, almost nothing because she intended to use them all to help get her Edward elected as the next Governor. This same home, the Governor's mansion, would be hers for the taking. Or maybe she'd have Edward build a larger and more stunning home for his new position. Edward's wife's fantasy was rapidly progressing when the name Laffite smashed it to smithereens. Her daydream was gone, and her full attention returned to Cayetana.

"Simone dear, I don't think you quite understood me. I said that Jean Laffite himself and his wife are with the General, along with my dear husband. They are engaged in conversation at this moment. Interrupting them at this point would be so rude, don't you agree? My, we need to show the Americans our culture and manners, do we not? Have no doubts; I shall be honored to escort you over to the General himself when he is available."

William's wife almost burst out laughing at the look on Simone's face. Thankfully, Simone had turned away to look for Jean and Tori, and this gave Cayetana another chance to goad the pair some more. "He is quite the hero, isn't he? So very dashing, if you ask me. Tori is stunning, isn't she? Quite the belle of the ball, and she has the American General quite taken with her. I hear that even his wife is taken with Tori, and she understands why her husband feels so in debt to them both. I overheard her thanking Tori for taking such care of her husband. Yes, Tori and Jean have the friendship of both the Jacksons. It always seems that the couple holds everyone's attention, good or bad. These days one could safely say all is good, though. Many hostilities have been put to rest; even my husband calls them friends."

A few of the ladies agreed as all eyes looked across the room toward the Laffites. "Did you know that earlier this evening, Jean and my husband William were joking with each other? They were telling the General about those silly posters they put up a few months ago. Surely, you remember? The rewards they both offered for each other. William finds the whole matter quite amusing now, as did the General. Hard to think of Monsieur Laffite as a pirate, looking at him now, don't you agree? Why I declare he looks more like a gentleman…"

"Cayetana, please," broke in Simone, "you can't possibly be serious? Gentleman, indeed. Why, have you forgotten that the man was charged, is charged, with many crimes? Both he and his brother, along with his worthless cutthroat friends, are outlaws and nothing more." She had let her voice rise and had gotten carried away, damn it. It did not bode well to show her animosity toward the Laffites just yet. "Forgive me. I am truly sorry for my outburst. It's just… well… so many of our fine men, like my Edward here, fought with the General and deserve just as much praise. I am just so passionate about my feelings when it comes to my husband. I do apologize." She looked at the gathering around her, calculating her next move. "I ask your forgiveness and understanding."

"Nothing to forgive, my dear," Cayetana said, patting her hand. "Now, if you will excuse me, I have other guests I need to converse with. I'll hurry, and then we can go and talk to the General. I do so want him to meet my dear and closest friends. You have not met him and I will be honored to present you."

"That will be most kind of you, but Edward has met the General, and he could do such introductions himself."

"Nonsense, I insist. One can hardly count a casual introduction and a few meetings during the war as knowing the General, can they? That is unless I am wrong, Edward. Did you maybe spend more time with him during the battle? You have never told us where you were, who you fought with. Such a heroic act, not bragging, I'm sure. Still, I would love to hear…"

Edward almost choked on his drink as the question was asked. He had no answers that would stand up to scrutiny. After all, he had been at his plantation readying himself for the victorious British. His mind raced with the implications of his whereabouts during the battle, and he knew it was a secret that he needed to keep, but how?

"Maybe at another time," Simone nodded. "I am tired of all the war talk, and Edward has agreed it's time to move past all the horror. Why he was telling me he thinks the General has overstepped his authority several times since our victory and that it's time he left and we all focused on the future. No offense to the American, mind you, just ready to begin living again without the threat of invaders. He knows talking about the battle can still upset many of us," she looked around at the other ladies and smiled gently. Edward is gallant enough to oblige me." She placed her hand on his arm and looked into her husband's eyes lovingly.

Cayetana would have pressed more but decided to hold her questions for another time. She and Tori both learned that Edward had not been seen near the battlegrounds, so he might not even have fought. After witnessing his response to her question, she decided that was closer to the truth; the man was a coward and still the enemy of the Laffites, she was sure. It was something to keep to herself right then, but oh, how she looked forward to telling Tori, Jean, and the man she loved that they had been right about the dandy and his partner in crime.

Cisco had walked over to join Tori and warn her about Simone's arrival. He slipped alongside Jean's wife unnoticed. The men were in an in-depth conversation about Dominique's exceptional skill and performance during the battle, and the women were so impressed that no one noticed Tori take a step back to stand closer to Cisco. Quietly, he whispered to Tori, "You look great. I find myself wishing you were available because, lady, I would love to show you what I could do to you." He was chuckling, and had anyone else overheard his remark, they would have been shocked, and he knew it.

Tori didn't mind his sense of humor, and looking at him now, she knew that he would remain dear to her, no matter what he said or did. They moved slightly further away from the group, and no one seemed to pay any attention except Jean, who, realizing who she was with, let her step away from his grasp.

"You don't look bad yourself for a dandy. Why, if I'm not mistaken, that young Southern belle, the one in the yellow taffeta by the window, is flirting with you. She has been trying for some time to gain your attention, hasn't she?"

He put on his sad face and quickly replied, "Tori, what I need is a woman, not some simpering girl, who would faint at the very thought of the things I would do to her."

Tori could not help but laugh out loud, and Jean, who had been talking to the General, looked over toward her with both puzzlement and admiration.

The General had not missed the expression on Jean's face and could not help but comment. "You have a beautiful woman there, Jean. I've been away so long from my wife Rachel that it gets more difficult each time we must part. Take my advice, don't let the days slip by you…" he hesitated and then added his last thought on the matter, "so that one day you find yourself wishing that you had spent more time by her side."

"General Sir, you could not have come closer to how I feel if you tried. She is lovely, isn't she?"

"Let's join them," the General said, taking Jean by the arm and walking a few steps toward Cisco and Tori. "I hope you do not mind? It looks as if the two of them are having a far better time than anyone else. Too many people are afraid to enjoy themselves, I think."

Cisco saw the two moving their way. "Looks as if we are about to have company, but before we do, I have to warn you. Edward and Simone have just arrived." Before Tori had time to react, Cisco greeted Jean and the General.

"Gentlemen, Tori here is impossible. Jean, your charming wife, I'm afraid, is determined to have me introduced to every available female here this evening." Tori smiled at the General before rapidly scanning the room, searching for her enemies. It took only seconds for their eyes to lock, and it was clear that Simone's hatred still burned within, carefully concealed behind her demure appearance. That bitch did not fool Tori one bit.

The General also had seen the couple enter and had recognized Simone. After all, who could forget such a woman? However, he could see that she was not the proper Southern lady by his standards, that he had first assumed her to be. She reeked of sexuality and enticement, a deadly combination when used skillfully, and by the looks of the woman, she knew exactly how to use both. In Jackson's opinion, she was a true Delilah, straight out of the pages of the Bible. 'Pity the poor Samson,' he thought.

Cisco had seen the look Simone shot Tori's way. "Enter the lioness into the arena," he whispered. Tori turned away from Simone's stare and faced the men once more, her attention turning to Cisco. She was determined not to allow the bitch or her husband to ruin this night for her, or especially the General's last few hours with them.

Jackson's glance at Simone left him cold and angry. He had seen how she covered her glare quickly by coyly turning her eyes toward him, and he had heard Cisco's remark. Simone had smiled briefly at him before turning her attention toward her husband, but the fact remained: she had upset Madame Laffite.

"My dear, I would not let someone like her upset you." The General's hand touched her arm and his eyes filled with a wise, knowing sort of look about them. The compassion that lay there also softened his words, giving them an edge of kindness and reassuring strength. "It would seem to this old man's way of thinking she is only jealous of you. I have seen such in my lifetime; trust me. Her kind is spiteful and vindictive, quite the opposite of you, my dear. The woman cannot hope to obtain either your looks or standing. I must confess that you are truly a woman to be admired. A kind and genteel woman, and I am honored to have made your acquaintance. Just remain as sweet as you are." He turned to Jean and added, "And you look after her; she has all the qualities of my own dear wife. We are lucky men, you and I," he laughed. Now, if you will excuse me, I will locate my wife and spend the rest of the evening with her by my side."

Tori was amazed by the man and his charm. His concern was genuine, but his knowledge of the fairer sex was so far off the mark. If only he knew, she thought. Calling her Tori, a woman to be admired, now that was funny. Tori felt like a liar and an actress, standing there, a person from another error, someone who knew about the many things to come. Who had, with friends, manipulated the battle and its outcome. A woman who could have told him about the treaty signed at Ghent. No, she did not feel worthy of being admired by the future president. Carefully she concealed her feelings and did what she did best. She'd be Tori Laffite, a woman of this era and nothing more.

Jean soon found himself chuckling, as did Cisco. Their mood, which only seconds before had been on the downslide, was now uplifted and cheerful. People around them turned to see what was happening as the laughter sounded above the hum of conversations.

Simone looked back at Tori upon hearing the joyful sound and misread the whole situation. In her blind fury, she thought that they had to be laughing at her. The bitch, Tori, must have said something awful about her to the General, and he must have believed the filthy lie. She was not about to let her get away with it. Not now or ever. In a voice loud enough to be overheard, she spoke to Edward. "Had I known that this evening was going to include the likes of her and that pirate, I would have turned down the invitation. My, it's awful… shameful if you ask me, the way people have conveniently forgotten that Laffite is a wanted man."

Edward agreed with her, as did several men standing around him. Some of the ladies who were still very jealous of Tori backed Simone up, but only by carefully whispering behind cupped hands. They feared being overheard by anyone who felt differently. Simone was about to continue with her onslaught on Jean's reputation and character when the Governor himself called the room to order.

"Ladies and Gentlemen. Before we go to dinner, I would like to bring your attention to our honored guest and my esteemed friend. The man who saved us all from British rule, General Andrew Jackson."

Everyone applauded, while still others actually cheered, the loudest of which was none other than Dominique You. Some of the ladies giggled like schoolgirls, not sure if his actions were appropriate but finding them amusing all the same. All eyes were on the General and his reaction to the outburst.

With no emotion showing on his face, Jackson walked over to the Governor and took his place alongside him, raising his hands in a signal that asked for silence.

"Speech," someone called from the back of the room and was quickly joined by the bellow of agreement from Dominique, who once again started applauding loudly. Then just as quickly as his clapping had started, he stopped, calling out for quiet. "Let the General speak. General Jackson, Sir, please continue," he said, bowing unsteadily, never taking his eyes off his hero.

"That fool is drunk," exclaimed Simone to those around her. "But then what does one expect of a pirate, I ask you?"

The gathering finally fell silent as everyone waited for Jackson to address the room.

"Ladies and Gentlemen, my fellow Americans, for that is what you all are regardless of your heritage or background." He looked briefly toward Jean and Tori before turning toward the Governor and continuing. "My wife and I want first to thank our host and hostess," he said, nodding in Cayetana's direction, "for having such a joyous gathering of friends here for this, my last evening in New Orleans. I shall miss you and your hospitality greatly. This is a fine and free state, filled with brave and proud citizens."

The room exploded into another outburst of applause and cheering that did not seem to want to stop. The Governor signaled for calm, and when the room settled back down, he asked the General to proceed.

"It is, however, not only I that you should be thanking for the victory that came our way. Thank also the brave men who fought alongside me. For those few, who gave their lives, so the rest of us could go on developing our grand country, in freedom and under our democratic laws, and not under the dictatorship of another country. May God rest their souls."

Dominique started to cheer again, but a sharp look from Jackson rendered him silent. "There is still one more person without whose help; we could never have won the battle," continued Jackson. "Without this fine Gentleman's help and that of his men, his supplies and dedication to upholding the American way, you can be assured that you would be entertaining the British here tonight and not myself. I am, of course, speaking of Mr. Jean Laffite." He turned and faced Jean, pointing in his direction as he did so.

Now Dominique did whistle and cheer, as did a few others.

Jackson waited for the noise to calm down again before continuing. "His patriotic act and heroism have not gone unnoticed. Indeed not. I, for one, have thanked him and owe him far more than I could ever pay. You too should be proud of your, and now, *my* friend. We should honor him tonight as the hero that he is."

If the cheering had been loud before, it was dim compared to the noise that erupted this time. It was a lusty, enthusiastic sort of sound, filling not only the room but the entire house. It grew even louder still as Jean and Tori joined the General and Governor, shaking hands and embracing one another.

Simone was devastated. Everyone was looking at Tori and Jean like they were gods to be worshipped. They were being treated as if they were royalty, standing there basking in all the glory. What did that stupid General know anyway, she asked herself? Jean was a pirate, a common lawbreaker, and she, for one, would not stand for any of this. It had to end, and end right then!

The Governor called for calm once again. He seemed genuinely pleased with himself, standing between Laffite and Andrew Jackson. He was making the most of the situation, a natural politician, placing his arms around both men's shoulders; he looked out into the sea of happy faces before him.

"Quiet… please."

The room hushed, but Simone's voice addressed the American General and all those present before he could continue. "Why, General Jackson, Sir, I'm sure that all of us here agree with you on some of the finer points your elegant speech touched on. But, Sir, is there not a little matter of our hero," she said, shooting Jean a nasty look, "being in danger of being brought up, along with his brother and men, on charges of smuggling?" The sounds of people gasping in shock rustled about the room. "Or was it piracy? I don't seem to remember which. Governor, you would know. Tell us, please, what were the charges that you issued?"

Adjusting his collar as if it were a bit too tight for him and then grabbing his handkerchief from his jacket pocket, the Governor began to mop his brow. The beads of sweat forming on his face glistened against his now reddened complexion. To say he was embarrassed was an understatement.

On the other hand, General Jackson stood motionless as he

listened to the words slide out of Simone's mouth, words that were as sharp as barbs, hitting their mark. He hadn't liked the woman from the beginning of the evening, and now he was more confident than ever that she was trouble. For whatever reason, it was evident that she took pleasure in trying to destroy the Laffite's evening, and he knew it would do his heart good to see her put in her place. Vixens like her seldom got their comeuppance in public, and he intended to remedy that.

Jackson responded immediately. "The Governor has no need to recall whatever Jean did in his past, Madame," he said, smiling at the Governor before turning back to face Simone and the crowd. "I am glad you brought up the subject, as I myself did not know quite how to handle the delicate matter. I would not want Mr. Laffite or his beautiful wife to take offense; after all, they have done for us." He smiled at Jean and Tori and then turned his full attention back to Simone.

"Now, it was kind of you to approach the matter for me, and with that task accomplished, I have something here that I would like to read, if I may." He reached inside his jacket and removed a letter. "I believe it will clear this problem up. With your permission then?"

He looked toward William, who sputtered. "By all means, General, please go ahead."

"It is a letter that arrived a few days ago, but I had wanted a time such as this to read it out loud in public. It comes by way of Washington and the President himself."

No one spoke or moved as the General read the letter. By the time he finished, it was clear that the President himself had sent his declaration of thanks and gratitude for Jean, his brother, and his men. "He also has… for their patriotic acts… agreed to bestow the Laffites and all Baratarians full pardons, of all and any past crimes. Not only that, President Madison went on to grant each and every one of the men full American citizenship.

Andrew Jackson finished reading and turned to hand the letter to Jean. "It is signed by President James Madison and dated February

6, 1815. Congratulations, Jean. You are now a citizen of the United States and a fully pardoned man. I only wish I could do more." He shook Jean's hand and then hugged Tori as laughter escaped from his glowing face.

The room went crazy. People hastened toward the couple to offer their congratulations, totally ignoring Edward's wife. Once again, Simone found herself being pushed aside as her so-called friends hurried to be included in the mirth and excitement surrounding the very popular Laffite and his wife. Standing next to Edward, Simone inwardly seethed. The bitter female watched the unfolding spectacle, and then she saw the General smile her way with a nod of his head and a wink of his eye. The man was obviously pleased with himself; he was taking delight in having said all he did. He had made her look like a fool, and more than anything, she wished Edward would grab her arm and escort her out of the gathering.

While considering her next step, Simone's eyes locked on Tori's, and rather than give the bitch the satisfaction of making her depart; she decided to play along. What else could she hope to accomplish without deepening her fall from grace? They could leave, but then that would serve no purpose. Their departure would only strengthen the glory that the pirate and his wife basked in. If they publicly snubbed the hero now, it would allow a total victory in the wrong camp, and that was something she could not have.

She and Edward could not just stand there, nor could they ignore the Laffites. The choice, for now, it seemed, had been made for her. The Spanish beauty took hold of her husband's hand and made her way toward the crowd of well-wishers. "I will see her squirm yet, my darling; just play along and remain by my side."

Edward had heard her whispered instructions but did nothing to respond. The time to challenge Victoria and Jean was not then, and he prayed his wife would maintain her decorum and continue to mask her disappointment and hate.

A line had formed out of nowhere; as each guest waited for their chance to congratulate the Laffites, before moving to greet the American General and his wife. He could wish the American all the best on his journey home and mean it. The faster this interfering friend of the city left, the better. While Simone inched forward towards Jean and Tori, her mind raced. They had escaped justice once more, and she had lost the chance to see them both ruined, but she swore she'd see them pay for her humiliation before the night was over.

Looking at the handsome face of Jean coming ever closer her way, Simone found her heart rate quickening.

Her lustful desire for him had not dimmed, and flashes of nights long ago flickered in her mind's eye. He should have been hers! His arm that protectively clung around Tori's waist should have been around her waist. In Simone's mind, she'd risked everything for the pirate, but then, she had not lost out completely, she mused. 'I am Madame Duval, the wife of a very wealthy and respected plantation owner,' she told herself. Edward satisfied her lustful desires in his own way, and then there was his wealth to consider. His standing in society... combined with his extravagant lifestyle, would offer her many opportunities to find another lover that would bring a spark of erotic excitement. Her gaze briefly landed on Jean as she continued to sort her feelings and plot and plan her next move. Even with his pardon, Jean would always be a pirate, while Edward would always be a gentleman of standing. How would Jean feel, she wondered, if he ever found out that she was the reason that he had lost his chance at becoming a wealthy plantation owner? Maybe one day, she would tell him about her part in taking the will away from them. How delightful that moment would be!

Her husband had stepped forward and offered his hand without hesitation. "My sincere congratulations to you both, to all your men and associates." His congratulations sounded genuine and honest, but as he babbled on and on, his words began to sound empty of the truth; his facade was dissolving. Realizing this, he curtly bowed his head and then moved quickly to greet the General and William. He left Simone to deal with the sticky situation she had created, and no doubt, knowing her, she'd deliver without hesitation or embarrassment.

'Coward,' Simone thought as she watched her husband slip to William's side, and in a flash, she knew her next move. She apologized for her actions and accusations in her most polite manner, asking for both Jean and Tori's forgiveness. Many people in the small crowd found her efforts to be humbling and genuinely believable; the woman meant each word.

Her good intentions, some whispered, were very evident and seemed sincere, even to the eavesdropping General. They did not for one second fool Tori though, who looking at Simone, thought it was a shame that the Oscars had not been invented yet.

"Madame Laffite, Tori," Simone said, reaching out and taking Tori's hand between hers. "I do hope that we may start over and put behind us once and for all any hostilities."

She was good; Tori had to give her that much. Then not wanting to ruin the General's last night with a scene, Tori smiled and answered politely, "Let us try."

"Oh, I am so happy you agree and that you can rise above our past differences. Let us start now, shall we? I, for one, would love to freshen up before dinner is served. Would you care to join me?" Simone tilted her head inquisitively to one side. Her face was that of pure innocence and friendship.

Just what she was up to was another question entirely. Cornered as she was, Tori had no choice but to accept the invitation or run the risk of looking like she was still holding animosity toward the now humble Simone. "I would be more than grateful for your company, and I agree, one would like to freshen up."

Edward looked toward his wife, knowing only too well that she would never forgive or forget. His Simone was up to something; that was for sure.

Jean was a little worried as the two ladies excused themselves from their company and headed upstairs. He started to follow his wife when a hand on his arm held him back.

"Let them go," said Cisco quietly. "She can handle herself. It's been coming for some time, you know? I would say that if I were Simone right now, I would be cautious. Tori can have quite a temper, and if my guess is right, she has had about all she can take."

Jean watched as the two ladies disappeared out of sight at the top of the landing. They were headed towards the lady's parlor, and whatever would ensue once there. His bet was Simone had totally underestimated Tori.

Jean realized that, for the moment, there was nothing to be done but wait and see what would come of such a meeting. The pirate turned to join in on the current conversation around him. He would check on Tori if she was gone too long, but Cisco was correct; Tori could handle herself; his hellcat was more than a handful when angered or pushed too far. 'Pity Simone, indeed, that female was about to get a rude awakening,' he thought.

On the other hand, Edward could not stand the suspense and wanted to have his say also. Given a chance, he intended to tell that pirate's bitch a thing or two. Besides, with all the commotion still going on around him, it would be easy enough for him to slip away unnoticed and have his chance to say a few things to the so-called fine lady.

ONCE on the landing, he quickly looked to see if he had been observed, and confident he had not, Edward turned toward the lady's parlor. Not wanting to be discovered hovering outside the door, he entered the darkened and empty room next to it and quietly pushed the adjoining door ajar. It was perfect. He could hear everything, and all he had to do now was wait to make sure they were alone before adding his words of threat to the woman he wanted to destroy. First, he would allow Simone her say, and then, once he was confident of not being interrupted, he'd let Tori know that neither she, nor her pirate husband, would ever be safe or free of his unwanted intentions to see them broken and in shame.

Excitement surged through his body, and he stood listening to the two unsuspecting ladies.

Tori sat down in front of the mirror to brush her hair and spoke to Simone in a very calm voice without looking her way. The room was empty except for the two of them, so she had no fear of speaking as she did.

"Come on, Simone. Out with it. All that shit about you wanting a fresh start is just that, shit, and I, for one, like it better when I know just where I stand."

If she had shocked or surprised Simone with her question and language, it did not outwardly show. Simone remained calm as she retorted, "Your mouth suits the whore that you are. You might have fooled Jean with your ways, but not me. I know you for what you are, a common guttersnipe."

Tori turned, putting the silver hairbrush down on the tabletop. "That's better. All that sweetness was turning my stomach like you do Jean's." Tori watched as her words accomplished their task. "After he found you out, for the tramp you are: how you mounted any man behind your husband's back and his, well… he despised you. So just who the hell are you to call me a whore or guttersnipe, with a reputation such as you have?"

These words did not put Simone out; they only fired up. "It only bothers you that Jean once loved me. That we slept together and the very words he whispers in your ears now, he told me first."

"Oh, please don't delude yourself, Simone. He has told me all about the two of you. About the fact that he never loved you, only enjoyed the sex. The pleasure you two had, he found on other nights in a bed at Rose's. Does that tell you something? You were just a passing fancy with him and nothing more. It's you who can't stand that he is with me. Now, that's more the truth, don't you think?"

Simone hated this woman who sat so calm and poised in front of her. She had to do something to hurt her, to wipe that smile off her face. "I think it is you who is the jealous one. After all, I am now a respectable married lady of society. At least I can hold my head up. No one will ever doubt my place, as they will yours. Jean is nothing more than a common pirate, a broke and penniless one at that, I hear. Maybe, if you are down and out like I think you will be, you could borrow a little something from my dear Edward to get you by."

Edward was about to join them when he stopped himself. His wife was doing a splendid job at ridiculing Tori. He would wait a while yet and enjoy listening before putting the crowning glory on the moment.

Simone was confident she had Tori where she wanted, so she continued. "Why, you don't even have any decent jewels. Every lady has them this evening. Did you have to sell the few that Jean was able to steal for you?"

This was it. She had touched a sore point. Tori's face was getting flushed, and her lips had formed a firm line. Gone was Tori's gloating smile. Simone thought she had found the weakness in her armor at last, and she reveled in the victory. She took off a gold bracelet from her wrist and threw it at Tori's feet. It rolled a bit before it landed a few inches away from Tori's shoes, where it fell on its side and ended up laying on the soft carpet, glowing in the lamplight. "Go on! Don't let me stop you from picking it up. Call it a gift of sorts to start you out on your new life with Jean. Your broken life." She was laughing at her. "I had wanted to destroy Jean and bring you down. Tonight, I thought I had lost; now I see I have won. This is far better than anything Edward or I could have come up with. Edward is very influential, you know. Your precious Jean will find it hard to get any kind of a decent living in this town, and you will live like you started, with nothing."

Tori bent down and slowly picked up the bracelet. Simone saw she was looking strangely at her; it was not anger or sadness; no, it was a look she could not decipher. Maybe it was a look of defeat? This was perfect; finally, the total degradation of the previously untouchable Lafitte's was at hand. Oh, the humility Tori was suffering; Simone laughed even harder. She grabbed at her sides, struggling to take in a breath, and then, looking at Tori, continued. "All the time, we planned and tried to ruin you and Jean. Why, I had begun to think that you had that witch Laveau, protecting you; not doing a great job, is she? Did you know, for instance, among other problems that have befallen your beloved Jean, that Jean was thrown in jail because of Edward? I see not. That should have worked, but oh no, he had to go and get out. Still, that is all irrelevant now, is it not?

Tori slowly stood up, and as she did so, she kept her expression blank and her fury under wraps. She just stood in one spot, twisting the gold bracelet around her fingers, while her eyes continued to bore into Simone. Tori knew that the evil woman was enjoying herself as the venom continued to spurt from between her lips.

"I will see to it that you and your husband are slowly blackened in this town. You will come crawling to me, and I might, out of the goodness of my heart, get you your old job back at a place like Rose's. Edward will be happy at that event, and I don't mind if he helps himself to your so-called charms. He will return to me after all."

Tori slowly walked toward Simone, stopping a few steps away. She spoke softly and calmly, looking into the burning eyes of her overly joyous foe. The person before her was genuinely twisted; of that, there was no doubt in her mind. She also now knew beyond a shadow of a doubt that there would be no peace for her or Jean. No peace, that was, as long as the Duvals were around. The fact that she'd openly admitted to plotting against her and Jean was unexpected. It was an error that Tori would now use against them both. It was time to strike back. Show her that all her dreams of destroying them would never come to pass.

"Have you quite finished? Because if you have, I would like to ask you something."

Simone cocked her head to the side. "You can ask all you want, but do hurry up. I'm starving, and I would think you would want to eat. Who knows when you will eat again as you will tonight?"

"I worry not, but you will begin to, I suspect. Have you been missing something lately? A valuable item that you hoped to hang on to?"

Simone looked at her with puzzled eyes. Had Tori gone mad? Had she pushed her too far, she wondered?

"I told you; keep the bracelet. You will need it."

"I am not referring to this," she said, holding out the bracelet and letting it fall to the carpet. "No, I am talking about a document that you had hidden behind a drawer."

Simone could feel the prickling sensation of something very wrong. What was she talking about? What document? Then it hit her. My god, was she referring to Leone's will? She had forgotten about it for so long. Watching Tori closely for any indication she was bluffing, Edward's wife struggled to make sense of what Tori was implying. It was true, she had hidden the will in her chest of drawers at the back of the top one, and those drawers had been sold with everything else in the townhouse. Could it be that Tori had been the one to purchase the...?

"I see you are remembering."

"I don't know what you are talking about," snapped Simone, turning to leave. "And if you don't mind, I wish to end this ridiculous conversation and go down for dinner."

"I think not. I think you and I had best finish this once and for all. The document I am talking about is Leone's will, as you well know."

Simone's heart sank, and she stood dead still trying not to panic.

"You had thought maybe that it was lost forever. How very careless of you. When it turned up missing, John Grymes thought it was Edward's work, but there was no proof until now. You know, if you had destroyed it right away, then you would have succeeded."

Simone turned to face Tori, unable to believe what she heard and yet knowing it to be the truth; the terrified woman felt a horrible fear creeping over her.

Tori could see the dread fill Simone's expression, and for the first time, she understood that for once, she'd outsmarted not only her but her husband too. "But you did not destroy it, did you? I wonder why? Could it be you intended to blackmail your husband? Well, dear Simone, the will is back, and Jean will go to court soon to claim what is his. I think it is you who will be in need of this bracelet, not I." Tori kicked it toward Simone. "Oh, and one more thing before I go to dinner, for I am hungry also. That small income, the one that you had from Adrian? I would say you should have been more careful; you could have kept that too, and it would be most welcome by you both in the days ahead, I am sure. But you see, my dear Simone, when you married Edward, you lost that too. Have you not noticed that the payments stopped? No? Ah well, you have had a lot on your mind, haven't you? I would hope Jean takes pity on you both and allows you to keep what you have bought with his money; it will help you until you find work. Maybe I can put in a good word for you over at that place like Rose's." Tori walked by the shocked Simone, who was trying desperately not to let Tori see the tears that were accumulating in her eyes: tears of anger, frustration, but most of all, fear.

She was about to physically attack Tori when the door to the opposite room sprung open. Both ladies turned to face the intruder and found a ghostly white Edward staring at them. He looked as if someone had struck him in the face, causing a great deal of pain and rage. His sudden arrival could only indicate that he had over-heard the conversation the women had been having.

Trembling, the dandy looked from one bitch to the other. He had to do something and fast before he lost everything. His first and only idea, leapt into his mind at lightning speed. All he had to do was grab Tori and hold her for ransom in exchange for the will. He would deal with Simone later. Until then, he'd use her to help him get Tori out of there unseen and keep her hidden under guard until Leone's will was returned.

His idea, however, had come too late. Voices were heard coming down the hall toward the parlor, and within seconds, a grinning

Cisco popped his head around the doorway.

Standing behind him were Jean and the American General Jackson. Both had a look about them that indicated they had been concerned about her, but Cisco's expression was one of anticipation and excitement.

"Everything all right up here?" asked Cisco. "You don't look too good, Edward, my man. Something wrong? Embarrassed, maybe to find yourself in the lady's parlor? The gentleman's parlor is the other way."

Cisco knew that Tori could take care of herself, but whatever had gone on here had to have been one hell of a knock-down, drag-out battle of wits with a big punch. There was no physical evidence of any violence, but Edward looked terrible, and Simone looked no better.

"Everything is fine," snarled Edward. "You will excuse us, as we are not about to remain in this house one second longer with the likes of this woman and her accusations that have hurt both my wife and myself." Edward grabbed Simone and pushed past the small group. "You will be hearing from my lawyer. You have not won. It's not over yet."

Cisco was bursting at the seams. He could hardly contain himself a second longer. He, like the others, watched Edward and Simone's hastily departure, and no sooner than they were out of the room, he popped out the one question on everyone's mind. "Tori, if you don't mind explaining, just what in the hell went on up here anyway? Those two seemed far from insulted; they looked like they were terrified of you."

Tori rolled her eyes and laughed before she relaxed and answered. "She got... no, they both got what they have had coming to them for a long, long time." She smiled at Cisco's grinning face and then looked at Jean and the General. "Jean, you will have to forgive me. I may have stepped out of bounds on this one, but she pushed me to it. That woman can be so infuriating. She just asked for it. I had no idea that Edward was listening. Anyway, I've gone and done it this time." Tori was sincerely wondering if she had gone too far. "I think I can sum it up, what happened and what I have done."

Cisco laughed. "Oh, this should be good. General, you see, Tori always comes up with the most fantastic explanations…"

"Cisco, please not now."

Jean said nothing; what could he say? It was best to hear what Tori had to tell them before he jumped to conclusions.

Seeing he was waiting to hear her explanation, Tori briefly told them how and what had happened, and when she had finished, it was Andrew Jackson's laughter that broke the silence.

He strode up to Tori and placed his arms around her trembling frame, hugging her to himself as he would have a child. "Jean, I would say that this little lady of yours has defended your honor and herself rather well. That Duval woman asked for it from what I can gather. Still, all in all, you had better go down at once. May I suggest you inform this Grymes fellow what has transpired… and the Governor too. You don't want to lose again, what should by all rights be yours, now do you?" His grim face and stern eyes spoke clearly to Jean. He may have just made a suggestion, but the man wished it to be followed as an order.

Jean could see the importance of informing Grymes immediately, knowing Edward and Simone the way he did. It was best to act swiftly, beating them at their own game. "Will you be all right, my lady?" He was not angry with her for spilling the news about Leone's will; instead, he was concerned that she had put herself in danger, something he intended to speak with her about later when they were alone.

"Tori will be just fine," said Jackson. "A good debate always drains one's emotions for a short time. Winning that debate, well… that helps towards a fast recovery. Wouldn't you say so, my dear?" He held Tori at arm's length and laughed.

"That I would indeed," agreed Tori. "Go on ahead, Jean. The General and I will follow as soon as I pull myself together. As for you, Cisco, go on and get out of here. The young girl won't wait forever, you know," she teased.

He all but bounced out of the room, pushing his way ahead of Jean as he did so. "Thanks, Tori, and you're wrong, you know, about waiting. For me, they always wait!

"Who's waiting where? What are you talking about?" asked a very puzzled Jean.

Tori grinned. "Nothing for you to worry about. Just go and find Grymes, and we will join you shortly. I promise to fill you in then. Now go on."

She seemed to be her old self again, and the General smiled in agreement with her. "I shall consider it an honor to escort your wife down as soon as she is ready to do so. You, on the other hand, had best do as she asks or like my own wife; I fear she will make you wish you had." Although he was joking, he had made his point. Jean turned and left smiling. It was nice to know that Andrew Jackson had a woman in his life as he had.

Tori looked into the tired face of the General, who was gazing at her with a far-off look in his eyes. "Andrew, is something wrong?"

"No, my dear, nothing is wrong. I was thinking of my wife and how you remind me of her and how much I miss her. I have seen so little of her this past year. I am always gone on one campaign or another. It's at times like this, like tonight, that I wonder if it's all worth it. I had not thought much on this subject until she arrived here on her own accord, mind you. She surprised me with her action, to do so, I can tell you. I think maybe she was trying to show me what these old eyes failed to see for so long."

Tori took his long bony hand in hers; feeling the cool, damp touch of his skin, she spoke softly. "General Jackson, Sir, could we talk for a second in private? I feel I have a need to tell you some things."

"Of course, and please, it's Andrew, remember? You can always feel free to talk to me. My wife thought you were in need of some advice, and I agreed with her. She is a wise woman, and it has not gone unnoticed that the evening was filled with a... shall we say certain hostilities."

"I did not think it was obvious to anyone."

"Nothing much escapes past my dearly beloved Rachel, and tonight was no exception. It is not her custom to attend such affairs as this gala. The woman is far more at home on our plantation than facing the public. Her time here has kept her busy, what with dinners, the theater and such. I believe she is in as much demand as myself. Did you know she always tells me to remain humble in my victories and remember that our love and life together mean more? That is why she made the trip to join me here, to remind me of our undying dedication to each other. Now that the British are gone, and my wife has joined me, I see the wisdom in her words. We owe you so much, you and your husband, please let me offer my services and a friendly ear."

"I have every intention to do just that, but I worry…"

"If it's about what you just did and how that husband of yours is going to react… well now, I would not worry your head over it. I'll talk to him if that's what you want."

"No, Sir, I mean Andrew. What I have to say has nothing to do with that mess. Please come with me before I talk myself out of what I so much wish to do." She took him by the hand over toward the window seat. "Sit here for a second," she said, letting go of his hand and quickly walking to the open door and pushing it closed. "Please hear me out. I know you might laugh at me, but you will remember this conversation one day, and you might smile then. I honestly can tell you; I know you will." She sat down next to him and looked directly into his gaze. "I saw pain in your eyes a moment ago, a kind of pain that most people don't know or have never experienced. It's wanting to be with someone you love and belong with but can't because of no fault of your own. I know because I'm in much that same position… differently, true, but still, the pain is the same, and I hate to see you hurt like you are. I also hate to think of you giving up on your dream."

He looked at her silently. Something in her eyes told him she spoke the truth and understood his agony and his loneliness. The only other person who could do that was his own dear wife, and he surely trusted her.

"What I'm about to tell you may or may not be the right thing to do, but I'm going to anyway. General, I am honored to sit here in this room with you. By having the chance to know the kind of man, you are. What I am trying to tell you is that I know you will make a fine president one day. I should be calling you Mr. President, not General. You will be president of this country, and you will make a difference. You and your wife will be together in the end. Andrew, it is all worth it."

The man stared back at her. How could she have known that it was his secret dream to achieve the office of president? An idea that not even his beloved wife was aware of. "And what makes you so sure?" his trembling voice questioned.

"It's not what I think will happen; it's what I know will happen. I can't tell you much, and time is short, but I will try my best to honor your question with a plausible explanation if you allow me."

FIFTEEN minutes later, Andrew Jackson escorted Madame Laffite into the dining room and seated her next to her husband. He was content to sit opposite the pair, and though he ate little, his spirits seemed high and his mood joyous. If the General's wife wondered why her husband's mood was so uplifted, she did not ask. Instead, she was content to spend the rest of the evening by his side. Together they would depart New Orleans early the next day, and in her mind, the great distance she had traveled to be with him had been worth it.

To all at the table, the evening was a grand success, and by night's end, everyone admitted they would be sad to see the American General leave. As Tori and Jean walked with Edward Livingston and Jackson toward the General's coach, the mood seemed to dampen slightly. The time for final farewells had arrived, it seemed.

Jackson turned to face his old friend. "We shall say our farewells here, Edward, that is unless you intend to rise with the sun as I do," he said, shaking Livingston's hand. "Stay in touch, and if you ever need a job, well, you will always have one with me." He turned to Jean. "So much I owe you, so little can I give you. You have my thanks and my friendship, Sir." He took Jean's hand and squeezed it with a strength Jean would have thought impossible for such a frail-looking man. Then it was Tori's turn. He bowed low and smiled at her. "Madame, thank you. It has been a delight and an honor to meet you." His face was somber, and Tori thought she could see the beginning of tears welling in his blue eyes. He reached for her and hugged her close, and she returned his embrace. Then before she knew it, the General was whispering in her ear words that she would never forget.

"The twenty-dollar bill. You did say the twenty-dollar bill?" He held her at arm's length, his face aglow and his eyes laughing. Color was flooding his gray face, and he actually seemed to be standing taller and prouder somehow.

"Yes, Andrew, I did." Tori laughed.

"That's what I thought. Gentlemen," he nodded toward the men. "Madame," he took her hand and kissed the back lightly. Take care of your lady, Mr. Laffite. She is extraordinary. Very special indeed. I will see to it that I follow your example and do the same with my wife. It is to her that I go right this second, and it is with her that I will endeavor to spend more time with." With that, he climbed into his carriage and signaled to his driver that he was ready.

"Just what was all that about, may I ask?" questioned Jean once the carriage was on its way.

"You may, but that is something for the General to know and for you to find out, maybe," she said, pulling at him playfully and adding, "Let's go home, shall we?"

"My lady. I thought you would never ask. And maybe I'll apply certain methods of torture to learn the secret you and Jackson share."

"You can try, Jean, but I can't promise you I'll break," she laughed, linking her arm through his as they happily prepared to leave.

Across town, it was a far different atmosphere. A storm was brewing. On the brink of disaster, two raging personalities were about to face off.

Edward had not said one word all the way home. The ride in the carriage had seemed to last a lifetime to them both. Each was going over in their minds all that had just happened. Once back at their townhome, Edward dismissed all the help, a sure sign of just how furious he was and a warning to Simone that she had best keep her wits about her.

He fumbled in the dark hallway, finally lighting a lamp from the smaller one that was kept burning by the front door. The nervous Simone wished he would say something, anything. He was brilliant and had the wealth behind him; this she knew to be so. All he had to do was listen to her; after all, they had to work together, for they had come too far to let it all be taken away from them now.

He was leading her upstairs, along the dark hall, and into their bedroom. Once inside, he closed the door and sat the lamp down on the dressing table. Then for the first time since they had left that horrible room and the Laffites, he turned and faced her.

Simone hardly recognized him; his face was twisted in a hate-filled rage. His eyes were dark and cruel. No reasoning or rationalization lurked behind them. She saw only madness, and she was terrified for the first time in her life.

Speaking through clenched teeth, he demanded answers. He was so close that Simone could actually feel his hot breath on her face. What scared Edward's wife the most, though, was that he seemed to have lost nearly all control of his temper, and he wasn't even drunk. As a matter of fact, he was stone-cold sober. His face was scarlet red, and his fist kept hitting the top of the small dressing table. Each time he slammed his hand down, it hit harder and harder, and his breathing got deeper and deeper.

"I have brought you here so we could be alone. So, you, my dear Simone, could explain to me what in the hell has happened." In a flash, he had taken her by both arms and pulled her a step closer toward him. "Just how did that bitch get my brother's will? How?" Edward's vice-like grip held her as his nails dug into her flesh, making her grimace with pain.

Simone started to cry, partly from the pain he was inflicting and partly from the terror that she was experiencing. However, try as she might, words would not form, and Simone could not answer him, let alone look into his crazed eyes.

He shook her violently, screaming "How!" his one word echoing throughout the house.

Panicking, Simone screamed back into his face, "I don't know!"

He seemed to consider believing her for a split second and then pushed that thought aside. He raised one hand, holding her firmly with the other. "Don't lie to me! Don't you ever lie to me!" His hand came down across her mouth, knocking her head sideways. Her bottom lip split open, and her blood was streaming down her chin as she screamed in pain, but he did not waver in his goal to know what and how he lost the will. "I want to know. I need to know everything. Do you hear me?" He took hold of her face and turned it up towards his. Then softening his tone, he continued. "Just maybe if we act right away, somehow we can salvage something." He stroked her face with the back of his hand gently. The old Edward seemed to be returning to her. "But I can't have any more lies."

Simone trembled from fear of his rage returning and knew the only way to prevent that was to tell him something that he'd believe. So, thinking quickly, she sobbed out a story, leaving out, of course, the fact that she had kept the document for her personal use. Instead, she told him that she had kept it in case another will had turned up. This way, they could have forged the one they had, making it look like the newer and updated version. In her mind, her quick thinking had saved her from his wrath. In Edward's mind, he wasn't so sure of her answer. He wanted to believe her, but how could he? She had told him that she had destroyed the will when in fact, she had not. If only she had done as he'd asked, they would be safe now, as Tori had so clearly pointed out. Now they stood the chance of having nothing, nothing at all.

Noticing how quiet he had become, Simone gently stroked his arm and said softly, "We have to do something. We can say that the will they have is false. Yes, that's it; they are, after all, broke and desperate. Who better to make up a new will to try and take the plantation away...the Governor, William, will help us. He is our friend, after all. Look, with him on our side, we shall win. Don't you see? They can't take this all away from us. I won't let them. You must stop them, Edward. You must!"

"And may I ask how do you expect me to do that? Once the will is shown, everyone will know it to be real. I'm afraid, my dear, that because of your stupidity and greed, you have lost it all for us. You and your cunning ways," he said with a deadly stare. "You're just like her." Then he yelled at her. "A stupid bitch! Do you hear me? You are a stupid bitch."

Simone was angry now. How could he call her stupid? After all the times she had saved him from sure disaster? "I am not stupid! If anyone is stupid, it's you, you spineless bastard! You had a lot of chances to get them. You could not even do that right, could you? No! I had given you all the support, all the plans, all my love, and still, you failed! I don't know what I ever saw in you! I should have taken care of Laffite myself!" She was shouting at him, forgetting herself and her fear completely.

"Yes, you should have. You two deserve each other. You could have taken care of the bastard all right, in bed. That's all you are good for; Tori had you right there. I'm the fool here. How I ever married you, I don't know. Giving you the Duval name was the biggest mistake of my life!"

The slap across Edward's cheek was so fierce that it stung the palm of her hand. She stared at him with a loathing glare and watched as he stood there scrutinizing her, stroking the red welt that covered one side of his face.

Never had a woman hit him before. Never, and by God, she would not get away with it. He came toward her, breathing heavy and eyes narrowing till they were mere slits. A thin line of blood trickled from the corner of his mouth. Edward wiped his chin with the back of his hand and saw the blood. He realized he had bitten his tongue when she had hit him. He lowered his hand and made a fist as he did so.

Simone could see that she had gone too far. He was beyond being reasoned with, and she would not even try. She turned to run to get away from him until he calmed down, but the dandy was too quick for her.

Anticipating her move, the angry man rapidly jumped into action and blocked the door as he turned the key in the lock. A sadistic smile crossed his face as he threw the key across the room. "Going somewhere, my love?" Completely panicked, Simone turned and ran toward the balcony doors in an attempt to open them and call for help, but she wasn't fast enough. His hands were on her shoulders, his fingers digging into her flesh. Squeezing extra hard, Edward spun her around to face him. His eyes were bulging, and his teeth clenched, causing the muscles of his jaw to flex. He was snarling like an animal, and then he lost control. His fists began to beat into the side of her head. Next, he punched her face, pushing her nose sideways. Edward ignored the blood that spurted from both the nostrils; he didn't even notice his fist was covered in the sticky substance. Blinded by rage, his other fist hit her again, only this time it was higher up and to the side of her temple. Her eye socket took the blow, and before Simone could scream out, Edward's next strike connected with one of her ears.

The ringing inside her head was followed by sharp pain, and a flash of light brought an unfamiliar strength to her arms. She fought back, and for a brief instant, she was free from his grip and his beating, but the woman had nowhere to escape to. Simone only had seconds to open the French doors and step outside. Out on the balcony like a cornered animal, she turned to face him. Rage over fear was now controlling her emotions and actions.

"Go on, hit me. That's all you're good for anyway. Hitting a woman is just your style, you coward. You would never hit a man, would you? No. You will never be half the man that Jean is. Do you hear me? Never!"

"I am more than his equal! It is you who is lower than Laffite's wife. At least she has her wits about her and is exactly what the pirate needed."

"Shut up! Just get the hell out of my life. Do you hear me? I want you gone."

"Gone?" Edward dropped his tone and spoke softly, with just a hint of sarcasm. "You wish for me to leave my own home?" Then he screamed as loud as he could. "I think not. You, Madame, have done quite enough, more than enough." He spoke to her then with hatred-filled words. "I intend to have you leave, and trust me, I will have my name removed from the likes of you."

"That will never happen. I will tell all I know if you even try!"

Edward reached out with his closed fist and hit her again. "Shut your mouth! You will never, ever threaten me again." He pulled his arm back and then swung at her, using the force of his body, he leaned toward her to enhance the blow. This time, his fist sent her flying up and backward, her back landing hard against the wrought iron railing. The instant she connected with the grill, it made an odd sound, as the wooden planks it was attached to lifted slightly. The iron grillwork was not yet permanently fixed in place, and the nails that had held it in place popped up and out one after the other. In seconds, the grillwork gave way.

Simone could feel it move as her body rammed against it and knew what was happening. In desperation, she screamed out his name as she began to fall."

Edward witnessed her beginning to fall, but try as he might, he could not prevent it. In slow motion, he watched as she slipped from sight, his name ringing over and over, echoing in his mind. He saw the look on her bloody and battered face, pleading with him to save her as she fell. He saw her arms reach out for him, and then there was nothing. Silence and total darkness surrounded him.

The dandy dropped to his knees and found himself crawling like a child toward the broken edge of the balcony. His hands grabbed hold of what was left of the grillwork while his eyes looked down at the ground below him. He did not know what he had expected to see; somehow, he hoped and prayed that she had survived the fall. His hopes were smashed, though, when he saw her lifeless expression staring up at him in the moonlight. How beautiful she looked laying there, smiling up at him with that gentle sort of look of hers that said, 'I love you.' Tears streamed down his agonized face as heart-wrenching sobs escaped with his every breath. He uttered her name over and over again in the darkness until there was silence. Only then did he begin to absorb the horrendous deed that had befallen him. His Simone was dead, and he had killed her. Nothing or no one could change that.

"What have I done?" he screamed into the night. "Why?" he pleaded. "What have I ever done to deserve this?" His body lay flat on the balcony, his head resting on one arm while his other arm raised up and down as his fist pounded on the floor until it hurt.

Then he was still, as his mind rolled and turned inward, refusing to accept any part of what he now needed to face. Like a curtain coming down on the last scene of a play, total insanity invaded what was left of his intellectual mind, ending his rational thinking. Edward Duval was beyond help. He had no more acts, no more curtain calls, and no reason to go on. He only wanted to crawl into that dark void inside his brain and cease to exist.

Seconds passed like hours, creeping by, and still, he remained lifeless, waiting and listening, but for what? He knew, only, that someone was coming. All he had to do was stay very still and wait.

Someone would arrive soon; then, they would help him. He needed to tell them about his wife, something, anything but what? What should or could he say? Edward quickly gave up struggling with this dilemma as he told himself an answer would present itself; after all, he was Edward Duval, and he was in control.

Dawn filtered into his brain, slowly arousing him. He stood and walked back into the bedroom as if in a dream. The man had not looked at his Simone. If he did not look at her, he reasoned, then maybe, just maybe, she would be all right. In that case, she, too, would walk into the room as he had. After all, what he thought had happened between them, could have been nothing more than a dream.

Once inside their bedroom, Edward looked into the framed mirror at his reflection, a reflection that returned a vacant stare. Still, he held out hope. Maybe all of it was nothing more than a nightmare. That was it; he'd had a horrible nightmare. If that was true, though, why had he been lying out on the balcony instead of in bed? He had to know! He had to look because something needed to be done. The man in the mirror tilted his head in the direction of the balcony, as if telling him to go and see. The image seemed so sure of himself to the dandy that questioning it was useless. In Edward's jumbled state of mind, he turned sharply and strode toward the verandah. He walked right towards the edge before stopping to look down. At first, there was nothing to register that he was even looking at her body, but then he laughed. It was a crazy man's laugh.

"Simone, don't you know it's not nice to lay with your legs exposed like that? What will people say, my dear? One does not allow so much flesh to be seen; other than by me… you can always show me. I understand, though. Your indiscretion is understandable I suppose. After all, you are so very tired, aren't you? That's fine, you rest. You will wake up feeling a lot better, won't you?"

In his mind, she smiled and spoke softly and lovingly to him. "*Yes, Edward. I need to rest now, but you have to make them pay. They have hurt me. Look, I am hurt. Don't you see? Look what they have done."*

His eyes left her face and traveled downward past her twisted neck. They followed the contour of her body, and then a scream of rage filled the air as he saw part of the ironwork sticking up out of her lower chest. The dark iron shaft matched the dried blood staining her once-beautiful gown.

The world around him began to spin, and he fell backward, tripping over his steps, as he tried to escape the image of her broken and blood-soaked body. He turned to face the interior of the house, his hands gripping the side door for support as he started to fall. Vomit spewed from his mouth, covering his hands and spraying the glass door as he fell on the carpet. Rapidly, he crawled on all fours toward their bed and away from the open doors, but still, her voice kept calling to him from the garden. How was she doing that? Why was she doing it? God help him; his wife would not stop! He had to make her stop.

Try as he might escape her, he could not. His hands covered his ears as he yelled at her madly. When that did not work, he struggled up and onto the bed, grabbing the sheets and pulling them around him. Next, he held the pillows in his bruised and blood-covered hands. He tried to smother the sound of her voice by placing his head between two pillows and crawling further under the covers, but that failed also. Simone was inside his head; she remained there laughing and taunting him, driving him crazy! His wife knew he hated being laughed at, and so he would find a way to silence her one way or the other.

"Stop it!" He screamed. "Get out, go away! Please, stop it," he pleaded, crying like a baby. Sobbing uncontrollably, he begged her to leave him alone. "I'll do what you want. Just stop laughing at me. Stop it, please, please. If you stop, I will listen to you. It took him several seconds to realize that the noise he was hearing was his own sobs and nothing else. When he held his breath to stop those, the room was still once again. Her voice was gone. Simone was gone, and Edward exhaled. He was alone at last.

No longer afraid, the man pulled himself out from under the mass of covers and stood up, looking once again at the mirror before him. However, instead of his reflection in the mirror, he saw Simone watching him.

"You know what must be done. I will see to it that you win. I will never leave you, my darling. I will be with you always." He stepped toward her, reaching out with his trembling hand. His Simone was there, and she was as beautiful as ever. Then she was gone, and all he saw in her place was his own image. For right then, that did not matter so much, as now, at least, he knew what had to be done; she was right. She had always been right. He moved about the bedroom with a purpose and cared only about carrying out her wishes. There was much to do and so little time. Just so long as she didn't laugh at him, he didn't mind having her with him. She could show herself and talk to him all she wanted. All he had to do was listen to his wife, and things would be all right again. His wife would help him get revenge on those who had harmed his love, and she would help him finish what they had begun so long ago.

First, he had to take some of the covers downstairs and make her comfortable while she rested. His wife was so cold out there. However, to do what he wanted, he would have to give everyone the day off. "Tell the niggers, all of them, to leave the front way. Don't need them disturbing the Mistress of the house," he mumbled. He, Edward Duval, would tell them to go. Tell them to go to the plantation and wait for him there. Yes, that was good. They would be walking for a few days. He would tell them all to be quick on walking. Day and night if need be, but they had to go to the plantation. The kitchen wench knows the way, so they best listen to her or be sold or worse. He'd put the fear in them. Yes, that was it. Simone didn't want to be disturbed. She wanted only to talk to him and rest. With the house empty, he could help her, listen to her, and no big ears would listen in. No one would go telling things they weren't supposed to. Simone's husband remained in one spot for a second and wondered what it was he should do first? Things were muddled up, and he needed help. He needed his wife. "Simone, I have a plan, a good one too but right now, what should I do?"

"*The key, Edward. Get the key off the floor. You locked the door remember?*"

Oh, she was good. Simone let no detail ever go uncovered. He would follow her instructions to the letter. They would all pay for what they had done, and his darling Simone was going to make sure they did, first things first, though. He had to see everyone out of his house. Yes, that was very important. He needed it empty so his wife could continue to help him. My, he felt so much better now that Simone was home. She was back safe and sound. They would never hurt her again. "I'm coming, my love."

"*That's good, Edward,*" Simone's voice inside his head spoke happily. "*That's very good.*"

~§ Seven §~

When they had returned from saying their farewells to Andrew Jackson and thanked the Governor and his wife for a glorious evening, they began to talk in earnest. They continued to discuss the problems about what to do or not do when they climbed into bed.

As they tried to sort out their next move, Laffite's wife began to worry. She tried to pay attention to what Jean was saying, but those tiny voices in the back of her mind would not stop. Her intuition was kicking in, and with it came a feeling of need to explain things to her pirate. She worried over and over about the latest twist in events and just what they meant. It was hard to ignore the thoughts that raced around in her head.

Tori had listened nervously to Jean and his grand plans for settling down and raising a family. How he would learn the ways of a plantation owner and more. While he talked on and on, the now panicked lady found her mind drifting in alternate directions no matter how desperately she did not want it to.

Tori was torn between promises still unkept and knowledge of things to come. Events that she had sworn to keep to herself and could have, if not for the way her love was carrying on about his life and their life to be.

She sat up in bed and tried hard to enjoy his plans for the future, but in the end, there didn't seem to be any other way out of the predicament she was trapped in. Jean had to be told; she needed to explain to him. The man had to know about Galveston.

Tori waited until his conversation approached the subject of Edward and Simone and what to do about them, and rather than face that discussion, she spoke up.

"Jean, I need to talk to you and...well... I'm a little frightened.

I want you to listen and to help. Could you hold me, please?" She slipped down from her sitting position and moved closer to him. Her voice was shaking, and that same haunting look that had filled her eyes for so long, the one that he had hoped never to see again, had returned. Without even hearing what it was she had to tell him, he instinctively knew what it was. What the love of his life was about to ask him would tear at his heart. Yet, he knew no matter how difficult he would do as she asked.

Leone's plantation was within their reach, which meant the lake would be too. She might have thought he had forgotten, after all this time, but how could he? Oh, it was true that the lake and what it could hold slipped his mind for days, sometimes weeks. It was also true that over the past few months, with all they had been through, the Duval plantation and the so-called time door had not entered his mind. Now, right then, holding her, it was the only thing filling his mind with dread.

He slipped his arms still further around her, holding onto her as if she were about to leave him. Jean wished they both would have forgotten that promise he had made so long ago, and the promise Tori had made to herself. Their promises now seemed like a curse to him. If only they could go back and undo such things. With such impossibilities, his mood was growing more somber by the second. Why was it that just when all was within his grasp, it could slip away? His lady, his love, could be taken from him, and he would have to live with that if it happened. He did not utter a word, nor did he want her to talk. He just wanted to hold her and keep her safe with him. He wished to forget the obligation that was now hovering about him like a dark cloud.

Tori finally broke the silence. "Jean, I've decided to tell you something about your future. Please don't say anything until I've finished because I'm afraid if you do, I'll lose my nerve." His hand caressed her back and reached up slowly to stroke her hair.

He ran his fingers in among the soft, silky waves and lifted it to his face. The smell of sweet jasmine filled his nostrils. Saying nothing, he just waited for her to continue.

"I know that I told you…that I didn't know anything more about what happened to you after the battle. Well… I lied; I do know more."

His heart all but skipped a beat as her words sank in. What was it she was holding back, he wondered? All thoughts of the lake and his promise vanished.

"In history, it is written that you don't remain in New Orleans. I don't know exactly when you left, but it was not long after the battle, from what I remember. You and some of your men, most of them that is, go off to a place called Galveston." Her voice was soft yet firm as she spoke. "It's on an island off the coast of what will one day be the free state of Texas. It's ironic in a way. That's where I first learned about you, on spring break as a teenager."

He had no idea what this spring break was but dared not disturb her to ask. He would have time later for questions.

Tori took in a long breath and then exhaled and continued. "It was South Padre Island or Galveston, and money was short, so we went to Galveston. I first read about you and some of your life while lying on the beach sunbathing. It was a small article in a local paper, but I still remember wondering about pirates and buried treasure." She giggled to herself and then gently pushed free of his hold. "I don't know anything other than that. You build a house there, the ruins remain, and I had thought about going to see them but didn't. So, you leave here, and you leave here soon, at least in my history, you do."

She decided not to tell him the part about him being run out of Galveston after a few years and returning to his life as a pirate on the high seas. He was, after all, the Gentleman Pirate who sailed off into history and was never heard of again. That was something which, for now, she would not talk about.

Jean exploded with relief. "You are worried over such a simple and trivial problem as that?" he laughed. "Oh, my love. Come here," he said, opening his arms to her, but she did not move.

"Jean, this is a problem. Don't you see? If you choose to fight for Leone's plantation and win... if you settle down there, you'll be changing history."

Jean grinned and twisted a long strand of Tori's hair around his finger. "I'm sorry, my lady, but I see no problem with settling down and raising a family. You, yourself, have often told me that from this day on, my life and what happened is a mystery, have you not?"

"True, but..."

"Ah... true and no buts. Who is to say that I did not settle down here and live out my life happy and respectable? Maybe you and I wished to remain together, untraceable and unknown? Could be, we sold the Duval place and moved to another part of America. We might even change our names and live out the remainder of our lives wealthy and content."

"I don't think so. How could you have stayed and gone to Galveston at the same time?"

"I am not sure. But I am confident of one thing, and that is you. I am a pardoned man." He took her chin in his hand and raised her head so she could look directly into his eyes. I am a citizen of America, and you and I are destined to live, from this day forward, together. If not on the plantation, then someplace else."

She tried to smile.

"Look at me, Tori. I don't have any more answers than you do, but what I do have, is a love so strong and so full that I know it to be all that my life needs." He was quiet for a while and then spoke as if thinking aloud. "You might be right about this Galveston." His mind began to race as ideas started to fall quickly into place. "I know what it is, you wonderful, beautiful lady. It is so simple... don't you see?" She did not see, but his face was so full of excitement that she felt he did have an answer. "I will leave here," he said, slapping the side of his leg. "I will sail to Galveston, but I will not remain there." The astonishment in her eyes told him he was right. "I see that you know this too?" He smiled at her. "Once we have my ship and my wealth, although not all at first... this is what we will do together. We will leave here, this house, this city. I will have money from the sale of the land. Grymes and Livingston have already begun to work on claiming back what was confiscated," he frowned. "That will take time, and we will have to be careful if we are to vanish."

"Vanish?"

"Disappear, you and me. We will leave Galveston and sail off into the sunset. We could go back to the island, our island. Be with Red and her husband. We will remain in paradise and grow old together there." In his mind, he could see it all so clearly.

Tori observed his happiness and excitement, and as it grew, it brought back the Jean that she had first known and grown to love. Gone was the worry over battles and plantations. The deep frown lines on his forehead had eased, and his face was filled with such a cheeky grin that she found herself smiling. Her Jean was once again the mysterious and cunning privateer.

"You could be right if you could make it work. Maybe, just maybe."

"No, maybe, Tori. You have given me the key to my destiny, and together we will return to where we began."

Flashes of the island and their time together filled her mind with thoughts of long tropical nights and warm lazy days. Could he really have figured it out? Is that really what happened to him... to them?

"I will meet with Grymes first thing in the morning and start things going. So many details have to be arranged and hidden. I find that sleep is the last thing on my mind. I have so much to do. You remain here and get some rest. Maybe even sleep."

She watched him as he moved about the room and dressed, all the time talking and explaining to her about the preparations that had to be made. Then he was off to his study to begin planning.

Suddenly the room was hers, chilled and empty. Something was not right, and Tori felt it deep inside. Her intuition was screaming at her to take heed while her heart was calling for her to ignore the little voices of doubt. Jean had made it sound all so perfect. Still, Tori's skin prickled with goosebumps, and a shiver caused her to pull the covers up around her shoulders. She needed to think and to face what could all too soon be the most significant move of her life.

The last time Jean looked in on Tori, she was fast asleep. Seeing her peacefully curled up on her side, with a slight smile on her lips, allowed him to relax. He had been so worried about her the past few hours as he worked in his study. The sounds of her walking back and forth upstairs had not stopped until near daybreak. Whether she had settled whatever was on her mind or whether sheer exhaustion had finally won over, he did not know. One thing was clear, though, Tori was sleeping so soundly that he knew he couldn't disturb her. If he were lucky, by the time she awoke, he would be back with the news that would set her mind at ease once and for all. Jean left early. His destination was Grymes's office to settle Leone's will.

THE morning was young with the promise of one of those rare, bright days ahead. The chill of the past few weeks had passed, and now with the warm sun shining brightly and the world set right, Cisco felt as if he was walking in a dream. Strange how fate could sneak up on you and change your whole outlook on things, he thought. What he needed most at that moment was a good strong cup of coffee to help him get himself together. Seeing Jean walking toward him was like seeing an answer to his dilemma. He wanted to talk to someone about what had happened to him. He had to share how he felt and who better than the one man who understood love, more than any other man he knew.

Jean saw Cisco standing on the corner, looking at him, anxiously shifting his weight from one foot to another. He also noticed that the young man was still dressed in the same clothes as the night before. Knowing this, he assumed that Cisco must have spent the night in the arms of a woman, and judging by the way he was fidgeting around, more than pleasure had occurred.

"Cisco, good morning to you." Jean's face betrayed nothing of his suspicions.

"Jean, my man. Just the person I need to talk with. Join me in a cup of coffee, won't you?" He had put his arm around Jean's shoulder and was guiding him into the small restaurant. Finding a table so early in the day was no problem. Most of the city was just now coming to life, and it would be another hour at least before some of the regulars would stop by for their beignets, freshly brewed coffee and meetings with friends.

Cisco placed a quick order and then turned his attention to his companion. "Java. Can't stop shaking with it, can't live without it." He was laughing nervously, running his hands through his hair. "Look, you'll have to put up with me here. I've been up all night, and man, you know what? Strangest thing, I'm not even tired."

"She must have been quite a woman. Single, I hope?"

Cisco shot him an astonished sort of look and then broke into his old familiar grin.

"No, she's not married, and for your information, I did not spend the night with her either. Can you believe it? I can't."

Jean sat back in his chair and frowned, thinking, this ought to be good. "You might just have to clarify yourself here. Unlike your Marie, I can't read your mind," he teased.

The two cups of coffee arrived, and Cisco's trembling hand picked up his cup, spilling some of the hot liquid down his shirt-front. "Damn it!" He quickly put the cup down and took several seconds to frantically wipe at the coffee stain before catching Jean's worried look.

"I'm not as bad off as I seem. In fact, I think I weathered last night well." Surrendering to the fact that the stain would not go away, he turned to his friend and said, "May I ask you something?"

"Please go ahead. Don't let me stop you. Knowing you as I do, I'm sure you will ask it anyway."

Cisco let Jean's remark slide, something uncharacteristic of him.

"Well, I need a man's advice on this one. It's about last night and a sexy young thing that walked into my life. And damn it to hell… well… I just don't know what happened. She turned out to be the prettiest, sweetest person I have ever known. I could have had a really good time, if you get my drift, but you know what I did?"

Jean shook his head no.

"Me, the Don Juan of New Orleans, turned down the chance of a lifetime. Instead, I made a date for tonight to take her to the opera. I hate opera. What in the hell is the matter with me, or dare I ask?"

Jean rocked with laughter. He tried several times to stop, but each time he looked at Cisco's face, he found himself hopelessly breaking up.

His young friend had obviously, and for the first time, fallen in love and, with it, gained a conscience. The best part was that the young fool was struggling against something that could not be fought. "Cisco, my friend. I think maybe you have become affected by the worst and best illness there is: It's called love, my friend, and you will have to face it. Your days of romancing the ladies of this town may indeed be numbered."

Cisco looked back at Jean with a confounded expression. "I was afraid you would say that. I never thought it would happen to me, and so damn fast. How can I be sure?"

"Think about it. What was it you did all last night?"

He smiled. "I walked the streets after we parted. I walked and thought about her, of how lovely she is and how soft and fragile. And you know what? I don't care if I am about to have to settle for one lady if she is the one. Jean, I just can't get her out of my mind, and it scares the hell out of me that I still want her."

"You have your answer, Cisco. Take it from a man who knows. And hear me, love is the most beautiful of all our emotions, but it can hurt like no other wound. It is like the moth to the flame, you see? We can't escape it, for it beckons us."

"Ah, but see," Cisco's voice went low and somber, "sometimes the moth gets too close and burns."

"Yes, love can consume, but true love has all the warmth and beauty of the flame in which the passion can grow, basking in its light. Love, my young friend, is what life is all about, and if you have found it, then don't let it slip from your grasp. Take hold and live life in its glow."

Cisco, taking a sip of his coffee, looked over the rim of his cup into his friend's eyes. After a moment, he said, "I don't know about you, but I'm ravenous."

"And calmer by the looks of the way you handled your cup," he laughed. "Love can make you either, my friend, hungry or sick at the thought of eating. You are about to see and experience life a whole different way. Never again will you go about each day as you used to." Jean was beaming as he spoke. "I am so happy for you and wish you all the best." He raised his cup in a toast. "May you be as happy as my lady and I. Speaking of which, she will have to meet this young love of yours once she hears the news. You know how she is and how she feels about you. We shall have you over for dinner." They both chuckled.

"You think she will put the poor girl through the mill?" Cisco quizzed.

"If that means what I think it does, yes. I am sure Tori will want to know all about her and how this young lady truly feels toward you."

"Well, I have no doubt that she will love her as I do. And as far as how she feels toward me, not Tori, my girl, she loves me, Jean, I have no doubt in my mind. She loves me as much as I do her. Now, I am famished. How about some food?"

THE restaurant had filled up as the two friends sat eating and discussing the finer points of love and courtship. Once in a while, someone would acknowledge Jean, and polite greetings of the day would be exchanged, but for the most part, the two friends sat relatively uninterrupted, enjoying each other's company.

Grymes stopped in for his daily breakfast and meeting with friends but, upon seeing Jean and Cisco, decided to start his day off with them. Besides, he could hardly pass up the chance to see what it was they were so involved in discussing. Cisco looked positively elated.

It took less than five minutes for Jean to tell Grymes about Cisco's latest dilemma, causing another round of joyous laughter and good wishes. Not one of them noticed Edward as he approached the table, followed by a somber-looking companion.

"Monsieur Laffite," said Edward in a loud, demanding voice, causing a hush to fall all around them. "You have taken from me that which is by birth rightfully mine, and you leave me no choice in the matter but to demand satisfaction." His hand came up and the leather gloves he held slapped Jean across the side of his face.

A gasp from another table was the only response. Not a soul moved or spoke. Jean stood up, pushing his chair backward across the wooden floor, making a scraping sound as it went. Grymes grabbed hold of Cisco and, without saying a word, kept him in his place.

Jean never took his eyes off Edward, and as he looked at the man, he knew that the time had come at last to finish the war that had raged on for so many years. He had no choice now. Edward had seen to that. It had become a matter of honor between gentlemen. So, without a trace of anger, Jean calmly reached out and took the gloves from Edward's hand. He stood for a second more and then returned the slap.

Then he spoke. "It did not have to come to this, and yet maybe it did. You have succeeded over the years in hurting those who I care deeply for. You have hurt my lady and your brother, who was our dear friend. It saddens me that it has come to this, but the choice was yours. It will give me great pleasure to meet your challenge. You, however, will have to be the one to name the place and... the choice of weapons, but one word of advice, Edward. This is between you and me and no one else. I want Simone and Tori to know nothing of this. Do you understand me? Nothing! If either of them finds out, the whole thing is off."

The Dandy's face darkened, yet the pent-up rage inside of him stayed buried. Simone's voice was in Edward's head murmuring, telling him to remain calm. "You have my word as a gentleman. This will stay between us, as it should be. As a matter of fact, Laffite, I find it in poor taste that you would even consider my actions as a gentleman to stoop so low as to involve either lady. It sickens me to even have to dirty my hands with the likes of you or your lady. My beautiful wife understands such matters and would wholeheartedly agree with me. I shall, however, acknowledge that this ugly affair will remain between us. So, the sooner we get this over with, the better for all concerned. We shall meet out by the field of Oaks at noon if that's enough time for you. As for the choice of weapon, I choose pistols.

"I would be glad to get it over with, as you so elegantly phrased it, but noon is not convenient for me. I have a meeting with John Grymes here," he said, indicating to John with a nod of his head. "A matter of a plantation. You do understand? Is one o'clock fine with you?"

"Easy Edward, don't let him get to you, my darling. He is just trying to unnerve you. Laffite is frightened, that's all. Why else would he delay? You have him now. You have him!"

His beautiful wife was with him. Her guidance was welcome, and he intended to follow it. She knew what she was doing, and that made him one lucky man. "If that's the time you choose to meet your death, then so be it. I have my second, and the doctor has been contacted. You will, of course, have your second ready, if any will stand for you?"

Breaking free of Gryme's grasp, Cisco sprang to his feet. He was disgusted by the audacity of the man. He loathed the very sight of Edward, and it would give him a great deal of satisfaction to help end the bastard's miserable life. "I will be Jean's second and believe you me; I will see to it that this here duel is a fair one. Do you get what I'm saying?"

Edward barely noticed, let alone listened to a word Cisco said. He had achieved what he came for. "Drink your coffee, Laffite. Enjoy what's left of your life. I will show the city of New Orleans that a true gentleman such as myself can overcome the likes of you, the scum of the earth. Or is it sea, being the pirate that you are?" He turned and looked around the restaurant and smiled. He bowed slightly as he spoke, "Good day, gentlemen," and then he departed.

As the two walked away, Jean noticed for the first time that Edward's second was carrying a long wooden case; it no doubt contained the weapons Edward intended to use.

The sight had not escaped Cisco's attention either. "You aren't going to let him talk you into using his weapons, are you? They could be rigged, fixed. You know what I mean. I would not trust him as far as I could throw him."

"I have no intention of letting him gain the upper hand, no matter how he tries, honest or otherwise. Come on; we have some things to attend to and less than three hours to do it in. One good thing Tori won't know about this until it's over. Grymes, you'll see to that, won't you?"

"Jean, I don't like this, not one bit. But asking you to reconsider is useless, I suppose?" The look on both Cisco's and Jean's faces confirmed his assumption. "I'll do what I can."

"It's called damage control," said a serious Cisco.

"Call it what you want. It won't be easy to keep this from reaching Tori. I bet half the city knows about it already!"

Tori had skipped lunch, choosing instead to sit in the warm sun and think about her awful dream. She had been about to sail off with Jean when a voice had called out to her. The voice had been Linni's, and then she had found herself at the lake. Kate was there, holding out her hands to her, telling her to hurry. She had seen it then, the doorway to her time, and standing on the other side, was her darling little girl calling for mommy.

By the time she moved toward her daughter, the dream had suddenly ended. It had been so vivid. But why now? What did it mean? She had almost come to the decision to leave with Jean… to sail off to the islands and accept her destiny when this dream appeared. How could she let go of her family and her life in the nineties when she hadn't even tried once to see if she had a chance of getting back?

After all these months of not thinking once about the lake, her family, and her trying to return, she now found herself consumed by the overpowering need to at least attempt it.

"Maybe that's why I feel so down," she mumbled. "I have to ask him to take me there, to keep his promise, so I can keep mine. God, how can I do that? Will he understand?" she said, looking up at the sky, not realizing someone was watching her.

"Don't think God answers out loud, not all the time anyhow. Things happen, and then they don't." It was Marie's voice that broke into her privacy.

"Cisco's gone and got his self into a heap of mess. Seen a vision myself last night. I feel, how'd you say just then, down? Yes, that about puts my mood right alongside yours."

"Well then, you had best come and join me, as misery loves company, you know."

"Can't say I do. What I do know ain't good, that be for sure. Trouble is all I feel. It's like you and Cisco. You knowing things, but not real clear like. That's how it is with me most of the time. I know things but ain't always clear. What I do know is, today ain't a nice day like the sky says it is. I know you will tell me it sure is a nice day, blue sky, but it changes even now. Look, the clouds are racing across the heavens, and soon the cold wind of death will follow." Marie looked up and around at the partly sunny heavens, her face deeply saddened. She looked at Tori then and walked toward her almost reluctantly. "I ain't sure I should be here, but I did hear about something that fits with why I feel this way. Maybe you have a touch of the gift, and you be feeling down cause of it too. I guess that you and I have been through the best of times and the worst. You are a good friend, and that's the only reason I am here."

Tori was starting to get worried. The look on Marie's face was similar to the look she had when Christopher had gotten sick. She reached out to Marie, grabbed her hand, and pleaded with her, her voice trembling with apprehension. "Marie, what do you know? What's wrong?"

"There ain't no easy way around this, so I'm just a goin' to say it as I heard it told to me, not more'n a hour gone. That Edward Duval, he done gone and called your Jean out. They be all set to duel this here afternoon, and Cisco, he's gone with him."

Alarmed and horrified, Tori dropped Marie's hand and stood staring at her. Her Jean and Cisco in a duel? People died in duels. It would be a sure bet that someone was not going to walk away from this one, but which someone? Edward would most certainly not play by the rules; that despicable bastard would make damn sure he won.

Bessy called out to Tori from the open doorway, "Mizz Tori, you have a visitor. It be that Mr. Grymes fellow. You want me to show him in?"

Marie shook her head no; she didn't need to speak or explain. "No! No, Bessy, you tell him I'm resting and not receiving any visitors this afternoon. Go on now, you see to it that I'm left alone."

"Yes, um, I'll tell him. Don't you worry none. Ain't nobody gettin' by old Bessy." She could still be heard mumbling as she disappeared inside the house.

Marie looked at Tori closely and frowned. "I think maybe he came here to keep you from doin' what you thinkin' about doin'. You're goin' to go and stop em, ain't you?"

"You're dead right there, but where do I go, Marie? Do you have any idea where or when this duel is to take place?"

"Didn't at first, but then that's what took the time gettin' here. You best change cause I got you a horse and the directions. If you is quick, you might get there in time. Cause Lord knows, you are

the only one that can stop it. The only one that fool Jean is a goin'
to listen to."

Jean and Cisco rode their horses quietly out of town to the place
that was well known to the locals. In years to come, the spot would
be replaced by another more convenient location, close to town,
called the dueling oaks.

Already New Orleans's reputation of foolish, hot-blooded young
men in duels and death was spreading far and wide.

Dueling in Europe had for years been a way for honorable men
to avenge a wrong against oneself or family. The tradition had
traveled across the ocean and found a place and acceptance in the
homes and lives of the young nation. Unlike Europe, where the
offense was more than often a serious matter, the young men of
New Orleans took the art of dueling to new heights. Many a young
Creole would lose his life or be severely maimed over such a trivial
offense as a spilled cup of coffee or an improper advance toward a
lady at one of the Quadroon balls. The deadly combination of too
much wine and misplaced honor would be more than enough to
trigger the demand for satisfaction, no matter how frivolous the
reason. With his honor, reputation, and family name at stake, there
would be no other choice for the young gentleman involved but to
duel. The earth beneath the dueling oaks would be stained forever
with needless blood.

Cisco's mood was as gray and dreary as the weather had turned.
Dark, dismal clouds filled the sky, adding fuel to his somber
thoughts. The cold wind felt like icy fingers of death tugging at his
sleeve. He shook himself, trying hard not to give in to his melancholy mood. Brighten up, he told himself. Death was not looking
for him or Jean. It was Edward, it called for.

Jean saw Edward standing next to his carriage, talking to his second. Three other men were present. He recognized one as the doctor and realized the other two to be the drivers of their carriages. Both blacks stood a short distance away from the area, close to each other and not looking too happy at having to be present. All means of etiquette had been observed and met so far as Jean could tell, but still, his instincts told him that something was seriously wrong here. He just could not place his finger on what it was.

As they approached, walking the horses slowly, he and Cisco surveyed the surrounding area for any possible ambush or setup. It was the younger man who spoke up for both of them. "Seems to be as you asked for, no sign of Simone or anyone else for that matter." Cisco rose up in his saddle to better take in the area around him. His nerves were on edge, and like Jean, he, too, had a very uneasy feeling. "Still don't trust the rat. His type don't fight, and when they do, the cards are always stacked in their favor. He's got to have something up his sleeve, I tell you. That, or the man's gone mad."

"I'm sure you're right, but then the man has been pushed to the brink. After all, he learned last night that he stands to lose everything, and a desperate man does desperate acts. Could be that this is just what it is, his only way out!"

They rode their mounts to within a few feet of the carriage where they remained, looking down upon the three men gathered there.

Edward shot a twisted a smile toward Jean. "Thought you might not show up. You could have sailed on the tide, but then you don't have any ships, do you? You have nothing but to go after that which is mine and ruin the fine name of my family." His smile vanished as he snarled. "That, Laffite, will not happen."

"Easy darling, don't push him. He's here, and you have him just where you want him. Listen to me, my love." He heard her voice so clearly that he was afraid that everyone else might hear her as well. "Shhh…quiet," he hissed, putting his finger to his lips, and turning toward his carriage.

Cisco looked curiously at Edward and then at his second, who also seemed to have noticed Edward's strange behavior. The doctor merely shook his head as if pitying poor Edward but said nothing. It was futile. Crazy or not, and in his opinion, the man was out of his mind; Edward was going to duel.

"*Show him the pistols. Do it now, Edward,*" Simone said in a light-hearted manner.

Edward reached for the box lying on the back seat. He carefully and tenderly opened the lid, exposing the two pistols that lay side by side. He lifted the container and handed it to his second, who in turn faced Jean.

"If you don't mind, Edward, I would like to use one of my own pistols. You may, of course, inspect it." He unfastened his jacket and reached into his belt, removing his weapon. He handed it over to Cisco, who held it toward Edward.

"I will do just that, and to show no hard feelings, you may look at the weapons that I have brought along." He reached and took Jean's pistol from Cisco's hand. As he examined the weapon, he continued to talk. "It seems to me that only a man other than a gentleman would think that they were anything other than top quality," he said, looking toward his second and the box he held. "You will find them in order." His voice had been smooth but laced with disdain. "Did you think that I would somehow stoop to rendering them inoperable?" he retorted.

"*Oh, Edward, please, the man's no fool. Stop this and get hold of yourself. Of course, he would think that of you. It's something that he would do. He is not a Duval. He's the scum of the earth, the slayer of women and children. Remember what he did to me, after all. You tried to make me feel better, but there is no better until the bastard is dead. Till he has paid for all, he has taken from us.*"

She was correct; he had to listen to his Simone. "Yes," he whispered to her. Then he looked directly into Jean's eyes, his mood once again calmer. "Fool. I have no need to meddle with the pistols. That act is beneath me. I am, after all, a Duval," he smiled. "I intend to kill you in a fair fight and with honor." His tone was deadly and very serious.

Jean judged that the man actually believed in what he was saying.

He also had reached the conclusion that he had slipped over the edge of sanity, and that made him a very dangerous and deadly opponent. A man that had nothing left to lose was to be feared.

Edward stepped up to Cisco and handed him the weapon and impatiently looked at Jean. "Don't bother. If you are ready, you may use your pistol. Let us proceed." He turned and walked to his second and took one of the pistols from the box.

"Doctor, you have agreed to officiate, and as such, may I suggest that to delay any longer is a waste of our time."

"As you wish." He spoke, sounding far more formal and official than he felt. "Monsieur Laffite, if you are ready?"

Jean nodded his head and dismounted, calling to one of the young black boys to come and take his horse.

Cisco slid from his saddle and handed the reins of his animal to the young lad and watched as he quickly led their horses away. He gave Jean his weapon and tried to say something but found that the deadly stare in Jean's dark eyes rendered him speechless. He had only seen one other duel in his life and had never expected to see another. Cisco listened as the doctor laid out the rules.

"You have a few minutes to confer with your second, at which time I will call for the gentleman to proceed. From that time on, neither second may move nor be involved until the matter is settled, and I myself have examined the outcome. Gentlemen, may God have mercy on you both."

Jean and Cisco walked from the meeting, standing a short distance away, just out of hearing range.

It was Jean who spoke first, placing his hand upon Cisco's shoulder. "I don't know how this will turn out. God willing, and with a little luck, you and I will ride away together from this place. I have every confidence that I have the upper hand, having fought before." His voice trailed off for a second. "I have never had so much at stake, so much to lose, and that alone gives Edward an edge. I find for the first time that if I could, I would walk away."

"But you have one hell of a reason to win. You have your lady, your love, and nothing could be stronger. Nothing is. Edward has his rage, and that will cloud his judgment. Unlike you, his wife is far from worth fighting for, while Tori, now there is a woman worthy of a duel." He felt like a football coach at halftime and wished he could put into words how much he cared for both Jean and Tori.

"You're right there," Jean smiled. "She is worth it."

"Besides," added Cisco, laughing, "the bastard deserves to die for all he has done and will continue to do if allowed to live." He would have gone on, but the doctor's voice rang clear in the afternoon air.

"Gentlemen, take your mark."

Cisco wanted to say good luck, but luck would have nothing to do with what was about to happen. It took nerves and skill and a good shot. Instead of good luck, "break a leg," he said softly, causing a stunned sort of look from Jean. "I'll explain it to you after this is over," Cisco laughed. "Just don't take it literally." Then he added, "See you soon."

Jean turned and walked toward his opponent. "I pray you are right," he mumbled under his breath. The two men stood inches apart, each trying to fathom what the other was thinking. Jean looked at Edward closely. He was either crazy or, worse yet, sane and very deadly. Something, however, was bothering the dandy. He could see it in the man's eyes, the way they stared at him vacantly as if he really didn't see him at all. Could it be that he was frightened to death at what was about to take place? Was he thinking about his wife and all that he was risking by this challenge?

Jean knew it was obviously his plan to kill him. He had to try and somehow regain his ownership of the plantation, and by Laffite's death, he assumed he would. Did he not know that it would all go to Tori if anything happened to him? Grymes had already drawn up a new will. The attorney had seen to it that Edward and Simone would never again have what Leone had left to Jean's son.

EDWARD was hardly listening to the doctor as he spoke, telling each man just what to do. Without much thinking, the dandy turned and faced in the opposite direction of his enemy, feeling Jean's back up against his. Simone was with him. She had stopped laughing and was now whispering instructions so softly that he tipped his head slightly to one side, trying to hear her voice more clearly. His face started to twist and twitch, his free hand opening and closing tightly. He was not scared or nervous at all; she had seen to that. He had a deadly purpose, and all his concentration was placed in carrying it out. He would listen to his beautiful wife and win. His body trembled with excitement as the seconds drew closer to the inevitable. He would end up with everything, and all to the thanks of his beautiful Simone. They would return to the plantation and live there, turning their backs on New Orleans and all its citizens. Yes, his lovely wife would be all he needed.

Edward closed his eyes as an unwanted thought filled his mind. Simone was dead, wasn't she? He had killed her. Panicked, he pushed that detail away. No, no, she was just sleeping in the garden; that's all he told himself. She was just a little sick; that was it, just like his brother. Only, this time instead of death winning, life would. Poor Leone, he had lost his battle. Yes, Leone had loved him, and Edward had loved Leone. It was Laffite's fault, his and his wench's. She would be next to be taken care of. What he had in mind for her was something far worse than death. She would pay dearly, wishing over and over that she had died alongside her pirate.

The doctor's voice sounded louder, causing him to pay attention at last. The man had stepped well out of the line of fire and, in so doing, was calling out to them. "I will start the count. Remember, ten paces, then turn and fire."

TORI rode as if the devil himself was after her, all the time trying to think if she had read anything, in any book, about Jean being killed in a duel or even fighting one. Could her role in history still be playing out, she wondered? Was it now her job to stop this fight before it could alter everything? When would the madness end? She did not care about the plantation anymore, and right then, she didn't even care about the lake. All she wanted was Jean's safety.

The cold wind whipped at her hair, bringing it down around her shoulders. The top of her blouse was catching the air and billowing out. This, in turn, caused the material to pull out of the top of her pants. Still, she spurred the horse on. "Please, please, dear God in heaven, let me be in time. Don't let Edward kill him, not now."

She prayed quietly to herself, unable to pray out loud, as the wind in her face would have taken her breath away. Not much further to go now, she thought, as she spurred the animal even harder, pushing it forward, begging it to find the strength and the will, to travel faster.

THE doctor started the counting, loud, slow, and rhythmic in his calling. "One… two… three…"

Edward's twisted smile encompassed his face. Simone had stopped talking, but he knew she was still with him. All he had to do was wait and listen for her. In a few seconds, Jean Laffite would be no more.

It was going to be so easy. All he had to do was turn and fire, and it would be over. Yes, that was all, but on the count of ten, never! Eight, she had said.

"*That's it; turn around on the count of eight. Careful now, listen, this is it.*"

"Four… five…" came the doctor's clear call.

But won't it be cheating, he asked her in his mind? I will inevitably be accused of murder.

"*That is if any witnesses were left to tell, but there will be none, will there?*" her voice answered him, laughing. "*You are so brave, and this time you will win my love."*

"Simone, my love, I will do it just as you said. As I kill Laffite, my second will kill his second. The doctor and the niggers will be next. Oh, how clever you are. I shall win. Jean's men attacked us, but I was strong, and I was the victor. As always, you are brilliant."

"Seven…" the doctor called.

"One more step. Now watch, my dear Simone, as he dies!"

Cisco did not trust Edward at all, and with each count from the doctor, he had moved slightly closer to the field and watched him intently. His eyes were riveted on the man's slow pace, his body language speaking clearly to Cisco's keen eye. He had been trained to closely observe each move; even the slightest action could tell him a man's intent. That's why he always won his fights, why he had earned his black belt so quickly. Yes, the martial arts had trained him well, and right then, it was paying off.

When he saw Duval break stride and begin to turn on eight instead of ten, he did not hesitate. He immediately screamed a loud warning to Jean as he raised his own pistol in defense. Everything happened so fast and yet went slowly in Cisco's mind. He saw Edward's second reaching into his jacket, but he hesitated, allowing Cisco the chance of one-shot that could save Jean.

Jean acted on pure instinct. Too late to turn, he dropped to the ground instead and instantaneously rolled over, just in time to see Cisco firing his weapon. The other man, Edward's second, was looking from the doctor to Cisco and then toward Edward.

It was the doctor who took a step toward Edward's second, and as he did so, he was relieved to see the man had no intention of reaching for his gun; instead, he removed his hand from within his jacket and left the weapon safely concealed against his chest.

Laffite thought the second's expression was odd; a mix of fear and shock was how he'd describe it. Not so strange, he thought; after all, he had just witnessed Edward trying to cheat. Seeing Edward's second was no threat, Jean stood up and looked toward his opponent. He wanted to see what, if anything, had happened to the dandy. Laffite was sure he had heard two shots fire, but he could have been wrong. Maybe it had been one shot and an echo.

THE force of being hit had knocked Edward off balance. His weapon had been raised toward Laffite's back, about to fire, when Cisco's bullet bored into his chest. Duval's arm jerked off to the side just as he squeezed the trigger. This slight action, while discharging the gun, unknowingly caused him to miss his mark. The dandy dropped his weapon when his legs gave out from under him. Quickly he fell to his knees, and then he buckled over onto the grass. His empty hand clutched at his chest while his face twisted in agony and hate. The stunned man had felt the hot burn of the lead as it ripped into his chest, followed by the explosion of pain that enveloped his brain as the bullet tore his insides apart. Its quick, deadly trip had pierced his soft flesh easily, and grazing a rib, the bullet finally came to rest next to his heart. It had nicked the main artery, sealing Edward's fate.

Only one thing filled Duval's mind right then, and that was to see Laffite dead on the ground. So slowly, he rolled over onto his side and moved his head so that he could look toward the area where the pirate's body was sure to be. Simone's name was on his lips as he struggled to breathe. "I did it, my love. We did it, and soon the doctor will come, and I will be all right. Simone? Talk to me? Why are you not talking?" Then in his head, she was laughing, not with him but at him. Simone was laughing hysterically, but why?

Edward's eyes followed the ground, looking through the grass toward Jean. His world was on its side, his cheek rubbing the ground as he strained to the angle he needed. Nothing made much sense to him at first, and it was hard to concentrate with Simone's laughing and the pain he felt. Then he saw what he longed for; Jean was down.

"Die, you bastard," he hissed, satisfied that he had mortally wounded the man. At last, he could understand why his wife was laughing. Simone was happy. He had made her happy; he had finally killed the bastard, Jean Laffite!

Then his twisted smile switched to disbelief as he watched Jean beginning to rise to his feet. Looking at the man, Edward could not find a mark on him. There was no sign of blood, not one hint of an injury. Laffite was not hit! He had missed. Once again, the pirate would be the winner, and he, Edward Duval, the loser of everything.

His mouth screwed up into a horrible grimace as his lifeblood pumped out of the hole in his chest. Simone's laughter was filling his head even louder than before.

"Like I told you, Edward, my stupid husband, Jean is way more a man than you will ever be. You lost...you, stupid man...you couldn't even kill him with my help!" Her voice was fading, until she was gone. His wife, his love, was gone, and soon he would join her.

"All because of you, you bastard," he tried to yell at Jean. "Damn you to hell," he mumbled, "I damn you..." and with one last searing pain, his world finally went dark. He could not see a thing, and the pain was gone, but he could still hear his Simone's laughter, and he despised her for it, and then it was silent.

TORI had seen the men walking and then the turning of one before the other. The sounds of weapons firing filled the heavens, causing a flock of blackbirds to take flight. Dear God, she thought, I'm too late, and still, she raced the animal toward the scene.

Both men had fallen, but which one was Jean? To which man should she ride? Closer and closer, the fallen men rapidly came into view, and in a flash, she was able to see that the one nearer to her was Jean, and he was standing up.

Screaming out his name over and over, she did not slow her pace until she was almost on top of him. Only then did she halt her breakneck speed and jump from the horse's back, throwing herself into his arms.

JEAN had seen Edward, but before he could do anything else, Tori's frantic call had made him turn away. He saw her galloping toward him like a wild woman riding the wind. In seconds she was pulling her mount to a stop. Sliding from the foam-covered animal, she ran into his arms, crying hysterically.

"It's alright," he told her as they clung to each other. "I'm fine. His shot missed me."

Tori squeezed him tighter in relief, and then finding her breath, she asked, "Is he dead?" She was afraid of the answer because she wanted him dead for all he had done. But, to actually want another human being killed was supposed to be unthinkable. Did she feel guilty for wishing him dead? Hell no, came her voice firmly in her mind.

Jean looked over to where the doctor was examining the body and watched as he placed his own jacket over Edward's remains. Jean had his answer. The dandy was dead all right, and not far behind the doctor, he watched as a very frightened second was running for his horse.

Edward's friend wanted no further part of this duel or of Edward. He had not been fast enough to stop what had happened, but the doctor had seen what he intended to do, and now all he wanted was to get far away, to avoid any questions. He would deny anything about the horrible part he was supposed to have played. Most of all, he would stay away from Laffite. If that man ever found out about his role in Edward's plan, he'd be a dead man.

The doctor walked over to Jean and Tori. A grim frown formed deep lines on his forehead as his lips pursed together in disgust. "Duval is dead. Hate these things; such a terrible waste of humanity. I knew his brother Leone, friends for years. Just glad he did not have to witness such an end. You know, of course, he must have been quite deranged. Turning on eight, as he did, and his second ready to do whatever they planned. He will have some questions to answer. If it hadn't been for your second, calling out as he did, I fear the outcome would have been more deadly for us all."

Tori buried her face still deeper into Jean's shoulder. He had come so close to death; she had almost lost him. The woman couldn't cry, but she couldn't laugh with happiness either. All she could think to do was to cling to him as tightly as she could.

Jean, who had been holding her in his embrace, also realized how very close he had come to being killed. He drew her still tighter in this realization. "I swear to you here and now, never again will I duel. My word to you, my love."

Suddenly she felt him stiffen. The change in his body as he went rigid alarmed her. As he pushed her away, she could see his face fill with a dread that caused her heart to race. Tori turned, and following his gaze, she found what had drawn his attention, and it caused her to scream. "No!" she cried out as she pulled free of Jean's grasp and began to run toward Cisco and his motionless body. Jean was at his friend's side in seconds, gently turning him over, revealing his bloodstained midsection.

"Oh shit," Cisco moaned upon seeing the blood oozing through his shirt.

"Hush, don't talk," Tori told him. Why she said that she didn't know; maybe it was because they always said something like it in all the movies. But hell, this was no movie; he had been shot for real and could be dying. "No," she mumbled, looking frantically back toward the doctor and calling to him. "Come on; Cisco needs help."

Cisco was conscious and alive; that was a good sign, and they had help right there; he would be ok, Tori assured herself. "Doctor, please, it's my friend! He's bleeding!" she cried, fearfully looking up into the man's face as he arrived by their side. "Don't stand there! Do something!"

The doctor ignored her anger and bent down by Cisco's side, his hands gently and cautiously feeling under his back. He looked up at Jean. "No exit wound. Here, I'll need your assistance." He was opening Cisco's jacket and pulling at his shirt. "I'll have to peel away the shirt here," he said, pointing to the bloodiest spot. "I want you to be ready to help me halt the bleeding should it be necessary." Jean didn't say a thing. He just knelt by his fallen friend's side, ready to aid the doctor in any way he could. While the doctor and Jean made an effort to examine Cisco's wound, Tori held her friend's hand and gently stroked the side of his face.

He forced a smile and even tried to laugh, "I don't understand *how* this happened. I got the bastard, though. I got him, Tori. He won't hurt you anymore. I don't understand how this…"

Tori could only shake her head. She had no answers for him. The sound of his shirt being ripped away as the doctor worked brought back memories of the field hospital; she had seen worse surely, and having assured herself of this fact, she convinced herself to look. Blood and gore would never frighten her again, having seen so much of it on that fateful day. Men and boys had lived with much worse; all Cisco had was a small bullet that the doctor would no doubt remove. Tori looked around and knew it was going to be hard, but they needed to get Cisco into the city and fast.

Laffite's wife turned her head to see the damage and watched as the blood began to flow even faster once the material had been removed and the wound itself was exposed. Jean ripped off his own shirt, and the doctor took it, bunching it up quickly. He placed it onto Cisco's stomach, and then he asked Jean for something to tie it into place.

Tori didn't hesitate; she called to one of the blacks standing near, "I need something to wrap around him; find something fast."

Wanting to do something to help, the youngest of the pair took his shirt off and ripped it in two. This he handed to Tori while trying not to look at the fallen man. "It be clean like. My mama made me change to come here said I had to look right cause it was the proper thing to do.

Tori handed the strip of material to Jean and helped him wrap it around Cisco's midsection while the doctor held him up.

Jean watched the bloody area as he used the shirt to hold his own now blood-soaked shirt in place, pulling tightly, hoping to stem the flow. For a few seconds, it seemed to be working until they both saw the slow trickle start, running down his side, falling onto the grass. Slowly standing up, the doctor looked toward Jean and shook his head from side to side. His face was grim, and his lips were turned down in a helpless scowl.

Tori spoke with strength and absolute calm in her voice that she knew Jean would not ignore. "Leave us alone. Please go."

The doctor looked at Jean, who stood and took him by his arm and walked some distance away. "They are as close as brother and sister. It's only right."

The doctor looked back at the pair and nodded his head. With kindness and understanding in his expression, he spoke quietly. "I'll stay just the same. She may need me. I am aware how strong she is and has been in the past, but this, this is going to be most difficult, especially if they are as close as you say." He took a step back and stood silently watching the wounded struggle, and upon seeing Tori make her move, he walked toward the two blacks to see if they knew anything about Edward's second and his despicable act.

Tori lifted Cisco's head and sitting down; she placed the top half of him in her lap so he could look at her as she spoke. "Why did you have to go and be so damn brave? You know that now I'm going to have to spend my days nursing you back to health, and you are going to be one hell of a pain in the ass patient."

Cisco smiled at her. She was so strong, trying to hide from him what he already knew. He had seen the doctor shake his head. He knew what that meant. There was no time for pretending here.

"Stop it, Tori. We both know that I'm not going to stay here with you." He put his lips together and tried to stifle a cough, and as he did, the pain caused him to grunt and clench his jaw.

Tori waited helplessly until the pain had passed. She was about to tell him he was wrong when he reached up and stroked her cheek.

"You know, it's kind of strange, isn't it? Us being here together like this." He shivered in the warm sun that peeked out from behind the wind-driven clouds. "It's cold." His hand dropped to his side.

Tori stroked his head and looked into his eyes while trying to smile and not show any fear. His eyes were getting glassy, and the pupils were large and fixed; they were not dilating, just like Christopher's had looked right before the end.

"Strange. It doesn't hurt anymore. Always thought it was supposed to hurt like hell, a shot to the gut." Another coughing fit hit, joined by an odd bubbling sound. His coughing was causing the wound to express the blood even faster.

Cisco squeezed her hand, too afraid to let go. "Tori, I guess I was not meant to stay here." He closed his eyes for a second, then opened them, a small smile creeping around his mouth, exposing a dimple that only showed when he grinned. He struggled to continue, "I was happy here...wanted to stay. Finally... I found someone to share my life with. You know, the girl in the taffeta dress? The one you pointed out, remember?" He was struggling hard to talk, his words dragging slower and slower as they came. "Seems as if I was wrong, though. I won't be staying, will I?"

Tori just stroked his hand between hers. What could she say? How could she tell him the words that she did not want to admit out loud?

Softly, in such a low whisper that she had to bend her head down to hear him, he continued. "I'm going back, Tori. I'm going home. It's all been a dream, right? Just a dream." A slight breeze blew up and over them. Its gentle touch lifted Tori's hair, blowing it over her face. "The wind is calling me. My world is full of shadows. It's dimming. Tori, it's getting dark. Was this real, all real? The other world, our world, is now calling me home." Tori had tears spilling down her face. They were dropping onto his shoulder, and she tried to wipe them off him.

"Now, you touch me. I should have got shot before." He gave her his last Cisco grin. "You're one hell of a woman." He tried to laugh but only smiled. He closed his eyes and lay quiet for a few seconds, and then he opened them and looked right at her. "Tori…"

"Yes, what? Anything you want, just ask."

"Don't forget me… and if you ever go back… well… look me up. Can't see you so good, too many shadows. What a dream…" he never finished.

His last breath whistled from between his parted lips as it left his body. His lifeless eyes were looking up to the sky that he no longer could see. She reached up gently and closed them. "I love you, my friend. I will never forget you or what you did. You were and always will be my best friend. You saved Jean's life. For that, I will cherish your memory." She looked into his handsome face; such a love for life he had had. She would never be able to hear his voice or laughter again, and yet, she knew that somewhere in time, he laughed and joked, as he always had.

Jean came to her side. He had seen the slump in her shoulders and the way her head hung low on her chest. He knew that their friend had breathed his last breath, and his wife needed him now. He got her to let go of Cisco's hand and to stand up and lean against him. She was crying softly, letting the tears fall gently onto Jean's shoulder. There was no need for hysterics or any room for anger. She did not want to leave him that way, just lying on the ground, but words would not escape her trembling lips.

Jean looked down upon the lifeless form of his friend, a man that he owed his life to and much more. How could he comfort his lady in her grief when he himself had a hard time dealing with it?

The sound of horses approaching and voices calling out to them drew their attention away from the tragic sight. Two riders came rapidly down the road, followed closely behind by a carriage. Even at the great distance between them, they recognized the driver. It was Cisco's Marie.

John Grymes and Thiac were the first to reach the sad scene, and dismounting, they walked to Tori and Jean, embracing them without speaking. Thiac pulled away to look at the fast-approaching carriage. "Boss, you best leave this to me," he said, walking back to meet Marie.

"I won't ask what happened. We'll talk later," said John, releasing Jean from his hug and turning toward Tori. "God. I'm so sorry, Tori. What more can I say? What can I do?"

"Nothing, John. No one can do anything. It's Marie; I'm worried about now."

She watched as Thiac greeted the carriage and talked briefly with its driver. He then helped Marie down and stood aside as she slowly walked toward Cisco's body. She did not look away from her lover and friend until she stood staring down at his face. Then she slowly looked up at Tori and Jean with tear-filled eyes. "I ain't about to mourn him, not like you think I will. I will miss him, as we all will. But it's the livin' that worry me now," she looked right at Tori. "You'll be a needin' some time by yourself, you and your man."

"Oh, Marie," cried Tori, opening her arms to embrace her friend. She walked quickly to her, and each clung to the other for a few seconds before Marie pushed her away. "I still can't accept it. He's gone. Really gone," said Tori shaking her head as she looked at him. "And Edward; he's gone too."

Jean spoke then to Marie, "Cisco saved my life. Duval turned early, and the doctor told me that before he could do anything, my second acted. His shot hit Edward just as he was going to shoot me in the back. If not for your man's action and quick thinking... His aim was excellent. Never knew he could shoot like that. I would say he aimed to kill too."

Marie looked over toward Edward's body and frowned. "Seems Duval asked for it, if'n you ask me." Tori was shocked by the coldness in her voice, and then for the first time, she thought about another woman who would be affected by the news. Simone would have to be told, and her reaction would be anyone's guess. "Who's going to inform Simone?" she asked no one in particular.

"No one," answered Marie. "Ain't no need." Again, Tori was stunned by the coldness of Marie's voice.

Tori knew the young woman suffered greatly by the loss of Cisco but was still surprised at how cold she seemed to be about it all.

"Well, someone has to. Jean? Someone has to tell her."

Marie looked at Tori and shook her head sadly. "Ain't possible. Afore I came here, I learned that she was found in her garden. Dead."

It was Jean's turn to be stunned now. "Are you sure?"

"Yes, em. Best folks can make out is Simone fell from the balcony above. Found her all covered up with bed covers. Her head on a pillow, and no one saw the iron sticking out her chest till they took those covers off. It looked like she was sleeping in bed, they said. Her face was messed up some too. Not from the fall, I was told. No, it came from his hands," she pointed at Edward's body. "He beat her somethin' awful. Peoples say how they heard the two fightin' real loud, her screamin' at him; then it went real quiet. No one would have thought much or found her so soon if'n it hadn't been for a nosy housemaid next door."

Marie looked at her Cisco and then back at Jean. "My man did what he came back to do. Nothin', you could have done to change it. That Edward was dead set on killin' you, just like he killed his wife. My Cisco, he can rest now. His job is done. But yours," she said, looking at Tori, "is not over."

Jean placed his arm around his wife, feeling the fear that swept over her. "Just what do you mean by that? What do you know, Marie? What does my lady have left to do?"

"That's up to her. Her destiny is her own choice. I can't help no more. I'll be taking care of Cisco. You two take care of each other." She turned away from them and, looking at Thiac, spoke softly. "You pick him up for me and put him in my carriage. Then you ride with me. You too, Mr. Grymes. The horses are needed elsewhere for another journey." She did not wait for anyone or would she answer any questions. Marie walked behind Thiac, who gently carried Cisco's body to the carriage as if he were a sleeping child.

John looked at Jean and then kissed Tori on the cheek. "Take all the time you need. You know where I am when you are ready." He shook Jean's hand and followed the others.

The doctor, who had remained silent up until now, added his words of help. "I'll take Edward's body back with me. You two take the advice of your friends and spend a little time together." He bowed slightly to them. "Madame, Monsieur Laffite." With that, he walked away, calling to the two slaves to assist him.

Tori looked at Jean and, not wanting to remain there a second longer, simply stated, "Let's ride."

For an hour, they walked the horses slowly, talking of all the good memories they each had of their friend and the way he had affected their lives. Then suddenly, Jean stopped his horse, looking at his lady quizzically.

"Tori, where is it you want to go?"

"Home Jean. I want to go home and be with you."

THERE was no funeral for Cisco. Marie chose instead to bury him in a safe and secret spot known only to herself and Thiac. No one questioned her or her reason behind her decision, even though it had seemed irrational. As far as the citizens of New Orleans were concerned, the handsome young gentleman had suffered an accident and, as per his wishes, had been buried quietly.

JEAN and Tori had been home for several hours when John Davis stopped by. Tori had sent word that they wished to see him and that it was necessary. The note had added that he was the only person allowed to visit until further notice.

The room was quiet, and a chill was in the air. Jean set about building a log fire and keeping an eye on his wife, who had been very quiet. She sat in a chair, sipping a glass of wine, and paid no attention to him or what he was doing. It was into this somber atmosphere that Davis walked.

The door had opened slowly, and the expected guest stepped into the room. Per his request, Bessy did not announce his arrival because he understood both his friends would be in deep mourning.

Jean had his back to the door, and Tori was sat in a chair; her eyes were closed, but judging by her tapping finger, Davis knew she was not asleep. The room was silent, and for a second, he almost turned to leave. However, putting off the inevitable would not stop the pain they all would feel for a long time to come. "Tori, Jean, please excuse the interruption, but I received your message and thought it wise to come straight away."

Jean turned to face their friend, and Tori opened her eyes, but neither spoke a word. Davis felt the need to break the ice and spoke up. "I am aware of the outcome of this afternoon's duel. There is no need to go into details, but I share that the result has hit me hard. Not as hard as you my dear." He looked at Tori, who had begun once again to silently let tears slip down her cheeks. If there was one thing he did not deal with graciously, it was a woman crying. "I shall miss him, you know, always will, but life has to progress, and I intend to work through the loss. The Opera house is going to be a hit, and I intend to take it on the road. Not the house Jean," he had seen the man's surprised and puzzled look. "The troupe those who I hire, will make a fine company. We shall endeavor to educate the public about the beauty of the..."

"John, please, no small talk." It was Tori who interrupted him as she wiped the tears off her face. "I am sorry, but the tears just come, and I can't stop them. Jean, I think maybe another glass of something stronger will help numb my broken heart a bit. He was like a brother... my friend... our friend, and did you know he had found love?" She let a small laugh escape her as she added, "He was so... so Cisco about it. That poor girl."

John interrupted her, "I was aware of the young lady in question and took it upon myself to address her father about the sad

218

circumstances before I came here."

"Oh, God! You didn't tell them he got shot at the duel, did you? We are telling those who need to know that he had an accident and…"

"Tori, please don't upset yourself. I was told by Marie what to say, and that was that. There is to be no service, no mention of his final resting place, and that's as it should be. He had told me before the battle if anything happened, that's what he wanted."

Jean handed Davis and Tori a drink and then picked up his glass. Raising it, he attempted to smile slightly. "To Cisco, who always did have a way of doing things that made me smile. I may never have understood him, but he was our friend, and he did well. He saved my life, and I owe him a debt of gratitude. Therefore, I will abide by his wishes as will my lady, won't you?"

Tori nodded her head and took several large swallows of the liquor Jean had handed her. "I don't think I could visit his grave right now if I wanted to. It's just too unreal to know he is gone. I need to keep busy like you, John, to keep my mind off all the sadness. The pain will ease; I know this, but damn, it's hard. Now there is just you that I can talk to."

Davis raised his eyebrow and began to say something, but Tori stopped him.

"Oh, right, Cisco said neither of you would talk about the future or engage in any more adventures to keep history on track." She finished her drink and stood up. "Forgive me, but I think I need to be alone right now."

Jean put his glass down and walked to her side. "My love, whatever you wish for, whatever you need to do, just ask, and I will see to it."

"I know you will. I have some decisions to make, and right now, neither of you can help me. So, if you will excuse me, I shall retire for the night." She turned to leave and stopped. "Damn it; I sound like I should, like one of…" she choked back tears once more. "Cisco hated it when I acted so proper sounding when there was no need. I am pissed off, hurt, angry, and very sad, but I am not beaten, nor am I going to continue acting this stupid part of a lady." She turned to face the men. "I am going to our room; I want to be alone. No one, not even Bessy, is to disturb me. Jean, you can come up later. You, I want and need. Sort out your business with John, and then bring a bottle up. I plan on fucking drowning my sorrows." With that said, she left the room, and Jean refilled the men's glasses.

Davis sat down and spoke to Jean. "She is taking this hard, but she is a survivor, Jean. I know that, and so do you. So, what is it you need to discuss?"

"I need advice, my friend, and as you are the only person who can understand Tori and know how she feels, you being from the same time, maybe you can help me. After this, I give my word that I will not mention another word about your origins."

"Word given and taken. One last time then, how can I help?"

THE weeks had slipped slowly by. The days were filled with meetings with Livingston and Grymes, who were trying to restore all that had been confiscated from the Laffites. Both Dominique and Pierre spent hours with Tori and Jean, waiting and hoping for their ships, what was left, to be returned, along with some of the goods and gold. Other meetings with Grymes concerned Leone's will and the claim of ownership of the Duval properties. For days Jean and Tori had talked about just what should be done with the plantation now that both Edward and Simone were gone. The temptation to remain in New Orleans and take possession of the plantation was strong. Then one night, knowing how he felt and wanting to please his lady, Jean asked her the one burning question he had. "History could be rewritten slightly, couldn't it?"

"I don't know, Jean. You are asking me to explain and expand on something that I have no idea about. I have asked myself over and over since Cisco's death, just what is my responsibility toward history." She was twisting a gold chain around her finger as she talked, pulling on the cherished locket, sliding it back and forth."

Did his death change anything? Was he meant to return, and by not doing so, has it all changed, our time that is? Or was he meant to die here, and by not returning, everything is as it should be?" Tori's tear-filled eyes looked at the man she loved, and gently she whispered her question hoping it would not hurt him. "Did our son have to die, and Leone, did he have to die to keep history on track, I ask you? Am I supposed to stay or go? I just don't know anything anymore."

Her tone of voice had a touch of anger to it. Then to add to her emotions, the chain around her neck snapped. The golden clasp had given way to her sharp tugging. Now her voice was filled with dismay and upset. "Oh Jean, look what I have done. It's broken," she cried. The locket was in her tightly clasped fist, with its chain dangling free, as she held it out toward him. "I don't even know what I'm doing, let alone what I'm saying." She was devastated and broken. The damn had finally burst, and all the bottled-up emotions flowed free at last. She broke down and cried. Cried for her lost friend, for her love of Jean, for herself, and for the decision she knew she had made.

"I'm sorry, my love. I never meant to assume that you held the answers. Look," he said, taking the locket from her. "Surely this is a symbol? I can have it repaired for you. That is a simple task. I can, if you allow me, mend that which is tearing you apart. Talk to me, Tori." Jean lifted her chin, and with his thumb, he wiped her wet cheeks.

She looked at him through her tears and tried to explain, but her tears came too fast to allow her to utter more than a few words. "I've..." she sobbed, "got to decide." She shook her head from side to side. How could she tell him? How could she do it?

"Tori, listen to me. Please let me help you. Maybe together we could decide whatever it is, one way or the other. Or have you already decided?" he asked her with a look of wisdom in his eyes.

He knew her so well. She should have guessed she could not hide it from him. For days, she thought her upset was well disguised, but now the ruse was up. "Hold me close; I need you to hold me; I need your strength."

Jean pulled her into his grasp and held her tightly. After a few seconds, he whispered into her ear. "Even in your sleep, you toss and turn like a ship in troubled seas. What is it, my lady? Come, tell me."

Tori knew the time was now. She could not delay any longer. "I want to go to Leone's house." She took a deep breath and added, "I need to go. That's the only way we will know if we should settle there or not, don't you see?"

He did indeed see. It was not just the house that was on her mind, though; it was the lake as well. That was the haunting memory that lurked deep behind her eyes. That was the only thing that had and would ever come between them, and it was time to face it. "Are you sure it's just the house and not something more that calls to you?" he asked her knowingly.

"I can't fool you, can I? No, it's not just the house, though that is a big part of it. It's the lake and the time door. I asked you years ago to help me return to it. You gave me your word, Jean." She pulled back from him. Her eyes pleaded with him for understanding. "I made myself a promise. I made my family and my daughter a promise. I have to keep that, don't you see? I have to try."

He pulled her close to him. Fear raced in his heart at the thought that he could lose her forever, should she succeed and return to her own time. But Cisco had not gone back, and Davis was still here; there was no reason to believe that the door worked both ways. However, he had to do what was right. "I am a man of my word. You know that. We will leave as soon as can be arranged, and one way or the other, we will face whatever awaits us together."

She could hear the pain and hurt in his voice. It killed her to think that he thought it was easy for her to try and leave him, to go back. She was caught in a living hell, for she now found herself genuinely torn between two worlds and two lives.

"Jean, can't you see? How can I make you understand? Whether

I'm to leave for Galveston and the islands with you or live on the plantation with you, it does not matter. What matters is that I have to do this. So, if I do sail off with you, it is with my heart clear and my promise kept. Cisco's death made me realize that life is too short and too precious to treat lightly. I have to live with my conscience. I made a promise to try to return to my daughter, and you made me a promise once to help me. We can't go on until we have both kept our word."

God help him, he did understand, and he knew as she did that it was the last obstacle in their way. Nothing else could or would ever come between them. It had to be done; his only prayer was that she failed, and he got to keep her with him. If that was wrong, so be it. He would gladly live with it.

MARCH was into its third week by the time the arrangements had been handled and legal documents sorted out. Grymes had drawn up official documents showing Jean Laffite as the new owner of the Duval plantation and properties. The court and its judge had hardly spent any time in its decision once Leone's last will had been presented. For Jean and Tori, it was a bittersweet victory. Neither celebrated nor admitted the apprehension they felt growing inside. They both secretly wondered how long they would remain at the plantation together... for a few days or for a lifetime?

❧ Eight ☙

Leone's house and the surrounding grounds had not changed in all the years she had been away. Riding up to the front, Tori half-expected Kate to come bustling out, followed closely by a warm welcome from Leone himself.

The new overseer was there to meet them and assured them that he would do all he could to help make the transition an easy one. In return, Jean reassured him that his position was secure. According to Grymes, he had done an excellent job running the place. Together they had gone over the books carefully, and he had even interviewed those who worked in the big house, some of whom remembered Tori. All were only too happy to have the new Master and Mistress in the place. Their friendly greeting was strengthened by their continued willingness to make Jean and his wife feel right at home.

Jean talked with Kate's replacement about the stable and asked who was in charge there, along with many other questions he wanted answered. While he was engrossed in conversation, Tori slipped away and entered the house, making her way to the one room she felt she had to face alone. Without hesitation, she placed her hand on the door handle and pushed it open.

The room was the same for the most part. The carpet in Leone's study had been changed because it had been impossible to remove the bloodstains, but his books and his desk sat just as he had left them. She touched the decanter of brandy and remembered the first time she had shocked him by asking him for a good stiff drink. A smile slid across her face. He had loved his brandy and enjoyed her company and their long evenings together.

So much had happened in such a short amount of time. She had run for her life with Leone's brother Edward, and the pain her disappearance had caused Leone remained with him, even after they found each other. Kate's death… Her eyes glanced to the spot on the floor where she had last seen her.

The monster was there too; Kane looked her way with his bashed-in face. The vision was vivid, and Tori blinked her eyes, telling herself that's all it was, a vision, a horrible memory, and then they were gone, but the room was cold. It had lost its warm and friendly feel, and now it represented a room of death and murder to her. A place where she had seen two people die. One she would always love. The other, she would forever hate. Here, she had killed a man and lost her mind while doing so. That was why Edward had fooled her so easily; she'd been in deep shock and not thinking clearly. If only Leone had returned instead of Edward, things might have changed completely. Maybe, Leone would have believed her and helped her find her way home. It was all too much to deal with.

Try another room, she thought; this one was not the best place to start after all. Tori ran into the hall, slamming the door behind her.

This would be the last time she would ever set foot in that room again, she told herself. But what of the rest of the house, was it going to bring terror or peace?

Walking toward another room in the house, her favorite place, helped her shake off the effects of the last one. There she experienced déjà vu. So many happy memories called to her. She could still see Kate in the kitchen and hear her humming the tune to Tommy's song.

She peeked into the dining room and was pleased to see nothing had changed at all. The room conjured memories of long dinners and gentle talks, fine food, and always the wines that proved to be spectacular and from so many different countries in Europe. Tori walked out of the dining room and into the grand hall.

There was the staircase, where she had made her first debut as a southern lady. The stairs she learned to master in the long gowns… these were happy times, filled with fond memories. But still, other darker times lurked behind each turn. She left the hall and went through the kitchen, stopping for a few seconds to look in Kate's bedroom. It was as if she had never left, and the new housekeeper was like her predecessor and kept the area neat and tidy.

Stepping outside from the kitchen and into the garden, Tori looked at the pathway that led to the gazebo. It reminded her of her first encounter with Edward. Facing the front of the house, she looked at the trail leading to the slave quarters. This only brought back images of the brutal, sick man, who had called himself an overseer.

Kane had been nothing more than a racist, murdering pig and a cruel bastard to the slaves. "Probably one of the best things I ever did was making sure you were dead," she said aloud before turning back into the kitchen.

The house held ghosts, both good and bad. She did not fear them, yet neither did she want to face them.

It would always be Leone's plantation, and if she remained in this time with Jean, she wondered if she could ever live within its walls? Even if everything were different, the lake would always be there, calling to her like it was right then. She could not live her life always drawn to its shoreline, and that is what would happen.

Sadly, Tori could not lie to herself about that. She would never stop trying to go back; she'd keep going to the lake as long as it was within her reach. How could she not, she asked herself? Who would ever understand that? How would she keep her longing away from Jean? He had to be protected and not know that his wife was always harboring the desire to stand by the lake and wait for the chance to leave. There was not a single person she could talk to about this, and she knew it.

The lonely female, who had so much to live for, intended to keep her word and visit the spot while they were here… but only when she was ready. She had to be sure that it was what she wanted. After all, if she stepped back into time and left Jean behind… could she live without him? Maybe the lake would offer the answer. If nothing happened, she would leave this place behind forever. It would be the only solution to the problem. If the lake did not take her home, she would be with Jean, begin a new life, and never feel so lonely or helpless again. With the lake not sending her home, she would be free to depart this plantation, knowing she'd kept her word. Tori would sail away with Jean but not to the Texas coastline; no, she'd ask him to take her to the islands, and there they would settle together.

Jean came inside, and Tori met him, smiling for the first time in days. "I think I had better show you around, and then we can sit down and eat. Did I ever tell you about the first time I came down to eat dinner with Leone?"

She was laughing and telling him the story again. He did not mind. Seeing her spirits lift made the story fresh and new for him. By the time they retired for the night, the house had a warmer feeling, and Tori wondered if she hadn't been too hasty earlier in thinking about leaving and not making it their home. Her last thought after closing her eyes was simple and offered a solution to her conundrum. It could be the amount of wine she had with dinner and the after-dinner drinks on top of that while she continued to tell the stories of plantation life and how she'd handled it all. The wine had clouded her thoughts, or had it cleared them? Morning would tell.

TORI had wanted to delay the trip to the lake for a few days, and Jean saw no problem in doing so. He, like his wife, was not sure he would ever be ready to go there. The few days, however, soon turned into four weeks.

There were many excuses: She wanted to ride around the land and show him all that Leone had shown her. Then she had wanted to change a few things in the main house and the slave quarters.

The old slave woman who had once worked in the big house and then lived in the quarters was gone. Another had taken her place as the healer, and it was her who told them that the older woman had died in her sleep. She had been buried in the slave graveyard, and

Tori had visited it with Jean. Once there, it brought back memories of Missy and her death, and looking at the old wooden markers, she shuddered. In her mind, it was not right that they were buried and forgotten. "Jean, can we have a fence put around here and get some gravestones, proper ones, for those buried here? Oh, and a building, a church for them and a meeting place, would not cost much and would mean a lot to them."

Jean smiled at her. "Always thinking of the ways to make amends for owning slaves, but I love you for it." I will see to it that this area is made as you want, you can help oversee it, and yes, a small building can be built over there." He pointed to an area that was clear of brush and halfway between the quarters and the graveyard. "It is a compassionate idea, and I agree. As long as we own slaves, and we will own them, setting them free would cause many problems, and as long as you understand that… we will treat them well, and any ideas you have, we will see to it that if they are not too out of the norm, they are met. I think that will keep you happy and all who work for us."

"You do have a memory, don't you? While we are at it, can we have some trees planted between the slave cabins? It will help keep them cooler in summer and, oh, maybe give them a bit of land for growing vegetables and such. Using the space between the cabins is not enough."

Jean laughed and pulled her to him. "I think you have many plans that will keep us busy, and may I say, they all, so far, will improve the plantation and everyone's lives. Come let's pay a visit to the Overseer's cabin, and you can tell me again what you want done there." He was happy because, to Jean's thinking, his wife was making an effort to have the plantation more of a home and not just a place where they would make money off the land. In his mind, Tori was leaning toward staying at the plantation with him regardless of what her history said he did. So, her actions and requests could mean she had no intention of leaving? He prayed they did, but he would not push her for an answer.

Little did Jean know all her projects were merely delaying tactics. Each idea took time to fulfill, and then, just when she thought she could not put it off going to the lake any longer, the weather changed, and wind-driven rain poured down, followed by a freezing cold snap. It was far easier to stay warm and safe by the fire with Jean, avoiding the subject, than it was to set a firm date for their lakeside visit.

As the days warmed up, Jean spent time with the Overseer, and Tori took the chance to visit the garden Leone had built for his wife. It was not a place that she wanted to share with anyone, not even Jean. All Tori wanted was to see the magical place and try to recall the happy days spent in the gazebo. While she visited beyond the walls, Tori slowly came to terms with what she needed to do.

The garden was changed; Edward had seen to that. The gazebo was torn down, and the small pond that surrounded it was nothing more than a muddy space. The stream that had fed the pond like moat had found another way to travel among the grand old trees. The stone bridge stood but was no longer needed. Tori turned away from the sad view.

Some of the gardens had been taken care of, but most had been left to grow wild. It was not the same wondrous place, and like the garden, she was changed. Edward had done that too. Tori was not the same woman who walked here with Leone, nor would she ever be the same again.

Realizing that nothing remains the same, she told herself the time had come, at last, to follow through with her promise. When she closed the wooden door and turned the lock, Tori knew in her heart she would never see beyond the wooden door or the high stone wall again. What was done was done, and it all belonged in the past. Now it was time to see where she belonged, in the future with Linni or in the past with Jean? As she walked back toward the house, Tori set a date in her mind. The clock had begun ticking, and soon, she would ask Jean to keep his word. Not right then, but very shortly, she would return to the lake.

FINALLY, with May upon them, the sun came out, and the whole world seemed to awaken from its long winter sleep. Spring filled the air, and with it came the time for them both to decide what was to be done. The planting season would soon be upon them, and decisions had to be made. Was this their home or not? Did they plant a crop or leave and sell? As much as he hated to push her, Jean had to know.

Laffite knew she was again having nightmares, and she would often call out for her daughter. His wife never said if she recalled these dreams, and he dared not ask her for fear of upsetting her. Tori was not sleeping, and eating had become a battle. It was because of this new state of affairs that Jean understood they could no longer delay making a decision. If his love was having a hard time trying to tell him it was time, he was going to make it easier for her. Jean loved her too much to watch her struggle, and as much as he wished they could just leave, he knew that would never happen. The clock had just stopped ticking; time had arrived to visit the lake, whether he wanted to or not.

THAT first trip to the lake had been the most challenging trip of his life. He had awakened her long before dawn and gently told her that he had their horses waiting for them. Tori had not said a word, just reached out and clung to him. That morning, the look on her face would stay with him for the rest of his life. Her expression held both anticipation and hope. Each emotion tore at her, filling her eyes with fear and filling Jean's heart with sorrow.

For two days, they had arrived at the lake before dawn, leaving the warmth of the house and traveling the short distance to the water's edge. They sat that first day together, looking and waiting, both so tense that neither dared talk. That night they had finally spoken about the event, and for the first time, they admitted that it was doubtful that Tori would ever see her way back to her own time again. Still, she had asked to go back. Tori could not explain it; she just had to go. Yet again, nothing happened, and again late into the night, they talked and held each other close. One thing had become clear to them; she could not make the plantation their home because the lake beckoned her, teased her, with the invite to try and see if there was a way to Linni. It would always call to her, and the pain was more than she could handle.

They arrived just as the sun was rising over the horizon on the third day. At first, they sat in silence, but then Jean stood and walked to the water's edge. He did not look back at Tori but spoke while scanning the lake before him. "Tori, maybe you are doing this wrong. From everything you have told me, I think you need to be either in the water or at least have your feet in the shallows." He turned to look at her, trying to keep a blank look. He raised one eyebrow as if asking a question as he waited for her response to his question.

"I see what you are saying, and it could be that. I just don't know."

Jean walked back to her and sat down. He pulled her closer and waited a few seconds before continuing. "Maybe you don't want to know because you don't wish to leave me. I thought a lot about this and if it's alright with you if something does happen, if the happening begins... I want to come with you. This way, you won't fear leaving me, nor I you."

She pulled free of him and began to respond, but he put his finger on her lips. "Wait, hear me out. As I said, I thought about this and about what Cisco always said. John, too, agreed with Cisco. What if the crossing takes you back further, or you turn up years ahead of when you left? You would be lost in one time or another without me. So, let me come with you. There is nothing here for me and most certainly nothing without you. What do you think?"

Tori smiled gently and then looked out toward the water. "I had not thought about you coming; after all this is your time, here and now."

"It is, but I have kept history, your future history, on track, have I not? Why then should I have to remain here?"

"I see your point, and yes, I would love it if you too came along. There will be problems, your I.D., the fact that you don't exist in my time... guess we can find a way around that. Nothing is impossible, and who would believe us if we told them the truth? You could come back to L.A. with Linni and me, and we could begin there... it could work out. Yet..."

"What is it? You seem troubled, and here I thought I had the perfect solution. At least it solved my dilemma of losing you."

"It's Texas, and you setting up there. If you come with me, then you won't go where history said you did and that in itself can change things. Who knows what the consequences would be if you don't do that? Plus, if you come with me, well, maybe that would change my destination, our destination... it's all so confusing, and I am torn, Jean."

"I see that, my love, and it's the last thing I want for you. If I am to stay here at your request, I will let you go... I gave you my word, and I intend to keep it. Let's say that if something starts to happen, we will decide at that moment..." He lay back, looking at the sky, and said nothing more.

Tori was more than upset and had had enough of the lake for one day. What she wanted was to go back to the plantation and have breakfast and forget for a few hours about the terrible decision she would have to make. Now that her mind was made up, she lay back next to Jean and briefly looked up at the sky, then closed her eyes.

Jean looked toward her and could tell his love was indeed suffering, so he decided to change the subject and take her mind off her dilemma by fishing for more information about her time while he still had her with him. "Tori?"

"Yes, what?"

"You have told me many times the story of how you came here and this campground you stayed at. We know how close the big house is to here... what I am wondering is this, was it there in your time, the house that is?"

Tori sat up and looked from the lake to the area behind them. "No, it was not there that I am aware of. Many of the plantations did not last the test of time. Linni and I took tours of Plantations along the River Road over the years. We saw Oak Alley and Nottoway, that one is huge, but both were built later than now; I don't recall when. I did not see Ormond, but I did get to see Destrehan. It was being refurbished when we briefly saw it. I never told you that did I? Or did I? Come to think of it, until now, I did not recall driving by the place. I have not thought about it in so long. So much has changed in my time from what it is now. Can we talk about this back at the house? I am ready to go." She reached out her hand, and he grasped it tightly.

"You are saying you don't want to go..."

"I'm saying, I want to go to the house for now. We will talk more later." She looked at the lake, then turned to leave. "Nothing is happening as far as I can tell, and right now, I feel I have more to think over. Much of what you said has me thinking. Let's just go, can we?"

TOGETHER they had decided to try one last morning, and if nothing happened, they would ride back to New Orleans. They would begin their lives free at last of any guilt. Jean would have kept his word, and Tori would know that she had done all she possibly could to reach her daughter. They would sell the plantation and use the money to start a new life in the islands. If by doing that, history was changed and the world learned what happened to the Gentleman Pirate Jean Laffite, then so be it. That future world would no longer be of any concern to either of them.

THE morning had been warmer than the last two, with the promise of an early summer hanging in the air. It was still crisp enough for her to wrap a blanket around her shoulders in the pre-dawn hours as she sat gazing out over the calm water. This time, they had left the horses on the other side of the brush and tree line at her request. Maybe, she thought, if the cove were just as it had been, void of any animal, then perhaps something would happen. As she sat there peacefully, her mind wandered with both sad and happy memories until one thought took hold of her. This would be the last time she'd ever gaze upon the mirror-like surface. The last time she would torture herself with 'what if?'

Daybreak had come and gone. The hours had slipped by until she could no longer deny the inevitable. Tori reached for his hand, and without looking at him, she stood up. "Jean, I need a few minutes alone." Slowly she walked to the edge of the water, and then she looked back at the man she would spend the rest of her life with. "Please, I need to say goodbye, this one last time." The blanket slipped off her shoulder, and she let it fall to the ground, not giving it a second thought.

Jean stood up and smiled gently. "I understand, Tori; you can take all the time you need. I will be with the horses until you are ready and my lady, know this, I love you and promise I will always do so." He did not wait for a response; it was difficult enough what she was doing. The tears filling her eyes told him such, but for him, joy filled his soul. Her words rang in his ears and his heart. His prayers had been answered, and he swore to God that he would spend the rest of his days loving her and making her happy. However, Jean was no fool; he knew that a part of her was grieving, and he wished that he could ease her pain. Guilt flooded him as he realized what his happiness was costing her. "Are you sure? If you wish to try again tomorrow, I am willing."

"No, there is no need. I could come here every day for the rest of my life. I could grow old and gray sitting here, waiting. Waiting for what, I ask you? Waiting for something that may never happen. Hell, I don't even know what it is I'm supposed to be looking and waiting for."

"Jean, go to the horses. Like I said, I just need a bit of time alone. I have to say goodbye in my own way. Then, we will leave for the city. We will go today and never look back." Her voice had trembled on these last few words, and he wanted to take her in his arms and tell her everything would be all right. Instead, he turned slowly away. She needed time alone, and maybe he did too. The pirate did not say a word, nor did he look back at her as he walked away. She was right, and he knew it. The most he could do for her at that moment was to give her the time she asked for and then never leave her side again.

Tori knew he had gone; she did not need to look. The sound of his footsteps crunching the earth as he walked had faded quietly away. Shortly after that, she could hear his voice softly calling to the horses off in the distance. The world was hers. The lake and all it held was hers, but she had not unlocked its secret. What had she expected anyway, she wondered? Sadly, she raised her head and looked out over the mist-covered shoreline of the cove she knew so well. Then she saw it, one white feather floating on the sparkling surface. Mesmerized, she watched it, and her thoughts raced back in time. So much had happened in the years since her arrival. Some of those times slipped her memory while others flashed vividly in her mind's eye.

When Jean had the fever, Marie had saved him. She had arrived, and when she agreed to help, the first thing she did came to Tori's mind. Like a movie playing in her mind, the image played out. Marie Laveau placed a cross on the bedside table, and a small candle was lit. Incense burned, and a large white feather was used to fan the smoke from the burning bundle of sage while prayers were spoken. Then in Creole, incantations were mumbled. It was symbolic, maybe more, whatever it had meant; she had believed the voodoo queen would save Jean.

This image vanished, followed by another. Jean had lived, but their son had not. Without wanting to, Tori saw another memory play out clearly. It was Marie standing, holding Christopher in her arms. Her voice rang in her mind. "If I were to tell you that I thought he will survive, I would be lying." Tori shuddered at the cruel memory, and then suddenly, she understood the meaning behind the feather!

The candlelight and the white feather were there to guide her loved ones. Cisco had had a white feather given to him by Marie. Maybe if he had not lost it, the feather would have guided him and kept him safe. They had helped bring Jean's soul back to her from the brink of death. The candle and feather were supposed to do the same for their son; bring him safely home to them. Instead, his tiny soul did go home, home to heaven.

Home! What a haunting word. For years she had thought of nothing else but going home to Linni. Now, as she stood there watching the feather float by, she wondered, could it be telling her that she was home after all. That for whatever reason, she was destined to spend the rest of her life with the man she loved and believe that her daughter was, would be, taken care of? A lump formed in her throat, and she swallowed hard. "Linni," she whispered. "Forgive me, but I did try, and I will never forget you. I will always love you, always."

The feather floated to the water's edge, and she smiled. Marie had been right when she told her that a sign would guide her. One last look, and then it would be finished. Her eyes looked up from the shoreline and across the expanse before her. However, unlike other mornings, the distant water was shrouded in mist, hiding its mystery underneath the glass-like surface. The sun was warm on her shoulders, and she stood deadly still, watching the swirling mist. Tears were filling her eyes, and though she understood the time had come to leave, she couldn't. It was as if something or someone was holding her there, but why? Tori moved one step closer and stood there looking at the view beyond but not paying full attention to what was going on before her. Her mind was filled with daydreams and images of all that had been and all that might be.

The time had arrived for the big farewell, the departing of one life, to move on to another; she understood that, but Tori felt as if she owed Linni and her family more. She owed them her prayers and her hope that they, too, could be happy and go on with their lives. They would never know what happened to her, as she would never know what happened to them, and it tore at her heart.

Tears ran down her cheeks, and silently she allowed them to fall. It was so peaceful and still; just what she wanted and needed to gather her strength to depart. Her tears would stop soon, and she would step away; she would go to Jean, and he would help her deal. He would be all the strength she needed. He was all she needed; he was the love of her life.

Tori was so deep in her thoughts that she almost missed it. Then it registered; the silence was deafening! The sensation hit her as surely as if a hand had struck her. "It's happening!" was all she could mutter to herself. Without thinking about what she was doing, her hands started tearing at her clothes. Tori knew she had to return the same way for some strange reason. The voice in her head told her, and she listened and acted without another thought. "I need to be naked. It has to be exactly the same," she told herself out loud. Her top came off in seconds, followed by first one boot and then the other.

Falling over, she pulled at her riding pants, which slid down and off faster than she could ever have thought possible. Now naked, she stood facing the lake, hesitating briefly. To wait could cost her the one chance she had. There was no choice but to try. So, she plunged in.

JEAN heard the splash. His head spun around, looking back toward the lake. He had covered quite a distance, walking the horses while waiting for his lady, but not so far that he couldn't hear her call or worse. There was no denying it; the splash could mean only one thing. His feet started moving before his mind told him he was running.

THE water was freezing at first; the shock of its frigid hold almost took her breath away, but still, she swam out toward the center of the lake, disappearing into the fog as she went.

Tori took long slow strokes, digging into the tranquil frigid depths with her arms and kicking hard with her legs. The icy cold stung her skin as her thoughts screamed at her, asking her just what in the hell she was doing?

The frightened woman swam harder when this happened as if trying to out-swim her own questions. Had she gone crazy? With water, this cold hypothermia would not take long to set in, and then what?

JEAN ran for all he was worth, his heart pounding from both fear and exertion. Somehow in between breaths, he was able to call out Tori's name; over and over, he called. To him, he traveled at a snail's pace, and no matter how hard he tried to speed up, the slower he seemed to go.

The lake was just over the small ridge, and it seemed to take forever to climb. He just couldn't get there fast enough. The cove where he had left Tori was just beyond the clearing, and without warning, Jean found himself standing at the exact spot.

At the lake, he found her blanket and clothes, but not her. The water was as still as it had been. Not a ripple or wave touched the shoreline. If anyone were out there swimming, the calmness would have been disturbed. Jean looked all around him, and upon not seeing a sign of Tori, he looked back at the lake and the fog that blocked his view.

It was in that one horrible earth-shattering second that he knew and at that moment, the only sound roaring through the heavens, like thunder on a summer's storm, was his cry of agony and loss.

SHE had just made her mind up to turn around and go back when she heard her name being called from what seemed like a great distance away. One long agonizing scream of Jean's voice carried on the breeze, swirling like the mist around her, fading fast as the slight wind itself died. Then silence.

She reasoned that he must have heard her, but she could not risk what little energy she had left in her freezing body to return his call. Tori turned instead and swam back into the mist-covered waters, heading toward him and safety.

Her strokes were long and slow, but instead of feeling her body weaken as she thought it would have, instead of the numbing freeze of icy water, she found tepid water hitting her face. Gone was the chill of the air in her lungs. Now, each breath she took filled her chest with warm, muggy air. Her legs hit bottom, scraping her knees on the sand. Still, the mist blocked her view, and it continued to do so until she stood up.

Deep down, she already knew what she would see, and as she emerged above the mist line, what greeted her eyes took her breath away.

As if in a daze, she walked out of the shallow water toward the small cove where Jean should have been standing. Instead, however, was a robe, bikini, and a coffee mug. Her head started spinning as she cautiously walked toward the objects, knowing as she did so just what they were and where she was.

Tori reached down, her hand trembling as she picked up her bikini and began to put it on. Her fingers were shaking so bad that she had trouble tying the strings. Next, Tori picked up her robe, knocking her coffee cup over. It went rolling over on its side, and she stood looking at it. No one had taken her robe; no woman had stolen it... as she recalled seeing all those years ago. Everything was just where she had left them. While looking at the cup, she unconsciously took the wet bandana from around her neck. It had slipped free of her head while swimming, and rather than have it where it now lay; she untied it.

Then a sudden realization hit. Tori knew instinctively she was being watched, and she knew who was watching her. Slowly she turned to look out over the lake, and there, way out, nearly in the middle looking back at her, was a lone swimmer. By some quirk in time, she found that she was looking back at herself for a brief second.

Frightened by this realization, Tori turned away and put the robe on. Her long hair she pulled up and out from under the garment, and then taking the bandana, she tied her long, wet hair up off her shoulders. Then Tori stooped and picked up the mug. It was easy to ignore the call for help, as she knew what would happen. No one was going to drown, and she was not about to mess with whatever the time loop tossed her way. One last look was all she would take, and a quick one at that.

The mist had closed in, and the image of the woman was gone. The Tori she had just seen in the lake had only just begun her journey, while this, Tori... herself, had come full circle. Ready or not, she was back, and by some strange fluke, time in this reality had stood still, or she had been lucky enough to return just about the time she left. It was all far too confusing, but one thing was a given, Linni was in the camp cabin... her daughter was within her grasp.

SHE did not know how she walked toward the cabin or how she looked when Dan saw her coming toward him. Tori would always remember him looking at her as if he were seeing a stranger and of how she sat and talked to him for hours, trying to explain what had happened. Nor would she ever forget the moment she was able to prove to him that it had not been a dream.

WHEN he had seen her walking toward him, he had been only too happy to assist her in her demands. Tori had begged to go to his cabin first and that no one was to know she was there. Thinking something awful had happened and that she could even be sick, he had agreed to tell Tori's friend that she would meet up with Linni and them later at the lake's beach. Once that had been taken care of, Dan had returned and sat for several hours listening to her talk. Tori did not go into huge detail, but she covered enough for him to look at her with a strange expression.

"So, that's when I saw you, and here I am, and God, oh dear Lord, what do I do now? How can I face anyone? Dan, please, you have to help me."

He looked at her lovingly and reached for her hand. "Look, there is a simple explanation to all this. Maybe you went down there for a swim, and with a hangover like you have, well, in all likelihood, you are still a bit under the influence. I think you fell asleep and had yourself one hell of a dream. Laffite was in it because Stirling talked about him last night, remember?"

"It was no dream, and I need to do something, tell someone about this, but who? If you won't listen and don't believe me, then… wait… I have it." Tori stood up and pulled the bandana she had on-off her head. It had been so early that morning that she had put her hair up and tied the bandana to keep it from falling. Until right then, she had forgotten about it. "Here, you go, look for yourself. This is just over five years of growth, and how the hell do you explain that if I am not telling the truth. No fucking dream can do this!"

Dan stood up and examined her hair, and stunned, he sat down. "I don't know what to think…"

"I do, and if that's not proof enough for you, look at this.

Remember I had a tan? Well, look, no more, tan!" She dropped her robe and stood to look at him with tears falling down her face. "See, I did not dream it. I lived it, and now I need to know what to do. What in the hell do I do, you tell me that?"

"Well, first off, I don't think you need to go telling anyone; think of Linni. Think of all the press and the nut jobs who will come out of the woodwork. Those will call you a liar and say this was all made up to get attention or money. They could even say you were the nut job and take Linni away from you. We need to protect you and your daughter. Until we can figure out just what to do, I think we need to hide this."

"How? Look, how do I hide this?" She lifted her long hair up.

"That's easy enough. Do you trust me?"

"I have no choice, do I? Oh God, I want to see Linni, I have missed her, and now… now I can't trust myself to see her and not fall apart."

"Tori, trust me, OK. I will go and get you some of your clothes. By the time I finish at the office, the girls should be down by the beach. If not, I will just flash my playboy smile, and your roommate will slip me something for you to wear, I am sure. Hopefully, that won't be the way it goes. Oh, and don't worry, I happen to have paid close attention to each outfit you wore since being here, so I know which room will be yours and what to grab. It may not match, but that won't matter. Tell me now about anything you really need, or you will have to wait till the friend gets back with your bags."

"Back where? I can't go anyplace."

"Tori, what do I need to grab besides an outfit? Concentrate here, and trust me, OK."

"Yes, Linni's Teddy Bear. He will be on the bed. She won't go any-place without him."

"One bear, done. It makes it easier to know which room is yours. Now, you stay here. Don't answer the door. Talk to no one. When I get back, you will dress while I go and get Linni. Then we will be on our way. No one will see you, and you won't have to talk to anyone.

Here, take this pen and write a note. Say I swept you off your feet, and we are flying home together, which is not a lie. I do happen to have a private plane at my disposal. I told you last night."

Tori frowned at him.

"Oh, right, last night was, what, five years ago? Guess this takes some getting used to. Look, you can tell Linni, your short hair was a wig, a joke. She will have to believe you, and when we get you home, you can get your haircut. After that, we will take it one day at a time, OK?"

"Really, you just came up with all this? You will do all that; you are going to help; why?"

"Call it a hunch, but I think we really connected last night. At least I did. For you, it's been a bit longer, I get that, but you felt it too, right? Hell, even if you didn't, I am not about to turn tail and run now. You are stuck with me, and we will sort this all out together. Are you with me?"

"I don't seem to have a choice, and you are right; we did have something special; I do trust you, and yes, I need your help. Just don't expect too much from me because I just don't know if I can ever…"

"You let me worry about that. Now, let's get things rolling. I might be gone a bit longer; I think it's best I check out and settle up at the office. That way, we can drive out of here, and no one will see you. If it helps, I will even settle up your bills, call it a gift, one that is supposed to buy me your confidence." He smiled, and his blue eyes squinted while he stood looking at her. He was thinking and added, "put in the note that you will call and talk in say around one today. That way, your girlfriend won't think I kidnapped you or something."

"Yes, that would help; she does tend to overreact. This is going to blow her away…"

"You do what you have to, and I will do my part. It's a long flight home, and that will give us plenty of time to talk." He hugged her and smiled. "I think maybe you can put your robe back on now. I do believe you, and after all, I am just a man who has fallen for the most complex woman one could ever imagine. Together we will get you through this; you have my word." He turned and left the cabin.

Tori put her robe back on and sat down on the couch. She was shaking uncontrollably. Jean… she had left Jean and would never know what happened to him. Her life was over, and yet it was not. She had returned home and would have to deal with it all. Dan was a lifesaver, and she knew she could trust him, but he would be asking questions, and how much should she tell him? Suddenly and without warning, Tori broke into a hysterical crying fit, and it seemed that it would never stop. She cried until there was nothing left but hiccups and a stuffy nose.

In a short time, this mother was going to hold her daughter in her arms once more, and that meant being strong. That meant no more tears, and as far as Dan, well, she would take that one step at a time.

❦ Nine ❧

New Orleans, Fall 1994

Tori realized the haunting memories of her past were still very much a part of her life. The harrowing experiences she had suffered before she married Dan had become a subject the two of them avoided. It was not her husband's fault, nor hers. It was just the end result of an agreement they had reached. The details about her' journey,' as they called it, were to be ignored because it was just easier that way. They had chosen to do nothing, tell no one, and move on with their lives.

However, for Tori, the incident was far from forgotten or ignored. Often, she found herself thinking about the years-long gone and those she had left behind. She lived each day, knowing her life was based on secrets and information—details that historians would love to know about. Dan was no historian, and maybe that was why it was easy for him to choose silence over anything else.

In the first weeks back, Tori had confided in him. He had heard her tell in detail the story of those five years and had asked many questions, never guessing the real torment his now-wife had been experiencing. Out of fear, love, and hurt, she had not told him the whole story, choosing instead to keep certain significant events to herself.

These events, which she referred to as her secrets, were the glue that stopped Tori from truly moving on with her life. She understood that, but for her to talk now and tell him everything could do more harm than not. Tori had grown to love Dan and hurting him was out of the question. On top of this guilt of holding back the rest of the story was another bit of information that constantly ate away at her very soul.

Dan thought he knew all about her' journey,' he most certainly understood that it dealt with the teen called Tommy. He, like Tori, knew Tommy from the campground, and both of them knew that from the very beginning, Tori wanted to contact him and tell him about Kate and Leone. However, Dan had advised her against revealing anything to anyone. His reasons had been valid back then, but now that she had the chance to contact Tommy again, valid had been tossed out the window.

If Tommy knew who he was and where he came from, Tori believed he could go on with his life without having questions about his adoption haunting him. Besides, she had given her word to Kate and even to Leone that she would talk to him if she ever had the chance. She had to tell him who he was, but that chance had never happened until now. Tori had not even sent him a letter or spoken to him on the phone.

After many arguments with her husband, Tori allowed him to think she had given up on the idea rather than run the risk of destroying their marriage. Dan's wife had bided her time, knowing the opportunity would present itself one day, and it had at last done just that.

So it was, on a summer's day, in the year 1994, Tori and her husband landed at New Orleans airport, both with different agendas. For Dan, it was to seal a deal and sign contracts, allowing him to begin building a flight department for an oil company. For Tori, it was to meet Tommy in person, without her husband finding out, and tell him what she knew. For her, there was no choice in the matter and once her mind was made up, going behind Dan's back to achieve her goal was, in her mind, justified. Tori just hoped that Tommy would believe her because all she had left since arriving back in her own time was a story, with no tangible evidence to prove any of what she went through was real. All shreds of evidence had faded with time and the only person in the world, who could corroborate that her journey back in time was valid, was her husband.

Discussing what she intended with her husband was not an option. Just as continuing to live, withholding information from Tommy was not an option either. She felt no shame in what she planned to carry out. In her heart, she knew that once her promise was fulfilled, there wasn't a scrap of doubt that her life would once again become her own. Her debts would be paid, and the past... her ordeal would finally remain buried, as it should.

ONCE they had arrived in the French Quarter, something buried deep inside Tori's soul stirred. When that happened, she knew she'd been right after all. There was no other explanation for all the emotions that flooded her mind and heart. She did not want to avoid any of it, not the sights, the memories, or the places she would recognize. Instead, she embraced the fact that she was back and on a mission.

Upon seeing the Cajun cottages, the narrow roads, and even while passing by the cemetery, she no longer feared the city because she believed her visit would not cause any harm. She was going to bring solutions to her plight and help a friend learn the answers he'd long been searching for.

THE entire flight, Tori's husband, had observed her closely. The woman he loved was strong, and she showed no sign of breaking down, but then she had not talked about anything to do with this move they were making. He had taken glances at her as he drove the rented car into the French Quarter. Though she was deep in her own thoughts, they did not seem to be upsetting her at all. Maybe, time had healed her wounds, and coming back to New Orleans was going to prove that.

After they turned off the highway and headed into the Quarter, there wasn't any chance to observe her without hitting someone or something. He had to go on her tone of voice and actions to guide him on how she was handling her emotions.

Dan was observing the roads. There were too many one-way streets for his liking. Too many pedestrians continuously thought they had the right of way, even when jaywalking. Add to that fact; that the town was packed with celebrating fans; he thought it better to drive slower than usual. "Here we go, turn Right onto St. Philip, that's what you said, and now we continue until we find Bourbon Street, right?"

"You got it. Just go slow; I have never seen it so crowded, and look, the idiots think the road is theirs to walk into. Crazy outfits, and will you look at the size of those drinks."

Dan laughed. "Party City, babe. Let the good times roll, remember?"

"Just don't roll over one of them, or our good times will be cut short."

"Come on, quit the teasing, and I promise to get us to our destination in one piece. One-way streets with people, taking their sweet ass time." Dan pushed the accelerator and moved across before the gathering party of tourists could hit the crosswalk.

"You realize you didn't come to a full stop just then. A California rolling stop won't work. I get why you did it, but let's not push our luck."

"Well, here's the next stop, and for you, see, we are not moving. Nothing is coming, so on we go." He was laughing. "Guess we had better get used to it. How's it looking your way?"

"You're fine, babe. You have plenty of time. There's nothing coming our way but people. I bet the locals stay out of the French Quarter when it's this crazy. I have a feeling we might do the same. I think this is the last stop sign before Bourbon Street."

"Well then, let's see if I remember your instructions." Dan moved the car forward and inched through the crowd to turn the vehicle onto Bourbon Street. "Left turn, onto Bourbon Street, then another sharp left, into the 'Lafitte Guest House' parking lot, which I will make as soon as this group walks on by. Here we go, up and over the sidewalk. Now, that was a smart maneuver, expertly handled, might I add. He turned off the engine and turned to look at his wife. "Told you I'd get us here in one piece, and to think you doubted me."

"Me? I didn't doubt you for a second, and you know it."

"Well, we have arrived, and I don't know about you, but I could use a stiff drink, and I'm starving."

"You are always starving," she joked. "Good thing this town is known for its food."

Tori, I have to ask you, and I promise I won't' bring it up again; I just have to know, are you OK? If this is all going to be too much, I can turn the job down, and we can remain in LA."

"You will not give up this job; besides, you don't have to. I am fine. Look, at first, on the drive from the airport, I did a lot of thinking, and I searched my mind and allowed myself to dredge up part of the journey and memories. They didn't bother me… not as I expected. We both know I have had a hard time dealing, and sometimes I wonder how you put up with me?"

"I love you, that's how."

"I know that I do; that's how I have managed to get my head together over the last few years. I think enough time has passed, and because we gave up dredging it up, what happened, well, it's just that… it's the past, and you know what?"

"What?"

"It's like it was all a dream. I am not even sure about certain facts and dates any longer. I may still have my down days and a few bad dreams, can't control them, but babe, I really do think this is going to work, and Linni is going to love it here. With you by my side, I can live anywhere, especially here." She leaned over and gave him a long kiss. "Now come on, I want to see if the room Stirling showed us is still the same. We may have lost contact with him, but we never forgot this place, and I am so excited we chose to stay here. Come on, I want to see it, and then I want to go out and find something to eat. I don't know about you, but a few drinks would be nice too."

It was just before six in the morning when Tori slipped out of bed. She found her robe on the fainting couch, as she called it, knowing full well that it was nowhere near one. The two-seater couch at the end of their bed was a beautiful touch and a convenient place to put their robes, but it was nothing like the authentic couches, nothing like her dear friend Marie's fainting couch. Tori quickly pushed the image of the woman to the back of her mind and told herself to concentrate on the now.

At least the room they were in had its own balcony, and because they had ordered this room, the one she had seen so many years ago, things were working out. Sitting inside to smoke was not a habit she liked. Besides, fresh air and a bit of time alone to clear the cobwebs would be good.

The room was dark due to the blackout curtains, but Tori knew it would be light enough for her to sit outside on the balcony by this time of the morning. Without disturbing her sleeping husband, she slipped into her robe before carefully searching to ensure the particular scrap of paper she had hidden away was secure.

She reached into her robe pocket and found the crumpled note with the phone number scribbled on it. Satisfied it was safe, she carefully made her way to the dressing table, where she remembered her pack of cigarettes and matches were waiting. Once she'd placed them in her other pocket, Tori slipped behind the closed curtains and apprehensively opened the balcony door. Gingerly she stepped out barefoot onto the wooden landing, leaving the door slightly open behind her. This was just in case her husband woke up and wondered where his wife had gone. Tori knew she'd hear him and could quickly let him know; she was just outside the room.

As she sat smoking her first cigarette of the day, Tori looked down Bourbon Street and could almost see where it met Canal Street. You could ride a trolley car just beyond Canal Street into the area now called the Garden District. It was there that many Americans had built their grand homes, beginning just before the Civil War. On the other hand, the Creoles and Cajuns had, for the most part, continued to expand in the opposite direction. She turned and looked the other way before sitting back down.

The 'Esplanade' was one prime example of this expansion, and yet, even that grand causeway had been infiltrated by 'outsiders,' as the locals referred to them. Some of the large old homes had been bought as investments over the years and now operated as bed and breakfasts. It was a lucrative endeavor, and as long as they kept the buildings to code and they maintained the look of a historical home, everyone seemed satisfied.

Tori had kept up with what was happening in New Orleans ever since she and Dan settled down in L.A. Tori had learned, in the years that followed the Civil War, the Crescent City and all her citizens had begun in earnest to blend old traditions and heal the wounds. Holiday celebrations, such as Mardi Gras, would emerge and gradually transform into a spectacular festival that let the good times roll. Once again, Tori smiled to herself and softly spoke the famous phrase in French. (*"Laissez les bon temp rouler."*) "Let the good times roll."

One tradition that had been forgotten was how New Orleans and the nation celebrated the victory of 'The Battle of New Orleans.' It was a national holiday right up until they decided to celebrate Independence Day on July 4th. She wondered how the populace of New Orleans had felt about that. They had lost the country's recognition of having been the only city to save the entire nation from British control and against all the odds at that.

The carriage she had heard approaching passed by where she was sitting. It did not even stop before crossing Bourbon Street. It just kept moving onward down the road. The horse's hooves, which had been plodding along slowly, began to pick up their pace. To make the animal move a bit faster, Tori had watched the driver raise the leather reins and flick them against the horse's rump.

It was then that echoes of a voice from long ago sounded in her head. She could hear her driver as clear as if he were sitting there beside her. "Don't you worry yourself, none, Mizz Tori. I will see ta it dat you arrives on time. Yes, um, I sure'n enough will. 'Cause if'n I don't, da boss, he sure a goin' ta be upsets like. An diss here old nigger, he don't need ta go an upset da boss none. No sur. I done know'd better fo sure."

She blinked her eyes to break her daydream. What she just experienced had happened in the past, and this was the present. Going back in her mind so clearly, after she had fought for so long to forget, was happing more and more since arriving, and strangely, unlike the last four years, she was letting herself feel and remember without hesitation.

DAN'S voice filled the bedroom as he checked on the order for breakfast. They had agreed to eat in the room while he got ready. It was a good idea, but neither of them had counted on waking up so early, and coffee was much in demand for him at this point.
He was not surprised to see his wife was already awake, and he rightfully guessed she had not thought of breakfast yet. If he knew her, she would be sitting outside, having her first smoke of the day. Tori always smoked outside and swore to him and their daughter she'd quit one of these days. When that day would come was anyone's guess.

He smiled, feeling very optimistic for the first time in nearly a year. If last night had been an indicator of how Tori was dealing with her past, he believed living happily in NOLA would happen. He slipped into his jeans and went to say good morning to his wife.

Dan walked toward the blackout curtains and drew them open, immediately squinting as the bright sunlight hit his face. He found himself in high spirits regardless of his hangover and the pain the bright light brought to his head. Realizing the door had been left slightly ajar for him, he smiled. She knew he'd come looking for her, and it warmed his heart to know that.

Just as he was about to step outside, the phone rang, giving him no choice but to return to his bedside and answer it. "Hello? Oh, yes, sir, Mr. McCloud. No, no bother, sir," Just getting ready for my morning cup of coffee. What's up?"

Tori walked back into the room and was shocked that she could hear McCloud's voice. The man was shouting so loud that Dan was holding the phone away from his ear. His boss was using a tone she never imagined he would use on his favorite employee. She stood and listened closer. It was not so much that she could make out the words being spoken; it was more that the man seemed alarmed and angry at the same time, and that had her worried.

Dan listened a bit longer before breaking into the one sided conversation. "That's impossible; they can't do that. The team checked the by-laws. I assure you we have the clearance to proceed." He sat on the edge of the bed and continued listening to his boss, who continued to rant on.

The sound of someone knocking at the room's door surprised her, and she looked at her husband, who covered the mouthpiece and whispered, it's breakfast. Can you get it?"

"Yes, will do; what's up?"

"Tell you when I get off the phone." He removed his hand from the mouthpiece and continued his conversation. After thirty long minutes, Dan hung up and rushed to get dressed. "Damn those idiots. I swear they are imbeciles who need me to hold their hands."

He walked toward his wife, who met him halfway with his cup of coffee. Dan's expression was full of concern. Whatever had gone wrong must have been something huge; because it was very seldom her husband's face gave up its poker façade. "Here, and two aspirin for the head." She handed him both and stood watching him as he took his first sip and the two tablets.

Dan let out a sigh. "Seems he messed something up. I tell you, sometimes I wonder how in the hell he became CEO of the company." He placed his tie around his neck as he continued to explain. "In all likelihood, I will have to miss dinner tonight. It looks as if we have to do a whole year's worth of work over and do it before noon tomorrow." Tucking his shirttail into the top of his pants, Dan walked toward her, pulling up the zipper on his fly and then fastening his belt buckle. Next, in one smooth action, he reached both hands down and scooped up his tie ends and stopped to stand in the middle of the room while knotting it.

"Tori, I am sorry, babe. You know if I could, I would spend more time with you before going in. Hell, I had planned on taking you to Café Du Monde."

"I would have loved that. There is always tomorrow, you know, or the next day?"

Dan smiled and continued dressing while he talked on.

Tori had stopped paying attention to him. Sitting in one of the chairs by the fireplace, sipping her coffee, she'd become lost in her thoughts as her husband rambled on.

Everything happens for a reason. It was strange how things worked out sometimes, and because it had, Tori realized she'd have all the time she needed to carry out her plans. Not only that, but she could do it all with no worries about her husband finding out what she was up to. Her biggest obstacle had been conveniently solved. He would not be nosing around the Guest House today and, with some added luck, not even until later the next day. She knew this to be so because, in the past few months, it had not been unusual for his team to pull all-nighters when it came to crunch time, and by the sounds of it, crunch time was upon them again.

Dan's voice broke her concentration. "You'll be all right, won't you?" He was standing at the end of the four-poster bed, papers in hand, ready to go. He opened his leather briefcase and placed the paperwork inside.

"I'll be okay, honey. I just need some more sleep; I seem to have a slight hangover." She smiled and then put on a stern face. "So, don't you call here waking me, or so help me, I'll get even by keeping you up all night, and then you can be as exhausted as I am right now."

"All night, huh? Sounds like fun."

Tori laughed. "You're impossible, you know. Go on and get out of here so you're not late. By the sound of your boss, that, my love, would not be a good way to start the day." She kissed his cheek and then escorted him to the door. "Seal the deal and make it airtight," she grinned. "McCloud can't do it without you. He'd leave some darn loophole, and you know that's true. We both know the company needs its own flight department and fleet of jets. You're the brains, you know, Captain."

"Make that Chief Pilot, if you please."

"Nice ring to it and a nice pay raise, which means maybe a bigger house?" She opened the door and stepped back, letting him pass. "I love you, and you will clear it up. We can look at the houses tomorrow or even the next day. Soon as I close this door, I'm going back to bed. One small pill and lights out." She hung the 'Do Not Disturb' sign on the door handle.

Dan looked at Tori and thanked the Lord for having such an understanding woman in his life. His wife believed in him and always encouraged him when he needed it. Happily, he leaned toward her and quickly brushed her lips with a light kiss. Tori gave him a slight smile, one that made her dimples show. This small action convinced him she was all right after all, that he could relax and concentrate on his work.

"Sleep tight. Love you, babe," he called back over his shoulder. He walked a short distance toward the stairs, where he stopped and turned to look at her. "Tori, no sightseeing without me."

"If it makes you feel any better, you know I'll wait. Remember I told you I would order some takeout? You weren't listening, were you? Tomorrow we will walk the French Quarter, and I will show you what I can. Now, go on and take the rental car; I won't be going anywhere." Laughing softly, Tori closed the door even before he had begun to go down the stairs.

IT had been several hours since Dan had left her, and she still hadn't made the phone call she needed to. First, she took a shower and then tried to call her daughter, completely forgetting about the time change. Disappointed at missing her chance to chat with her daughter, Tori called out for some food to be delivered to the room. She told the local sandwich shop that if the delivery boy wanted to earn a bit extra, he could add two bottles of red wine and a six-pack of beer to the order, and just before she hung up, she added a six-pack of soda also. The shop owner had agreed and, shortly after that, delivered what she had requested, no questions asked.

TORI had procrastinated long enough. It was now quite simply time to start the ball rolling; after all, there might not be a better chance. She walked toward the phone with nothing left to occupy her and no reason not to put her plan into action.

Her next move was why she had come along on the trip to start with, and if all went as she hoped, it would free her from all her torment. She just prayed that not telling the whole truth to her husband was a forgivable sin. The thought of going to church and asking for forgiveness had occurred to her once, but the idea of both the church and telling the story to a stranger kept her from doing so. Besides, God understood her reasons, and God was everyplace, not only in a building.

The piece of paper with the phone number felt like rough sand-paper in her hand. Looking at the numbers and knowing she was about to do the one thing she and Dan had agreed she should never do, made her feel a bit guilty, just not enough to stop her. After all, if everything worked out and her husband did manage to find out what she'd done, he would be understanding and support her, especially if she were to explain why she had acted on her own in the first place. At least that's what she told herself and to think otherwise was stupid.

Tori stood for a few seconds, staring at the phone. "Please let him listen to me," she said out loud. "And you, your voice, or whatever the hell you are, inside my head, just shut up. I'm ready to do this; watch and see if I'm not."

Tori picked up the receiver, and instantly the sound of the dial tone filled the room. She thanked her lucky stars that it would be a local call. That meant no long-distance charge would turn up on the bill. Dan would not discover what she'd been up to when it came time to check out. He was always a stickler for details and would have spotted a long-distance charge to an unknown number. Looking around the room, she smiled. At least she could make the call in the comfort and privacy of their room and not have to search for a public phone booth.

Suddenly there was a loud beeping, followed by a voice saying, "Please hang up and dial again." She had taken too long to dial the number, but the interruption spurred her on instead of putting her off. Her finger pressed down the button on the base of the phone, where the receiver sat. Thinking she'd hung up, immediately the phone stopped its annoying voice and beeping.

Tori was determined to place the call right away, so she lifted her finger off the connection, and as soon as she heard the dial tone, she began to press buttons. A different tone sounded with each button she hit, and she found herself thinking how unlike the rotary dial phone it was. Her mother insisted that the earlier version was the better of the two types, but that was neither here nor there.

Tori frowned, and her finger hovered for a second before she pressed the last four numbers in rapid succession, then she waited.

Her heart felt like it was beating in unison with these final beeps, and her grip on the phone was so tight that her knuckles were visibly pale. The palm of her other hand was cupped over the mouthpiece, which seemed ridiculous, even to her. This strange action, though, was deliberate. It would be the last obstacle before talking. To be heard, she'd have to remove her hand, which was the deal she'd made before dialing. Once she removed her hand and spoke to Tommy, there would be no going back.

It rang a few times before someone picked up, and when she realized her call was answered, the breath she'd been holding released in one burst. It sounded somewhat like when one blew out a candle, and she was relieved that her cupped hand had stopped the person on the other end from hearing it.

A young woman had answered in a friendly tone, something she had not expected. There again, she did not know what to expect, and for a second, she panicked. Having a female answer had not been a part of her scenario when she had thought things through. Tommy was supposed to pick up, so Tori had almost hung up when he hadn't. When she heard the woman use the camp's name, she somehow managed not to back down.

Her voice was frozen, and Tori was beginning to doubt herself. She knew what she had to ask, so why wouldn't the words come out? Instead of responding to the friendly voice on the other end, she just stood there, terrified to continue and more afraid not to.

"Hello. Hello, anyone there?" The young woman's voice didn't sound annoyed, just puzzled.

Tori's mind was spinning with options, and not one of them coincided with her plan. 'Take a breath, and talk. You can do this. You have to.' "Ah yes. Is Tommy there? I'm an old friend of his. I'd like to talk to him if I may?"

She had surprised herself. The tone of her voice had not even hinted at the panic she was experiencing. Still, Tori was losing the courage to continue with each passing second. What if he didn't remember her? Surely, he'd remember Linni, and if not, what then? She chewed on her lower lip and stopped only because the phantom voice inside her head made itself known again.

The irritating inner voice quipped. '*Well, stupid, if he remembers her, he has to remember you, and you can bet your life, he remembers.*' Tori closed her eyes and tried to block the sarcastic-sounding response to her question. She didn't need her subconscious telling her anything at this point. That's what the voice had to be because if she were listening to voices in her head, that would indicate she'd lost it. Only crazies hear voices, let alone speak back to them, she reminded herself. No, all she needed to do, was stay on track. That and reassure herself that the voice in her mind did not mean she was not going nuts.

Her conscious thoughts were rational, like what she was doing right then. Her thinking voice, inside her head, was something everyone had. The other one, the voice that just popped up whenever, well, maybe that was way beyond ordinary, and it was a given; not everyone had it happening to them. She'd never once heard of anyone hearing his or her subconscious talk. That inner voice, whatever it was, defiantly had to be ignored. She had ignored it for years and never once told Dan about it, so if she had silenced it once before, she could now. All these thoughts were flashing through her mind as she waited, and then it happened.

"Yes, Ma'am, Tom's here. He just walked in; if you hold on, I'll fetch him."

"Hold on? She has to be kidding me. If he does not pick up fast, I'm hanging up," she mumbled. '*The hell you will*', the voice snapped. '*You know you have to go through with this. I hate to tell you I told you so, but I told...*' Suddenly a mature male voice sounded in her ear.

"Yeah, Tom here. What can I do for you?"

Tommy had taken her call, was all she had time to think about before answering him. "Hello." Tori quickly pulled herself together and remembered what she had rehearsed to say. "Tommy, do you remember me? This is Tori. Tori Wilkinson. Well, it's Morgan now.

You knew me at the campground as Mrs. Wilkinson. My daughter Linni and I have stayed at the campground three, or is it four times? We typically stayed around this time of year. Our last time was nearly five years ago. That made it our fourth, come to think of it." What the hell was she saying? Of course, the kid knew her, and babbling, like an idiot, was going to ruin it all.

"Yeah, sure I remember you, Ma'am. I don't tend to forget my friends, you know? That's how I felt, still do, even if we have lost touch. How's the little one doing?"

"Not so little anymore. She's great. Thanks for asking. It's nice of you not to be upset with me, after all, this time."

"Well, Miss Tori, it's not hard. No bad feelings here, just maybe a few curious questions, that's all? You and your daughter were the only folks that up and checked out that summer way before the booking ended. You were the subject of quite a lot of gossip, you know. Seems that everyone thought you'd been swept clean off your feet. Romantic like, by a particular guy, who loved fishing. I remember him too. He checked out at the same time if I recall." He was chuckling, and while he had his moment, Tori took in a deep breath and slowly released it before continuing their conversation.

"Tommy... I mean Tom. It's Tom now, isn't it?" Her voice sounded shaky, and Tori wondered if he'd noticed.

His voice, on the other hand, was calm. His Southern accent was full of musical highs and lows, just like she remembered. He did not let on if he noticed how awkward she was, and she thanked God for that. He just kept on talking as if the two of them conversed often. "It was Dan something; he paid his and your bill and gave the campground an excellent tip. Gave me fifty bucks, and that was a shock, I can tell you. You know me, never was able to keep my allowance for long, so fifty bucks was huge, I can tell you. After that, I felt grown-up-like, and I had people call me Tom, not Tommy. I was all right with Tommy in Junior High. You gave me my first paying job. You surprised everyone and trusted me to babysit Linni and her friend Sarah. I recall it was so you and the gals could sit down by the lake and party. Never forget you or those times. Damn, it's good to hear from you."

"I feel the same way, Tommy."

He laughed at her, calling him Tommy. "Look, we go back a few years, so anyways you want it, the name, that is. Call me Tom, Tommy, whatever you like. Guess I better ask you, what can I do for you, Ma'am? Do you need a cabin?" His tone of voice had turned quite serious, and it shocked Tori. She was about to ask him if everything was ok when he laughed and continued his conversation. "Sorry about that. Dad just walked by. No need for him to know who I am speaking with. Had to make it sound all business-like. Good thing you called, though. Might be the last season we rent out. Folks are thinking of closing down after this summer."

"Oh, I am sorry to hear that; I have always loved the place."

"Yeah, well, Big RV Park down the way took most of our clients. Small mom-and-pop place like this can't compete. Don't have the funds to do it right. Now, will you look here? I'm just going on and on. Sorry, Miss Tori. About that cabin?"

Inhaling deeply, Tori rushed on before she chickened out. "I am sorry to hear that about the campground. After the first time, we just kept coming back because it was more like a home away from home. Dan, too, he told me it was his second year staying there when we met. He loved the fishing. He's who I married, you know?"

There was a sudden sound of loud laughing, and she listened as he happily congratulated her. "I knew it. You and Mr. Dan had left because he did sweep you off your feet. Wait until I tell my folks. They were worried at; first, you know. When they hear this news, they sure are going to be happy."

"Now, I feel guilty. Please tell them we never meant to worry anyone."

"I sure can, and they will understand."

"Glad to hear that. Anyway, I'm in town with Dan, staying in the Quarter, so I'm not calling for a cabin. Nothing close to that." This was it. No backing out now, Tori told herself. But, before she could go on, Tom's voice broke in.

"He's still a fishing nut, right? Got us a few of them here now. If you're wanting to ask if he can fish the lake, he's more than welcome; you just tell him so, you hear?"

"No, it's not that either. You see, I have some news for you." Tori paused slightly as her thoughts continued to race. 'Here goes, it's now or never; please let him listen.' "Tom, it's about your birth mother. I know you're not going to believe this. You see, I know who she is." There was a long silence. "Hello, you still there, Tommy? Look, I'm sorry to blurt it out like that. I know I'm rambling on and on. I'm just so nervous and all. Tommy? Are you there? Please answer me."

"Yes, Ma'am. I'm here. You say you know who my mother is? How could you possibly know that? Is this some kind of joke? Cause if it is I…"

"No, Tommy. It's no joke; I promise you. I would never joke about something like this. I can explain, and I will, just not on the phone. I would like to see you in person so that I can tell you everything. Can you meet me? I am at Lafitte's Guest House on Bourbon Street, room number twenty-one. I will let them know at the desk that you are coming to visit."

THINGS happened quickly after that. After hanging up the phone, Tori called downstairs and explained she was expecting a guest. She gave them his name and asked that he be allowed to come on up once he arrived. Once that had been taken care of, Tori did not know if she should cry or laugh; she'd done it. She'd started the ball rolling, and there would be no going back, no more hiding secrets, and long ago promises would be kept. She sat down with her cigarettes and a glass of wine to wait for him. The wait was not a long one.

A large plastic container of cut-up fruit and two subs arrived from the same deli. They were for Tom. The food she'd ordered earlier still sat untouched. Tori couldn't eat a thing. Ever since she'd hung up, she found herself worrying about what to say and how to say it. The stress had squashed any appetite, but what it had not done was squash her thirst.

On the dressing table now sat three bottles of red wine. Tori had opened one earlier and poured half a glass. Liquid courage, she told herself. Besides, it felt good to take the edge off. Tori sighed heavily; it was a sigh of anxiousness. She just wanted to get this part of her plan over and finished. Lifting the glass again and hesitating for only a second, she began to drink one small sip after another until the glass was empty. Determined not to be tempted to pour another drink, she paced the floor, going over how she would explain herself to Tommy. Tori even tried sitting outside and smoking while their room was being made up, but it had not helped calm her in any way. So, once she was alone in the room again, she had given in and poured another full glass of wine and took a seat in one of the chairs, swearing she'd only take a sip of the wine now and then and no more. She'd just lifted the glass to her lips when a loud knock sounded.

The abruptness of the knock on the door caused her to jump, and that movement jerked the glass. In seconds she'd spilled some of its contents onto her cotton blouse. Feeling like a kid, who'd just been caught sneaking a drink, she put the glass down and dabbed at the spill with a paper napkin. A second knock sounded, and this one was louder, followed by a male voice.

"Miss Tori, it's me, Tom."

Panicked, she ran to the mirror to see how nasty the stain was. Right away, she saw her reflection, and even though the stain wasn't that large, it was right there for all to see. Not knowing what else to do, she began rubbing it furiously with a paper napkin and quickly realized she was failing miserably at its removal. "Great. Just fucking great. He's going to think I'm drunk and crazy!"

She caught a glance of her terrified eyes, and for the first time, she felt slightly overwhelmed by what she was doing. Staring at her image, she tried to hide the panic she saw in her expression. What she needed to do, was to put a fake smile on her lips; failing that, a blank expression would have to suffice. She brushed her hair away from her face and tried a small smile again. No matter how forced it looked, it would have to be enough because there was nothing left to do except answer the door. Tommy would just have to accept her as she was.

She hurriedly approached the door and, without further hesitation, opened it to reveal a tall, self-assured young man. At first glance, she didn't recognize him. He had grown and matured so much. Gone was the awkward teen from years ago. Standing in front of her now was a young man who looked so much older than his years.

"Ma'am. I hope I'm not too early? Just couldn't wait, you saying you had information on my mother and all..."

"No, not at all. Please come in." Tori could not help but compare the young man standing before her with another person she remembered only too well, and she swallowed hard. Tommy's hair was shoulder-length, and the loose curls fell softly around his temple and neck. His skin was too dark to be white and too light to be passed off as black. It was the color of 'cafe au lait,' the shade given to him by his father.

'Black is black, no matter how white you look,' a male voice echoed inside her head from the past. This time, it was not the voice of her subconscious; instead, it was the memory of a man she despised and hated to her very core. Immediately, Tori shut down that image. She was not going to pay any heed to anything other than the critical issues at hand. Tori continued her scrutiny of Tommy. He had his father's eyes; they were a pale blue color that could change to a shade of green if the light reflected just right. 'Mixed blood always outs in the end,' the man's voice laughed. Pushing this memory away was more complicated because she had to block the image that went along with the voice. To do that, she had to concentrate hard.

Tom looked around as if all the answers to his questions would somehow miraculously appear on the walls of the Guest House room. Satisfied that would not be the case, he walked to the open balcony door and stepped outside.

Tori studied him as he walked around the bed toward the open veranda door to look at the street below. She needed to calm down, and she had to go through with her intentions no matter what. The door to room 21 closed, with the Do Not Disturb Sign still hanging from the handle. Now, she could concentrate on her task and Tommy, so she followed him out onto the balcony, where he stood looking down at Lafitte's Blacksmith Shop.

The resemblance to his father was stunning. The way he was standing, legs slightly apart, with his hands on his hips, was just how his father stood when thinking.

They had the same nose and pointed chin. His skin was several shades lighter than his mother's, yet she could see Kate in Tommy as well, especially in his demeanor. His soft-spoken manner and gentle smile reminded her of the kind women she'd known.

Tori recalled the way Tommy was good with children, especially with Linni. Hell, he got along with all the other kids at the campground. In this trait, he followed his mother too. She'd been great with the younger girls under her charge and even with the children down in the quarters. Tori blinked back, the tears forming in the corner of her eyes. His mother would have been so proud of her son. How had she kept the information from him for so long, and why? Especially when he had every right to know where he came from?

Tom turned to face her; it was his turn to scrutinize the woman before him. "You've changed yourself, Ma'am. The tan's missing, and you did something with your hair... it's lighter and cut shorter. Matches the new you... in an odd way. Not odd, just different; that's what I meant to say. It's shorter and straight. Last time I saw you, it was much longer and curly." He looked at Tori and took a step toward her. "Ma'am, you don't look too well if you pardon me saying so. You sure you're all right?"

"Yes, Tommy, I'm fine. Just a little tired, that's all, and maybe a little wound up. Spilled my wine; I'm so nervous." Her hand went to her chest where the stain was, and she briefly rubbed at it. "Not to worry, it'll come out in the wash, I'm sure." She turned and walked back inside toward the dressing table, picked up the open bottle of wine, and carried it to the small table she'd placed in front of the antique two-seater couch. She sat down, pulled her glass across the small table toward her, and topped it up. "Please have a seat, Tommy."

"It's Tom." He forced a polite smile as he sat down in one of the chairs by the fireplace.

"Tom," she said after taking a sip of her drink. "I'll try to remember that."

"Ain't hard," he smiled. "Look, I'm about as nervous as you are. So, what's say, you just spill the beans."

She nodded, placed her glass on the table, and picked up her nearly empty packet of cigarettes. With her fingers trembling, she lit up and blew her first drag high into the air, watching the pale smoke dissipate before talking. Then, without looking at him, she spoke. "You must forgive me; I didn't think to ask, do you want something to drink?"

"No thanks, just want to hear what it is you think you know."

"Right then, I'll get to the point; just bear with me." She took another sip of her wine and put the glass down before looking directly at him, yet not holding eye contact for longer than a few seconds. "The only other person that knows the story I'm about to tell you is Dan. We've been together for nearly five years. About a year after our stay at the campground, we got married, and he adopted Linni as his daughter." She inhaled again and blew the smoke downward. Then looking directly at Tom and this time without looking away, she continued. "Shit, he'd have a fit if he knew that I was telling my story to someone, let alone you."

Tom leaned forward with a grim expression on his face and anger in his voice. "You mean he's kept you from telling me information about my family? He had no right! Why'd he do something like that?" Furiously he stood up and headed back toward the open balcony door. He was trying very hard to compose himself, something that, with each second he stood there, was getting harder and harder to do. All he could think about was that Miss Tori's husband had kept her from telling him who his mother was. Why'd he do that, and what gave him the right to play God?

Tori reacted quickly. She stood up and was standing by his side before he stepped out onto the balcony. She took hold of his arm firmly and guided him back to the small couch, where together they sat down. One was calm, and the other was fuming, and both knew the tension needed to be diffused and fast.

"Tom, it's not what you think. You'll understand when I tell you everything." She patted his knee and tried to reassure him. In response to her touch, all he did was move his knee away from her. He stared at Tori as he edged his whole body sideways until settling on the far edge of the couch.

Tori felt for him and understood his dilemma. The sad thing was, he had no idea about hers. "Look, it's going to be a long afternoon, and I think it's best if I just start at the beginning if you're ready?"

"No better time than now," he said with an edge to his voice. "So out with it. I'm ready, been ready my whole life, I reckon."

Tori took a deep breath and closed her eyes for a moment. Tom said nothing, afraid that he would lose control of his senses if he did. He always did have a quick temper and now was not the time to show it. The young man bit the inside of his cheek as he waited for her to begin. He was out of there if she sounded nuts because she sure as hell was not making any sense to him so far. Then there was the known fact that liars always look away when dishing you a load of crap, and she'd just closed her eyes, a dead giveaway in his point of view.

When she opened her eyes, she saw, in her mind, a young boy in front of her. A young Tommy wanted to know about his mama, about the woman he loved but he couldn't see her face. The woman he could hear in his dreams. Her voice remembered and stowed away somewhere in his memories. The lullaby she sang to him, the one he'd never forgotten. Throughout time, that lullaby had been the link, joining mother to child. He just didn't know it yet.

Tori's voice quivered as she began. "The only way you're going to believe, what I have to tell you, is if I tell it all. God help me; it's not going to be easy." She took another sip of her wine. "All I want is for you to listen and wait until I'm finished before saying anything. No interruptions, no questions. Agreed?"

Tom studied the woman's face. He could see that she was upset. Worse than that, the female looked somewhat terrified. What was it she knew or thought she knew? One thing was for sure; he knew he'd have to agree to her terms to find out.

"Look, Miss Tori, I don't know what it is that you have to say. Whatever it is, I agree, I should know it all. I've waited my whole life to find out who I am and where I came from. If you know something, please…I need to hear it. I'm not going to judge you or the information. If what you know turns out to be true, then I'll always thank you. Regardless, if it's good news or bad, I need to hear it. If it does not check out, well, at least, you cared enough to tell me." Tom scooted toward her and reached out, taking her hands in his. He noticed that they were hot and damp and as he squeezed them to reassure the frightened woman, he felt her relax a little.

"Tom, I can't rest until I tell you; I know that now. After you hear what I have to say, I hope you will forgive me for not telling you sooner. You see, you are tied into helping me, as much as I am to helping you. I desperately need to tell someone the whole story. I understand that now. Guess I knew it all along, come to think of it. My story holds answers you are looking for, and it holds the key to my peace of mind."

The look in her eyes scared him. He'd never seen anybody with that look, except in movies, and it was always when somebody was about to say something awful. Hell, this wasn't a movie, he scolded himself. This here was real life, and folks don't always have bad news looking like that, did they? "I'll listen, don't you worry none. Seems like I don't have a choice in the matter anyway, that is, if I want to find out what it is, you think you know. Just understand I'm here for you."

For the first time since Tori had dialed his number, she could breathe a little easier. He was caring and compassionate, and he'd agreed to listen. "You are just like your mother. She was a good listener and very kind. I knew I was right to talk to you."

Tom's expression changed from caring and kind to shock and disbelief. "You knew my mother? You are sitting there, telling me you talked with her?"

Tori held her hand up to silence him. "I can explain it all, and I will. Trust me. Just trust me, ok?" Seeing him sit back and nod his head, she reached for the cigarette in the ashtray and put it out. Then she picked up her glass of wine and took a large gulp.

To an anxious Tom, it looked like she was stalling when suddenly she sat back and smiled at him. "Now, I'd better get started before I lose my nerve. That or you think I'm crazy and up and leave. Just remember, you agreed to hold all questions until I finish. No interrupting, please," she begged. "You see, Tom; I fear if you break my line of thought, I might not be brave enough to continue." She gave him a little smile and then nodded her head. "Right then, let's begin." Her hands were shaking as she reached for another cigarette.

Tom picked up the bottle of wine and topped up her glass. He placed the half-finished bottle on the table and took the book of matches from her trembling fingers. He struck one and held it close enough for her to reach. It was then that he noticed his hands were none too steady either. He wondered if it was because he was excited, nervous, or just plain frightened of what he may learn. Tori watched as he blew out the flame. He caught her staring at him, with eyes looking like they would burst into tears at any second. It made him feel really uncomfortable, to say the least. He needed to do something, anything, to break the awkward situation.

Calmly he stood up, looking at the dressing table, which she was using as a makeshift bar. Besides the two bottles of unopened wine sat a plastic bucket, which served as a cooler for two tins of soda and two of beer. "If you don't mind, I think I'll have a can of soda." Tom knew he was the one stalling now, and he hoped that drawing out his actions would give her time to get her emotions under control.

"Not at all; take what you want. There are more in the fridge and some beer in the kitchen. It's right behind us, fills the end of the hall. You can't miss it. The way I figured it, you are old enough to drink now, right?"

"You could say that. Twenty-two is legal, far as I know." He forced a grin when he faced her holding a can of soda. "Most of my friends and I, we've been drinking in the quarter for a few years now. Some of them serve you if you act right." He sat down in one of the chairs by the fireplace before popping the can open. Then changing his mind, he stood up and dragged the chair closer to the small table and Tori. He sat back down and smiled at her.

"Actually Tom, you are way old enough; in fact, I can safely tell you your age is maybe one year older than you think. I don't recall if Kate told me your birthday, but she did tell me your age when she lost you."

Tom was stunned and about to ask her to explain but stopped when she interrupted him. "Not now, Tom. I'm sorry. I am getting ahead of myself. Please don't ask me how I know. Look, I can begin by explaining this much first. When you were found by the lake in seventy-four, everyone thought you were two years old when in fact, you were three, maybe closer to four. You were shy and did not talk too much. Your favorite number was two. When we met, you thought you were fifteen years old but you were closer to sixteen. This is ninety-four, so by my calculations, you're twenty-three. So, if you want a beer, go ahead. Just know that none of what I just told you will ever be a fact in the eyes of the law. There is no way to prove what I just said. So, there you have a bit more knowledge about yourself, and I hope by the time I finish, you will have a full understanding of who you are and where you came from. Now that bit of information is cleared up, maybe it's time for me to start. Just remember, you gave your word; no questions until I am finished. I promise you I won't skip ahead of myself again."

Tom placed his soda on the table before leaning back and fixing his eyes on hers. He was bursting with questions but decided he would play by her rules.

"I have to explain it all and not stop or skip around; I know that now." Looking at Tom, she decided that maybe it was better for him to sit across from her. In this way, he could see her face as she talked, and perhaps, he would be able to tell that she was not lying to him.

Tom felt like he wanted to scream at her. All he wanted was for her to just up and tell him her side of whatever it was. He needed to pace the floor or do something other than just sit and wait. So, he did the next best thing, he picked up his soda and took a long drink before putting down the almost empty can.

During this entire time, his eyes had not left hers. It was true he would rather be drinking a beer or some of the wine the woman was going through, like water. But, one of them needed to stay clear-headed, and he thought it had better be him. Besides, he figured the way Miss Tori looked; she needed the wine way more than him. If she was telling the truth, then his age had just skipped ahead and her claiming there was no way to prove it sort of messed with his thinking. He had no choice, but to wait her out, to get the rest of the story and see if at least some of it could be proved.

One thing was sure; Tori was not the same carefree woman of a few years ago. The very fact that she was smoking showed him that. It had been Tori, who caught him trying to steal a cigarette at the campground when he was a lot younger, and Tori who had given him that long lecture about what a terrible habit it was. She'd made him promise that he would never touch another cigarette again, and he hadn't. His word was his word, and he was proud of that fact. Looking at her sitting there, inhaling the menthol-like nobody's business, saddened him. He wondered how long she had been smoking and why she had started again?

"Before I begin, Tom, I want to let you know that I will be referring to you and your age, as we all thought of it back then. Other odd facts may seem out of place, but I will do my very best to clear them up after I finish. I think maybe the hardest part for you will be not to interrupt me. You just have to trust that for me to remember every detail, you have to keep your word and not distract me. I don't want to keep repeating that, but it's essential.

Tom nodded his head, indicating that he understood. He had agreed he would hold all questions until she was done telling him her information. So, there was nothing left for him to do but sit back and wait silently. After all, this couldn't take very long. For half an hour or so, he could keep his mouth shut. Yes, he'd keep his word on that until she was ready for him and his questions, and he'd bet his life, he'd have plenty of those for her.

The silence between the two broke as Tori started to talk, and in a matter of minutes, he was swept up in her story. Her words were so descriptive that he could easily envision it all in his mind. It was like watching a movie in his head, and there was no way on earth he was going to interrupt her. In later years, Tom would remember how he'd had no idea when Tori had begun to tell her tale that it would change his life forever.

"YOU see, Tom, it was my hair. I had it tied up in a bandana of sorts. I always rode with it tied up, and I had not thought to remove it when I jumped into the lake. It was not until I was back with Dan, trying to explain to him about five years of my life, which had been less than ten minutes here, that I remembered that the proof was my hair. Remember? It was shoulder length and permed. Well, in five years, it grew, and when I let it down, well, Dan had to believe me. Then there was the matter of my tan. I did not have one!"

Tom sat there looking at her. Her hair was short and straight. No five years of growth there. She had told him one hell of a story, but could he believe it? Any of it?

Tori saw him struggling with what she had told him. After hours of talking and opening up, he still had his doubts. "Look, I know how hard it is, and trust me, at times, I have had to ask myself if I'm crazy, but the simple fact is this. It happened. If you are wondering about my hair, I had it cut again. I tried to erase all ties to Laffite at that time. Found out you can't erase love or memories."

Tom stood up and walked toward the open balcony door. Morning had arrived in the French Quarter. It was not a surprise that they had been up all night. Five years of past history had taken that long to tell. He ran his fingers through his hair. Strange, he wasn't even tired. He was mixed up, though. He wanted to believe her, mostly because of Kate and Leone. It would give him an identity, but time travel?

"Tom, please come here for just a few minutes longer." She watched as he turned toward her. "I did not know until now if telling you was the right thing to do, either for you or me. You see, Tom, even Dan does not know the whole story. Oh sure, he knows most of it, but how could I ever tell him about Christopher? You are the first and the only other person that will ever know the whole truth. Can you believe that? By me telling you, it's helped heal my pain some, but what have I done to you? Have I helped, or do you think my tale the raving of a crazy woman? Have I, in some way, made it better or not?"

"Tori, ma'am," he said, sitting back down by her side. "If I could believe in your story, I would have to say that yes, it would help. But, ma'am, you ask me to sit here and tell you something that I can't. If it helped you to talk, then we should both be glad for that, but the fact remains, it's just a story. Your story, not mine."

His sad face tore at her heart. She had made it worse for him after

275

all. How could she have ever expected him to believe her? "You can talk to Dan. He won't be too happy with me but let me worry about that. He will tell you. You'll believe him, won't you?"

"Ma'am, it's not that. Don't you see? I need more'n him telling me he believes you." He stood up. "Now, if you don't' mind, I think I had best be heading home. You take care of yourself and maybe before you leave, we will talk again, but Tori, don't call me. Let it be my choice, all right?"

Tori would not let it end like this. She wanted him to know that it was the truth, but how? He wanted proof, actual proof. Then it hit her; she just might have it after all.

"Tom! Wait a minute. I have an idea. I know just how to prove it all to you. The question is, are you brave enough to face it? If you give me just a little more of your time and come with me, I'll give you your answers and proof. I am talking about physical proof. What do you say? Will you do it?"

Tom turned back to face her. The woman was dead serious. She really believed she could prove it to him. A small glimmer of hope took hold inside of him. Who the hell was he to say she couldn't do it, he asked himself? "Well, I've spent this much time listening to you; what's a bit more? I guess it's worth it one way or the other."

"Oh, Tom, it's worth it. You wait and see. It will all be worth it."

ᕫᕫᕫ Ten ᕫᕫᕫ

Tom sat in his parked car on St. Philip Street, anxiously awaiting Tori to join him. He was less than a half a block away from the guesthouse and would see her as soon as she stepped onto the corner of Bourbon and Philip Street. Tori had said that she needed only thirty minutes to take a quick shower and take care of a few other things.

To Tom, those thirty minutes had felt more like thirty hours. If it turned out that the wild story Tori had just finished telling him was true, it would change the way he looked at life. It would forever alter his attitude, not only about himself but also about how he lived and would continue to live. Part of him was excited, and the other was frightened to death.

True to her word, Tori appeared in exactly thirty minutes. He found himself gripping the steering wheel while watching her walk toward his car, her step lively and her face full of excitement. Taking a deep breath, he told himself to take it easy.

The car door opened, and she slid into the front seat next to him. There was not a hint of fear or doubt in her manner. "Well, this is it then," she smiled. "I left a note for Dan, just in case he comes back to the room before we get back." In a more serious tone, she added, "I hate lying to him, but what choice do I have? I don't want him to worry, and he would never understand this. Anyway, it's best if he thinks I'm off shopping after an early breakfast."

Tom looked concerned. "You sure you want to do this, whatever this is? I mean, I've been thinking about it. I can't figure out how in the hell you intend to give me concrete evidence." He hated to sound so pessimistic when she seemed to be so sure of herself, but he had to play devil's advocate, especially if it meant saving them both from a big letdown.

"I'm not positive that I can find you concrete evidence," she said, her smile slipping away. "But, yes, Tom, I want to do this. If I find what I'm looking for, you will have no choice but to accept the story. If it's not there…well…what I've tried to show you might still convince you."

Tom's mood lifted a little as excitement started to take hold. He felt terrible for having put her good spirits in jeopardy and wanted to cheer her up.

He wanted to give her back that self-confidence she had had only a few minutes earlier. "Look, when you were telling me the part about my mother last night, I have to tell you that I did have flashbacks of a dream I used to have as a child, and it did sort of fit. What I mean is, the description of that plantation…it *could* be from a life I once knew, but right now, it all seems so hard to believe."

"What I have in mind is far more tangible than fleeting memories, wishful thinking, or déjà vu feelings. In the next few hours, I hope I can show you something tangible. Two things, to be exact. Things that will erase all doubts." She touched his arm lightly to reassure him that she was sure of what she intended. Then sounding confident once again, she asked, "Are you ready? Because if you are, let's get started, shall we?"

Tom was more than willing. "As crazy as this seems, I think that I do believe. At least a small part of me does. Still, some tangible proof wouldn't hurt any. What do you have in mind?"

"First stop is not far from here, and I could use a drink."

He shot her a fearful look. "It's only nine-thirty in the morning. No offense, but isn't it a little early to be…you know?"

She laughed at him. "Or a little late, whichever way you look at it. Jean used to say, 'the sun's setting over the yardarm somewhere. Don't worry, Tom, you'll understand in just a few more minutes. Just trust me and go along with me from this point on, okay? It's very important that you listen to me, and please, do as I ask."

Once again, he told himself he was stupid for going along with her, but she seemed so in control, much more than the afternoon before. Something in him trusted her or at least wanted to. He would just sit back and see.

"Come on; we can walk the rest of the way." Tori gave him no chance to question her. She opened the car door and climbed out. The anxious woman had to get him to follow her and didn't want to allow him one second to change his mind or figure out their destination.

They walked back the way she had come, and Tom frequently looked at Tori in an attempt to find out where they were going or what she was thinking, but she never faltered in her stride or gave any sign of her emotions. Her face remained blank.

At the corner of Saint Phillip and Bourbon, she finally stood still, looking at him as she dictated her orders. "Just act like a tourist and go along with whatever I ask or tell you to do, okay?"

She was off again before he could answer her, calling over her shoulder, "Come on. Stop dawdling." She had turned and was headed up Bourbon Street when suddenly she disappeared into an open doorway.

"It's Laffite's Blacksmith Shop!" he said aloud, following her rapidly inside.

The interior was dimly lit and empty, except for the bartender, who sat on a stool watching the television that hung above him. He was finishing his burger and didn't acknowledge them until they sat down at the far end of the bar.

"Can I help you, folks?" He said, wiping the corner of his mouth and taking a sip of his coffee.

"You sure can, if you can fix a good Bloody Mary," said Tori. He smiled at them, putting his cup down. "Ain't a bartender around that can do it better than me, that's for sure. Fix you right up. And you?" he looked at Tom.

"He'll have the same," she said quickly, giving Tom no choice. "Had a great night, but boy are we paying for it now," she laughed, putting her hand to her head.

"Know what you mean. This city can do that to you. Where you folks from?"

"I'm from California, and my friend here is from the Big Easy. He's been showing me around. I just wanted to come back here for a quick pick-me-up. Loved the place so much last night," she lied easily. "This bar, it has got so much atmosphere about it. Do you mind if I take a look around?"

"Don't mind at all. Most folks just come in and drink and party. Not many folks know or want to know the history of the place, though," he said as he mixed their drinks. "Locals and a few history buffs know. Spect you know already," he said, looking up at Tom.

"Me, sure. It's Jean Laffite's place, or should say was, right?"

"That's what they say. I did some reading up on it myself when I came to work here. If you have any questions, I'd be happy to answer them." He placed the drinks down in front of them, a friendly smile on his face.

"I'm a writer," said Tori. She took a sip of her drink. "Ummm, really tasty."

The bartender beamed; he was proud of his concoction and her compliment but didn't seem interested in the fact that she was a writer.

Tom picked his glass up and took a large gulp. Bullshit on the writer crap, he thought. Just what game was she playing? He was about to try to catch her eye when she continued her conversation as if he wasn't even there.

"I've written a fiction piece about Laffite. This place plays a significant role in my story."

"That so?" He seemed pleased.

"My name's Tori. This is Tom, and you are?"

"Walter's the name."

"Nice to meet you, Walter. It does my heart good to meet someone who knows about this old place. I have read and studied Jean Laffite and different locations connected with him for years but have always returned here." She was walking toward the fireplace in the center of the room.

"I was told that this was the forge."

"That's what they say. Most of the building is as it was; it's historical, you know. Can't change anything in here or outside anymore."

She smiled to herself, turning away, afraid that he might see her expression. If only he knew how much it had changed over the years. True, the outside still looked as it had, but he was wrong about the inside. For one thing, she could tell him that the floor had all been one level. There had been no such step up; just past the fireplace and looking down at the concrete floor, she frowned. There had been no such flooring either.

She stepped past the fireplace, paying it little attention when her eye caught the painting facing her on the far wall. Hanging there in all its glory was what was supposed to be the likeness of Jean Laffite.

Now there was something that would have made him furious, she thought. It looked nothing like him at all. Tori walked closer to inspect it, frowning as she did. Her handsome, dashing Jean had been made to look like an evil character, dressed all in black. Her temper was close to exploding, but she decided not to let it get to her. *No,* Tori told herself, *she'd be like the real Jean Laffite, who, unlike this stern-looking image, would have laughed at such a painting. It's just so hard to laugh, though,* she quietly thought to herself, hoping somehow that Jean could hear her. She was angry that the whole world did not know him as she did, nor would they ever. Her anger gave way rapidly to sadness. Nothing inside the cottage was the same.

It was nothing but a bar from the front entrance to the rear. Small wooden tables were up against the wall, each sitting two, while larger tables filled the interior. Unlit candles sat on each table. Some tables still needed cleaning and chairs that needed straightening for the new day, and she assumed that the morning crew would soon be in to take care of all the tidying up.

What little light that filtered in from the open door, or side windows, was just enough to allow her to see the actual condition of the establishment. The walls were raw bricks in places; the beams and wooden floor above were darkened with age. 'That's just it,' she told herself. 'The building is ancient and considering all it must have gone through and seen over the years, it is a miracle that it's still standing.'

She looked again and smiled. It was in better condition than she had first allowed herself to admit. Sauntering toward the back end of the bar, where the piano sat with its stools placed around it, Tori stood still. That was the place she and Dan had met Stirling, and again she wondered what had happened to him. Wherever he was, she hoped he was happy and who knew, maybe one day their paths would cross again. As that thought passed, she continued her exploration.

It was essential to remember the cottage as it had been in the past, to find just what she was looking for. The memories became stronger as she reached the back. It was as if the walls were talking to her. The building was filled with the residue of a time many years ago, and she could feel it. How many people came here each day to drink and party, she wondered? People, who would think it nothing more than a funky old pirate's bar, never going beyond their first impressions. How many would walk toward the back, like she was doing right now, and feel the presence of the building's ghosts and appreciate the history that surrounded these walls? Not many, she figured. Ah, but those who did: what an experience, what a trip.

Tori was getting her bearings slowly but surely. She had to be sure of herself before she started to retrieve what she had come for. It could only be in one spot, a spot so easy to find in the past but not so easy now. With the interior so altered, that spot would be harder to locate but not impossible. Tori saw the side door that exited into a small courtyard. In her mind, that area held many visions of the bygone era. Now, it merely held more empty tables.

She tried to open the door, only to find it locked.

"I'll let you have a look that way if you'd like," called Walter. He had walked from behind the bar and stood by the fireplace, all smiles, watching her.

"That would be great if you don't mind, that is. I hate to be a bother."

"No, bother at all. Here, I have something to show you out there; most folk never see it, and those that know about it, well, the folks have a name for it. You being a writer and so interested, I figure you will love this." He opened the door, and the pair of them stepped outside.

Curious, Tom followed them. By the time he stood in the side doorway, Walter was already standing on the far side of the small patio area, talking with Tori. They were standing in front of a brick wall, looking down at a planter of some kind. Nothing so odd about that; however, the look on Tori's face alerted him that whatever she was looking at in that planter was significant in some way. Walter was still talking and turned to face Tom as he continued.

"See, some say it was a water feature; not sure about that. Come over here and see this; the little lady is quite taken with it." The bartender smiled at Tori and continued on as Tom stepped up and stood to look at the amazing site. "The greenery has overtaken it, and I pull it off and tidy it up when I can. The locals call the art or statue; whichever you choose, they call it 'Lovers in Stone,' and I can't tell you much else about it, sorry to say."

"Well, I think it's lovely, and thank you for showing me, but I need my drink right now. In fact, Walter, could you set us up a couple of your best whiskey shots? That should help us. I will be right in; I want to tell Tom what he missed."

"No problem, come on in when you are ready; I will have the shots waiting." He left them and made his way back inside, oblivious to the strange reaction Tori was having. Once he was out of sight, Tori looked at Tom and shook her head as tears filled her eyes.

"What gives? I don't get it?" He looked back at the large statue of a man and a woman lying side by side. Am I missing something?"

"Do you remember the part of my story, the part on the island with Jean? Remember that you laughed a little when I did not fool him in the water with my double back?"

Tom took a second and then nodded his head. "Yes, well, you made me blush too, if I recall. The two of you, making love on the beach part."

"And do you recall what it was Jean told me?"

He had to think about that. "I am not sure, but he said something about loving being there with you. Yes, he wanted to stay like it forever. The look in his eyes told her he was remembering and connecting the dots."

Tori looked down at the statue. "And, he said that one day, he would have a statue made of us laying there like we were. He memorized each detail, and now," she pointed at the statue, "this is the result. It can't be a mistake or coincidence." Tori reached down and touched the faces of both stone statues. This is us, no doubt in my mind. He did it, had it made, and he left it here knowing I would see it. Tom, I don't know about you, but I need a shot, maybe two." Tori pulled herself together and forced a smile. "Come on; I need to get you your proof before I fall completely apart."

"I think I will join you on that one." Tom walked slightly ahead of her, and when they reached the bar's side door, he felt her grab his arm.

"Give me just a few, will you. Keep old Walter entertained. I need to scope out where it is… what I am looking for."

He just nodded and joined Walter at the bar where two shot glasses were waiting.

Tori looked both ways from where she was standing. Directly in front of her was a wooden door marked 'Ladies.' Now, this was a new addition. "Everything original, my ass," she said under her breath. Then quite suddenly, she found herself giggling. This would have made Thiac laugh. He had thought the idea of a toilet inside anyone's home the sickest thing he could ever think of having inside.

Tom called to her from the front of the bar, and she strolled toward it to join him. She turned her head to look over at the side-wall once again on her way. Her mind was racing, and the upset of a few minutes ago was forgotten. She figured it had to be just past that piece of shit artwork. Counting the number of windows and looking back toward the side door, she made a mental note of the approximate location to start her search. Just how to go about it undetected was going to take a bit of ingenuity on their part. Step one completed. On to step two, she told herself.

Tom sat sipping his drink, watching her as she approached him. For the life of him, he couldn't see what she hoped to show him here. What actual proof did she have in mind? Sure, the statue bit had been unnerving, but it could also have been part of a ruse. She could have known about it and worked it into the crazy story. "I'll take a second shot if you don't mind."

"I think you better stick with the Bloody Mary and go easy." Looking at his expression, she softened. "You can have mine, but that's it. We still have some driving to do after this."

Tom frowned. Tori had not mentioned going any other place. Again, he wondered what she was up to?

"You know," said Walter to them both. "This place is said to be haunted by Laffite. Those, including myself, have heard things late at night or real early, like when it's deathly quiet. Not so much down here," he said, looking around. "Mostly upstairs."

Tori's eyes looked up at him. "Upstairs, you say?" So, she was right. The stairs still did exist. They would stand behind the bar; that's why she had not seen them. "Do you think I could take a look?" 'Maybe it hadn't changed as much upstairs as it did down here,' she thought. 'If it had, it would be fun to see how much.'

Walter's attitude changed visibly as he looked away quickly. His voice was sharp. "Can't let you do that."

"I'm sorry. Did I say something to offend you?"

"No, Ma'am. It's just that it's private up there. Just a small apartment of sorts, nothing you would want to see anyway."

Tori had the feeling he was hiding something but didn't have a chance to investigate further. His look softened toward her. "But there is this," he said, pointing to the wall behind the end of the bar. "Now, this might be of interest to you. Have you seen it before? The writing that's here?"

Tori looked to where he was pointing and could not make out any writing, nor did she know what he was talking about. "No, I can't say that I have." She moved closer to see more clearly.

Walter smiled and continued. "No one knows who wrote it or when—kind of a mystery, like the statue, outside. One of the other servers has the name of the artist who made it but not the reason why. Anyway, the writing is old though, much older than the statue if you ask me. Been there for years. I had it translated once, being I don't read Italian. Look, I'll shine the flashlight on it for you." He aimed his light up at the spot on the wall, and slowly Tori could make out the inscription.

Her glass fell to the floor as her recognition of what she was looking at sunk in.

Walter's words stopped halfway through his translation as he turned to see what had happened.

"Oh, I'm so sorry. It just slipped. God, I'm so clumsy!"

"Don't worry, none. It's nothing that can't be cleaned up. Still got to charge you, though," he chuckled. "Fix you another one if you want? Put it in our plastic cups; no more broken glass." He chuckled to himself.

"Yes, yes, please do. You positively make the very best Bloody Mary I have ever had. You agree, Tom?"

He was staring at her and snapped out of his daydream-like state. "Yeah, sure do. Too good to be throwing around like that."

"I fully agree with you," she said, turning back to Walter. "I'm so very sorry."

"As I told you, it's all right. You forget about it. I'll clean it up as soon as I fix you another one." He looked back up at the inscription and asked, "You still want to know what it all says?"

"Yes, please," she answered excitedly. She waved her hand at Tom, "Come on over here and take a look at this, will you?"

Stepping away from the front of the bar, he walked toward her, careful not to step on the broken glass.

"As far as I know, it says, '*Love passes time. Time passes with love.*'"

Tom held his breath. Now, he knew why Tori had dropped her drink with that just-seen-a-ghost look on her face. She could read the Italian saying before Walter had had a chance to translate it.

"Interesting saying. What do you think it means" she asked, blatantly lying?

The bartender was back mixing her a fresh drink. "Don't know, but there are those who say Laffite himself put it there right before he sailed out of New Orleans."

"Look, you mind if we take a seat over there?" Tori pointed toward the small table by the sidewall. I would like to write that down before I forget it."

"Fine by me, go ahead," he handed her the new drink.

"I'll clean up the mess and then take care of business. If you have any further questions, I'll be right here."

She took Tom by the arm and led him to a small table between two windows. "This should do it." She pulled out the chair and sat down, looking around her. "It should be right about here. The problem is getting it without being seen."

Tom pulled out the opposite chair and sat down, taking a large swig of the drink. "What in the hell are you talking about?"

His mind was still swimming after seeing the inscription. For a few brief seconds, he had considered that she already knew it was written there, like the Lovers in Stone. It could be that this was all part of an elaborate scheme to fool him. However, he quickly rejected the idea, realizing that she had been just as shocked as he was upon seeing those words scratched into the brickwork.

"Tori...I remember you telling me about the locket and the inscription. It's the same... isn't it?"

"Oh, it's the same," she said, her voice breaking a little. "I do not doubt that Jean wrote it for me to find. He knew about this place becoming what it is and must have known I would come here. It was his way of letting me know..." she stopped talking. Walter was cleaning up the broken glass and was within hearing range of their conversation.

Tom lowered his voice. "That's not it. What we came here for?"

She shook her head, still watching Walter clean up while pretending to write down notes. Tori was biding her time. Nothing could go wrong if she was extremely careful, and Tom followed her instructions. Having mopped up the mess, Walter returned to his seat behind the bar and turned the channel on the small T.V.

"No, it's not why we are here. What we came for is behind one of these bricks, right about here," Tori said, pointing to the wall down by her side. "The trick is going to be finding it and removing it without being caught."

Tom looked horrified. "Are you crazy?"

"Nope, not yet anyway. Now, all you have to do is keep an eye on our friend over there. I'll do the rest." She was already probing with her fingers at an exposed area.

Tom watched as her hands searched frantically for a specific place on the wall. 'What could she be looking for,' he wondered again? Sitting there like he was would be no help, so he begrudgingly looked away to keep his eye on the man behind the bar. Thank goodness he seemed more interested in the previous night's receipts and the television than he did with his customers. Tom only hoped it stayed that way, but if Tori didn't stop carrying on as she was, that might not happen. The woman asked to be caught if she didn't keep things down.

"Come on, be here," she said impatiently. "I know it's here."

"Tori, for God's sake, lower your voice," he begged.

She listened to him but still kept whispering to herself. "Sorry. Bad habit of mine, you know." She looked back at the wall. "Jean, damn your hide. I need your stash. "Look, finding the words isn't enough. Nice touch with the statue, but damn it to hell, I need more."

Suddenly she fell silent. The brick under her hand had moved slightly. The mortar around it was loose and cracked. Some had even fallen away completely.

'This could be it,' she thought. "Oh, please let it be," she begged softly. The woman pushed a little harder, and then reaching into her bag, she brought out her nail file. One quick look toward the bar told her she was still safe. Again, Tori turned her attention back to the loose brick, pressing the metal blade into the space between the red brick and the crumbling mortar. She pushed and poked at the area while applying an extra effort to gain entrance to the hollow area beyond. Tori knew it would be found once the brick was removed, and not worrying about the mess she was making, her fingers worked at prying the old brick free of its resting place. Mortar fell to the floor in small bits and pieces. If the bartender looked their way or, worse yet, came over, it could pose a problem. She had to conceal the dust and particles and do so by scattering them with her foot.

All this time, Tom kept looking from Tori to Walter and back again. He prayed that no other customers would come in too. "Tori, please hurry up, will you? Whatever it is you think should be there, a hell of a lot of time has passed, and it may be gone. Have you considered that?

Instead of looking at him with anger, she shot him a look of triumph as, finally, the brick was far enough out of the wall for her to grab hold of it. In a few seconds, she would know.

"Damn it," her angry voice snapped loudly. It made Tom jump, and Walter looked over toward them.

"Need two more drinks over here," Tom called out, smiling. I'll come and get them and settle up the tab while I'm at it."

Walter nodded and went about making two more of his specials, seemingly unaware of what they were up to. Tom breathed a sigh of relief, and then he shot Tori a worried look. "What's wrong? It's not there; what you are looking for? It's the wrong spot?"

"Nope, right spot," she held the brick up for him to see before quickly lowering her hand out of sight. "The hollow area is still there, so we may just be in luck."

"So, what's up? Why the sudden outburst?

"I just broke a nail."

"You did what?" The two of them laughed, breaking the tension.

"Broke a nail, you heard me. Will you just listen to me? I could be arrested for disfiguring a historical landmark, and I'm complaining about my nails."

She was grinning, and her eyes were sparkling. Even in the dim light, Tom could tell she was as excited as he was. The only difference was that he didn't know what he was supposed to be so worked up about.

"Don't do a thing till I get back." He got up and, taking his wallet from his back pocket, walked to the bar. Tom told himself to remain calm and to act naturally. He could not give the bartender any reason to pay them the slightest bit of attention.

Tori watched as he paid the bill and picked up the two drinks along with a piece of paper. She could not hear what was being said between the two but hoped that it would not cause any problems or delays. She was just so damn close. Tori held the brick at her side out of sight and placed her free hand on her empty glass.

Tom placed the new beverage in front of her, along with the piece of paper. It was a guest receipt and written on it was the translation of the inscription. Tom explained, "I had to tell him something about your outburst. Couldn't tell the man the truth, could I? So, I said you were making notes and thought you got the translation backward.

He wrote it down for you."

She looked at her companion. He really surprised her. "Quick thinking. God, you're good. Thanks." She took a sip of the drink and looked toward the bar. Walter had returned to his T.V. show and had turned his back on them.

"Well, it's back to work. Here goes. Keep an eye out, OK?"

Tom didn't know which one to watch, the bartender or Tori, and what she was doing. In the end, he flashed his eyes continuously between them both.

Tori was reaching into the small space, and then as her hand disappeared into the hole, she took a sharp breath. "Thanks, Jean, you did remember. I can feel something, almost got it." She took a deep breath and held it while she struggled to grab hold of whatever she had found. "Got it!" Her hand came out holding a small leather pouch, and quickly she dropped it into her open bag. Then she placed the brick back into its original position and kicked at the floor one last time, scattering any visible sign of fallen mortar.

"Drink up," she laughed, picking up her glass and downing the contents. "Trust me; you're going to need it."

Tom did as she said and followed suit. Then before he had time to utter a word, she was up and on her way to the outside.

"Thanks," she called back to Walter.

"Good luck on the book," he answered. "Hey, before you go, what's the name of it?"

Tom looked dumbfounded, while Tori just acted as if it was the most fundamental question to be asked.

"Legends of New Orleans," she answered him, "and when it comes out, this place is going to be very popular. Good luck to you!"

TOM and Tori walked quickly and headed for the car. Tom laughed aloud, waiting until they turned the corner onto St. Philip before shouting at her.

"And you said I was good!" He opened her door and then went around to the driver's side. "You weren't kidding, were you? You have the pouch…shit. It's all true! I mean, how else would you have known where to look?" Grabbing her arm, he said, "My God, do you know what this means? You really did know my mother." His eyes filled with tears as any doubts he'd had washed away.

"You mean, even if nothing is in the pouch, you still believe me, one hundred percent?"

"How in the hell could I not?" he replied. "To tell you the truth, I was afraid that it would turn out to be a lie. I wanted to believe you."

"Well, sitting here like this won't tell us what we have, will it? Let's take a look, shall we?" She reached into her bag and removed the pouch, placing it on her lap.

In the daylight, Tom could see that it was made of thick brown leather and was gathered at the top by a long strip of cord.

The pouch pulled open easily after her fingers had carefully untied the leather cord. She watched Tom's face as she turned the pouch upside down so the contents could fall out into her lap. Tori did not need to see what was falling; she already knew what the pouch contained.

Tom stared as the sound of coins broke the silence in the car. His eyes rounded in sheer delight as a small heap of gold coins landed in her lap.

"Holy shit! Will you look at that? You're rich! You done gone and won the biggest lottery of all!"

Thirty-five coins had dropped out, shining in the morning sunlight. Holding one between her fingers, Tori turned it over slowly and said, "You know, Tom, up until this moment, it could have all been a dream. I have often wondered if it was not some trick of my mind… that I was not nuts. Now, I have proof of my own. Look, here it is." She handed the coin to him. "It's all true." She looked off into the distance in a daydream-like state. "Crazy as it seems, it was so long ago, yet it was just around five years ago for me."

Tom held the coin in his hand, almost afraid to look at it. He then turned it over and over in the palm of his hand, examining it closely. "This is a Spanish gold coin and in mint condition." He reached over and took another coin from her. This one is American. Do you know how long it's been since America made gold coins? I've only seen one in my lifetime, up till now. It was a twenty-dollar gold piece-my dad's. I know the date on it; it's 1903. This is much older."

Tori had spread the coins on top of a road atlas. She was looking at one or two closely while Tom looked at the rest of them.

"They're all in perfect condition and the dates... Tori... they're all way old! I don't know about the Spanish ones, but a few here have dates; here's one dated 1815..."

She reached out smiling and took it from him. "That one is mine."

"What are you going to do? These coins are worth a ton, not just in the weight of gold, but much more to collectors, I'm sure. They're in mint condition... how, are you going to explain where you got them?"

Tori looked at him and smiled. She already knew what she was going to do with her share. "You can make up your own answer to that question, but please come up with a story other than the truth and sell them discreetly. Dan and I will help you if you want. I haven't told you, but we are moving here. Going to look at some homes in the Garden District." Her eyes went to the small pile of gold coins. "Guess I will have the house of my dreams and you, I will have you to talk to, as much as I want." She counted out fifteen coins and handed them over to him. "I need to let the past go. I don't need a lot of publicity and unwanted questions. Tell whoever you take them to that an old relative gave them to you, or maybe not. Let Dan make some inquiries, and we will go from there. My husband is very well connected with those in many different fields. He will do his best to get the top price and keep it quiet."

"You mean you're giving these to me?" he asked. "But why?"

"Because in a way, they belong to you too. I want you to have them. Call it paying off a debt I owe to your mother and father."

"So, what are you going to tell your husband? I mean, about how you got them and me, what about me?"

"I am going to tell him; I asked you to meet me, I told you about Kate and Leone, and then you helped me retrieve what was left for me to find. Nothing more than that, ever. Some things need to remain between us, you understand. Our friendship will remain, and you can promise Dan that you won't talk about my adventure or what I told you. There's only one favor I'll ask you in return."

"Name it," he said softly.

Tori looked out the window and sat quietly.

He loved her so much, not just because of the coins he now held. She had given him much more than money could buy. He had an identity, and he knew about his parents, and best of all, they had learned about him. "What is it? Please, you can tell me." He didn't like the look that appeared on her face. It was the same tormented look that she had the day before and most of the night.

"I want to break away from the past. I want to put Jean's ghost to rest, so to speak. It's time to let him go. You understand I won't stop loving him, but I will move on and live life as he would have wished. To do that, I have one last place to go… and now that you believe me… I hope you will help me. I want to go to Christopher's grave. Will you take me?"

He understood her pain and her need to go there… to complete things. Also, she needed a friend to go with her, and who better than him? Tom knew she could not and would not ask Dan to take her because she had kept the baby a secret from him. No, it had to be him. Tom put the coins into his jean pockets, never looking away from her questioning eyes. He started the car and asked, "Which way?"

They had to stop for gas, and Tori took the opportunity to call the hotel. Dan had not returned, and she had no messages. They were soon on their way with a couple of cans of soda, heading toward Baton Rouge. She told him to exit at one point and explained that it was a short detour. She'd tell him when to turn, then Tori fell silent, and Tom allowed her the time she needed to prepare for the next step.

He focused on the countryside they passed through. Thoughts and questions rambled around in his head, intermingling with his emotions. His feelings were just as mixed up as ever. In just over twenty-four hours, his whole life had turned upside down. He was the son of Leone Duval. He'd never been abandoned by his mother, Kate. He'd simply stepped forward in time, leaving them behind. He looked over at Tori, who smiled slightly.

"You must be remembering a lot," he said. "I don't know which is harder. Me not knowing what it was like… the people, the plantations, the way of life… or you having to live with the memory… and the secret of it all," he said, taking his eyes off the road and looking at her momentarily. "Have you ever thought of telling anyone else?"

She shook her head. "I don't know yet. In the beginning, when I first came back, Dan and I wanted to tell someone else. Someone who could maybe help me get over the shock. And believe me, it was a hell of a shock. It's like I lived two lives, in two different times, and died and came back here again. However, the more we talked about it, the more we knew we had no proof. Sure, my hair was long again overnight, but it could have been that it was never really short in the first place. We could be accused of creating this great big hoax just for the publicity and the money. The talk shows, magazines, and maybe even a tell-all book," she laughed.

"We had to think about Linni, also. People would think I was crazy or a liar, neither of which would look good at a PTA meeting if you know what I mean."

"Well, you could have gone and gotten the coins like we just did. They would have had to believe you then."

"I had thought of that too once, but I wasn't sure anything would be there, so I put that out of my mind until today, that is. Besides, don't you see? They could have said that it was planted beforehand by myself or an accomplice. Sure, it would be an expensive hoax, but that's what they would have settled on in the end. No one wants to believe in time travel," she said, looking out the car window.

He thought about the idea of her planting the coins. To him, it was absurd, and he quickly discarded the possibility.

"Besides," she continued, "I couldn't do much because of … well… I didn't want to reveal the whole story. Didn't want Dan to know all of it. You're the only person that knows the whole damn mess from beginning to end. About Jean and the baby—something that I have not, and will not ever, be able to tell Dan." She took a breath, "I hate keeping it from him. I'm not ashamed of what I did and how I felt, but I just can't hurt him. I can't run the risk of his not understanding why I didn't tell him initially. He asked me to marry him with no doubts in his mind from the start. He loves me, and I know he loves Linni very much. It's been hard on him, but he has never given up on me. That's how much he loves me. So how could I ever tell him that I loved Jean more than my life, that we had a baby—how would he feel if he learned the truth? He thinks I had a fling with the pirate and nothing more. Don't get me wrong, I love Dan more each day, but a part of my heart will…well, you know. It has to be this way. In a short time, I will cut all ties with the past. After seeing the grave and saying my goodbyes, it will be over, finished, and I will go on with my life."

Tori sounded like she was trying to talk herself into believing what she was saying, and Tom was not so sure she was doing the right thing. He was helping her cover up a huge lie, and he'd have to live with it. Although he suddenly felt uncomfortable, he was compelled by his need to help her; he had to continue. She had been through so much, and in the end, she didn't have to come forward and tell him anything. The woman was the bravest he had ever met, and he would die before he'd let her down.

"Get off here and turn toward the town of Destrehan; there is something I want to show you."

The car made the turn, and Tom grinned. He knew where she was taking him. She was going to see the plantation or what was left of it. "What was this area like back then?" The Mississippi was on his left as they headed north, and the land was dotted with large trees and small communities.

"Pretty much as I told you. The distance that took us less than an hour to cover would have taken more than half a day or longer then. That depending on the weather and conditions of the road." She pointed ahead and towards the left. "Slow up; we're almost here. If you pull off to the side in front of Destrehan for a moment, I'll try and describe it to you as it used to be."

He saw the large house and pulled into the small car park on the side. He had been to the more popular and flamboyant plantations such as Oak Alley, but never to this one.

"It…the house looks the same…but the grounds have changed. I'm sure it would break my heart to go inside. Marie and J.D. were so proud of their home and the two wings he added as their family grew. I arrived here after that first Christmas and can tell you it was grand, yet simple. It was a home filled with love and lots of children."

"Do you mind if we just walk around?" he asked. "You could describe it all to me then."

"I really don't want to, Tom. It's just so hard to see what has been taken away. For instance, the view of the river is gone. It was never like that." She pointed across the road to the high levee that faced them. "When I used to visit, the driveway curled up and split off just about there," she said, pointing, "so the carriage could drop off its occupants, either at the front or the back." Sitting up higher in her seat, she continued. "There used to be a separate kitchen, store-house, and drying house.

The slave cabins, about nineteen of them, were down toward the fields. There were others, but those were the only ones I ever saw. And there were large sheds that J.D. kept his machinery in.

Marie used to play with the children out on the grass, right over there, among her flowerbeds. At the end of the day, we'd all watch the river, enjoying the different scents that the breeze carried in while the children played in the garden," she said, smiling. "A low thick hedge enclosed the whole garden, and there were a few oak trees. Some up to sixteen feet in height and all the walkways were bordered by large crepe myrtle trees." Her voice had softened, and sadly she added, "Gone. It's all gone now. Oh, I know the house is there, and the Grand Oaks are here, but it's not the Destrehan I knew, and no one I loved is here; they are long gone."

She shook her head as if trying to remove the sadness. "They had their townhouse in the French Quarter, as you know, but Marie loved it here in the summer, and this is where she raised her children. She was a wonderful woman and a great mother, not to mention one of my best and dearest friends. And J.D. was, in his own right, quite a man. I could tell you so much about him, more than any of those tour guides could, that's for sure," she chuckled. "Take, for instance, the huge marble bathtub off Marie's bedroom. She implied that it had been a gift to them, from none other than Napoleon Bonaparte himself."

Tom laughed. "So, you told me last night but Napoleon?"

"Don't look at me like that," she smiled. "You wanted to know, and I'm not making it up. They knew a lot of important people, both here in this country and in France. Why one of them, the Duc de Orleans, came to stay with them once. He later became King Louis Phillippe of France."

Tom was impressed. He viewed the house with a whole new attitude. 'If only old homes could talk,' he thought. They were so much more than just bricks and wood; they were the past standing in today.

"J.D., as I called him, was elected the first state senator from Louisiana. That was in 1812, I think. Marie hated him being gone so much and being the family man he was; he resigned without serving out his term. Good thing too, if you ask me. Jackson needed his help. He was one of the men on the committee that helped bridge the gap between the citizens of the city and the General's military. He may have had something to do with Jackson's agreement to meet with Jean; I'm not sure, but it wouldn't have surprised me."

"How did Jean and J.D. meet? After all, they seemed to come from two entirely different worlds, if you ask me."

"Not so different as you think. I never got a straight answer out of either man on that same question, but from what I gather, they had met when Jean started using what is called the Harvey Canal. He used it as a shortcut into New Orleans," she grinned. "It worked out very nicely for all involved for quite a while. Anyway, that's how I think they met, though they could have known each other in France, I suppose. Anything is possible."

"You're telling me!" he said, letting out a massive sigh.

"We need to get going. I still have to see the graveyard and get back before Dan returns."

He started the car again and pulled out onto the empty roadway, continuing north past the grand old home. He turned the car around and drove the directions given to him. It was not long before they were traveling up the River Road to where Jean and Tori had buried their son.

THE idea came to him while he was driving, and he spoke with such determination in his voice that Tori had no doubt he would succeed: "I'm going to study, and I'm going to see to it that more of the past is preserved for future generations. Tori, I'm going to use these coins to go to college. I'm going to become a historian and maybe even a curator at the museum one day." He turned toward her. "I will keep one gold coin too and have it mounted. I'll wear it to remind myself of where I came from."

"You know, I think your mother would have liked that. Leone would have been proud of you too. You are a lot like him, determined and strong in your convictions. Yes, they both would have been very proud of you. They were." She looked away from him. Tom was becoming very emotional. Tears filled his eyes, and she didn't need him crying on her right then. She required his strength for what she was about to face.

THE graveyard had changed over the years. It was still a tiny cemetery compared to others like the St. Louis graveyard found in the French Quarter. The aboveground tombs were the norm there, but here, some of the dead lay buried beneath the ground, among the trees. Tori was happy to see it was still a peaceful and harmonious place. The only sounds to disturb the tranquil atmosphere came from the birdcalls overhead.

They both looked around, and even though the cemetery was smaller, it still overwhelmed them. The sheer number of headstones revealed that many had been buried here after Christopher. For decades the place had been used and even expanded beyond the older region behind the iron fence. The newer section, closer to the road, was kept up, and most of the headstones and graveside adornments were far from weathered, even though many dates read from the early 1900s.

The whole area, old and new, had a natural, peaceful atmosphere, just like she and Jean had hoped it would. It was like having a small slice of heaven on earth for those who buried their loved ones there. Though rundown and overgrown in places, it was evidently still being taken care of. Some of the closer graves even had fresh flowers placed on them, and the grass was trimmed and tidy around them. Some families, it seemed, had not forgotten their loved ones resting place.

Walking through the old iron gate, the two of them could hear the sound of someone raking leaves and humming to himself as he did so. Off toward the far end, just about where the fence stopped, they saw an old black man working diligently. He hesitated only briefly to look up, and upon seeing Tori and Tom, nodded his head, smiled, and then went back to his work.

Looking around her, as she walked toward the back end of the oldest part of the graveyard, Tori could see some of the older graves had not been attended to in years. They'd been long forgotten and left for the elements and time to claim. It was a sad sight for her, but then, those graves lay undisturbed, and that is what she and Jean had wanted for their son, to rest in peace.

Walking slowly, she witnessed many gray headstones that the rain and unattended attention had worn smooth. Some markers had weathered the years a little better, sheltered from the elements under large old oaks, but even these stones could not escape the ravages of time. Their inscriptions were fading, erasing the names and dates of those lying beneath them.

Stepping carefully among the graves, for there was no clear pathway, Tori and Tom both noticed that quite a few of the old stones were leaning precariously to their sides. In fact, more than one old stone looked as if a good wind could finish the job time had started and topple them.

Tom moved closer to Tori and asked the obvious question: "How you going to locate it? I mean, this place has had so many new graves since then. Shall we split up? You tell me what to look for."

"That won't be necessary, Tom. Don't you remember what I told you? His grave had a tree planted by it, and if you follow my gaze, you will see for yourself. Over there is a large, old tree and something tells me that under its shade, one of those graves is the one I seek. It's in the right location and… it's the largest tree. There were not so many back then…just let me look."

Tom took her hand as they made their way toward the tree. Then, as if drawn to it like a magnet, Tori walked up to one single small marker that rested amongst the tree's roots. Nearly half of it looked like it had grown into the large roots of the tree. "Silly, the tree grew into the headstone. Guess we didn't think about that. Tom, look at the rest of this stone; it's surrounded by grass, weeds, and more roots. That could be a good thing."

Tom could see the top half of the marker, but whatever had been inscribed there had weathered away. The lower half, however, seemed to have been protected. The part that was encased in the trunk would be impossible to read, and there would be no way to get to the inscription, even if it remained, but maybe there were words lower down that could identify who it was that lay there.

Tori realized that the mighty old tree had wrapped itself around the stone, pushed it to an odd angle over the years, and kept it there. It could have pushed the stone completely over if it had kept on moving against the object in its path, but it had not grown in that direction for some reason.

Tori smiled gently. "I think one could say that the tree is cradling this headstone. At least I'd like to think that."

Standing there looking at the small headstone and the trunk that encompassed it, Tom decided it was surreal and unnerving. He looked away and then walked past Tori to the other side of the massive tree. "I thought you said a tree was planted near his grave; this one seems to…"

"It's his." Tori kneeled and pulled at the weeds and grass that grew close to the stone. "Look here, the inscription is faint, but not all the words are completely gone." Trembling, she ran her fingers across the face of the stone and tried to read it nonetheless. "The name could be Christopher," she whispered. Tori's fingers lightly traced the few indents that remained. then her hand moved lower to make out the beginning of another inscription. "Taken away from us too soon."

Tom knelt by her side, scrutinizing the stone. There was an ample blank space after the first words, but more stone remained to be seen above ground, hidden by grass and dirt. Tom's hand ran over the flat area, then he pulled up the remaining grass by its roots and dug away some of the soil and debris. It was clear that something had been written there, too, at one time. "Look, here, these few words are clear. Most seem to be buried in the tree's roots, but these are clear, they say, "on in our hearts." Tori gasped.

The tree had consumed the first part, but that did not worry Tori, who softly uttered the complete phrase. "Whose memory will always live on in our hearts." Her eyes filled with tears as she said the words out loud. Knowing that what she had found was her son, Tori lowered her head and then rested one of her hands on the top of the stone. "Hello, son," she whispered. "I don't know if you know this, but your daddy was right. You are always in my heart, as I'm sure you are always in his." She could feel the stinging of her tears as the pain buried deep down inside her made its way to escape and be heard. Grief-stricken, Tori cried softly, not only for her son but for the memories that she would forever leave after this day. Her son would remain as he should, a part of history.

"Tom, can you leave me alone for a bit…please?"

It broke his heart to see her so sad, yet she was stronger than most he had ever known. He understood her need and knew that she would be all right without him standing there. So, without a word, he left and walked back toward the iron fence to give her some space.

TOM walked to the fence and the old man, who was still working, at tidying the grounds. "Mind if I join you? She needs some time alone."

The black man stopped what he was doing and looked up into Tom's face. He could see the hidden heritage in the stranger's features, giving them something in common. The man was maybe half black, but that didn't matter to him, full or half; he was a brother, and besides, he was respectable, asking politely if he could join him. He put down his rake, looked over toward Tori, and then back at the man standing in front of him. Something told his old bones that the young man was not the normal curiosity-seeker. He got plenty of those, looking for ghosts or whatever. Most just left when he chased them way, but this couple was different somehow.

"Ain't been no one buried over there in years. Folks these days wants themselves buried fancy-like. Got to have themselves laid in some big fancy spot, not run down and old like this is." He spit off to the side and leaned up against the fence. Reaching into his pocket, he took out a packet of chewing tobacco and offered some to Tom, who politely refused, so he preceded to fill his cheek with a fresh wad, then he replaced the packet very carefully, paying great attention, so as not to spill any. Once that was taken care of, he looked over at Tori again. The woman was on her knees, cleaning the small area at the base of the old tree. He could tell she was crying too. "Ain't never seen, no one come here, to take care of no grave like that neither. I been a takin' care of this place for long as I kin remember. Know every grave. That one, there, it's too old for any kin. How come she goin' on like that? Like it's some kin of hers or somethin'?"

Tom looked into the man's face and into his weary eyes that lay sunken above his hollow cheekbones. Gray stubble clung to the man's chin, and his clothes looked old and worn but clean. He had a serious look about him, yet he also had a gentleness in his persona. His face held kindness and, in its expression had wisdom written in its many creases. The creases formed deep furrows in his leather-like skin from his forehead clear down his neck, and Tom thought he was the kind of man who had a thousand stories to tell and no one to tell them to. Those wrinkles, the one's surrounding his mouth, made it appear as if he were about to smile. If he were a bitter old codger, then those lines would have to droop downward in a permanent scowl, but they didn't. At that second, Tom decided the man had the kind of face that you could trust.

"If I told you that she did have a claim to the grave, you would only want to know-how. So, could you please trust me? All you have to know is that soon she will leave and we won't be back. My friend just has to make peace with herself and her memories."

The old man listened to Tom's words and could see that the kid was not telling him a lie. God had seen that he was a good judge of character. Hell, he could tell the young man all about his gift, about being able to judge people and all. Like he had earlier, he'd been a good judge of character then. The man wondered if he should tell this new visitor that they were not the first on this day to pay attention to that grave? He was pondering that very thought when he saw the exact figure from early that morning, making his way over to where the woman knelt.

TORI had stopped crying. She was kneeling deep in thought as the sunbeams filtered down among the tree's branches. She watched as the shadows danced upon the grass and around the headstones. They seemed to play a game of chase with the golden sunlit. These spots would appear and disappear with each breath of wind. Maybe her son played here among the shadows and sunlight. Maybe on moonlit nights, he climbed trees and enjoyed the beauty of the place? Tori hoped so. One last prayer and she would leave. A deep shudder ran the length of her body as Tori knew that what was buried here would remain and the past would keep its secrets. Tori lowered her head and closed her eyes to pray. It was time to say goodbye.

During her prayer, a hand came down upon her shoulder, resting gently, as if not wanting to disturb her. The shadow of the person behind her was blocking out the rays of sunlight on Christopher's gravestone, but unlike its dancing partners, this shadow did not move.

Reaching up, she held the hand in hers, never taking her eyes away from the grave. It was nice to know Tom cared how she felt and that he had joined her. Tom was the one person Tori could lean on right then, knowing that the grieving woman began to pay attention to her surroundings and him. She could feel the warmth of his skin and the dampness of his palm in hers as he gently but firmly squeezed hold of her hand. It came as a shock when it registered in her mind that it was not Tom who was standing next to her. His hands would never feel so warm and frail. Tori turned her head and looked at her shoulder, where she saw that the hand on hers, was that of an old man.

This was odd and still more confounding because she could not get free of its solid grip. The old hand that grasped hers was as firm as Tom's could ever have been, but she was sure it was not Tom's. Had she looked so desperate, crying at an old gravestone, that some stranger had taken pity on her, she wondered? Tori turned to face the man to explain that she was all right, but the words never left her mouth.

The old man standing over her was partially obscured by the sun shining brightly behind him. Squinting, she tried but could not focus on his face at all. The hand that was gripping hers became even tighter when she tried to lean to one side to get a good look at him. Whoever he was, his hand was now squeezing hers, almost to the point of hurting her, and still, he did not talk or show any sign of releasing her. Panicked by these actions, Tori looked to see where Tom was. Her intention was to call him to come and help her because something was not right; she could feel it. However, before she had time to locate Tom or anyone else, let alone call out, the stranger before her took a few steps to stand by her side.

Tori's eyes followed the man's movements, and the moment he stepped out of the sun's glare, his face came clearly into view. He was old, but she knew him immediately, and all she could do was gasp. Calling out for Tom was now the furthest thing from her mind.

The man's dark eyes gazed into hers and held her captive. Even if she had wanted to look away, she couldn't because somehow, she had to make certain it was him and not some trick of the light. He just stood looking at her as if he'd seen a ghost; then, he nodded his head slowly in acceptance.

Tori would have known those eyes anywhere…and in any era, at any age. They were the same eyes that had haunted her dreams every day for years. Even though not a single word had been uttered, they both had come to the same conclusion. While still trying to understand what was happening, Tori let the man help her up, pulling her to within inches of his chest, where she fell into his arms. She clung to him as he did to her. No words were uttered as they were not necessary; their actions spoke volumes, and silently both stood for what seemed like an eternity.

His hair was gray, and a fever's heat pumped out of his thin body. His shirt was soaked from sweat, causing the material to cling to him. The strong shoulders that had once been broad and square now sagged beneath her grasp. He shuddered weakly, and this movement alone gave her a reason to speak.

Somehow Tori managed to utter her first words to him, words mixed with the taste of salty tears. "Jean, I don't understand... how?" This was all she could say as fear and doubt raced in her mind. Tori couldn't even bring herself to raise her head from his shoulder, too afraid that if she did and looked closer at him, he would not be her Jean after all.

One of his hands came up to her head and stroked at the side of her face tenderly, and still, he did not speak; instead, he swayed a little, holding her as close as he possibly could. For a while, his embrace was as strong as ever, and he held her like he had so many times, and yet still, she refused to fully allow herself the possibility that the man was real, that he was Laffite.

Tori pushed back from him, trying to get a better look at his face. "Here, let me get a better look at you. Oh my God, I'm not dreaming. It *is* you!"

"That it is, my lady," said the old familiar voice. "And it really is you." His body slumped a little, and she felt him weakening. Then, as if he had no energy left, Jean let himself lean against her body for support and tried to gain his balance but was failing to do so.

"Come and sit over here," she ordered while helping him to the shady side of the large tree. "You're exhausted. I can see it, and you're not well."

He sat down, finally releasing her hand to do so. Then the old pirate leaned his back up against the tree's trunk for support. Immediately he patted the ground in an invitation to join him. "My lady, my love, Tori. You are as I remember you. It seems time has been far kinder to you than to me. You are as beautiful as the day I first laid eyes on you, or more like night," he laughed hoarsely, remembering how feisty and full of fire she'd been that night at Rose's. Then sadness filled his expression as he added, "and as beautiful as the day I lost you."

It was him! His voice was so familiar; his features had changed, but his spirit was the same. There was no longer a shred of doubt in her mind. On acceptance of Jean's identity, many unanswered questions and thoughts flooded her brain. However, the most prominent thought of all was that Jean, her Jean, was here looking at her and still loving her.

He smiled. "It would seem to me that we both have been brought together once again. And he, our son…" Jean coughed as his hand grabbed his chest, halting his speech.

Tori took his other hand in hers and watched as he tried to relax and catch his breath. The man was ill and needed medical help; that was obvious. He had a fever; that much was evident, but his eyes were clear, and he had his wits about him. She assured herself that whatever ailed him was not serious and that a few antibiotics would do the trick: he'd be fine.

"Sorry, my love. As I was saying, we're together again because of our son and…just in time."

"Jean, you need a doctor; any fool can see that."

"No, my love, what I need is to explain to you what happened. That is why I am here. So, for once, sit and listen…" he said, trying to smile as his fingers stroked her palm. "I crossed over three days ago and knew right away; I was in the right time. Some future you have here." His face filled with wonder like that of a child's. His eyes sparkled, as she had so often seen them do, as he continued. "I have seen for myself all that you told me about, well, nearly all," he grinned. "I have seen the carriages that go without horses, the things that fly in the air... the size of the boats," he coughed again, then added, "and the barges on the river. The ships that travel up and down... not a sail among them. All as you told me. But what did they do to the city? I could not find my way around, and people in this time are not so trusting. Not that I blame them much, me looking as I do." He shifted his position a little so he could look easily into her face as he talked.

"Some have helped, but I was weakening fast and knew only one place I could go that I could find. I got here early but left to get some water and look at the river. One has to have a backup plan, and here I had no plan at all except to reach this place." He fell silent, and she waited for him to continue. "When I returned here to the graveyard, I thought myself dead, for you were waiting for me. I could not believe my eyes or my heart. You are young, and for that I am..." he hesitated. "I had an image in my mind, you see. I carried this image..." Again, he paused, looking at her closely. "I am old, and I imagined you the same way, but I found you are here and as beautiful as ever. I am not dead, am I?" He coughed again, sounding worse than before.

"No, Jean. You're not dead, but you surely will be if we don't get you to a doctor."

Tom had walked over to join Tori as soon as he saw the stranger approaching her. He had seen them hug and then sit together. For his life, he could not understand what had prompted Tori to act as she had, and by the time he joined them, it was clear something was up.

Tori turned to face him. Whether he believed her or not, she would need his help getting Jean to a doctor. "You won't want to believe me, but it's true. Tom, this man is Jean, my Jean. Tom, he's here."

Tom's face was blank, and she thought maybe he did not understand her. "Jean, Laffite! Tom, please, I am not lying. This is Jean!"

Her young friend's body stiffened at the news. Sure, the man was dressed strangely, but most of the bums around the city were. That did not make him the pirate that they had talked about. He searched the stranger's face for any sign resembling the description she had given of Laffite. However, what he saw was the old man scrutinizing him just as closely. His outfit looked like a poor pirate outfit that was sold for Halloween. His boots were leather and engulfed his legs, stopping just below his knees. A hint of a gold chain around his neck caught the sun, but it was only a glimpse. Maybe, he thought on that chain was a coin. Maybe a date on said coin could help confirm what Tori was suggesting.

Jean's face softened, his deep creases relaxing. "Tori, this young man looks a lot like Leone. Can it be that he is the young Tommy you told me of all those years ago?"

Tom's eyes lit up at the reference to his father. Only the real Laffite could know about Leone, but before he had a chance to respond, Tori started speaking.

"I see your memory is as good as ever. He is one and the same, but you need to stop talking. We have to get you to a doctor." She began to get up.

Jean's hand reached out and pushed down on her shoulder, shaking his head as he did so. He pulled himself up to a higher sitting position. "It's not going to do any good, I'm afraid. I have seen a doctor. True, it was hundreds of years ago," he chuckled, "but I doubt that even your doctors could do anything for me now. Leave it be. Let's just sit here for a while and talk. Come join us, lad. I assume that you know about me and my connection to this lady."

Tom nodded his head. "Yes, Sir. I know," he said, running his hand nervously through his hair. "This is a hell of a shock, you know. Give me a few to wrap my head around this, will you? Hey, why don't I get us a couple of sodas from the car."

"That would be great," answered Tori, without taking her eyes off Jean.

Tom left them without saying another word. He needed to get his head together, and they could use a few more minutes to themselves. This time travel thing was absolutely messing with his mind. First the coins, the solid proof he'd asked for, and now he was looking at the man Tori swore to be, Jean Laffite himself. Jean Laffite was here, but what was next? The man was ill; anyone could see that. Getting him to a clinic or E.R. would mean him producing his identification, a driver's license, or even a social security number, both of which the pirate would not have. Tori was worried that was plain enough, and that had to be the reason she was not thinking clearly, not realizing the problems that now faced them.

TORI moved closer to Jean's side, sitting with her back up against the tree trunk, allowing him to lean comfortably against her. She wanted to take him for medical help but knew that to try to do so before he was ready would be like trying to move a mountain. Once Tori accepted that she was able to calmly and rationally talk with him without a trace of panic showing. First, she explained to him what had happened to her the day she crossed back to her time. He listened to her every word while looking toward Tom every now and then. It seemed he was taking his time getting some sodas, whatever they were?

He had fallen silent and seemed distracted. Tori desperately wanted to get him to pay attention to her. Squeezing his hand in hers, she spoke with her voice breaking up as if the words themselves hurt to utter. "You know, not a day has gone by that I haven't thought about you...about us." Tori shifted into a more comfortable position. "I even started reading everything I could about you and about the years after I left."

Tom joined them, hesitating at first to sit down. "Here," he said, handing Tori a can of soda. "Sorry it's not ice-cold, but beggars can't be choosers, I suppose."

Jean said nothing, but Tori could see that he found Tom's way of speaking amusing. She popped the top of the can and took a swig before handing it to her pirate. "Jean, try this. It's not what you're used to, but it's wet."

Jean had startled at the sound of the can popping and then quickly composed himself. Again, his old grin filled his expression. "It seems to me that if I am to keep you happy, I must oblige you." He cautiously put the can to his parched lips and took a sip. "Not what I call a man's drink, but then as you say, it's wet." He grinned as he handed it back to her before turning to Tom. "Do you know that this woman has the damnedest ability to always get her way? That or getting herself into situations where she did not need to go."

"She does have a certain ability in that direction," grinned Tom. "She got me to bring her here today. It's the last place I would have ever expected to be."

Jean turned back to Tori. "Glad you came," he said, patting her hand.

"Jean, what happened to you after I left? I mean, I know what happened; you're here, but what did you do all those years? I couldn't find one thing in all my reading that told me much. I even tried to find a link, anything referring to me, even Christopher... but nothing. I phoned...called...talked to someone at the Cathedral and asked them to check their books. Sort of lied to get them to look."

Jean shook his head and chuckled. "Told you she has the ability to get her way, and now, even lying to the church." He coughed as he laughed, and when he settled down, he smiled at her, admiration clearly showing on his face. "Go on, what did they find there?"

"You know just what they found. His christening records are gone. Did you have something to do with that?"

He laughed softly and looked at her with that old familiar twinkle of mischief.

Tom had to admit that even now, in the winter of his years, Jean had a roguish, handsome look about him. With a shower, haircut, and some new clothes, he would easily present himself as what the ladies called a grey fox. Yes, the younger pirate must have been quite the man in his day. Tori had not exaggerated at all. Watching the pair interact like they were, was like having a glimpse of how they had been back in the day.

Tori half-smiled at Jean. "Don't you go giving me that 'who me?' look, Mr. Laffite. You know very well that I can see right through you. Always could, always will. I know some of what you did or what history said you did. I only want to know what really happened." She looked at him and then softly pleaded, "Ple-e-e-ease."

"You talk about knowing me, huh." He looked toward Tom. "That's how she gets you every time, with that pleading look of hers. That coy, soft, loving appeal tugs at your heart so much that the battle of wits is a lost battle," he chuckled.

His Tori had not changed a bit, and he was so glad. "I'll try to explain some of what happened, but this old mind is not as clear or quick as it once was."

"Liar," she pushed playfully at his side.

"Well then," he stroked his unshaven cheek and then pulled at the goatee, "let's say, I will tell you that, which I think is relevant, starting with the most obvious. I take it you must have asked the Cathedral to prove a point. After all, they do keep such good records."

His chuckle made Tom grin and Tori smile.

"Oh, you devil. You did do something, didn't you? But, how on earth did you manage it? I mean, that's the church we're talking about. I was told the records of Pierre's children; they were still intact."

"Had no reason to disturb them," he stated.

"You had told me often enough that in your time, this time here, there was very little known about my life. I chose to help keep it that way. If you stop interrupting me, I will tell you what I did."

"I do not interrupt you. You keep avoiding the subject," she said, trying to sound serious.

Tori was teasing him, and he knew it. It was as if time had stood still in their relationship. They were acting as they always had, and his heart filled with love at the memory. Still, he had to be careful. To tell her too much would be a disaster, and to tell her the reason why he had imagined her as an old lady…that was something he had to consider carefully.

Tom sat still, watching and seeing the interaction between them. He understood now, only too clearly, the pain their parting had cost them. Tori's life with this incredible man suddenly became very real to him.

Jean took the can from Tori and tried another sip of the strange liquid, and handed it back to her. Neither Tori nor Tom spoke a word. They just sat under the shade of the tree and listened to the pirate's deep, methodical voice as he continued.

"You remember our friend Nicholas Girod? The mayor? I see you do." He looked at Tom. "He was not only a friend but the mayor of New Orleans for a while. Very helpful to both my business and myself at times, as my love knows only too well." He looked toward Tori then. "More so after you left. He resigned as mayor in September of 1815. I will not detail his personal life or his dealings with myself. I shall say that he died a very wealthy gentleman," He winked again and grinned. "Let me say that due to his prospering, and thanks to my aid, he owed me a favor. After he became the church's warden, the warden of the St. Louis Cathedral, that is, it was easy enough for him to help me out. He was not in that position for long and maybe not even officially, but it mattered not. He was trusted, respected, and never questioned, as far as I know. He was known to be devout in his faith. It worked out for all involved." Jean had an inscrutable grin covering his face when he shared this last bit of information. He was delighted by the memory of what he had been able to accomplish.

"So that's why the records aren't there. Why there are pages torn from the book. You devil you. You never change, do you? Still up to your old tricks. What else did you do?"

"My whole life, after you left me, was, as you said, filled with old

314

tricks. That and loneliness." His face saddened as his voice softened. "Now, I have to tell you something else. I don't know if it is written in your history books or not, but I would not want you to learn of it by reading it. You shall hear it from my lips." He looked gently at her then. His whole attention was on his wife, and it was to her that he explained the next part of his life.

"I took a mistress. It is as simple and as complex as that. I will tell you that I never stopped loving you. It does not excuse what I did, but she never filled my heart, only helped with my loneliness."

Tori's eyes were filled with compassion and understanding beyond anything he could have hoped for. "Oh, my Jean, my love, I would not have expected you to stay alone. I know where I stand. I am secure in your heart, always have been. Just as you should know that you are and will forever be in mine."

Jean smiled at this, but the smile was fleeting. "There is more. You have a right to know, and I have to tell you. It was to Catherine's arms that I went. It was there that I sought refuge from the loneliness, the wanting of you."

"The young Catherine Villars?" Her voice was shaky, and her tone sounded a little shocked.

"One and the same. She was young and had always loved me from afar. Even my brother Pierre, her sister, and mother thought the arrangement a good one. Never did I lie to her about you or my feelings. She never asked for me to love her, and for that, I will always be a bit ashamed…nor did she pry into where you had gone, and I never gave an explanation to anyone. Marie and Davis knew."

He lowered his head, wiping at his sweat-filled brow. His fingers squeezed his eyes closed. "We had a child, a boy. He was named after Pierre." He looked up at his lady, a pleading look in his eyes, asking for forgiveness or at least her understanding.

She reached for him and hugged him close. Tori did not utter a word. There was no need. Then after a few minutes, she sat back and smiled at him. "Did you really go to Galveston?"

"I did." The subject of his mistress and child was now closed as far as he was concerned. He was glad for the change of subject and loved her for doing it. As always, she knew him so well. "When you left, I returned to the city. Not right away; it took me days to leave that lake and you behind." Turning to Tom, he said, "I sat there every morning hoping to join her." He spoke to both of them, looking from one to the other as he continued. "I went to Grymes and had him sell the plantation. My name was not on the deed or the bill of sale. Took some fancy maneuvering, that one did, but Livingston and Grymes, well, that's what they got paid so well for. Handling odd requests of mine was a frequent event before and after I left the city."

Tori raised her eyebrow in acknowledgment of this information, but she did not question him.

"Livingston and Grymes both continued to try and reclaim all that was taken away from me. This included my ships and my merchandise, but as time went by, it became only too clear that the tide had turned against me. Knowing about Galveston, I set about arranging with a few close friends, Sauvinet, Girod, and Blanque, to purchase some of my fleet back for me. When I had a few ships, not all, but more than enough, my men slowly came to join me once again. It was no Grand Terre, but I built a house, and the settlement was more established than anything before. I was like a man possessed. I drank, I swore, and I set sail with my brother, Pierre. It did not last long, but you knew that, didn't you?"

She simply nodded her head.

"After that, a storm raged inside of me. I left Catherine, the boy, and many others on Galveston… and tried to return to New Orleans, but to no avail. Dominique left my side at this time, choosing to remain in the city. I can't say that I blame him. He did become helpful over the years and was always ready and willing to help me when I was in need. I returned to Galveston one last time, and it ended sadly. The Americans gave me no choice, so I burned it all down and sailed off, never looking back."

Tori smiled softly. "I know you did. I have spent years doing

316

research, reading everything written about you. I even looked up everyone I met and read about them. Made a list, hoped that somewhere in their memoirs would be a mention of you. I did learn that it was Pierre that died in the Yucatan and not you. It is his body that was buried there. I am correct on that, right?"

"You are. I saw a few of our friends over the years but held them to secrecy. I gather they kept their word. After I fled Galveston, I was angry, and if not for my crew, I think I would not have lived long. They slipped me into New Orleans to visit Dominique, and it was at this time that Marie Laveau reached me, and I took hold of my life. She is a very wise woman and a good friend. Everything I did after that was with you and your time in mind. I was honorbound, after all. It became a game for me, a challenge, and one that you have confirmed I won." He coughed hard, buckling over, his hands grabbing his midsection.

Once the coughing fit had subsided, Tom stood up and helped Tori move the old pirate to a more comfortable position. He was so exhausted and weak that it took both of them to get him positioned. Once he was on his side, Jean rested his head in Tori's lap, looking up into her face.

For so long, most of his life even, he had carried a vision of her in his mind. It was the vision of the last time he had held her, many years ago. Jean would not tell her about that sad day. Their lives had always been entwined, and he would not change any of it. All he had to do was convince her that her world and life would not end because his had too. Laffite clearly saw that destiny had given them a gift to see each other one last time and not have to leave this world alone.

All the time Tori was with him in the past, she worried about changing the future, and as he looked at her, he found he finally understood that. He would not do or say anything that would change what was to be. "Tori, history did not give up on me, nor would I give up on you. I knew that whatever I did, you would read about it in your own time, and my love, I did not want you to suffer, thinking 'what if.' So, I simply…" he started coughing again.

She held his head up until he quieted down. He sipped a small amount of the soda that she offered him before pushing it firmly away. "What does it matter what I did or where I went? I think that I rather like the mystery man I have created," he said, his dark eyes staring intensely into hers.

"And you did a damn fine job of it if I might say so," said Tom.

"Why, thank you, Sir. I believe I do agree with you there. Still, the story is not over, is it? I am here, after all. I had no intention of ever trying to come to this time, but when I learned that I did not have long left…" Jean grasped hold of Tori's hand, "well, you were all I could think of once again. So, I returned to New Orleans and our two dear friends. Marie Laveau and John Davis. I really had no idea that this time anomaly would work again, let alone for me. If I could not get to you…that was what I was thinking. If not, I planned to visit this place and make my peace. I was going to come here to our son, and I was going to see to it that…well, that's another fact we shall talk of soon. Anyway, I got to come here instead. Thanks to those two and my insistence."

Tom looked at him and couldn't help but ask the one question he knew Tori was also thinking. "How, how did you do it?"

"Well, I had good instructions and a lot of luck." Jean looked at Tori. "You see, I begged Marie, and she talked with John, and we knew I could try one last time. Not the lake…no that was impossible. It was the way John and Cisco came to us…the alley late at night. I stood there until there was silence. We both know what that stillness is, don't we? There was nothing, but suddenly there was this loud noise from somewhere up in the heavens.

When I looked up, I could not see anything, but I could hear it, and without thinking, I started walking, searching for whatever was making the roaring sound. I walked down the dark alley, trying to follow that sound, when I finally saw it. The big thing you had told me of that flew in the sky. A plane is what you called them; I recall that now. It simply appeared in the heavens, and I knew I was here, in your time. Besides, the whole town had lights, not gas or candles, and everything was… but I have no need to describe that. Part of this outfit belonged to Cisco, Marie had kept it, and I used it. Marie said I needed something to connect me to your time and to you." He closed his eyes and whispered, "I had both, and then I found you… that's all I ever wanted to do. Forgive me; I never meant to travel here. I had given my word…"

Tori leaned over and drew him into her embrace. He had never stopped loving her, and now he was once again by her side, but was it too late? What could she do? What was going to happen? Looking at both Tom and Jean, she guessed they were wondering the same.

A man's cough broke the silence and caused all three to look to see who had joined them. Tom had forgotten about the old black caretaker, and now he stood a few feet away from them, staring at them in wonder. "I been listening behind this old tree, and if my ears hear right, I would like a talk with you."

Tori nodded her head affirmatively. She did not care if he joined them one way or the other. If he had heard them talking, what difference would it make? No one would believe this old bum, in her arms, was Jean Laffite. They would say he was a crazy old man. No, her Jean was still safe.

The caretaker sat down in front of Jean. "Me old bones ain't doin' what they used to. These here young'uns don't know of old yet. Here," he said, reaching into his back pocket and pulling out a small metal flask; he held it out toward Jean.

"You need this. It's got more punch than that there sugar water. Go on, take a swig."

Jean took it, his hands fumbling with the top as he opened it. He lifted the flask to his lips, stopping briefly to smell the container under his nose. He smiled and then winked at the old caretaker. Happily, he swallowed a large gulp. His face reddened as his eyes watered. "Thank you." His voice sounded hoarse from whatever it was he had swallowed. "Now, that's a man's drink," he added, handing the flask back.

The old man took it from him and frowned. "You really this Laffite fellow?"

Jean nodded his head. "You can say that whatever is left of this old man is Jean Laffite."

The black man looked at all three of them carefully. "Well, if you are who you say you are, you can prove it by answering my question."

"If I can, I don't mind."

Tori objected. "We need to go, not sit here and chat as if nothing is wrong." She wanted to get him to the doctor, but Jean shook his head. He silenced her with one look and then turned his head to face the black stranger.

"Go ahead, ask your question. I'll just have one more swig from your flask, though, in payment." His face held that inscrutable look. Jean was up to his old tricks again, thought Tori. The pirate pushed himself up to a sitting position again and reached out his hand.

The old caretaker handed him the flask. He wanted to know about the story that his family had passed down from generation to generation. If it were just a story, this man obviously couldn't have known about it. He could still be Jean Laffite. However, if it were true, the real Laffite also had to know the story, and it would prove beyond any doubt he was who he claimed to be.

"Well, there is this here legend in my family, a story that you might remember. It took place after the Battle of New Orleans. Yes, Sir, the big battle. The story goes that you set a black slave free. A young boy he was, not yet a man. Old enough to help you out, though, he was. Now, can you tell this old man, the name of that there, slave? The one that you set free?"

Jean looked at the man and handed him back his flask. He had to think. True, he'd set a lot of his slaves free over the years. The first being shortly after he and Tori were at Grand Terre. Still, there was one he would never forget. It was the young boy Thiac had taken under his wing, the boy who had saved his life during the battle.

The one that, when it was over, had used Jackson's name. "Can't seem to remember his first name but seems to me the boy you are talking about is Jackson. Is that the one? Used to be so good at names," he whispered.

He was weakening, and even his cough sounded different, not as forceful as it had been. Tori hated to see him like he was, and it worried her. She looked at him and could see the disappointment in his eyes at not being able to give the old man the full name.

"I think the name was David. Jean, you know. Isn't that the boy; you told me about him, the day you sent him to Thiac for a job as a free man."

The fog lifted as the years slipped away, and he clearly remembered. "Yes, that is it. It was David Jackson. He named himself after the General."

They all looked at the caretaker for confirmation that he had the right name. The shock and surprise on the old man's face told them that it was.

"Praise the Lord! You are *him*! Aint no one knows that story around here. I don't tell it no more. Folks, they don't care none, and anyways, they thinks it a lie. Everyone's great, great, great, granddaddy was with you or knew you, but then I always knew that the story was true. I ain't got no one to pass it down to no more. My boy, he got killed over in Nam. Me, I'm the last. Monsieur Laffite, my names the same as my ancestors, as all the first-born boys in our families were called. I'm David Jackson, Sir, and I owe you. My family owes you. Anythin' I can do to help you, you name it. Lord, this is just the damnedest thing." The man was so overcome by his emotions that he pulled out a red piece of cloth he used for a handkerchief and blew his nose and wiped his tear-filled eyes.

Tom went over to the man and helped him to his feet. "Let's take a short walk. Leave them alone for a while. Got any more of that booze, or whatever it is?"

"Sure do, right over that way, in the shed," he pointed to the small structure at the back of the graveyard. You just follow old David, and we will go and find us some. I think we both needs it."

The two headed off together, and as they walked, Tom looked back over his shoulder. "Won't be gone long. You two behave yourselves."

Tori looked into Jean's weary face. He was staring at her with such a strange smile. "David Jackson... Seems that fate has once again been working. Who would have known? Tori, my love, I need to ask you something." He shivered slightly. "I am so tired. So cold."

She moved closer to him, letting the top half of his body lay in her lap. Flashes of Cisco's death came and went. She told herself Jean was not dying. He just needed to see a doctor-that was all.

Laffite looked up into her face, forgetting his question for the moment. "Been a long, long time since I've been in your arms. It feels good. Feels like I've come home." He closed his tired eyes and rested for a while.

Tori watched his breathing, which was shallow but steady. She waited silently while she studied him. His face looked so peaceful, and his skin was still tanned, giving him that seafarer's rugged look. She could say that the lines which ran deeply across his face were etched by the sun and wind and not by old age.

His silver hair was shorter than it had been but still fell softly below his collar, as was the style of so long ago. When his eyes opened, Tori realized that she could still lose herself in their dark depths.

He began again with his story. "When I lost you, I made my mind up to keep my word, to honor your wishes. I did, too, for so many years. I gave my word after all." He closed his eyes and continued talking, more to himself than to her. "I never searched. So many years there were without you." Jean opened his eyes and looked at her sad expression. "What have I done? I never meant to come here... I did... never thought it would work," he lied, "it just happened." He rubbed his eyes and then slowly shook his head side to side. "Let's not talk of this; it makes us both melancholy to do so. I am glad that you are in your own time, that you found your

Linni and family again. Your life is as it should be, while mine is almost over."

Tori looked at him. "How did you know I found Linni? I have not spoken of her."

"Tori, it stands to reason; if you found Tom, you found Linni. Listen to me; you have so much to live for."

It sounded like a good-bye speech, and she wanted no part of such a thing. "Will you stop talking like that? Look, we are going to get you to a doctor, and you will get well. Then I can show you so much. You will see all the things I used to talk about."

He raised his hand to her face, stroking her cheek. His finger traveled down the side of her jawline, and then he outlined her lips.

"So beautiful, so strong. Listen to me now. Just listen. I am dying, and it is right for me to do so. There is not enough time to get me back, and I doubt that it was meant to be. I am where I am supposed to be. We are here, you and I, to end what began so long ago." He turned his head away from her and looked over at Christopher's tiny grave. Our son loved you so, just like I do." He looked back at her. "The boy has been alone long enough. Tori see to it that I join him. Lay me to rest next to him, but no marker. No one must know. I want to be left in peace with our child."

Tori began softly crying again. She did not want it to end like this. Laffite's lady would not let him go, but she would promise him anything if only to get him to rest a bit and then go to a doctor. "You have my word on it, Jean, but that will be in the future, not now. You just need rest, that's all. I do give you my word, though."

Once she had given her word, he relaxed and smiled at her. "Please don't cry. You have no need, my love. You have brought me such happiness. Such love. You are here with me now." He lifted her hand to his lips, kissing it lightly. "You did not forget me."

"I will never forget you, Jean. How could I?"

Placing her hand over his heart and holding it there, he spoke. "I will always have you in my heart."

"And a part of me will always be Jean Laffite's. I love you now and always will." Her eyes were filling with more tears, and he did not want her to be sad or be filled with regret.

"I wrote something many years ago. Wrote it for you. I was trying to find a way to put it where you would read it. It was a problem that I did not solve. It is solved now, though, as I can recite it. It goes like this—my lady. Time is as fluid as the sea I sailed upon. Its currents like the days washing you along on life's journey. The kindest, most beautiful gift time ever deposited upon my shore was you. The cruelest its waves ever became was the day it swept you from my life. And now it seems, in its grandest moment, I am to be put adrift in the mystery of its depths. Or rather, set free to sail upon heaven's ocean above. Upon which star I wonder will I wash ashore? Wherever time and tide take me, I go full of love and in peace. Let me no longer be an anchor to you. Instead, let the memory of us calm your soul and set you free to sail the most glorious oceans of them all…the one called life."

"That's beautiful." Tori was truly moved. How could she not be, she asked herself? After all, it was his swansong. Her pirate was saying his farewell.

He smiled up at her. "No tears, my love. Here, I have something for you." Jean was struggling to remove a gold chain from around his neck. "It's yours. It really is." The sheer effort started him coughing again, but he was determined to remove the chain, which he did by pulling it over his head. "Here, take it. I think it is the reason I found you…"

She held out her hand and watched as the thick gold links, on which hung a round gold ring, dangled from his fingers. He dropped it in her open hand. "There, it's back." Tori looked at it closely and saw that the ring was not like anything she had seen before.

"It is called a Möbius. Sort of a symbol of infinity, or something close to it." He coughed violently, and this time his hand came away with blood on it. "I think maybe you will understand one day. I have carried it with me, and it has given me the strength to continue when I had need. It will do the same for you. It is our symbol, our destiny."

Tori held the gold ring to her lips and kissed it.

"I hope you will forgive me for taking so long to return it to you…" he said, smiling weakly, "but after all, I gave my word to not look for you, and a gentleman always keeps his word."

Looking at him, she tried to remember him ever giving the piece to her and could not. Maybe, he was confused, but rather than confront him, she held the ring close to her heart and smiled at him. What did it matter anyway? He had kept it with him, and she would now keep it with her, always.

"It is done," his raspy voice softly sounded the words. Be happy, my love. I am suddenly not so cold, for I am always going to remain warm in the memory of what we have shared." His hand left hers and came up to her face, touching it briefly. "This image is the one I get to take with me." Then his hand slipped downward, knocking hers off his chest.

Tori would not feel his heart stop beneath her hand. She did not have to. She simply knew Jean Laffite had, at last, gone home.

Tori let out a stifled cry and gently moved him off her lap. Then she dropped her head down onto the chest of the man she had loved and shared so much with, her gentleman pirate.

Tom and David ran to her side. It did not take words to explain what had happened. Her face and her actions told them. Tom knelt and placed his arm around her waist, lifting her off Jean.

"We have to bury him here," was all she said.

"But, Tori, I don't know if that can be done. We will see about it later, okay? We will do what we can. Come with me. David will call someone to take care of him."

"No!" she screamed at him. "You don't understand. I gave my word! I promised him." She turned to David. "I said he would be buried next to his son, just as he wanted. I gave him my word.

Oh, please, David. You have to help me." She turned back to Tom. "You both have to help me. I can't let them do an autopsy or try to learn who he is. Don't you see, I gave him my word."

Tom panicked. "Tori, I don't know if that can be done. His death has to be reported and a death certificate issued; so much red tape."

Tori shook her head. "I don't give a rat's ass," she yelled angrily. Then she tried to control herself, struggling hard to soften her plea. "He has to be buried here; he has to!" She pushed Tom's arm away and dropped to the ground to lay her head down on Jean's chest.

It was David who spoke next, kneeling beside her. "Listen, I owe this man a debt. My great, great, great granddaddy never did get to pay him back for what he did. He saved his life and set him free, and he always said that he owed him. Our whole family owed this man. The story, it been goin' a long time and now, well it seems to me that this is how the debt is a goin' to be paid. I know some folk, and I know how we can git this here done. It goin' to take some money, but if you willin', I kin git him buried right where you want…on this here, very day. I will see to it that the Jackson family that's left, it being me, of course, finally pays back the debt." He scratched his head. "Seems it was meant to be anyway. Like God, his self is giving me a chance to even the score. Why else do you suppose I be here? I ask you that…if not for this?"

Tori stood up and smiled gently at him. "I think maybe you're right. If I have come to realize anything in the past few years, it's that everything happens for a good reason. Don't you worry about the money; you can have whatever it takes to get the job done and then some."

THE sun hung low on the horizon. The summer breeze was cooling down as the long day gracefully paved the way for the blanket of nightfall. Tori ended her day holding on to Tom and David's hands. The three of them were alone, standing in front of a fresh, unmarked grave.

"I owe you, David. Without you, this could not have happened."

"You don't owe me nothin'. No, Ma'am. I will be joinin' him along with my family in a few years, God willin' that is. I'm goin' to be a hero. Yes, sir-ree. I was the one that put thin's right. My ancestor, he's a goin' to be very pleased with me. Yes, Ma'am, pleased is not the word. Don't you go a worryin' about this here little secret that we got neither. I ain't a goin' to be tellin' no one. Hell, ain't anyone ever goin' to believe me no how and I ain't a goin' to do nothin' but keep an eye on thin's round here till the good Lord calls me."

Tori hugged the old man. "Thank you."

David was quite touched by the hug and a little embarrassed. "You have my address. Write me sometime or call. I gave my phone number too. Who knows, maybe we can just sit and talk when thin's are healed some." He nodded to her and walked away, humming the same tune that he had been humming when they first arrived.

Tori looked at the grave. Strange, she thought. She was not as sad now as she had been. She knew that Jean was finally at peace, and she herself could go on, free at last.

Tom had left her side to get the car, and in a few minutes, she would leave this place, never to return. She took the gold chain out of her purse and looked at it closely before trying to lift it up and over her head to put it on.

"Want some help putting it on?" said a familiar voice behind her. It was Dan! But how could it be? How did he find her here? She turned to face him as he walked forward, opening his arms to her.

"Come here. Seems to me you need a hug." Seeing she didn't move, he added, "It's all right. I know what's happened. I've talked with Tom. Good thing I got back to our room when I did. He called me, and I came right away. Oh, my darling, what a shock. You should have told me. I would have helped you. Don't you know by now that I love you? That I would do anything for you?"

Tori fell into his arms. He was so good to her, but would he understand if he knew the whole story? She would have to tell him now, no more secrets between them. It was the right thing to do.

Standing there holding her, Dan looked over her shoulder to the fresh grave. He would have liked to have met the man who lay beneath that soil. The man who helped his darling Tori when she needed a friend and had no one to trust, no one to turn to. Then his eyes went to the small gravestone nestled in among the tree roots. He noticed that someone had tidied it up and put fresh flowers on it. At first, he thought nothing of it, as his main concern was Tori. Dan stepped back and took the chain from her hand.

She did not try to stop him and only watched as he looked at it. "There's something I have to tell you. There was a locket he once gave me. What I never told you was the locket held a baby's lock of hair. That locket is gone, but he wanted me to have this." Did he hear her when she mentioned a lock of baby hair? God, this was difficult. He needed to know, and she had to tell him.

Dan nodded and placed the chain around her neck. Slowly, the whole story began to form in his head. The missing pieces, he knew she had held back, and now it all fell into place. This is what she had hidden from him. This was the thing that she had feared he would not understand, and that would hurt him if he learned about it. The fact that she had had another man's child! That was what the small gravestone was, the one next to Laffite's grave. That's what the locket had been about. Her son...their son! My God, what she had gone through, for all these years, just to protect his feelings and their love.

Dan looked at her, and in a very gentle voice, filled with compassion, he spoke. "I love you, as he must have. I understand that. You two shared so much, but you are free now to tell me the whole story. That is when you are ready, and Tori, you can tell me all about the child."

He knew! Her husband, he knew, or was he guessing? How could he have come to such an obvious conclusion?

Seeing the questioning look behind her eyes, Dan reached her arm and turned her around to face the grave. He pointed at the small headstone and then touched the disk with his fingers, lifting it up for a second before letting it fall back against her skin. He kissed her tenderly and held her face gently between his hands.

"You must have hurt so bad. Why didn't you trust my love enough to tell me? I would have listened and understood. After all, he loved you as I do. We had that much in common, if nothing else. I understand you really loved him, and it does not take away one bit from how much I love you." His words caught in his throat. "The pain of thinking you could not share this with me, that is hard to understand, but nothing like what you have suffered. No wonder the sleepless nights, all those years, and then the not wanting to talk about any of it. Oh, my poor baby." He held her closer and tighter.

She was crying softly, speaking barely above a whisper. "I do love you, Dan. I do. It's just that I didn't want you to doubt that. When I came back and told you in bits and pieces of what had happened to me…well, it was just easier to leave out the parts that were so painful. Then as time went by, I just couldn't tell you out of fear. I had grown so close to you and needed you. Then I fell in love with you, and I just couldn't." She fell silent and took in a couple of deep, ragged breaths.

"It's true a part of me did love Jean but believe me when I tell you; I love you. I just need time to come to grips with all this."

"I know that you silly girl, and you will have all the time you need," he said as his eyes filled with tears. For Dan, it seemed he loved her even more now than he did before if that was possible. She had been living a lie to protect his feelings. What more proof did he need of how she felt about him?

"Look, Tori, I know that you will always think of him; that is only natural. But sweetheart, what we have is so strong; it will carry us forever. Don't doubt that. He is your past, and he is gone. How can I be jealous of a ghost? I am thankful that he was with you when you needed him. Thankful that you found your way back to Linni and me. That's more than enough to prove that what we have is not broken; it is growing. Do you believe me?"

She wiped the tears from his cheeks, first with her hands and then with gentle kisses. "How could I not? I believe you, and I love you so much."

Dan smiled at her. "In time, we will talk of your life with him, all of it. When you are ready to share, I'll be waiting. Now come on, it's time to head back." The two walked together hand in hand, out of the graveyard and through the little iron gate, toward Dan's car.

Tom waved at them and called loudly so that they could hear him. "I'll call you at the guest house tomorrow. We'll get together then, Tori. After all, we have a few things to sort out, a few items to do something about. Take care of each other. Jean would have wanted that." Then he climbed into his car and pulled onto the road.

Dan looked at his wife. "A few items? Dare I even guess?"

"You would never guess in a million years. I will tell you all about it on our way back to the guest house."

Tori climbed into the car and watched as Dan joined her. "You ready?"

Smiling slightly, she answered him. "I am."

Looking through the car window, Tori saw the sun had set, leaving the sky a delicate pink. The soft light shed a warm glow across the land, and as they pulled away, she looked toward the graveyard one last time. There, for a fleeting second, Tori thought she saw Jean. A young Jean Laffite, holding their son, and they were waving happily at her.

She wondered if it was the tears clouding her eyes or perhaps nothing more than wishful thinking? Blinking, she found the image had gone, but not her tears. However, they were now tears shed out of love, not great sadness. Tori knew in her heart that all was as it should be. The woman, who for so long had waited for the time to share everything, took hold of Dan's hand and squeezed it gently. She had her place with him, as Jean had his with history and their son. Her hand went to his gift, and she held the Möbius tightly. Tori remembered his words and smiled at the thought of the secret that lay buried by the tree. "I rather like the mystery man I have become," he had told her just a few hours ago. Smiling quietly to herself, she whispered, "so do I, Jean. So do I."

❧ Eleven ❧

Garden District New Orleans 2034

The tall, dark-haired stranger had his hand in mid-air about to knock a second time on the grand old home's door when to his amazement, it swung open. Instantly dropping his hand, he tried to conceal how dumbfounded he was. The stranger could not stop staring at the girl while, at the same time, he found that it was impossible to utter a single word. It was as if all pent-up emotions had gripped his mind and prevented him from any further action. For him, at that moment in time, his eyes had locked with the females and hers with his. Strange, the man thought; he could hear the sound of music coming from around her head, and he wondered how that was possible? One thing was certain, standing there without speaking was not going to get either of them anywhere, and to that end, he forced a smile and hoped his expression was pleasant enough. Still, his eyes bore into the young female, who stood her ground.

In a quizzical tone of voice, the girl spoke, and not to him, he was sure. As she reached for her ears, she spoke clearly into the air. "Music, pause."

Jean stood there, looking at the spitting image of Tori; true, it was a younger version, but the resemblance could not be denied. It was this experience that had him frozen but not fearful. Inhaling deeply, his voice almost whispered, "Excuse me, I apologize if I startled you. It seems my knocking was insufficient to overcome what you have there." He nodded his head in the direction of her hands. The teen was taking out both earbuds as he continued. "Can you hear me now?"

She frowned. "Of course, I can hear you; it's turned off—my fault for having it turned up so high before. Sorry, I didn't hear you knock. I thought I heard something, just never thought it was the door. Most people ring the bell. Guess you aren't most people. Can I help you?"

"I believe you can. I am an old friend…look, Linni, we may never have met, but it is not you that I have come to visit. I am here to see…if I may have a word with Tori?"

The teen looked at the man, whose eyes held her gaze. He was dressed a little odd, but odd was nothing out of the ordinary this week in New Orleans. It was, after all, Tall Ship week, and many dressed as pirates or wenches. The stranger who stood before her had half a costume on; true, his shirt was white, and the kind one would call a pirate's shirt. It lay loosely laced up across his tanned chest. His boots were knee-high, but his jeans were not in character. Most costumes came complete with pants that fit the era and a hat, but her visitor had chosen not to go full out, leading her to believe he was not a local.

She had never met him before nor seen any photos of him, yet he called her Linni and asked to talk to her Nana. Surely, he didn't think she was her mother?

"Did I say something wrong? I do apologize again for startling you. I can assure you it was not my intent."

"You called me Linni. Why?"

"That is not your name?"

"No. Linni is my mother, and she has been missing in Egypt for two years. I thought everyone knew that. All of her friends know about it, all but you, that is."

"I did not know; forgive me. I apologize again for my lack of understanding. You look very much like your…well…you look like my friend Tori. I just assumed…look it's been a long time for me. You might say I have been traveling and so…"

"I look like my Nana? Wow! You too? I get that a lot around here. My name, by the way, is Dominique' a French name chosen by my mother and Nana. Friends call me Domie for short. I told Nana that if she could shorten her name to Tori instead of Victoria, I get to shorten mine. Good trade if you ask me. You say you are a friend of..."

"What I should have said was, Tori is a friend of my family, and as I am in town, I had hoped to pay her a call."

Dominique looked at him closely. There was something odd about the man, but she liked him. Her Nana didn't get many visitors these days. So, if this stranger was who he said, well, it could be a good thing. Having someone to talk with besides herself and visiting nurses, would cheer her up. Plus, if her Nana was busy talking, she would be free to talk on the phone without worrying she'd miss something. "Can I tell her who is calling?"

Jean had not expected this question; in fact, he hadn't even thought about meeting anyone other than Tori. Now, here before him stood Linni's daughter...Tori's granddaughter, and even though he was so close to finding his love...the time...the year was wrong. It was obvious he had traveled too far into the future. That could be the only explanation as to why Tori's granddaughter stood before him.

"Ah, Mister, your name?"

"Yes, yes, of course. Please inform Miss Tori that a family member of the Destrehan's wishes to visit. That should do it. However, in case not, tell her Jean awaits downstairs."

"Destrehan's, right, and your name is Jean, just Jean? Ok, don't know why I am doing this, but come on in, just Jean. You can wait here? Don't try to take anything; as you see, you are on camera." She pointed to the small objects with tiny flashing green lights mounted high up on the wall.

"I assure you, Dominique...sorry Domie, that I will remain standing right here until you return."

The girl smiled brightly before turning to begin her climb up the grand staircase. "Ok, then, I will be right back...music mode off... set call for Robert, in fifteen minutes." With that said, she picked up her pace and ran up the stairs, stopping briefly to look back at Jean once she reached the landing. Upon seeing he was remaining just where she'd left him, Domie walked away and disappeared.

She had spoken to the air again about her music, and someone called Robert. It was perplexing as Tori had never told him of such strange actions. Then he rationalized that she couldn't have, as he was now certain beyond a doubt, he had come to Tori's future, not the place and year she had returned to, the very era she had once left via the lake.

Jean had been left standing in the hallway, feeling entirely out of his depth. The girl had spoken but not to him, not to anyone he could see either. Music and calls to a Robert had been talked of, but how this request would be handled, he didn't have a clue. His eyes looked up at the tiny black boxes with the blinking lights, and he wondered just what else would surprise him? Obviously, he was in the right place, or he hoped so. The girl's mother was a Linni. Tori's daughter was Linni, but now…now there was a Dominique. Her name alone spoke volumes; it could not be a coincidence she'd been named after someone who lived long ago and was adored by Tori. Then there was the fact that the family resemblance was so strong. Tori's granddaughter looked so very much like her. All facts supported his conclusion that he was in the right house, just the wrong era. It was a quandary that had him perplexed. Should he remain or leave and try again to reach her time?

He looked around him and saw that on many of the walls hung paintings of Louisiana landscapes. Slowly he turned to face the wall directly behind him and observed the closest framed pictures. Jean stood dead still as he looked from one picture to the next. All the images seemed to be of New Orleans French Quarter, places he recognized, but his eyes spotted something else. This gilt-framed picture stood out; it was what Tori had told him was called a photograph of this fact, he was sure. No painting could ever be as fine or accurate as what he beheld. There, standing in front of the house, with a welcome home sign hung over the porch railing, was his

Tori. Next to her stood who he assumed to be Linni. Tori's daughter was holding the hand of a young girl that had to be Dominique. She looked about six years old, and she was waving at something or someone. However, it was to Tori's face his attention went. She was older than he had last seen her, and she was leaning on a cane. Maybe an accident of some sort had required her to use it?

Then he spotted another larger framed photo a few feet away. The image was of a much younger Tori; she looked almost the same as he remembered her and by her side was a tall blond man. They were standing in front of a sold sign, and again he recognized the house behind them; it was the same one he was now standing in. The pair looked happy, and Jean began to doubt himself for the second time. Maybe, he should just leave; he did not belong here, but then again, he didn't feel he belonged anyplace without Tori. Did he have the right to upset her life just because he missed her? What had he been thinking?

DOMI entered her grandmother's room and saw right away that she had turned off the screen and was lying in bed staring at the ceiling. "Nana, can I show you something on the screen, please?"

"Show me what exactly," she questioned weakly. "I thought you were going to get the mail and make us something light to eat?"

"You hardly eat, and you know it, and no, I have not got today's mail, but I have someone downstairs who says he wants to visit you." Domie picked up a remote and clicked a button. "Honestly, Nana, I don't know why you turn it off like this. You know all you have to do, is say off."

"Just an old habit, I guess. Like the image on the screen-saver I keep and won't change." She smiled at her granddaughter. "Go on then, show me what you have."

On the wall, opposite the bed in which Tori lay, was a screen that filled most of the area. It had been built right into the wall itself and framed to look like a work of art, when an image or screen saver was turned on. Once activated, the image was so clear that for a second, one could almost imagine they were looking out of a window. There, on the modern-day device, was displayed a three-dimensional photo of a sunset in the bayous.

"Screen, show front hallway and entrance, split-screen, both views." She looked at her Nana. "Wait until you see him. He claims he is here to visit you. Really quite strange; he thought I was mother, and he called you Tori. No one outside of family calls you that. Said he was a Destrehan, or something like that. His name is Jean something or other."

Tori's eyes went immediately to the screen, which was flipping through images of the house. Domie had turned to look at the images and missed the reaction the old woman was having. "Did you say visit? He wants to visit? Domie, you know I don't like visitors." Her voice was filled with apprehension, but her expression was one of curiosity.

"I think you might like this visitor. Here see for yourself." The screen changed one last time and froze. There before them was a split image of the hall below. The man in question, whoever he was, had his back to the camera, and it was apparent he was looking at the photos hanging on the wall. "Audio on… Jean, whatever your name is, can you turn and face the camera, please?"

Tori gripped the bed sheets and held her breath but not for a single second did she look away.

JEAN heard the voice that seemed to come out of thin air. One of the small black boxes had emitted the girl's voice, instructing him to look at it. So, he turned and looked up at the object and frowned. Things were indeed very different from anything he was used to, and again he never recalled Tori telling him about such objects that replaced servants. He had to admit that having a housekeeper was preferential, not this odd way of introducing oneself to something or someone he could not see.

"Zoom in. There, do you know him, Nana?"

The wall was now just one large headshot of the man Tori never dreamed of seeing again. The shock caused a sharp chest pain that she ignored. "Can't be possible," she murmured.

"What, Nana? Do you know him? I will ask him to leave..."

Tori inhaled deeply and shook her head no. "No, just give me a second; let me think here." 'Could it be possible after all these years?' Slowly, she exhaled while her eyes remained transfixed on the image of Jean Laffite's face. He was dead, died in her arms years ago, and yet, there he stood, looking up at the camera. How and why now? Her hands relaxed as she studied his face. Time is a tricky thing, and there would be only one way to sort out what was going on. Like it or not, Tori would meet with him; she had to. God help her; it was far more than learning the answer to so many questions flying around in her mind; no, she desperately wanted to see him, talk to him. However, she had to remain calm and not show a single shred of how she felt right then, especially to her granddaughter.

"Dominique, I recall now, yes you can show him up, but give me five minutes to ready myself. As a matter of fact, my dear, just give him the directions where to find me, and then you can see if the mailman has been. Let us visit alone. You may check in on me later."

Her Nana had just called her by her full name, something she hardly ever did. Whoever this Jean was, he had rattled her. "Are you sure? You look kind of strange. Nana, is everything alright?"

"Everything will be. He told you the truth; the gentleman is a family friend, grown-up since I saw him last, that's all," she lied. "Just do as you are told, and Domie, in a little bit, you might pop up to see if we are in need of anything. Now, do be a dear and don't keep our guest waiting. Remember, five minutes."

"Yes, Nana. If you are sure, that's what you want? I never stopped to think if you would be up to a visit."

"It is what I want, and I am perfectly healthy enough for a visitor."

Domie beamed. "I told you that you might like this, didn't I? You can watch on the screen, or change it, whatever you want. I'll be back in a bit."

Once her granddaughter left her alone in her bedroom, Tori studied the image carefully. There was no doubt in her mind; it was him. He didn't look much older than the day she left him, and now, he was about to see her, and she was old. If he saw her now, it would be the last image of her he would carry for years to come. He would know her as an old invalid until he found her again. She had been young when he died in her arms. The image of an old, sick Laffite was what remained in her mind until now.

Maybe it would be better if she just sent him away, but how? Knowing him, he would not go, not now he had found her. "God, give me strength, and please, whatever I do, please help me not say anything that I shouldn't."

Tori watched as her granddaughter talked to the man, and then she spoke softly toward the screen. Computer stop recording and erase today's files. Restart recording at eleven pm." She sat back, thinking. 'That should be enough time for a visit, and then I will send him away. There will be no trace of him ever being here.' "Screen off. No, no screen, turn on bayous image."

Tori sat looking at the bayous, and panic took hold. "Shit, what have I done? What will he think? Oh, Jean, why now, you should have stayed away." Tori reached for her brush and quickly began brushing her long grey hair. Satisfied it was the best she could do, she opened the bedside table drawer and pushed everything into it and out of sight, leaving the top empty except for an old-fashioned oil lamp.

JEAN heard Domie coming long before he saw her. The young girl was smiling brightly as she came downstairs. "Yep, Nana said she would see you. I have to get the mail, and then I have to talk to

Robert; I said I would. I don't know how long that will keep me, but I will be up in a bit to see if you need anything. So, you go up there in five minutes," she pointed at the stairs. "Turn to the left at the top and take the hall on your right. Her room is the door at the end. Word of warning, Nana gets tired fast, and we all try not to upset her. Have to say, though, I saw her smile and get quite excited when she saw you. Still, can't believe she knows someone I don't. Guess you were a kid when she last saw you. Hope it cheers her up talking with you. I've got to run, or I'll miss my call. Up the stairs, left then right, and you can't miss."

Jean watched as the young girl walked out the front door. She didn't seem to know anything, which meant Tori had kept her secret about the past. He looked again at the photo of his love, standing with the blond man. Maybe she kept the secret to herself and told no one. If keeping her past was what she wanted, he would abide by it. As of right then, he would begin to make his way up to her room. He'd take his time; after all, she had requested he wait, but knowing he was this close, Laffite couldn't wait.

He climbed the stairs slowly, thinking as he went. What would he find when he entered her room? Why did she get tired easily? Hell, he should have asked Dominique more questions, but it was too late now.

JEAN saw the door was left ajar and beyond it, somewhere in that room, was the woman he had crossed time to be with. He stood still when he reached the door and listened. His hand was flat against the wood, and as he slowly pushed against it, moving it slightly inward, he stopped and held his breath, wondering if he should knock?

"Just come on in, will you? I, for one, can't take the excitement or the delay. Jean, if it really is you, show yourself."

That was all he needed; he pushed the door wide open and stood looking at the frail woman propped up in bed. Neither spoke a word; they just stared at each other. Then, with tears streaming down her face, Tori held out her arms. "My Jean, it is you."

In several long strides, he was by her side. In seconds, she was in his arms, and together they sat in a tight embrace. Tori could feel his heart beating against her chest, and Jean could feel her warm breath on his neck. He could also feel how painfully thin she was, and that was when he understood everything. His Tori, the love of his life, was indeed old and frail. The words Marie had told him echoed in his mind. "You may not like what you find, but then you need to find what you don't want to admit. You belong to history; both of you do but not together."

Tori pushed him away and looked into his eyes. Her thin, aged hand reached up and stroked the side of his face. He, in turn, wiped the tears on her cheek, then he leaned forward and kissed her forehead. "My love, it would seem you have once again managed to get yourself into a difficult situation." He tried to make light of what was a most hurtful sight.

"And you are, as always, are a smooth-talking Gentleman Pirate. I would say it is you who has gone and got himself in a difficult situation. Why now, why here and how?" She coughed a bit and then lay back against her pillows. "So, are you going to tell me? Did you swim into the lake…or find another way, maybe?"

"What does it matter how I am here? What matters is that I am by your side. However, it would seem that I traveled, a bit further into the future, than intended, and if you don't mind me saying so, I am just in time, maybe? You are ill. I can see that, but how ill? Talk to me."

"I wish you hadn't come. I hate that you see me like this while you are still as handsome as I recall."

"To me, you are as beautiful as the day I laid eyes on you."

"Liar." She grinned. "But it does make an old lady feel special. I have a thousand questions, as I am sure you do."

"Then let us make the most of our time together." His hand reached out and took hers. You are and always will be the most important person in my life. As long as you need me, I will remain by your side." He pushed a long strand of hair away from her shoulder.

"I won't ask you to do that…to stay here with me."

"You don't have to."

"Well then, for a short time, you can sit with me; if I have your word, you will leave and go back to your own time. Please, Jean, your word."

"As much as I would like to stay, I cannot give you my word…"

"If you do not, I will have Domie show you out…"

"Please, let us not fight over something as silly as this. I give my word, there, is that better?"

"It is."

He looked around the room and spotted the large screen on the wall, displaying a three-dimensional image of a bayou at sunset. "Is that where I think it is?"

"It is, but even the bayous have changed. You would not recognize the bay or the coastline. Let's not talk about that. We need a drink, you look like you could use one, and I know, I sure as hell can. Screen, find Domie."

Jean watched as images of the hallway and then a living area appeared on the framed wall. "*Domie found.*" Tori smiled as she saw her granddaughter talking on the phone. "Audio on… Domie, this is Nana. I want you to do me a favor. Please go into my library and bring me up two glasses and the bottle of brandy, and one of the whiskey too—some ice for me, and maybe something to snack on. And Domie, thank you, my love. You were right. I am enjoying my visitor. We have a lot to catch up on."

Domie didn't even look up as she held the phone away from her face. "Told you, Nana. I will be right up. Give me ten, ok?" The phone was back by her ear before Tori could respond. "Screen, show bayou." The bayou photo flashed back on.

Jean looked at Tori. "Nice view, great invention, but I would rather look at you."

"And, I you. So, where shall we begin? What happened when I left? I have often wondered. For years, I felt so guilty, and then Dan helped me, and slowly I went on with my life, knowing you had with yours."

"Ah, so that's the blond man in the picture downstairs. He is the same man you told me about, the one with you the night before your swim?"

"The one and the same. He saved me, Jean. When I returned, I was a mess, and he was there. He took care of Linni and me, and he loved me…loved us. I married him, and we bought this home. I have been here ever since. In a way, it was a connection to you. Don't get me wrong; I loved Dan; we had a good life together. He understood how much you meant to me. We just never talked about it once we moved in."

"I am happy he was a good man, that he looked after you when I could not."

"Funny, that's what he said about you."

"Will I have the honor of meeting him?"

"Afraid not. Dan passed away almost ten years ago. Then, Linni and her daughter moved in. Her husband travels a lot; he will be home tomorrow. He is a good man, and I have been blessed to keep my granddaughter close by. Linni, she was lost to us…"

"I am sorry to hear that." Jean reached behind Tori's head and lifted the pillow up a bit higher. "There looks a bit more comfortable."

"Enough about me; there is not much to tell beyond what you now know. So, tell me, what happened when you found me missing?"

Jean was about to talk when he heard Domie call out. "A hand here if you don't mind. Jean whoever…quick before I drop something."

Jean got up and quickly walked to the door and saw the girl standing in the hallway trying to balance a tray, on which were glasses, plates, food, and one bottle. In one of her hands, besides the edge of the tray, was another bottle that she had a hold of by the neck, and it was slipping.

"Here, let me take the tray; you save the bottle," he laughed.

"Thanks, thought I had it made but guess not. Nana, I have what you wanted. You know the doctor said no alcohol with the pills, but hey, what's it going to do, kill you?"

Jean was shocked by what she had said, but he did not show it. He placed the tray down on the bedside table and took the bottle of whiskey from Domie."

"Nana, you been cleaning up a bit," Domie's eyes had scanned the tabletop, and knowing what should be there and wasn't, she frowned.

Tori grinned. "I have what I need, and if I don't, I will call you. Jean and I have much to catch up on, so thank you for the tray. You go and do your studies or whatever. I am in good hands." Her eyes went to Jean, and he nodded.

"OK then, I will be downstairs or in my room. Dad said he'd call when his flight leaves London, and I don't want to miss that. Jean, whatever your name is, don't let her talk you into anything and only one drink, with tons of water. I am so happy to see you looking more like your old self, nana. I mean that. Just don't overdo it. Later guys." Dominique pulled the door almost closed when she left and stood outside listening to see if they noticed.

Tori spoke first. "I will take a shot of the brandy, and knowing you, the whiskey?"

"I will, and you, would you care to eat something?"

"No, just hand me a drink. You were about to tell me what you did when I left."

"I was? Funny, I don't recall that."

"Stop teasing and explain to me how on earth did you find me? How long after I left did you wait?"

"I waited by the lake for days; how many, I am not clear on that. After a while, it became clear that I needed to find another way to you, and Marie, along with John Davis, both knew of another opening. It was the way Cisco and John came, and if they did it through the same alleyway, then surely it was a place where such things happened more frequently. I left the plantation weeks ago, and with the help of our friends, I am here."

Dominique was satisfied that all was going good even if she could not understand much of what the visitor was explaining. They were talking softly, and for her, that indicated this Jean, whoever he was, understood that her nana needed no stress or excitement. 'So far, so good,' she told herself. 'I'll check back later, but for right now I have more important things to do.'

Two things were on Dominique's mind. Her boyfriend and a phone call. Besides, her nana would be furious if she thought she was spying on her. The night nurse had called in sick, and she was kind of glad. Her nana had not looked so happy in such a long time, and she obviously wanted to keep her condition a secret because all her meds were now in the side drawer. No, if the nurse came, she'd ruin everything. Besides, when the time came, she'd make sure the nightly meds were taken, and the room was set up for the night.

For a while, Tori had slept, and Jean had sat quietly on the bed by her side. It was during one of these quiet times that Domie had entered the room on the pretense of picking up the tray. Her nana was sleeping peacefully, and Jean was sitting on the bed by her side, holding her hand. He had let Tori's head rest on his chest, and when he had seen Domie enter, he placed his finger on his lips. She got his meaning and held up two of her fingers and mouthed the words, *'I'll be up in a few hours.'* Jean smiled and nodded his head. Tori's granddaughter would be back in to see how they were in two hours. Until then, he would take care of his love.

346

TORI woke up, and before she even opened her eyes, she felt him by her side. He was no dream. Her Jean was really with her. After all this time, all the years of wondering, Jean had found her, and she now knew that the first few weeks after she crossed back had been a living hell for him. That's when he had approached their friends and listened to what they both had to say. He had used them and their help to make the journey to locate her.

For him, her trip had happened only a few weeks ago; for her…she had buried him many years ago—the how and the why of what was happening right then needed to be explored, explained. However, before she said anything to him about what had happened when he had found her at their son's grave, she had to think.

Tori kept pretending to sleep as she recalled all Jean had told her so far. Listening to his slow regular breathing, she began sorting through their history. She had known some of his stories because she'd learned what she could by doing research. When Jean had found her in the cemetery, at Christopher's grave, he had told her a bit more, and now, today, she had learned even more. History, it seemed, was turning out the way it was supposed to or was it? Why had he died in her arms so many years ago? There seemed to be no rational explanation.

In the first few hours together since he arrived at her home, her pirate had never mentioned seeing her again. How could he? Jean would not see her again until he was an old man. This was the most upsetting truth in the matter, and Tori's mind kept going back to the image of him in the graveyard. But as she lay there, a realization came over her. Something strange had begun because she realized the image from the cemetery was fading in the recesses of her memory. Maybe it was because now she had a new vision to hold dear. The image of Jean Laffite as a dashing younger man was hers to hold. Here sat her husband, lover, and lost pirate who looked so very much like the man she had first met and remained with for five years. Could this be the reason time had allowed him to find her? Had time a role to fulfill? Was she meant to die with the image of a younger Jean accompanying her to whatever awaited? Had it brought him to her when it did, so he had an image of her as a young Tori, not the old woman she was now?

It was clear at last. Here he was, young and as handsome as ever. He had no knowledge of what was to be because he was not old yet and had not made that last trip across time,' she thought. This trip had to be his first, and God help her; she had to make sure it would be his last, or next to last.

She stood a chance of preventing Jean from taking that last trip, but should she? One thing was sure; Tori understood she'd have to remain careful with her story until she understood more about what was happening. For just a little bit longer, the frail woman decided to go over in detail as much as she could recall, of the day he had found her, the day she had buried him.

TORI opened her eyes and moved, lifting her head up off Jean's chest. "Jean, can you please hand me a glass of water and if you don't mind, there is a pill container, the blue lid. It's in the side table drawer. I need one; it's past due."

Jean was up and walking around the bed before she could push herself up on the pillows behind her. He opened the drawer, took out the one container with the blue lid, and opened it. "How many?"

"Just one and some water?"

"Here you are" he handed it to her. "Domie came in a while ago and took the tray. She left this for you." He opened the bottle of water and handed it to Tori.

"She's a good girl. I don't know what I would have done without her. She reminds me of myself. Headstrong and stubborn." Tori swallowed the pill and waited a second before sipping a bit more water. "I detest water. How about another sip, maybe of something stronger? I won't fall asleep again, I promise."

Jean half-filled the small glass and then filled the other to the top for himself. "Here," he handed her the glass. "Better not tell Domie, or she will kick me out." He raised his glass in a toast and then consumed the contents and put the glass down. He winked at her, "needed that."

Tori began to laugh, and just as suddenly, her chest felt like it would explode. The pain was sharper still, and it took her breath away. The glass in her hand dropped, and she hunched over.

"Tori, what is it? What's wrong? Should I call for help?"

Her hand reached out for his as she uttered the word, "wait. It will pass, just please, the pills, the long box; I need one or two."

Jean opened the drawer and found the long-looking box. He opened it and took out two small white pills, which he quickly showed her hoping they were the right ones. Tori nodded her head and opened her mouth. Jean did not hesitate; he placed them on her tongue and anxiously waited.

"Don't need water; they melt. It's passing; nothing to worry about. Just give me a moment."

It tore at his heart to see her in pain, and he wanted to call Domie, but Tori had been adamant not to. All he could do was wait, and if she did not look any better, he'd call her granddaughter regardless of what she wanted.

"Jean, can you help me here?" Her hands were struggling with a gold chain around her neck. "I want to give you something. Please, help me take it off."

He leaned forward and took the chain in his hands. Slowly, so as not to tangle Tori's hair, he raised the chain up and over her head. Once he had done that, she leaned back and closed her eyes. He watched her and saw that she patted the bed beside her without opening her eyes. "Join me, please. It was so nice, having you so close after all these years."

Jean walked around the bed and climbed next to her. He raised her up, slipped his arm under her shoulders, and pulled her toward him. Then he gently moved her head and placed it on his chest.

"Do you have it? The chain, do you have it?"

"I do. It's right here in my hand."

"Look at it. The gold ring on the chain is called a Möbius. See how it is made and how it loops up and over. It's a symbol of infinity, and I have worn it ever since I lost you. It has been… no; it is the link that joins us; I understand that now. You will in time too. It has helped me through tough times, and now it will help you."

Jean turned the ring over in his fingers and then looked down at his love in wonder. She had kept the memory of him with her all of her life.

"I had thought about having it inscribed with '*Love passes time. Time passes with love,*' but it didn't need those words to remind me of you."

Jean smiled. His love had remembered the saying he had inscribed on the locket he had given her after their son's death. They were the words he had scratched into the cottage wall on his last visit to New Orleans. "You remember! Do I dare ask did you find the writing on the cottage wall?"

Tori laughed softly. "I did, and I saw the sculpture in the side courtyard. That was your doing, wasn't it?"

Pleased with himself, he smiled softly. "It was. I had hoped you may find them and know I was thinking, remembering all, and that I kept my word about the sculpture. That afternoon, on the island, I told you that I would have one made. You recall that afternoon, do you not? I said I would remember it forever, and I gave you my word that I would have the image of us sculpted."

"You did, and you kept your word. I have a thousand questions still. Today, arriving here to be with me…tell me, and be honest with me, how often have you tried to find me?"

He grinned and then frowned. "This is my second trip. My first was unsuccessful, but I did have time to commission the statue before returning to my time. It would seem that the way I came has a short amount of time that it is open. I was here less than twenty-four hours. I had to leave or find myself forever in the wrong time. So, after realizing it would be a daunting task trying to locate you, I returned the way I came before that doorway closed, which Marie felt was happening less and less. Don't ask me how she knows such things, but she does. I had a long talk with Marie, and it was decided I could try one last time; only one more time would she allow me to do so, and here I am."

"Do you recall what year that first trip took you to?"

"I do, but it matters not. My visit was short as I knew I needed to find the right time to locate you. I did not travel far enough ahead in time to locate you. A mistake I hoped to rectify with Marie's help. She agreed to assist my endeavor and made a few suggestions, but this time, well, I came too far forward, and yet I am pleased to have found you and do not regret for a second my decision."

Tori frowned. Jean had never mentioned anything about this trip to her when he was in the graveyard. Briefly, she wondered why not? Then another thought came to her, and it seemed to hold the key to everything at once. She touched the Möbius. "Look, I have worn that ring every day of my life. Whenever things got difficult, I would hold it. If I needed strength, I would think of you. I would think of us. Jean, I want you to wear it and promise me that you will go back to your time. You go back and don't try to find me again. Stop looking before you get lost in an era where I may never be found, and you find yourself trapped with no one you know. Live your life, my love, be happy and do what it is you were destined to do. When things get difficult, and they will, hold this and think of me. Do not linger here; you do not belong..."

She closed her eyes to rest a moment and to gather her thoughts. A flash of an old pirate close to death came once more to her mind. That had been the image she carried for years, and it had saddened her. Again, she wondered if she should tell him that it was he who gave her the Möbius right before he died? However, telling him frightened her. After all, she never mentioned or hinted that she had given it to him while he lay in her arms dying. Now, here she was in his arms on her deathbed; Tori understood that fact to be the truth; she did not have long to live. The pain in her chest was constant now, and it had never been so before. It was bearable but also a messenger telling her that her heart was weakening, and no pills could stop what was happening. Her Jean had found her just in time, it seemed.

Tori squeezed her eyes closed for a few seconds. Everything was so confusing. It had been so long ago that afternoon in the grave-yard, but she did recall how he had claimed the Möbius was hers and that he was returning it. Back then, Tori had not understood the significance of what he implied. She'd thought him merely confused. Now she understood what he meant. Jean knew she had given it to him just as she now understood Jean had given it to her. 'So where did it come from? Could she…dare she question him? Better he did not know his end,' she assured herself. How could she explain him giving her the ring without telling him more? If she kept it a secret, Jean would live a long life and do things that only the Gentleman Pirate Jean Laffite would know of. The man would create the mystery surrounding him; he'd live and always with the knowledge that his word was his honor. Once given, Jean would keep it; there would only be one more trip for him, one time where he would break his word and right to do so, it seemed.

Tori looked into his eyes and smiled slightly. There was wisdom in not telling because if she did, Jean would keep trying to find her in the right era, where they could be together again. Also, as much as she wanted to know what he did, where he went, and how he lived, leaving no clue or a few clues to his hidden identity, that too was best left unspoken. It was all so tangled and yet so clear. History was on track, and if they had changed it, how would they know? The answer was they would not because, for each of them, the moments they lived in were their history, their time.

Then a thought hit that made a bit more sense to her. Jean had found her in this time because of the 'Möbius.' That was the link, not what he wore or where he crossed through time. Tori recalled him telling her before he died that Marie and Davis had thought if he wore a few of Cisco's things and carried a few modern-day coins, it would help him cross to her. He would find her if he thought of her while moving through the portal. She now understood, as he would one day, that it was the draw of their love and the gold symbol that was now around his neck that would guide them. The gold Möbius belonged to them both, and it would always find its way to each of them when the time was right and it was needed. That time for Jean was now; hers had been years ago.

'Oh, what a complicated issue time was,' she thought. But not so complex that she did not realize everything happened for a reason and that they had come full circle. Because of her, what she kept from him, and what she had given him, he would have the courage to live, to remain in his own era until he felt the need to find her again. By doing so, by finally breaking his word, he would get to take the image of her as a young Tori with him when he died. It would not be the image of an old woman that he now saw. 'Both of us will have an image of our younger selves to take with us on our last day,' she told herself.

If only she had the strength to explain it to him, if only she could…if only she had known back then, would it have changed things? What would happen if she told him now? Could she find the strength to break the circle? Would the truth shatter whatever strange link bound them together?' Tori was worn out, yet knowing time was slipping away and that she had a huge decision to make, she closed her eyes to ponder the mystery and try to come to terms with what she should or should not do.

TORI had fallen silent and seemed to be resting comfortably. Whatever pain she had felt had passed, and the medicine was working. 'Maybe that's all she needed, to rest and take her pills,' he thought, but he knew it was not so in his heart. Jean had placed the chain over his head and laid the ring against his bare chest to please her. His free hand moved to the object, and he held it, wondering how such an object could bring him peace and strength?

Feeling him move, Tori stirred and opened her eyes. Seeing the chain around his neck and the ring on his chest, she smiled.

He saw the happiness in her eyes because he had taken her gift, and he smiled. "I will wear this until the day I die; you have my word."

"I know you will...Jean, you have given me your word; now you need to keep it. Return this night and do nothing more than that. Don't linger or spend any of your time trying to learn about yourself, as tempting as that may be. I did all the looking and reading years ago. I even tried looking up all of our friends along with you, and for some, I read accounts that have been handed down; for you, there was nothing that anyone could prove beyond legends and stories. My love, you will do that; you will create your destiny and do so knowing that I know you lived on, doing things your way."

"You read about our friends, my life? History turned out as you hoped, and I became the enigma you said? I am so much more..."

Tori panicked; was she right in her silence? He had to go back, but not knowing...could she do that? "Please, you will go home and stop trying to find me." Tori took a deep breath; as the love of his life, she had always been honest. True, there had been times that she, Cisco, and Davis kept things from him, and maybe if they had not, history would have found its own way. Could she...should she tell him? In a moment of weakness and loving him as she did, Tori decided to tell him all she knew because what harm could it do? "Maybe if I explain...yes, I have something to tell you...you must listen and..."

This time, the pain was so bad that it felt as if something very heavy was sitting on her chest. Tori struggled to catch her breath, and she gripped Jean's hand, knowing what was happening to her. Time was rapidly running out, and she still had so much she wanted to tell him but knew now that she wouldn't. Another more powerful pain gripped her chest, and she felt her heartbeat skipping wildly. For her, time was almost up.

Jean held her close, but she twisted her head to look into his face.

This was the image she would take with her, the young Jean Laffite, her soul mate in time. 'How strange time was. Even with all the hardships and years apart, how wonderful life had been, it had been an epic adventure,' she thought. In a whisper, Tori uttered her last words. "I love you, always have, and always will. Set sail Jean; I will wait for you upon your star…"

No more words left her; there was only the sound of a soft exhale and then nothing. His lady, his love, had left this world and him. His only comfort was that she had died in his arms and would always know how much he loved her. The gentleman pirate's eyes filled with tears, and he let them fall. Slowly he pulled his arm free, and then he stood up and walked to the foot of the bed. Once there, Jean lifted the ring in his hand and placed it on his lips. "My lady, rest now, for I will keep my promise to you." He put the ring back on his chest and took a step back. Tori had a slight smile on her lips, and he was happy that she had left this world in his arms and not alone. He had found her and lost her, and now was the time to depart. He had a promise to keep; he'd always kept his word to her no matter the pain or the cost. His word was all he had left to give her, and for his Tori… he'd do anything…always.

It was late, and the house was quiet. Quickly he descended the stairs and reached the front door just as the grandfather clock began to chime. It was nine o'clock. He looked up at the small black boxes and saw that the small green light wasn't flashing. Whatever that meant, he did not care.

Jean looked back upstairs and nodded his head. Dominique would find her Nana and know in her heart that she had not died alone. As for him, he opened the front door and took a deep breath before walking outside. Jean turned briefly and closed the door softly. He stood for a second and thought of his love. The image of her was clear in his mind. He wished he could carry an image of a young Tori with him, but it was not meant to be. His hand reached again for the ring that was next to his skin. It didn't matter how he remembered her, just that he would never forget her.

Jean Laffite turned, then walked away into the night and into history, knowing her gift was with him. This Möbius would be his lifeline, as it had been hers and the words echoed in his mind as he made his way along the city sidewalk.

'Love passes time. Time passes with love.'

The End

The Möbius strip or ring, also called the twisted cylinder, is a one-sided surface with no beginning or end. The design of a Möbius strip shows that the two sides, which are referred to as inside and outside, are joined together and become one side. The Möbius shows us we are unified in some sense, connected in an endless ribbon. This symbolizes unity and oneness and the concept that we're all on the same path, a path that is never ending, with no beginning and no end.

Epilogue

When I finally typed those two words in book five, 'the end,' I began to look back over Tori's adventure and see all she had accomplished. While Tori is fictional, as are other characters, the time and places she finds herself in are rich with legends, actual events, and many known historical figures.

Flipping through the pages of the five books, I recalled all she had witnessed, each detail of her journey and her struggle to survive while maintaining histories timeline as she knew it. It was then I began to wonder what happened to the many people who crossed her path, just as I imagine you might. So, I started scrutinizing numerous notes for any pertinent details that could have escaped me, notes that explained in greater depth the lives and deaths of many.

The first task was to recall the names of all Tori had come to know, and no matter how briefly they met, each was important. After creating this list, I attached a short biography of those who had significant roles and played a part in her life and history. The outcome of this endeavor is a list that you, the reader, might appreciate now that you have completed the whole epic tale.

It's easy to say I was shocked at the sheer number of historical people that turned up between the pages. Even though Tori did not personally interact with all the historical people listed, they each had roles in all that occurred during this crucial timeline. No stone was left unturned while researching every individual in the saga, especially Jean Laffite.

As you know, Laffite vanished, becoming one of the most prominent legends of New Orleans today. While everyone has a theory about where he went and what he did, no one can confirm beyond a shadow of a doubt the truth behind his disappearance. My idea of what happened to the Gentleman Pirate is simply that, but one that fits the narrative nicely and keeps an air of mystery surrounding him.

I invite you to scan the lists of historical characters and the other shorter notes I compiled to understand this epic saga better.

Having completed the first two lists, adding a few of the historical legends and events between 1810-1815 seemed only fitting.

Also included is a list of actual locations from Tori's travels that you can visit most days. If you are lucky enough to do so and recall Tori's adventures in the past, maybe you can bring her saga to life in your mind's eye in a way you never thought possible. Imagine visiting Destrehan Plantation and standing in the room where the ball was held or going upstairs to view the parlor where Tori, Jean, and their friends rode out a violent hurricane. You can even take the time to see the marble bathtub rumored to have been a gift from Napoleon.

While walking the French Quarter, visit Laffite's Blacksmiths Shop, the local bar that our heroin came to know so well when it was just a Creole cottage. Stroll down Pirate's Alley, where you may find yourself sensing the ghosts of the past all around you. The Cabildo houses a museum full of the history and artifacts of New Orleans. You can even see the jail cells where pirates and other unlikely souls were held while awaiting trial.

If you can make it, take a trip to Chalmette Battleground. The center displays many artifacts and even shows a short movie explaining The Battle of New Orleans, which, as you now know, was the last battle to be fought on American soil with a foreign enemy.

A reenactment of the battle takes place every year on the anniversary of the final victorious battle, and those involved are more than willing to interact with you and answer your questions.

If you are lucky to be there while my cannoneer friends fire several blasts across the area, it will shock your senses. The sound echoes in the heavens from these small cannons, and after hearing them, you will better understand how all those in the city in 1815 sat in fear listening to the roar of much larger weapons. Not only cannons of Andrew Jackson's force but also those of the British and the American Vessel, the Carolina.

It's wise to mention at this point in telling Tori's story; that I took a writer's privilege with some of the characters, their roles, and actions. One such liberty was with the historical figure John Davis. His story, in the book, came from documents of the era. It would be nice to think the man would chuckle, knowing I turned him into a time traveler. There again, who's to say he was not? Every detail learned about this man, and all he accomplished is true. As to his role in breaking Laffite and his men out of jail, well, that is a stretch of the strange circumstances surrounding their so-called release.

Another major figment of my imagination was to make the Governor's young wife a spy. This idea came as I needed someone close to William Claiborne to report all they overheard. Cayetana was perfect; after all, it's history that she ended up marrying John Grymes after her husband's untimely death.

While I kept each character in their own timeline, the yellow fever outbreak that Tori witnessed did not happen until many years after she departed in 1815. By researching the horrific epidemic, I could bring the terrifying events of that incident and incorporate them into my story. The descriptions of the heinous outbreak were taken from old letters, newspapers, and medical books. Though graphic, the gory details of the illness, also known as Black John, along with the actions taken by the populace, are an accurate account of what happened during such outbreaks.

I also took the liberty of adding on a few years to the age of Marie Laveau. I had a plausible explanation in the storyline but thought it best to let the reader know that as far as her birthdate goes, history has it where she would have been far too young in this story. Everything else about her, the legends and tall tales and descriptions are as accurate as I could make them. Marie's legacy lives on, and her gravesite is visited by those who tour the tombs in Cemetery #1 and #2.

The Duval Plantation is pure fiction and is based on the histories of such grand estates that once existed throughout Louisiana. Even though all the characters involved around this plantation are fictional, their daily life and working conditions on such an estate are based on facts. Many plantations fell into ruin over the years or were destroyed and forgotten. The Duval plantation could easily have existed and fallen victim to time, so searching for it is futile, unlike the other two in the story, which you can locate. These two plantations were lovingly restored to their former grandeur. Both offer tours and even allow you the chance to spend the night. Destrehan has two creole cottages onsite, and the Ormond Plantation has rooms in the main house and an excellent restaurant.

The running of a large estate and the description of the slave quarters and their daily lives took hours of research and many tours throughout Louisiana. One such expedition was to the Whitney Plantation; (not in Tori's story). It's a tour I highly recommend. The plantation is dedicated to the memory of the enslaved African people and all they endured. Hundreds of their names are inscribed on a wall, and each year more are added. They are brought to the plantation from the descendants of slaves or found among papers by researchers. If you plan a visit, book ahead of time as it is very popular, and the tour groups are kept to a size that allows each individual the chance to ask questions. Once the tour is over, you are free to roam the gardens.

As Tori learned and was exposed to a life that she in no way agreed with, we also learned the hard truths of the era. One interesting fact which came to my attention was plantation owners and their overseers were supposed to live by the 'Code Noir.' This document explained how they were to treat enslaved people, but many ignored its guidelines, more so in later years. While offensive today, the language spoken, and the terms used were commonplace in those times. I had no choice but to use the same derogatory terms and describe the violent actions considered acceptable by the day's standards.

Last, I intended to have you, the reader, thoroughly immerse yourself and discover, along with Tori, many truths about this era, 1810-1815, and its people without realizing you were also receiving a history lesson.

New Orleans rich history goes well beyond the party city it is today. Its role in saving America from British rule is not widely known or taught throughout our schools. I am constantly amazed that such an important battle is not more widely known here or around the globe.

While the good time's role (laissez les bon temps rouler) let us each remember the bravery of those who fought against all odds to save our young nation.

Historical Figures in the Legends of NOLA

All of the following played essential roles in our history and in Tori's fictional adventures:

Jean Laffite: Known as The Gentleman Pirate. He arrived in New Orleans after his brother Pierre, a little before 1810. His birthplace is unknown as is his birthdate. Some claim he was born in France; others say Santo Domingo. He was highly educated and the reason why Andrew Jackson was able to guide his army to victory against the British. The man remains a true enigma to this day. Many books have been written about him and many more have speculated about what happened to him after he left Galveston Island. The man simply vanished into history and became a true legend.

Pierre Laffite: The older brother of Jean Laffite. He arrived in New Orleans around 1802, and like his brother, his life is a mystery. His birthplace and date remain unknown. He'd suffered a stroke which left him with a slightly crossed eye and very weak. Before Pierre took a mistress, he was married, and they had a child together, but Pierre was not one to settle down. He had at least two mistresses of color who gave him children. The descendants of these children live in New Orleans today. The date of his death is known; he died in 1821 near Dzilam de Bravo in the Yucatan Peninsula.

Dominique You: He arrived in New Orleans with Jean, and some say he was the older brother. His full name was Alexandre Frederic Laffite according to some records. He was a member of the Masons, and when he died on November 15, 1830, he was given a full Masonic funeral, and the city of New Orleans closed for the day when he was entombed.

Vincent Gambi: Vincenzo was his given name but went by Vincent or Gambi. He was Italian and one of the most violent and blood-thirsty pirates that worked with the Laffites. He died in 1819

Chighizola/Chez Nez *also known as* **Nez Coupe:** Born 1787 in Genoa, Liguria Italy. Died 1870 in Barataria Jefferson Parish Louisiana. He was one of Jean Lafitte's lieutenants. "Nez Coupe" as he was known because half his nose was cut off. He fought in the Battle of New Orleans, and after Jean left for Galveston, he and others settled in Grand Isle, La. He died in 1870. His descendants still live in Grand Isle.

Madame Chighizola: Genevieva Celestine Encar born in 1790 married Chighizola. She died in 1842

Renato Beluche: Born in New Orleans in 1780 to René Beluche and an unknown mother. René owned a wig-making business, which was a front for smuggling operations. He owned a plantation in Chalmette, Louisiana, and held the deed to the cottage known today as Lafitte's Blacksmith Shop. The cottage he rented to the Laffites, it's where Pierre kept his mistress. He joined Jean Laffite and became a pirate before fighting in the Battle of New Orleans. He died peacefully in Puerto Cabello in 1860.

Charles Deslondes: 1789 – January 11, 1811) was one of the slave leaders of the 1811 slave revolt that began on January 8, 1811. He led more than 200 rebels against the Plantations along the Mississippi River toward New Orleans. Charles Deslondes worked as a "driver," or overseer of slaves, on the plantation of Col. Manuel Andre or Andry, who owned a total of 86 slaves. Deslondes was, ostensibly, a loyal slave driver, a slave who also oversaw his brutal master's vast plantation. Deslondes was feared by slaves and trusted by white plantation owners. Deslondes was among the first captured by dogs after the battle. The militia did not hold him for trial or interrogation. Charles Deslondes had his hands chopped off, then shot in one thigh & then the other until they were both broken. He was then shot in the body and before he had expired was put into a bundle of straw and roasted! His dying cries sent a message to the other escaped slaves in the marshes.

Marie Laveau: born September 10, 1801 – died June 17, 1881. Marie Laveau started as a hairdresser for the wealthier families of New Orleans. She was the voodoo queen of New Orleans and used her magic by incorporating Catholic saints, African spirits, and Native American Spiritualism. A network of informants supported her divinations. She developed these connections while working as a hairdresser in prominent white households. She excelled at obtaining inside information on her wealthy patrons by instilling fear and awe. During her later life, she and her daughter, also known as Marie, practiced voodoo, and this was how she could appear to be in two places at once. Marie used her trickery and knowledge to remain in power, but in the end, she turned back to the church and its teachings. To this day, many visit the voodoo queen's tomb. Marie Laveau died peacefully in her home in the French Quarter.

Jean Noël Destréhan: born Jean Noël Destréhan was born in 1754 and educated in France. He married Marie Claude Celeste de Logny. His wife's father, Antoine Robin de Logny, built for them the Destrehan Manor House in 1787, which is still in St. Charles Parish and now open for tours. Later, the couple had two more wings added to the original house to accommodate their total of fourteen children. Destréhan was a prominent Louisiana politician and legislator. He was also a mercantilist and planter. His plantation produced sugar; his brother-in-law Etienne de Bore perfected the sugar granulation process making shipping of the final product far easier. Destréhan was a member of the Louisiana Territorial government from 1803 to 1812. Speaker of the territorial house of representatives from 1804 to 1806. He ran for Governor in the first gubernatorial election but lost to William Claiborne. Destréhan was selected to serve in the United States Senate instead, but he resigned within a month. It is known that he maintained the canal known today as the Harvey Canal. It links the Mississippi river to Barataria bay. Laffite used this canal for his smuggling and was said to visit the Destréhan plantation. Destréhan was the first Vice-Mayor of New Orleans in 1805. In 1812 he was elected as a United States Senator, just after Louisiana became a state. However, he resigned less than a month after his election before even qualifying for office, possibly because he did not speak much English. Destréhan served as a Louisiana State Senator from 1812 to 1818. During this time, he helped to draft the Louisiana Constitution. 1811 German Coast uprising, the largest slave rebellion in American history occurred. Destréhan himself served on a local six-member tribunal at the conclusion of the revolt. The Destréhan's plantation was the location of the St. Charles Parish slave trials. Three of Destréhan's slaves were among the eighteen conspirators who were executed, and their heads placed on spikes along the river road.

Jean Noel Destréhan died in 1823 at his plantation home and is interred near Destréhan, Louisiana.

Marie Destréhan: was born 1770, in Louisiana, died in 1824. She married Jean Noel de Tours Destrehan in 1786, at age 15. They had 14 children, with only 11 surviving beyond childhood. The following were introduced to Tori. Antoinette Celeste. Etienne. Justine. Nicholas Noel. Marie Elizabeth. Nicholas Guy Noel. Elenore. Louise. Bienaime. Leonie. Rene Noel. Marie Celeste, and Amelie

William Charles Cole Claiborne: Born in 1775, died November 23, 1817, he was an American politician and was the first noncolonial governor of Louisiana. Claiborne supervised the transfer of

Louisiana to U.S. control after the Louisiana Purchase of 1803. This transfer upset the Creole and Cajun citizens, who disliked him for many years after. He won the first election for Louisiana's state Governor and served through 1816 for a total of thirteen years as Louisiana's executive administrator. He won the seat in a surprising upset with majority votes against J.D. Destrehan and Jacques Villere. Livingston and Claiborne negotiated the aid of Jean Laffite to defend NOLA from a British attack late in 1814. The governor's first two wives, Eliza Wilson Lewis and Marie Clarisse Duralde died of yellow fever in New Orleans within five years of each other. The second marriage produced a son, William C. C. Claiborne, Jr. In 1812, Governor Claiborne married a third time to Cayetana Susana Bosque Y Fangui and after his death, attorney John Grymes married her. William Claiborne was the third great-grandfather of fashion designer Liz Claiborne.

Cayetana Susana Bosque Y Fangui: Cayetana Susana Bosque: Born: August 11, 1796 in New Orleans. Died August 6, 1881. She married: William Claiborne at age 15, who became Governor of NOLA. "The marriage lasted five years, and they had two children. After his death, she traveled to Europe and returned to New Orleans to marry the socially popular US Attorney, John Randolph Grymes. They never divorced but separated when she moved to New York City. In 1836, she purchased land on Staten Island and built a villa she called "Capo di Monte" (Top of the Mountain). Members of the Vanderbilt and Cunard families built mansions on what became known as Grymes Hill. The area is still known for its luxury homes. She moved to Paris, where she could converse in seven languages. She died there in 1881. Her obituary described her as "beautiful and accomplished, superbly endowed by nature and charmingly cultivated."

Jacques Villeré: born April 8, 1761 died March 7, 1830. He was the second Governor of Louisiana after it became a state. 1784 he married Jeanne de Fazende. Together they raised eight children. He was a member of the convention, which drafted the Louisianan's first state constitution. He served with distinction in the battle for New Orleans as major general 1st Division of the Lousiana militia. His plantation Conseil located downriver from the city, was overrun by the British army. He was a close friend of Destrehan and highly respected in the Creole population.

Captain Samuel McCutchen: 1773-1840. He was a merchant and mariner from Pennsylvania. He served in the Navy before moving to New Orleans. He married Rebecca and took ownership of Ormond Plantation. Together they had nine children. After the Battle of New Orleans, he moved to British Honduras, where he introduced a sugar plantation production.

Colonel Richard Butler: 1783-1840 served in U.S. Army before leaving Philadelphia for New Orleans. He built the Ormond Plantation house after his ancestral home. He later sold one-third share of Ormond to Captain McCutchon and moved to Bay St. Louis. No reason was given for this move, and he and his wife never returned. They died from Yellow Fever.

Jean-Bernard Xavier Philippe de Marigny de Mandeville: 1785-1868. Jean was born in New Orleans. He was married twice and had five children. He was a planter, land developer, and Politician. His paternal grandfather was a French nobleman; his maternal grandfather was the royal treasurer of the colony. He entertained royalty in his New Orleans home and lived a lavish lifestyle. At 15, he inherited his father's plantation east of New Orleans' Veux Carre. His education continued in England, where he became an avid gambler. On his return to New Orleans, he brought back the game of Craps. He founded the "Louisiana Race Course," now the Fair Grounds Race Course. In 1806 he had his plantation subdivided and sold plots to help pay his gambling debts. In 1811 and again in 1814, he was elected to the New Orleans City Council. 1822-1823 Marigny served as President of the Louisiana State Senate. Eventually, he lost his fortune gambling and died impoverished. He was buried in St. Louis Cemetery No. 1. His mother, father, paternal grandfather, and paternal great-grandfather were interred in St. Louis Cathedral.

John Grymes: December 14, 1786 – December 3, 1854 was an attorney in New Orleans. He was a member of the Louisiana state legislature, U.S. attorney for the Louisiana district, and aide-de-camp to General Andrew Jackson during the Battle of New Orleans. In 1808, Grymes arrived in New Orleans on May 4, 1811. Grymes was appointed to the office of U.S. attorney, serving until December 1814, when he resigned his post to represent the pirate Jean Laffite. Many speculate he was working for Laffite in secret for many years before representing the brothers openly. Grymes was a law partner with Edward Livingston, and both were members of the "New Orleans Association," along with the Laffites. Grymes was a Freemason. On December 1, 1822, Grymes married Cayetana Susana, widow of the first Louisiana Governor William C.C. Claiborne.

Thiac: He was most likely born in St. Domingue (Haiti). Thiac was a free black man and a loyal friend to Laffite. He had a smithy located at 174 Levee after Laffite left the city. While his name pops up in many places, not much is known about him other than he is constantly linked to the Laffite brothers. I surmised that he arrived in New Orleans when Jean did. There are writings saying he was arrested for receiving smuggled goods and stolen slaves. There are no records of his death that Tori could locate.

John Davis: Born approximately 1773, died 1839. Davis opened the Theater on Orleans on an avenue between Bourbon and Royal Streets. Construction began in 1806, but the opening was delayed until October 1815 because of the Battle of New Orleans. After a fire, it was rebuilt (with the adjacent Orleans Ballroom and reopened in 1819, led by émigré from Saint-Domingue, John Davis. Davis became one of the significant figures in French theatre in New Orleans. The theatre was destroyed by fire in 1866, but the ballroom is still used. John Davis engaged architect William Brand to design the Orleans Ballroom (Salle d'Orléans) next to the theatre. For gala events, the ballroom could be joined to the theatre, where temporary flooring was laid over the pit, making one enormous ballroom. The facilities also included gambling rooms "for those unlucky at love. The first American gambling casino was opened in New Orleans by John Davis. The club, open twenty-four hours a day, provided gourmet food, liquor, roulette wheels, Faro tables, and other games. He introduced Poque a version of the British card game Brag, which Americans transformed into Poker, using a fifty-two card deck. Davis also made sure that painted ladies were never far away. Gambling was outlawed in Louisiana territory in 1811, but New Orleans continued to enjoy the prosperity brought by gambling, and the law turned a blind eye for years due to its popularity.

Andrew Jackson: (March 15, 1767–June 8, 1845) Before being elected to the presidency, Jackson gained fame as a general in the United States Army and served in both houses of Congress. In the war against the British, Jackson's victory in 1815 at the Battle of New Orleans made him a national hero. A victory that could not have happened without the aid of Jean Laffite and his men. Jackson's hatred of the British stemmed from his youth. He and his brother Robert were captured by the British and when Andrew refused to clean the boots of a British officer, the officer slashed at the youth with a sword, leaving him with scars on his left hand and head. Within two days of arriving back home, his brother was dead, and Andrew was in mortal danger of dying. After nursing Andrew back to health, Elizabeth volunteered to nurse American prisoners of war on board two British ships in the Charleston harbor, where there had been an outbreak of cholera. In November, she died from the disease and was buried in an unmarked grave. Andrew became an orphan at age 14. He blamed the British personally for the loss of his brothers and mother. After arriving in New Orleans on December 1, 1814, Jackson instituted martial law in the city as he worried about the loyalty of the city's Creole and Cajun inhabitants. At the same time, on advice from his friend Edward Livingston he formed an alliance with Jean Laffite and his men. Jackson formed military units consisting of volunteers in the city. Note here, Jackson was a Freemason, as were Livingston, Grymes, and Dominique You, among others in the story. Jackson received some criticism for paying white and non-white volunteers the same salary while serving under his command. These forces, along with U.S. Army regulars and volunteers from surrounding states, joined with Jackson's force in defending New Orleans. Jean Laffite supplied him with weapons, flints, and men without which the battle surely would have been lost. The approaching British force consisted of over 10,000 soldiers, many of whom had served in the Napoleonic Wars. Jackson had only about 5,000 men, most of whom were inexperienced and poorly trained. After the battle, the British retreated from the area, and open hostilities ended shortly thereafter when word spread that the Treaty of Ghent had been signed in Europe that December. Jackson's victory made him a national hero, as the country celebrated the end of what many called the "Second American Revolution" against the British. There is much more behind this former President, and given the time, I highly recommend reading about him.

Racheal Jackson: Rachel Jackson: June 15, 1767–December 22, 1828. She was the wife of Andrew Jackson, the 7th President. She lived with him at their home at The Hermitage, where she died just days after his election and before his inauguration in 1829. Her first marriage was not happy, and the two separated in 1790. Believing that her husband would file for divorce, she returned to the family home. When Andrew Jackson moved to Tennessee in 1788, he boarded with Rachel Stockley Donelson the mother of Rachel. The two became close, and shortly after, they married. Rachel believed that her husband had obtained a divorce, but as it had never been completed, her marriage to Jackson was inadvertently bigamous and therefore invalid. On the grounds of Rachel's abandonment and adultery, her soon-to-be ex-husband was granted a divorce in 1794. After the divorce was finally legalized in 1794, Andrew and Rachel wed again in a quiet ceremony. Unlike Jackson, Rachel never liked being in the spotlight of events. She would consistently warn her husband not to let his political accomplishments rule him. An example of her warnings is after Jackson's victory at the Battle of New Orleans; she warned Jackson not to let it tempt him to value his glory over his own family. Rachel died suddenly on December 22, 1828, of a heart attack, given her symptoms, according to her husband, which was "excruciating pains in the left shoulder, arm, and breast." That her death came right before Jackson left for Washington, and he lingered at the Hermitage until the latest possible moment. His love for his wife was to him beyond words. Jackson always blamed his political enemies for her death. "May God Almighty forgive her murderers," Jackson swore at her funeral, "I never can." She was buried on the grounds at The Hermitage wearing the white dress and shoes she had bought for the Inaugural Ball.

Mayor Nicholas Girod: (April 1751—September 1840) He was the fifth mayor of New Orleans, from late 1812 to September 4, 1815. His inauguration ceremony was conducted in French because Girod did not speak English. He prospered as a commission merchant and owner of extensive property in New Orleans, especially in the American quarter. Girod was quite a philanthropist. Girod welcomed General Jackson on his arrival and thoroughly co-operated with him in the vigorous resistance to the British. It was well known he hatred the British more than the Americans. He was a devotee of Napoleon, and in the spring of 1821, Girod built and furnished a house at 124 Chartres Street, near St. Louis Street, "The Napoleon House," to be in readiness for Napoleon Bonaparte. Nicholas Girod was one of the sponsors of the plot to rescue the emperor, along with Dominique You, one of Lafitte's lieutenants. The plan failed because of the death of the emperor before they had a chance to rescue him. For a short time, he served as warden of Saint Louis Cathedral.

Mr. Nicholas Girod died on September 1, 1840 at 9 P.M. at the age of 90, at his home located on the corner of St. Louis and Chartres Streets. His former residence in the French Quarter is now known as the Napoleon House and is a restaurant. Both New Orleans and Manderville, Louisiana, have a Girod Street, named in his honor.

Jean Joseph Amable Humbert: (22 August 1767–3 January 1823) was a French military officer who participated in several notable military conflicts of the late 18th and early 19th centuries. In 1810, Humbert emigrated to New Orleans, where he established a relationship with Jean Laffite. After he acquired his privateer papers, he began working with the Laffites. Humbert fought in the Battle of New Orleans while wearing his old French uniform during the battle. He was a known Mason.

Madame Poree: A lady of society who opened her home to around 75-100 females during the Battle of New Orleans. While this female turned up in several manuscripts Tori was unable to learn anything else about her.

Captain John Henley: 25 February 1781 – 23 May 1835. Born in Virginia. He was a commissioned Navy Officer who commanded a major delaying action as Captain of the Carolina. Though his ship was destroyed he along with his crew survived.

Mr. John Dick: 1764-1833 United States District Attorney who prosecuted Pierre Laffite. During the trial, his enormous dislike of John Grymes came to light. The two men in the fall of 1814 fought a duel, in which Grymes was shot in the calf and Dick got a serious wound to one thigh which left him with a limp for the remainder of his life. He died of consumption at age 36, leaving no surviving children.

John Henry Holland: 1785–1864 John Henry Holland, lawyer, city official, and Masonic leader Holland moved to New Orleans before 1803, served as sheriff of Orleans Parish, and was the jailer when Pierre Laffite was in the Cabildo. For many years he was associated with the Masonic order in Louisiana. He was grand master of the Grand Lodge of Louisiana from 1825 to 1828 and again from 1830 to 1839. He died in New Orleans on March 29, 1864.

Jean Blanque: He was a member of the Louisiana House of Representatives. He did not arrive in New Orleans until 1803. Laffite sent a warning to New Orleans with his fastest courier, who could arrive in a day. He sent a copy of the British offer and a plea for the release of his brother and a stop to the 'persecution' of his privateers and even volunteered himself, his men, and supplies for the defense of New Orleans to Jean Blanque, who gave it to Gov Claiborne. Blanque died in 1816.

Marie Adelaide: The only facts known about her is she was born in St-Louis-of-Jeremie Parish Santo Domingo. There are no known images such as paintings or drawings of her. She and Pierre Laffite had one child born before 1808. They had a daughter born in 1810.

Catherine Villar: Younger sister of Marie Villar and linked to Jean Laffite as his mistress but it is unclear if this is so. Rumor had it that they had a son who they called Pierre. She had a total of seven children. There are no known portraits of either Catherine or her sister Marie.

Marie Louise Villar: born in 1891 in New Orleans, she was an Octoroon and sister or Catherine Villar. There is no known image of her. Some books list her as a mistress of Jean Laffite.

Edward Livingston: born May 26, 1764, in Clermont, New York, Livingston served as both U.S. district attorney for New York and mayor of New York City (1800), resigning all offices while coping with yellow fever (1803). He was John Grymes law partner and good friend of Andrew Jackson. During the Battle of New Orleans, Livingston served as aide-de-camp, secretary, and military interpreter to General Andrew Jackson. He was a Freemason and also represented the Laffites after the battle trying to get them their ships and goods back that had been taken when Grand Terre was burned.

General Packenham: 19 March 1778–8 January 1815 was a British Army officer. During the War of 1812, he was commander of British forces in North America from 1814–1815. On the 8th of January 1815, Pakenham was killed in action while leading his men at the Battle of New Orleans. His body was returned to England in a barrel of Rum.

Additional Historical Figures

The following people also played roles in the books and in history in the years before and after the Battle of New Orleans.

Captain Andrew Holmes
Revenue Officer Walker Gilbert
Felicidad Fangui
Pierre's son Pierre
Brigadier General Morgan
Pierre's children
Mentioned Andry and Son Gilbert
Jean Baptiste Sauvienet
General Keane
Admiral Cochrane
Captain Nicholas Lockyer
Captain McWilliams
Captain Percy
Commodore Patterson
Colonel Ross
Chief of Staff Alexandre Berthier
Mentioned Mr. John Holland
Arsène Lacarrière Latour
Mother Superior Marie Francis Olivier de Vizin

Destinations
from the story that you can visit:

French Quarter
The Garden District
Jackson Square
Cabildo
Café du Monde
Lafitte's Guest House, now Lafitte's Hotel and Bar
Lafitte's Blacksmith Shop which is a local bar. Also, when visiting
Lafitte's Blacksmith shop, be sure to ask to see the writing on the
wall and in the courtyard the statue that Tori called "Lovers in
Stone."
Cemetery number one and two
Area known as Congo Square, it's where free colored and slaves
would meet
Destrehan Plantation
Ormond Plantation
Grand Isle
Grand Terre
Ursuline Convent
French Market
Pirate's Ally
Battle Ground at Chalmette
Destrehan Canal or Harvey Canal as it is known today
Barataria Bay
Theater d' Orleans
Bayous
Saint Louis Cathedral
Terrebonne Bay
Parisian Avenue des Champs-Elysees
Tomb of Marie Laveau
Tomb of Mayor N. Girod

Tomb of Dominique You
Tomb of William Claiborne- Metairie cemetery
Town of Donaldsonville
Baton Rouge
Sight of Marie Laveau house in the French Quarter
Sight of Andrew Jackson's headquarters in the French Quarter
The area of Cat Island and Last Island
Mayor Girod's home that was built for Napoleon
The area known as The Temple can be seen from an airboat adventure in the bayous

Historical Events
that occurred during the
story's time frame
1810 -1815

Louisiana became a state
The election of the first Governor of Louisiana
Strong Hurricane that hit New Orleans
Earthquake north of Baton Rouge
Battle of New Orleans
Battle at sea off the coast of Cat Island
Destruction of Grand Terre
The arrests of Jean Laffite and his men
Jean and his men let out of jail on bond from charges of piracy
The arrest of Pierre Laffite
The duel between John Grymes and Mr. Dick
Pierre's escape from jail
The plague of Black John or yellow fever
Jean Laffite's meeting with Andrew Jackson
The meeting between Jean Laffite and the British
Jean Laffite supplies Andrew Jackson with men and weapons
The arrival of the British outside New Orleans
The battle against the British
The slave uprising
Andrew Jackson's trip down the Mississippi to survey the fort
The gathering of the women during the battle
The celebration for Andrew Jackson's victory
The wanted posters for Laffite and his response with a wanted
poster for Claiborne
The full pardons for Jean Laffite and his men along with gaining
citizenship
John Davis opens his casino and hotel

The story of Chez Nez and the gold thimble is a family legend
The story about Napoleon and the rabbits
The story of how Bernard de Marigny threw his gold plates into the river after the Duke of Orleans (who became King Louis Philippe) ate off them. Bernard by all accounts considered no one would be worthy of using them again.

Acknowledgements

First, I want to thank my family, who visited New Orleans countless times over the years so I could do my research. Before the internet, it was the only option and one that I relished as it allowed me to immerse myself in the history and cultures, both past and present day.

I wish to thank the Louisiana Historical Association and the Research Center on Charter Street. The personnel there never let me down or ceased to amaze me. One of my proudest moments came when they accepted copies of my books for their archives.

The Destrehan Plantation was not open to the public when Daniel, my husband, and I first came upon it. They were battening down for an approaching hurricane when we pulled onto the grounds. Mr. Joseph Maddox listened to my husband's plea and was gracious enough to give us a personal tour and explain the house's history and that of its former owners. We have since returned to visit Destrehan Plantation many times, and though our paths have never crossed with Mr. Maddox again, I wanted him to know that I did my best to keep the historical facts correct as promised. From the shell of a neglected building all those years ago now stands a proud and fine example of a historic plantation. It is open for tours, and I highly recommend a visit.

I also appreciate the work done by my son Dylan. His creative ideas and talented photography allowed him to design each book cover. I wish to thank my daughter Drena Bathemess for taking the time to write the blurbs. Anyone who knows me understands that it would be another book in the making if I had to create a blurb.

To my dear and talented friend MaryChris Bradley, there are no words that can express my deep gratitude for all your help and wisdom. Without you, this book would still be sitting on my computer.

I would also like to thank the fine people at Lafitte's Blacksmith

Shop found at the corner of Bourbon and Saint Philip Streets. It was because they were always willing to talk about the building and its history that I was shown "the writing on the wall." May I suggest, if you are ever in New Orleans, that you visit this bar and ask to see the writing and the statue I called, 'Lovers in Stone'. I won't put a spoiler here; let us say you will understand this recommendation when you read the story. I guarantee it will give you goosebumps.

If you find the Blacksmith shop too crowded, cross the street to Lafitte's Hotel and bar. Once there, you get to step into the building as Tori did at the beginning of her adventure. It's the same hotel that Stirling showed her and Dan. You will recognize the entryway, and if you have the chance to stay there as a guest, be aware there is more to this establishment than you know. After all, they say the French Quarter is known for its ghosts and hauntings. The decor and atmosphere are pretty remarkable, and the staff is always welcoming and helpful.

Finally, with all my heart, thank you to Jean Laffite and Tori, for letting me tell their story and for never letting me give up. Together, we somehow always found a way to validate the historical events that unfolded in their epic adventure. It was hard saying goodbye, and it was not until typing Jean's last words that this author could finally let go.

I was surprised to find myself typing his words while working on a different story and genre. I had begun writing 'The Wardrobe' when the Gentleman Pirate spoke his last words. The note started with 'Time is as fluid as the ocean I sailed upon,' and before I knew it, I had his farewell. Yes, that small note found at the beginning of each book was how he said goodbye to Tori, me, and you, the reader.

Wherever time and tide took our pirate, may he rest in peace.

About the Author

D.S. Elliston lives with her husband, Dan—her best friend and biggest fan—and four rescued cats and two dogs that they babysit when their families travel. Together, they enjoy the three grandchildren they are blessed to see often. The couple reside in Florida and enjoy the company of friends and family. While she admits to relishing her time spent writing, she sometimes struggles with computers and modern-day technology and is grateful to her children and grandchildren for their continued help.

Her love of history was the foundation for this series. Dedicated to research, New Orleans shines in her account of the history of its people and culture. Weaving historical facts into a fictional story is her passion and near obsession. Her goal is to entertain while teaching readers about an often forgotten past. In addition to reading and writing, she loves to cook, paint and travel and looks forward to working on her next book.

Made in the USA
Monee, IL
10 December 2023

48788750R00216